PRAI

The Fourteent

"This debut novel deftly captur _____ ...u me cusp of an uncertain future. The characters' choices are difficult, their solutions complex. At times charming and funny, at others intense and heartbreaking, Dragonette depicts a complicated chapter in our history with precision and depth, and renders it with compassion, understanding, and grace."

—Patricia Ann McNair,
author of *And These Are the Good Times*

"This deeply felt novel took me back to the time when hopes of the future slammed up against the realities of war, and when the fate of young men was determined by a number in the Draft Lottery. It's a re-immersion for some, for others a book to learn what all the fuss was about."

—Patrick T. Reardon, author of *Requiem for David*

"A compelling, original book and a great read. It's at once transporting to an incredible moment in recent history and still distinctly modern, as a story of a young woman finding her independence, her voice, and her place in the world—an unpredictable, emotional, and gripping ride through to the end."

—Josh Lohrius, author of *The Breaking of Goody Boothe*

"Rita Dragonette's novel reveals what I have known for a long while—that she is a writer of great talent and integrity who in-fuses this debut work with an energy and vision that lifts it far beyond the ordinary coming-of-age story. This is an important book, not to be missed."

—Gary D. Wilson, author of *Getting Right* and *Sing, Ronnie Blue*

"Dragonette transports readers to a college campus in 1969 when flunking out meant front lines. Judy's journey represents the complexity of every generation's timeless effort to align conscience with action. This debut novel, neither idealistic nor fatalistic, offers the unique perspective of a young woman facing her own private rebellion."

—Elizabeth Wheeler, author of *The Asher Trilogy*

"This novel magnificently arcs the distance between the deeply personal and the global. It sharply depicts a seminal point in history, while tackling universal questions about how we measure the need to act versus personal cost. Dragonette has given us a work of recent historical fiction with profound relevance for today."

—Barbara Monier, author of *You, in Your Green Shirt* and *Pushing the River*

"A compelling novel about the Vietnam era with a morbid similarity to events in today's world. A coming-of-age story of students, their loves and fears, and the polarization of political thinking. A wonderful read for those who remember, as well as younger people who will identify with the unrest."

—Ellis Goodman, author of *Bear Any Burden* and *The Keller Papers*

"The struggles around integrity and the coming-of-age narrative of 'Judy Blue Eyes,' the protagonist in Dragonette's well-structured and -versed story, though they represent that of a generation during the Vietnam era, are very relevant to what we face today."

—Jian Ping, author of *Mulberry Child*

"This story is beautifully written with compassionate and thoughtful narrative and engaging characters who play out all the angst of the era set on a Midwestern college campus when America was at its most vulnerable. Dragonette shows us what we can be, both in our best and our worst." —*Windy City Times*

The
Fourteenth
of
September

The Fourteenth of September

A Novel

Rita Dragonette

SHE WRITES PRESS

Published 2018
Printed in the United States of America
ISBN: 978-1-63152-453-0 pbk
ISBN: 978-1-63152-462-2 ebk
Library of Congress Control Number: 2018938550

For information, address:
She Writes Press
1569 Solano Ave #546
Berkeley, CA 94707

She Writes Press is a division of SparkPoint Studio, LLC.

Book design by Stacey Aaronson, cover illustration by Paul Sahre

To my mother
For, and despite it all

"There will be an answer, let it be."
—Lennon / McCartney

PART ONE

September 1969

Chapter 1

ON THE SECOND MONDAY OF SEPTEMBER, JUDY TALTON put on the new jeans she had run through three washing cycles and the fatigue jacket she had found at the Salvation Army resale shop, went to the Student Union, and, for the first time, took a seat on the freak side of the Tune Room.

She chose an empty table, one of dozens occupied by student radicals and other misfits, against a wall splattered with as many posters *against* the Vietnam War as *for* next month's homecoming game. She glanced across the room's wide central aisle at the matching tables filled with the neat sweaters and slacks of the sorority, fraternity, and other straight types on the Greek side. She watched the entrance as students walked in, paused at the top of a short flight of stairs, then chose their side: Greeks or freaks.

She drew her stack of books close, as people landed at her table spraying drops from shaken umbrellas and complaining about the quick intensity of a storm that had just hit. The room filled rapidly to capacity. Too many people and too much distraction, she thought, watching her plans drip away with the rainwater. She should go. What was she thinking, anyway? That she could just change her clothes, walk in here, and somehow her life would work itself out?

Suddenly, the crowd parted, revealing two guys poised at the top of the stairs, water sliding off their olive drab ponchos.

"Reserve Officer Training Corps, two o'clock," said someone near Judy.

"R . . . O . . . T . . . C, ROTC," came the murmurs along the freak side, ramping up in volume as some of them elbowed each other at the affront. They pronounced it ROT-ZEE, like Nazi.

Monday was drill day on the Quad, as Judy knew well. These two must have been caught in the rain. Why else would they risk coming here in full dress? She had to get out.

She rose, but her exit was blocked by a tall figure in a long duster and a pancake hat who was moving from a nearby table toward the ROTC guys. She realized she wouldn't be able to leave without crossing between them, so she sat back down. The guys had taken off their ponchos, revealing their full fatigues, and were now sitting on the bottom stair near the Greek side.

"Hey," said the guy in the duster, "afraid of a little rain? You'll hold up really well in that jungle you're headed for." A few snickers echoed from the freak side.

The ROTC guys glanced up briefly, then ignored him as they rummaged through their things, sandwiches suddenly materializing from under layers of olive drab.

"Any artillery in those backpacks? I thought you all got toy guns to go with those spiffy outfits?" the duster guy said, stopping a few yards in front of them, hands on his hips. "Drop them when the lightning hit, did you? Not very gun . . . g ho, now is it?" He drew out the "gun" part of the word for maximum effect. The snickers multiplied. The rest of the Tune Room quieted down, watching. Soon, the only sound was heavy metal spewing from the jukebox that gave the room its name.

The ROTC guys stared at him, expressionless, as they continued to chew on their sandwiches, one coolly picking wilted lettuce off his lunchmeat.

"Cut the crap, freak," said a voice from the Greek side. "Let 'em alone."

"Oh, I get it," the duster guy went on. "You don't really need guns, do you? Because ROTC lets you 'place out' of the jungle, doesn't it? Right out of the Gen Ed of the infantry and into the honors officer class."

Laughter surged from the freak side. "Good one!" a voice yelled.

"Straight to officer school so you can boss around the rest of us when the Draft Lottery sends us off to Saigon." He turned back toward the freaks, spread his arms wide and took a bow.

"I said let up, smart ass," said a very tall Greek, standing to support his threat, his fair face pinking up, color streaking along the part of his short hair.

"I will not." The duster guy turned toward the Greek. "I'm offended," he said, dramatically clutching his chest. "I'm deeply offended that these members of the war machine on campus are here, suited up, throwing their dirty conflict in our faces."

"Here he goes again," said someone at Judy's table.

"What do you mean?" she asked, leaning in to hear the girl next to her who was trying to explain.

"David can't stand ROTC," she said, pointing to the speaker in the duster. "Says it's condoning the war. He tried to get it thrown off campus last year, and he's pissed he couldn't. He can't let it go."

A full-body shudder knifed its way through Judy. She craned her neck to see if there was another way out.

By this point, David and the Greek were standing in the middle of the central aisle trading increasingly heated jabs.

"So, you don't agree with the war. Fine," the Greek said. "But these guys are just like us, doing what they think is right, don't you get that, asshole?"

"There's *nothing right* about this war and *no one* should be fighting it, don't you get THAT?!" David sneered back.

Cheers rose from the freak side.

A few paper cups and other debris flew from one side of the room to the other.

"You're just against them because you're yellow," said a guy in a letterman's jacket, stepping up next to the tall Greek.

A projectile in a bun hit David in the back, sliding down to leave a trail of mustard on his coat. The Greek side howled, some of them standing and throwing whatever vending machine food they'd been eating at David.

"War lovers," he yelled back, twirling to avert the rain of bread, meat, and condiments. His hat was knocked off his head, revealing thin dark hair hanging just shy of his shoulders.

"Screw you, longhair," said the Greek, advancing closer to David, pointing his finger like a weapon. "America is a free country and ROTC is their choice. Let 'em do what *they* want, not what *you* want."

"Their choice? That's funny," David said, pointing to the ROTC guys. "They can't even vote yet. *We* can't even vote yet. Go ahead, defend them," he waved them off with a limp hand gesture. "Sounds like you're all dying to go to Vietnam with them anyway."

"Yeah, dying," came another voice from David's side. "And that's just what you'll do." The freaks shrieked with glee.

"That's all this war is about anyway," David went on, standing his ground. "Some old guys play politics while we die. ROTC is their way to suck us into it right here on campus . . . and you want to let them keep doing it."

The rain of food slowed and there was a strained pause, as if the crowd was trying to grasp what David had just said.

"Someone has to fight for our freedom," blurted the Greek, his face now as bright as his red sweater.

"I . . . fight . . . for . . . peace," David said, stabbing his finger at his chest with each word.

"Oxymoron, freak. You even know what that means?" the letterman said. "Or do you just get the 'moron' part?"

With this, most of the guys on both sides of the Tune Room leaped to their feet, cheering on their champions in the center aisle.

"Choosing ROTC is free speech," said the Greek, nearly spitting his words.

"Yeah, free speech, and this is mine." David raised his fist, chanting, "Hell No, I Won't Go!"

"Then don't go, but you have no right to stop them."

"I can try," David said, with a sneer. "Like you said, it's a free country." He changed his chant to "Free Country," rhythmically punching his fist with each repetition. Two other freaks stepped into the aisle and joined him.

"It's only free because they're willing to fight," said the letterman, shrieking over the chanting.

At a gesture from David, a few of his cohort stood and picked up the chant "Hell No, We Won't Go!" In response, the Greeks pelted the other side with foam dishes and spitballs. Soon, a shower of the tin ashtrays that littered each table followed, scattering cigarette butts into rainwater footprints, puddling down the aisle's slick wood flooring.

Most of the room was in on it by this time: from one side yelling at David, from the other egging him on, chanting louder and louder. A beefy Greek tore off his jacket and stepped into the aisle, fists raised, but he slipped in the watery ashes and skidded, nearly clipping David and another freak. Judy cowered, waiting for the punch, as he scrambled to his feet.

At that moment, the tall Greek started singing "My Country, 'Tis of Thee," joined immediately by most of the other Greeks, even the girls. Everyone still sitting on both sides now sprang to their feet, vocalizing loudly, trying to drown out the others. Judy's table was up. She felt she had to rise with them, softly joining the "Hell No" chant. An orange peel grazed her shoulder.

The ROTC guys were sitting quietly, heads bouncing back and forth, following the action. Judy lifted herself up on her toes to get a better look over the heads in front of her. They were now wiping their mouths and gathering up their sandwich wrappings. One crushed his bag of chips in a single hand and stuffed it into his backpack. The other stood and walked slowly and deliberately toward David.

"They're going to go at it," said the girl next to her.

"They can't fight in uniform," Judy said, before realizing she had spoken out loud.

"Get your outfit and your buzz cut out of my face," David said.

The ROTC guy stopped, took off his cap, and down tumbled thick, shoulder-length hair, which he shook with delight. David stopped mid-shout. Even from the back, Judy could tell he was shocked silent, frozen to the floor. The whole room seemed to gasp, then exploded into laughter as the ROTC guys walked out together. At the door, they passed the campus cops, arriving late to break up the brawl.

Judy slipped out, unnoticed but shaken. The rain had stopped. She went to the Quad and climbed up the stairs to the statue of the university's founder. She looked across campus for the two ponchos and watched the recruits as they walked along the path toward the dorms, both with caps off, long locks bouncing to their stride.

JUDY was up all night gathering her courage to try again. If she waited too long, she knew she would lose her nerve, and she had promised herself she would finally do this now, on her birthday. She walked back into the Tune Room the next day and again took a seat on the freak side.

She was thankful the room was relatively quiet, with only about a third of the tables occupied compared to yesterday's crowd. She tried to appear casual, focusing her attention on a copper-haired guy in a fringed jacket struggling with the collapsing corner of the banner he was trying to hang. STUDENT MOBILIZATION COMMITTEE TO END THE WAR IN VIETNAM. JOIN SMC NOW. She wondered if she should offer to help, or if that would be pushing it.

Relax, she told herself. This could take hours, or many visits, or maybe nothing would happen at all and maybe, just maybe, that would be best. She opened her biology book and slowly flipped the pages as if she were studying, looking up every now and then to see who had come and gone or changed seats. She felt claustrophobic and fanned herself to brush away the smell of steamed meat, strong coffee, and cigarette smoke. At one point, she noticed the banner was in place and the guy had disappeared. She swiveled to see if she could spot his red hair in the crowd.

A clipboard suddenly appeared under her nose.

"Sign this," a voice said. "It's important."

She looked up. It was that girl from her dorm in her usual leather headband, perfectly faded bell-bottoms, and braless top, her nipples impossible to miss in the chilly room. Judy planted her feet to steady herself.

"We can't let them fire Swanson," the girl went on. "It's a farce. We know the real story. They need to hear from the students."

"Shouldn't I read it first?" Judy asked, feeling she should say something like that to show she wasn't a pushover. She hoped her voice sounded even.

"You don't know about Swanson or you don't support him."

"I—"

"You have to choose, you know," she said, tapping her pen

against the metal clamp of the clipboard. "Or are you going to tell me you're apathetic?" The girl sat herself down, happy for the opening. She dropped the clipboard on the table and leaned in close, emitting a wave of warm patchouli. Judy felt a little sick to her stomach.

"Let me explain." The girl lit a cigarette and pointed it at Judy to emphasize her words. "It's such bullshit to claim it's Swanson's teaching methods. They could at least have the guts to admit they want him out because he's an activist." She slapped a hand on the table. "So, we need to vouch for what a great professor he is, and they'll have to keep him. You get it now, right?"

She shoved the clipboard across the table. It hadn't occurred to Judy that she might be asked to sign something. She made her signature as illegible as possible, using a modest public-school *J* versus her usual initial plume.

She had seen the girl many times before, always in the thick of campus antiwar activities, often with Professor Swanson. She envied her looks—an incredibly right combination of Cher and Grace Slick—and admired her ability to punctuate a sentence with a dramatic flourish of her cigarette, as well as the way she sang out "Oh, wow," when impressed or excited. From a distance she seemed intimidating, even scary. But now, as she ran her index finger down the full length of her substantial nose, leaving an ink trail that caused them both to giggle, Judy was charmed.

"I'm Vida," she said, wiping her stained finger on a piece of Judy's notebook paper. She took a long drag and tilted her head back to watch the smoke as she exhaled. "I knew you'd get here eventually."

"What?"

"I saw you sitting in the back at the SMC forum at the beginning of the semester, and at the Lottery Countdown meeting at the dorm last week. I even saw you sneaking out yesterday after that great anti-ROTC action. Wild, wasn't it?"

Judy inched her seat back. Why had Vida been watching her?

"It was just a matter of time." The girl leaned back and raised her chin to blow another trail of smoke. "Everyone who *knows* ends up at the Tune Room," she paused, "at least this side of it."

Who *knows?* Judy struggled for an answer.

"So, what's your name, anyway?" Vida finally asked.

"Judy," she answered, adding quickly to take the focus from herself. "I've never heard the name Vida before."

"It's Albanian, next door to Greek. Isn't that a riot? Greek without the matching sweater set, I like to say. I used to hate the name, but now I like that it's different. Gives me distinction, along with my nose." She offered her profile and grinned.

Judy couldn't believe she was so friendly.

"You a freshman?" Vida asked.

"No, sophomore."

"Really? Well, I'm definitely the oldest sophomore on campus. I took a semester off to help the national SMC get its act together and some other shit. So I'm twenty."

"I just turned nineteen . . . yesterday."

"Interesting," Vida said, raising an eyebrow. "A kick-ass time for a change."

Judy stiffened. "What do you mean?"

"Maybe I'm clairvoyant," Vida winked. "Or maybe it's not too hard to figure out that you showing up here on your birthday might mean something."

Maybe Vida knew more than she was letting on. "It's actually the day *after* my birthday."

"Details." Vida dismissed the fact with a flip of her hand. She took another drag. "My boyfriend has the same birthday as you, and he's trying to pretend it isn't important, either. Really sticking his head in the sand."

"How so?"

"Hello! The lottery? They'll get their numbers by their birthdates? It's not a problem, though. If he gets a low number, he's going to Canada. I've checked it all out. I'm a poli sci major."

"Doesn't show a bit," Judy said, with a smile.

"You?"

Judy gave the answer she had rehearsed. "I'm science."

"No shit. I wouldn't have guessed it. What kind of—"

"Just science. Pretty boring," she said quickly, pointing to her biology book. She needed to change the subject. "So, you said everyone who *knows* comes here. What does that mean?"

"You can't define it," Vida said. "If you *know*, you just do."

Judy felt flattered, though she wasn't sure exactly why. She allowed herself to relax and joined Vida in surveying the scene.

She was aware the Tune Room was a converted bowling alley here in the Union's basement, but now, looking around, realized how perfect the layout was for the Greek/freak divide that had begun to separate the campus since the announcement of the pending National Draft Lottery. The entrance, once used for concessions and shoe pick-up, was a great no-man's land. The wide set of stairs offered a perfect stage to pause and check out the scene before stepping down to the lower level and choosing to sit on your preferred side of the two-alley-wide aisle that had been the focus of yesterday's near riot. The long aisle led all the way to the jukebox and a wall of vending machines at the far end of the room, where the pins would have been.

She used to think it silly to call this place the Tune Room, like on *American Bandstand* or something. But sitting here now as the music played, watching feet keeping time, fingers tapping against textbooks, lips mouthing the words to the latest Blood,

Sweat, and Tears song, her own leg now bobbing up and down, she thought the name was just right.

She felt an elbow against her ribs.

"David's here. Center stairs." She followed Vida's pointed finger to a tall guy poised, scouting the room. The navy-blue pancake hat and the long olive-green coat that trailed behind him were unmistakable. He was the jerk who had heckled the ROTC recruits.

"Over here," Vida shouted.

David halted, then spread his arms wide, calling out, "In-A-Gadda-Da-VIDA!" as he headed down the stairs to their table.

He hugged Vida, and with his face still tucked over her shoulder, gave Judy a full, head-to-toe scan. When he took off his hat, his hair fell over the top half of his face and he shook his head to fling it back. Judy had to catch her breath.

"Meet Judy," Vida said, as the two of them drew apart.

"Judy Blue Eyes," he said.

She smiled in surprise at the recasting of her dull name, but lowered her head. It was a reflex. Her eyes had always attracted too much attention. Large and teal, they were ringed with dark, heavy lashes, a surprise since her blonde-brown hair was on the light side of dishwater.

"Judy Blue Eyes," David said again. "Look up."

She raised her eyes without lifting her head and realized David had bent toward her, expecting her to say something. He smiled, and she noticed his bottom teeth were crooked, but in an appealing way. She wasn't prepared to like him.

"Hey, man," a voice called, and both Judy and David turned toward it.

Standing before them was a huge guy she would have bet played football in high school before he went shaggy, with bushy sideburns and an attempt at a moustache.

"Howie," David said, shaking one hand firmly with thumbs interlocked, grabbing his forearm with the other.

"Meet Judy Blue Eyes." David waved in her direction.

Howie grinned and launched into the chorus of the new hit song, "Suite: Judy Blue Eyes."

"Dew do do da dew, DO do dew do da dew." He played an imaginary guitar to accompany himself, fingers following the notes he sang up and down the scale on phantom strings.

David joined him. Judy looked down again, embarrassed, but couldn't help smiling into her chest.

After two choruses, Vida interrupted. "It's Judy's birthday."

"Ah," David said, "the fifteenth, the Ides of September, are you an omen?"

"Ha!" cracked Vida. "Hitting on her with Shakespeare? Is nothing sacred?"

"It was yesterday, actually, the fourteenth," Judy said, excited at the attention.

"Sorry, that date's taken," said a John Lennon look-alike, who put his hand on Vida's shoulder. "I seem to remember a big party in my room last night with a sign that said HAPPY BIRTH-DAY, WIL that proves it."

Two guys came to the table with big grins.

"Thought your teeth were going to drop out of your mouth yesterday when that recruit took his hat off," one of them said, laughing, while the other whacked David on the back. "A military freak. No way you saw that one coming."

Judy put her hand to her mouth.

"Two-faced bastard," David said, shrugging the guy off. He slid his chair back, annoyed. "He can't have it both ways." He pounded his fist on the table. "ROTC is the war machine. If he's in it, he's complicit. Period." He stood up. "Pardon me while I get some actual organizing done."

"Vida." He angled his head, suddenly very official, and they took off to talk to people at a nearby table. The two guys followed them.

Judy's head was spinning with the boomerang of David's shift—from jerk to nice guy, then back to jerk again. She realized she still had her hand over her mouth. She fanned her fingers and curled them off, one by one, in a gesture she hoped would look casual.

"You don't mess with David and ROTC," Wil said, sitting down next to her.

"Those guys are probably just in it to pay for school," she said.

"We know that, but it's hardly the point at this stage of the war," he said to her, but his attention stayed on Vida at the other table. He watched her with wide-tracking eyes, head bobbing to the conversation she was having, though he couldn't possibly hear what was being said. His arms worked their way around to cradle the clipboard she had left on the table. He no longer seemed to remember Judy was there. She realized it was up to her to break the silence.

"So, it's Will, right?"

"That's Wil with one *l*," he specified after a long pause. "Wilfred, as in Owen."

"Are you related?"

"In my mom's head."

"Are you a poet?"

"I wish."

Judy wondered if she would be able to get a full sentence out of him. "Vida says you're planning on going to Canada if you get a low lottery number."

"Vida says a lot of things."

More people gathered as the morning went on, pulling up

chairs and joining the ever-growing collection of tables, jamming them close together. By early afternoon, the many people who circled around Vida had come and gone and come again, the Tune Room their base between classes. There were faces with catchphrase names: Wizard, who "played a mean pinball," as he demonstrated on the Union's two machines; Fish, who was Tom Fisher; RoMo, who was Rosemary Molotsky, the girl who had been at her table the day before; Achilles, who had a last name ending in "opolis"; and Meldrich, who just went by Meldrich. Howie's girlfriend, Marsha, also joined the group but seemed out of place in a crisp, collared shirt and a necklace that looked like it might be real gold. She was very pretty but kept pulling at her hair, fingering the strands from ear to shoulder and checking the lay of her bangs against her forehead.

It was dizzying trying to remember everyone, and Judy appreciated how often Vida salted her name into the conversation. Amazingly, they all seemed happy to meet her and add to the chorus of "dew do do da dews." Maybe the trite flower-power slogans she had heard since the Summer of Love were true after all, and the freaks accepted everyone. Or maybe Vida was right and she really did *know*. It didn't matter. It was all going much better than she'd ever imagined. She was so glad she'd come back after yesterday.

And she was having fun. They were witty, quick with a quip, or a clever way of putting things. It was as if it were a contest among them they enjoyed tremendously, especially Vida, who continued to banter with David about Judy's birthday.

"*Et tu,* Judy?" David asked when Judy agreed with Vida about the Ides being only in March. She had no idea, really, but it was fun to gang up on him; so much so, she didn't realize she had missed half of her one o'clock chemistry lab until just before two, when Vida stood and gathered her books.

"We can't cut Swanson," she said to David and Wil. "While this petition is going around, we need to be sure his class is packed so they'll think he's the most popular teacher on campus." She tucked her clipboard under her arm. "I'm going to get every student there to sign it."

"See you tomorrow, Judy Blue Eyes." David grinned at her, showing his askew teeth. She felt her face heat up. As he walked away, she noticed a long dark spot down the back of his coat.

She was sorry her section of Swanson's class didn't meet until the next day, but realized she could still catch the end of her chem lab. On the way, her pace approximated the three-step of a cha-cha-cha to the "dew do do da dews" running through her head.

Maybe she could pull this off after all, she thought. Maybe she really could.

Chapter 2

PETE LOOKED UP OVER THE BUNSEN BURNER.

"You're late. You're never late." He pointed to where he was on the lab sheet.

Judy blushed as she pulled a petri dish out of a drawer to begin her part of the experiment. As they worked she started humming. "Dew do do dew . . ."

"What's with you?"

Pete, or as most called him in his program, Pirman, was a great guy: a math and science natural who was happy to coach her in her toughest subject, and a straight-as-an-arrow, compulsive dater who bragged that he had gone out with every girl in his senior high school class except two and who had tried at first to add her to his list. He was also a "hick," as she teased him, from downstate who was financing his veterinary schooling through ROTC. They had met at a mixer for students on military scholarships the first week of freshman year. The dating issue was a hurdle in the beginning. Judy didn't know why his type of clean-cut looks no longer appealed to her; however, once they got past that, Pete had become her first genuine guy friend. But since then, Judy felt, he had developed an annoying knack of being able to see right through her.

She kept humming and reached over him for the mercury thermometer.

"Earth to Talton." He snapped his fingers in front of her face.

The thermometer slipped from her hand and rolled off the

end of the counter. Pete moved quickly to catch it but missed. It hit the ground, shattered, and they were immediately surrounded by shiny globs rolling around on the floor.

"Don't touch anything," yelled Professor MacNeal as he rushed toward them. "Just step back carefully. You don't want to get any of it on your skin."

"Mercury poisoning?" Pete said to Judy. "You trying to get rid of me faster than the Viet Cong?"

"That's not funny, you know."

"Hey, gallows is all we got." He waited for her laugh.

"Maybe it's time for someone to do something about that," she answered in a near whisper.

Pete scrutinized her face so long she had to look away. He made her feel he knew where she'd been all day and that she knew better.

They finished the experiment and once class was over, Pete picked up her books along with his own. She sighed and followed him to one of the benches that lined the path from the Science Building to the Union. It was still warm enough to sit outside.

"Is this going to be another 'America, Love It or Leave It' lecture?"

She teased him like this often but knew he wasn't rabid, like her father, who actually had that slogan on a bumper sticker on his car. Pete was just doing what he had to do, like she was, he would remind her.

"What's up, Talton? You changed dorms, you hardly talk to me unless I'm tutoring you in chemistry, and what's with the jacket?" he flicked his finger against one of her metal-buttoned pockets.

"Don't tell me you've become clairvoyant, too."

"What?"

"Never mind."

Judy squirmed as she considered how much to tell him. On one hand, she felt she could trust him completely, but this was new and dangerous territory.

"Did you happen to recognize that song I was humming?"

"Huh?"

"Dew do do da dew, you know, it's 'Suite: Judy Blue Eyes.' I was called that today, Judy Blue Eyes, not Talton."

She examined the rooftop of the neighboring Administration Building while he waited hunched, forearms on thighs, with that open, you-can-tell-me-anything-look she knew he could hold forever.

"How are you feeling about your ROTC program these days?" she asked.

"Same as always," he said slowly, cocking his head in anticipation.

"Really?"

"I thank God for the full-ride scholarship that will keep me from having to work in a hardware store in Lincoln, Illinois, for the rest of my life," he recited, like so many times before. "You know that."

"I guess what I mean is, how are you feeling about the war?"

"What is it this time, Judy? The lottery? Look, it's not all bad. At least everyone will know, either way, and some guys will be able to get on with their lives."

She shuddered, hearing Pete spout the party line, and shifted on the bench away from his gaze to look straight out over the Quad.

"You know this summer my father kept describing me to his American Legion buddies as someone who has 'her head on straight,' not like all the hippies and protestors out in the streets."

"Yeah . . . and?"

"I didn't like it. Pete, do you think that just by being in our programs it's automatically assumed we approve of the war?"

"I don't go there. It's not up to us to approve or disapprove."

"I guess that's my point. Now that we're in, is anything still up to us?"

He sighed heavily, staring down at his feet. "I focus on the degree, Judy. That's the payoff. Don't overthink it."

She stood up and put her hands out for her books.

"Be careful," he said, handing her the stack. "You've got a lot to lose."

Chapter 3

JUDY WAS SLEEPLESS WITH BOTH EXCITEMENT AND FEAR that night, up at dawn the next day, counting the minutes. She bounded into the Tune Room as soon as her morning classes were over but stopped cold at center stairs. Where were they? She noticed a sorority girl from her dorm watching her from the Greek side and quickly looked away. She stepped forward, then back, feet rocking. She couldn't start all over again, could she?

"Judy!" She turned toward the voice and saw that it was Vida calling. A loosening wave of relief worked through her as she hurried to join their crowded table. Vida and David scooted to make a place for her.

"Meet Michael Morgan." Vida gestured toward a fierce-looking older guy with a yellow-blond mustache and matching hair, cut sharply to his jaw. He was wearing a jean jacket with a large peace sign on the back, hand-painted, roughly, in bright blue.

He gave Judy a slight nod then returned to the conversation underway.

Vida whispered they were making plans for the protest.

"Swanson said he thinks a petition will do it," said the real Greek guy, Achilles. "He doesn't want things to get too out of hand."

"He thinks a petition will work for anything. No imagination," David said.

"The Trots are holding education meetings in the dorms, so

everyone understands the issues," a girl with blonde hair said. RoMo, Judy remembered.

"Do those socialist motor-mouths think they can run this gig, too?" Meldrich asked.

"They've got a point," RoMo said. "If you haven't had a class with Swanson, the administration's argument might sound reasonable."

Familiar faces of people Judy had met or who'd drifted in and out of the Tune Room the day before jumped into the debate. Wil, Vida, and RoMo seemed to be reasoning out what activities would make the biggest impact, while Fish and Achilles ranted about how the administration was just making up false evidence so they could oust Swanson before something called the Moratorium could get going. David and Meldrich just complained about whoever these Trots were that seemed to be threatening what they were doing. Judy couldn't really follow, but worked hard to appear like she did, nodding and imitating the reactions of Vida, which seemed the safest bet.

"We need something big," Michael suddenly announced. "Maybe a march, if it's the right kind. We have to make a move that'll drive home the point."

"You're not worried it'll blow our thunder before the Moratorium?" Vida said. "It's only a month away."

"There's no such thing as too much thunder." He slapped a small red book on the table: *Dare to Struggle. Dare to Win.*

Judy watched and listened as Michael went on to talk about how the administration needed to see teachers and students standing side by side, and how they all had to step up since Swanson could only take a backseat at this point or they would kick him out for sure. That's the plan they needed to work on. When he was done, he locked eyes with each of them until they agreed. He skipped Judy, passing from David to Vida.

There was something wrong with Michael's right hand. When he wanted a cigarette, he tapped the pack against the table with his left until one broke loose. Sometimes it was more than one, and the extras would roll away until someone stopped them, silently lining each up in front of him. Once, he picked up a cigarette with the filter on the wrong side, the tobacco end facing his mouth. A girl next to him took the cigarette from his fingers and righted it. All the while Michael kept talking, and once the cigarette was in position, he put it in his mouth, lit it with a plastic lighter from the same hand, and continued.

The girl was small, with limp hair and a plain, flat face. She was knitting, working pure white yarn, and Judy was amazed it remained snowy among all the cigarette ashes, coffee cups, food, and other debris spread across the table. She didn't say anything and didn't appear to be listening to Michael, yet seemed in tune with each of his movements, slightly inclining toward him when he got excited and gestured broadly.

"And let's keep control," Michael said, wrapping up. He stood up, and the girl rose with him in a single, synchronized motion, yarn packed and ready to go. "This is no time for the Trots to take over or we'll be sunk for the Moratorium." He put his arm around the girl's tiny shoulders and leaned heavily as they walked out.

Vida got up and Judy hurried to follow her to the vending machines.

"What's the Moratorium?" she asked.

Vida stopped and gave her a look. Judy wanted to melt into the floorboards.

"You know, the national day of demonstrations against the war. October fifteenth."

"Oh, yes," she pretended to remember. "And—"

"Michael?" Vida read her mind and moved close, answering

in a whisper. "Well, he's older, like twenty-three or even twenty-four."

"Is he a student?"

"He's technically a philosophy major, but he never goes to class. Michael is our *glue*," she said.

"What's wrong with him?"

"No one knows. No one asks. Only Sheila, 'Sweet Little Sheila,'" she sang the name of the song.

"The girl?"

"She's our age," Vida said. "They're together."

"And the knitting?"

Vida had turned her attention to shaking the vending machine to accept her quarter.

"That's her wedding dress."

"It is? But . . ."

"That's what she says." Vida gave the machine a kick and reached for a cellophane package. She handed Judy one of the two Twinkies.

When they returned to their table, Howie was singing again, playing his air guitar.

"I've got it!" Howie said, "Marsha, My Dear," altering the name of the girl in the Beatles song.

"Give me a break," Achilles said.

"Isn't the lyric really '*Martha*, My Dear'?" Judy asked Marsha.

"Yes," she said, laughing, "But David has a song for all the girls, as you know, Judy Blue Eyes. So, Howie's been racking his brain for one that works with my name." She rolled her eyes as the three women stood next to the table, watching Howie continue to sing and "play" his guitar.

"Hey, man," Wil leaned over, mock-punching Howie in the arm. "You're messing with my god's words here."

"Who knows, maybe it's 'Marsha, My Dear' when you play

the album backwards. Paul's dead anyway. He won't give a shit," Fish said, repeating the myths about the White Album. "If you're gonna argue, do it over a decent song, *zeeze*," David said, making a buzzing sound through his uneven teeth that Judy thought was kind of cute.

Wil threw an empty cigarette pack at his head, unleashing a spray of tobacco bits across the table into everyone's food. As David brushed them off his books, he knocked over Fish's soup, who in turn retaliated by crumbling up a foam coffee cup and showering Wil and David with white beads that stuck in their hair. Meldrich overturned an ashtray now full of the spilled soup into David's upended pancake hat. He raced from the table with David at his heels, screaming to Achilles for help.

"Not worth my energy unless it's Clapton," Achilles answered.

"Come on, you know Alvin Lee's faster," Wizard said.

"Speed without soul," Achilles yelled, "You *do not* compare Cream with Ten Years After in my presence." He jumped on Wizard as if to strangle him.

As the roughhouse continued, Vida stood between Marsha and Judy, her arms around their shoulders. When the guys started throwing food and wrestling on the floor, she pulled them close and said quietly, "Behold, ladies, the men who are going to change the world."

Chapter 4

A WEEK LATER, JUDY PAUSED COMING OFF THE CAFETERIA line at breakfast before heading to her usual table.

"She's over there with all the noise, by the window," her roommate Maggie said, coming up behind her.

Judy glanced in the direction of laughter, saw Vida holding court at a packed table in the corner, then quickly turned back and put her tray down opposite Maggie, as always.

"Who? What are you talking about?"

"You've been hanging out in the Tune Room with her crowd since the semester started." Maggie took a bite of toast, watching Judy's face as she chewed. "News travels fast."

"So?" Judy took her time cutting her entire plate of pancakes into bite-sized pieces. "I've made some new friends. Why shouldn't I? After all, you go home every weekend." She stuffed two forkfuls into her mouth at the same time.

"What do you think you're doing?" Maggie asked.

Judy chewed slowly. "Right now, I'm eating my breakfast so I won't faint in Swanson's class."

"He's supposed to be a communist, you know."

"You really buy that bullshit?" Vida sat down and threw her foot up on the empty chair next to Maggie. "That's what the administration wants you to think. Swanson teaches political science, and that includes Marxist theory. Are we to assume we're so stupid we'll be brainwashed? What about all those business majors running around being anesthetized with capitalism? Should we be afraid of them, too?"

"You're not supposed to put your feet on the chairs," Maggie said, in her sing-song, tattle-tale voice.

Vida's eyes did a slow pan down Maggie's pink mohair pullover and gray slacks, all the way to her loafers. "I'm quaking."

She turned to Judy. "There's a big meeting to organize the protest tonight. It's off campus. I have to be there early to set up, but Marsha's going to head over around seven. Why don't you come with her?"

"Sure, of course," Judy agreed. She didn't dare look at Maggie.

Vida turned back toward her table and gave Marsha a thumbs-up. "Oh, and David will be coming with you guys."

Judy smiled and felt her face flush. Maggie starting tapping her fork on the edge of her tray.

"It'll be the same people who'll be coordinating the Moratorium, so you'll see how things work," Vida said.

"Seven, I'll be there."

Vida kicked the chair back, ignoring Maggie, and headed back to her table.

"The Moratorium?" Maggie said, now waving her fork. "With that bunch of dirty hippies? Who wears a sleeveless T-shirt without a bra in the fall, anyway? Are they why you made us move to this dorm? What do they think of your . . ." Her eyes got wide as she stopped her litany of questions. "You haven't told them, have you?"

She sat with fork suspended in air and mouth open. "Ha!" she said, finally, then whistled long and low. "Your mother's going to love this."

"Don't you dare say anything if you run into her this weekend. I mean it."

"Whatever you want," Maggie said in her whiny cadence. "But if she finds out, don't blame me." She picked up her tray and left.

Maybe her mother was right about Maggie, Judy thought. Magpie, she called her: small brain, big mouth. She pushed away the rest of her pancakes. She hated to agree with her mother about anything, but really, Maggie should be on her side. Judy had agreed to sign up as roommates with her when they first came to Central Illinois University, the biggest college on her program list. She really wanted to meet new people, especially from the city. She was also sick of Maggie always pushing her brother Rick onto her, but they had gone all the way through elementary and high school together, and she knew Maggie would be hurt if she said no. On top of it, she was always trying to ingratiate herself with Judy's mother, which made them both roll their eyes.

It had worked itself out, anyway. Freshman year Maggie spent every weekend taking the Greyhound bus back and forth to Belmont Heights to see her boyfriend, Danny, and continued doing it now that he was in junior college, still living at home. Judy couldn't understand it. She was sure Maggie would end up, in order, pregnant, married, and working at an hourly job, like all the other Belmont Heights girls. It was almost contagious, which is why Judy was intent on getting as far from that life as she could and only went home on holidays, when she absolutely had to. She felt like college had opened the door to her way out, and she was determined never to get sucked back.

Judy watched Vida's group pack up and move out of the cafeteria. She thought David smiled at her while returning his tray, but he could have been laughing at something Marsha said.

Why shouldn't I make new friends? Judy asked herself. She wasn't about to let Maggie bring her down, not when things were finally starting to happen. What do I care if Maggie does slip and tell Mom? Wasn't that the whole point? Wasn't that part of "the plan"?

Yes, she and her mother had a plan. Or rather, her mother had a plan for Judy, for as long as she could remember.

"You need to go to college to be able to take care of yourself. You don't want to rely on anyone else, not even a husband." Judy was sure that in their mother-daughter code what that really meant was "and then you can be on your own and out of my hair." It also meant the ticket to avoiding what her father felt was the highest professional achievement for a woman.

"If you can type, you can always get a job," he would say, and her mother would catch her eye as affirmation that her way was best.

Judy did not disagree. The career path for Belmont Heights women was either to be an office worker, a waitress, or a hairdresser, with milestones of early marriage and rapid-fire pregnancies. It had even trapped her brilliant mother, who had once seen the world, her bitterness now propelling them both. At least they agreed that college was Judy's goal, though neither one of them knew how it would be paid for. Figuring it out was harsh, and her mother had little patience for what she felt was Judy's slow understanding of what she had been trying to instill, practically since she was in the womb.

"Start saving now," her mother would say each week as she handed her the quarter for the elementary-school savings plan. "Because you know as well as I do, if there is any money for school at all, it will have to go to your brother. After all, he's the boy." She repeated her warning often. Judy wondered if she was saying the same thing to her younger sister. She thought they had plenty of time to save; her brother was only seven.

"Things don't just happen by themselves," her mother had repeated, time after time. "Save half of what you make for college," she had instructed Judy throughout her years of babysitting and working summers at the park district.

Once Judy hit second-semester junior year of high school, making a plan for college had become an obsession for her mother. The kitchen table was regularly covered with loan applications they really couldn't qualify for and pamphlets offering scholarships for strange majors like chemical engineering or business administration. Her mother never asked Judy if she was interested in these careers. The information just appeared. The lesson was clear; get out any way you can, sweat the details of desire later, if at all.

Encouraged by her advisor after winning a student prize for a story she wrote about a young woman living in France, Judy applied for a teaching scholarship. She hadn't planned to tell her mother but couldn't keep it a secret because she had to include financial information.

"Don't put all your eggs in one basket," was all she said.

Judy never showed her the rejection letter when it arrived. She took some comfort in the fact that she had been a finalist but knew her mother would only see the failure.

Judy panicked then. She checked out everything she could find, but the liberal arts options for the English literature she wanted to study were incomplete: partial tuition-relief stipends or debt forgiveness, if you agreed to teach for five years. All her saving had netted her only enough for a single year's tuition and room and board.

One weekend late in first-semester senior year, just before final applications had to be in if you had a prayer for any financial aid, Judy came home after a movie with Maggie, got into her pajamas, and went to pull down the bedspread. On top of her pillow was a brightly colored brochure. It was about a scholarship that paid for everything. It was for nursing. It was from the United States Army. She hadn't thought her mother would go that far.

She walked up the stairs and approached her mother, who was sitting under a lamp darning one of her white stockings. She knew she had heard her coming but continued sewing, waiting until Judy was right in front of her, holding out the brochure in a silent question.

"Well," she said. "Can *you* think of another way?" Judy turned her back.

"It was good enough for me," her mother called after her.

Judy was notified she had been awarded the scholarship in early February 1968, right after the beginning of the Tet Offensive. She received her instructional packet in April, right after the assassination of Martin Luther King. Immediately upon high-school graduation, right after Robert Kennedy was shot, she was inducted into the United States Army, where she was to stay for her four years of college—two at CIU, then a transfer to Walter Reed—plus three years' payback, a total of seven years. She knew that meant she most likely would be going to Vietnam. The war had been going on so long, in one form or another, that she didn't remember a time without it, and now she had grown up to the age where she would be in it. Her life was starting to feel inevitable, and she had yet to turn eighteen.

"Vietnam is where the action is," her mother had pointed out, "like when I was overseas with Patton." Judy had watched the war reports on television and seen the protests at the Democratic Convention. "Action" wasn't the word she would have used.

For graduation, her mother gave her a wristwatch with a second hand, like the one she used to take pulses, and her own pair of bandage scissors, its blades deformed into an awkward, lazy-L angle.

The afternoon Judy began packing for college, her mother motioned her into her own room. She stopped at the foot of the bed in front of the cedar chest that had always been off limits.

They stood side by side as her mother slowly raised the lid, releasing a strong scent of wood and stale air. Judy opened her mouth to breathe. Inside, lay the uniform her mother had worn as a nurse during World War II, shiny gold buttons against olive wool. Her mother gently caressed the caduceus pin, then carefully detached it from the lapel without disturbing the jacket's sharp folds.

"First time it's been off since '46," she said, handing it to Judy. "Of course, you'll get your own once you earn your RN, but you might like to have this until then."

Judy fingered the entwined serpents of the insignia as she listened for the umpteenth time to the story about how medical personnel stayed overseas for six months after VE day to help liberate the camps and deal with all the displaced persons. She envisioned her life in lockstep with her mother's . . . forever. Would they share war stories, she wondered. Would her life stop in the middle and turn bitter as well?

They took a photograph of Judy at the swearing in, and everyone noted how much she looked like her mother . . . and like a nurse.

There was no way she would let Maggie ruin it for her. All her mother would need now was to hear that Judy was hanging out with antiwar protestors. Maybe she should pave the way a little, soften her mother up. A short note, a hint about what she was thinking. Nothing her mother could use against her.

Chapter 5

BY THE TIME JUDY ARRIVED AT THE PROTEST MEETING WITH Marsha and David, the basement of the Lutheran church was nearly full. Angry voices were competing with an earsplitting banging of metal on metal.

"Let's get this show on the road," said a guy in a ragged sweatshirt as he pounded the rim of a table with a hammer serving as a makeshift gavel. Judy recognized him from the Tune Room. It was Wizard.

"But the SMC chaired the last two meetings," yelled a short guy with pitch-black hair and chalk-white skin.

"That's the Student Mobilization Committee to End the War in Vietnam to you," Wizard said, pointing the hammer at him. "What can I say, the people have spoken. Wait till next time. You Trots are used to that."

"Fascist," the black-and-white guy said, plopping down on the floor.

The room had hard fluorescent lights, orangey imitation wood paneling, and the slight smell of kitchen garbage. It was furnished with metal folding chairs and oblong tables arranged in no discernible order.

People were perched on every surface: in chairs, on top of the tables, on a low bank of cabinets along the back, and in the preferred position, cross-legged on the floor. Judy followed David and Marsha as they wound around, looking for a spot to land.

David pushed through, and they settled on the floor right in front of what appeared to be the head table, where the speakers would be. Judy dodged a girl who almost stepped on her hand and crouched defensively as people popped up and down around her. She scooted up when five new students joined the Black contingent and needed more floor space. She ended up sitting next to the defeated Trot and looked at him sympathetically, but he ignored her.

"Foiled again, eh?" David said, leaning over Judy to taunt the Trot. "Isn't democracy beautiful?"

He gave David a dirty look and turned in the opposite direction.

"It's an established fact that Trots have no sense of humor."

"Who are they, exactly?" Judy asked, whispering to David, so the guy next to her wouldn't hear.

"Pests," David said loudly. "Irritants."

"Seriously . . ."

"They're YSA, the Young Socialist Alliance, the Trotskyites, as in Leon . . . Trots. Get it? There're only a handful of them." He pointed out a few who wore red buttons that read PERMANENT REVOLUTION. "But they're everywhere, run for everything. They never win. Still, they take over the floor, won't shut up, and think they rule the world."

Judy nodded to Vida, who was wandering around eating a sandwich, chatting with various people, including one of the Trots. Vida knew everyone.

"Where's Howie?" Vida mouthed to Marsha.

"Studying."

"He should be here," Vida said, moving into earshot.

"Big test tomorrow," Marsha said. "He has to pass or else."

Another bang of the hammer brought the noise in the room to a halt, but it immediately ramped back up. Vida gave the black-and-white Trot a brilliant smile, then maneuvered to sit between Judy and David.

Eventually, Wizard gained some control and laid the hammer on the table. Judy watched a girl next to him quietly move it out of his reach. He raised his voice to be heard over those who continued talking.

"Come on, we've got work to do here," he said. He told them they needed to show solidarity with the teachers' union, which was lobbying for a substantial raise after nothing for three years. It wasn't going well, so it was gutsy for them to rock the boat defending Swanson at this point. "Let's show them how much we appreciate their involvement."

"Yeah, Workers of the World, Unite," someone yelled.

"Power to the People."

Voices joined in. Every shout was greeted with cheers and clenched fists pumping the air.

"First off," Wizard said. "Let's introduce the man himself: Professor Swanson."

He stood up, all in rumpled corduroy, sport coat and pants in unmatched shades of brown. He took the floor comfortably, as if he were about to begin class.

"I'm a teacher. I love what I do and want to continue, end of story," he said. The room exploded with applause. "At the same time," he continued, once the noise died down, "I'm an individual citizen with opinions of my own and don't feel that I should have to sacrifice one for the other. My goal is to help you learn to think for yourselves—not to agree with me, necessarily—but to be sure you fully understand the decisions you make and how they will shape the person you'll become." The applause started up again, and Swanson quelled it with both hands. "That said, I'm honored that you here have decided to support me, and I promise to try always to be worthy of your confidence."

The crowd noise hit its previous peak, punctuated by eardrum-piercing whistles. It took Wizard quite a while to achieve

sufficient quiet to announce the representative for the teachers'
union, a middle-aged man neatly dressed in slacks and a muted
plaid shirt. David whispered that he was a math professor.

"Without the students, we wouldn't have the voice we
need," he said, then went on to explain the danger of firing a
tenure-track professor.

He stopped after a few more words, but rather than return
to his seat at the head table, he joined a small group of other
teachers sitting in an orderly row with their hands folded in
their laps. One nodded, and another shook his hand as he sat
down.

Wizard stood again and told them the issue the gentleman
from the union hadn't mentioned was that the vote was only
two weeks away, and there had been no sign they had moved off
firing Swanson.

"They're lining up witnesses," he said.

"So what are we going to do?" a voice asked.

"How about our own witnesses?" Vida said. "We could get
hundreds of students to testify."

"Let's march," a voice called out, cutting her off.

"How about a bonfire in front of the electrical building, real
close up by that glass wall so they'll see the reflection all the way
to town?"

"Let's burn Jones in effigy," said a big guy in a flannel shirt
with a bandana wrapped around his head. "Nothing like fried
university president to get attention." He stood and took a turn
with both arms raised to draw applause and cheers that grew in
volume as it went on.

A little movement, like a reflex, rippled down the line of
teachers.

Judy couldn't tell if Wizard had lost control, or was just letting the ideas run.

"Attention," he said finally, banging on the table with his hand, now that the hammer was gone. "They're going to kick us out of here in about twenty minutes, and we have to decide. So, what I'm hearing most is that we march, right?"

The crowd was quieter now, muttering in agreement and losing focus as Wizard and others assigned responsibilities for getting the word out. Some people were starting to put their coats on to leave.

"The march needs teeth," said an angry voice from the back of the room. Judy turned with the rest of them and saw Michael.

"We march all the fucking time," he said. "Hell, all this movement knows how to do is walk. You want attention, you'd better be willing to do more than just stroll around campus carrying cardboard."

There was a stunned pause, arms halted halfway into sleeves.

"Like what?" someone asked.

"We . . . need . . . a . . . boycott," Michael said, punching every word. "We need to shut the university down!" he shouted, gesturing with his fist.

"Yeah, shut it down!" the bandana guy yelled.

"Fuck classes!"

The people at the head table huddled while the crowd began to chant.

"Shut it down! Shut it down!"

Judy watched each teacher fold their arms across their chest, one or two muttering into the ear of their neighbor, heads shaking.

Swanson stood up and called for order.

"Now let's remember . . ." He waited for quiet. "Let's remember a boycott is a tactic that will have student ramifications. It's going to impact grades, the students on probation . . ."

Judy thought he was a cool head, just like in class.

"We can't be selfish," David said, up on his feet. "Oppression is oppression. We have to sacrifice for justice."

Heads turned toward him, yelling in agreement.

"My issue aside," Swanson said. "We're all union members. If we push too hard, we could all be out."

The line of teachers evened out as they sat up straighter.

"What are you losing now in an administrative police state, slave wages?" David challenged.

David and Swanson were the only ones standing.

"Maybe you should teach the administration a lesson?" David went on.

Judy thought she saw a movement, but the line of teachers remained rigid. The room began to murmur.

"Let's stick to the point here," Swanson said.

"I thought the point was free speech . . . yours! And now you tell me to shut up?" David yelled.

"What about the draft?" Swanson said. "If classes shut down, you're all vulnerable." The room went dead quiet. "I really appreciate your efforts, but let's consider our activities in context. A boycott can be an effective tool, but we may need to save it. Remember the lottery is coming December first."

Swanson's comments punctured the zeal of the crowd, and David and Michael were overruled. It was eventually determined there would be a march from the Student Union through town and back to the Administration Building. People were assigned to pass leaflets to build support. The teachers agreed to attend en masse. The meeting broke up and they filed out, David stomping ahead. Judy turned to look for Michael. He was sitting by himself, smoking.

Chapter 6

"MICHAEL'S RIGHT. WE NEED THE BOYCOTT TO MOVE OFF center on this thing," David said as they walked back to the Tune Room. "Swanson's full of shit."

"Well, it *is* his job that's at stake," Marsha said.

"It's bigger than that. He's a pussy, and now he's made them all pussies."

"Did you see the teachers' faces?" Judy said. "They really pulled back when we started talking about the boycott."

"Nah," David said. "Union members understand these tactics. And they know they wouldn't have a prayer without us."

"Didn't you think the meeting was odd," she said. "All those people talking over each other?"

"Odd?" David stopped in the middle of the sidewalk, shaking his head. "You just don't get it, do you?"

Judy went silent and followed them back to the Tune Room, where they joined a group also fresh from the meeting. They were on their knees unrolling banner paper down the center aisle, all the way to the vending machines.

"Hey, can you do this poster?" one of them asked her, the copper-haired guy she had seen the first day. "I need one that says ROTC OFF CAMPUS NOW."

Judy hesitated. "Shouldn't we be sticking to the Swanson issue?"

"Same difference," he said. "So try this one. It needs to say SWANSON STAYS OR STUDENTS GO." He handed her a marker.

She approached the sign-making gingerly. She didn't want

to make another mistake but soon got wrapped up in the excitement. It was like working on the homecoming float, she thought. It helped that Wil had settled beside her and was now very friendly, chattering away about what he was sure was the real meaning behind every song as it played on the jukebox.

"Work hard, kiddies," Michael said when he arrived, without a word about what had happened at the meeting. He sat down and began reading *Notes from the Underground,* looking up to check on them as he turned each page. They worked, ate, smoked, laughed, and debated boycott tactics. The guys argued about the specifics of the lottery.

"You won't be able to do shit," Meldrich said. "They're going to take the dates of every day between 1944 and 1950—which means the days *we* were born—throw them in some big roulette container, shake 'em up, and then start pulling them out. First one's number one to be drafted, second one's number two."

The guys got more upset as they talked, while all Judy could think about was a story she read in school called "The Lottery," where lots were drawn to choose who would die.

"We've got deferments," Howie said.

Michael snorted behind his book.

"You got something that guarantees that?" Fish said. "Might as well fold it into a paper airplane and see if you can ride it to Canada."

"We goddamn better still have deferments," Howie said again.

It took Judy a while to realize that Wil had become quiet once the lottery talk started.

Meanwhile, RoMo calmly orchestrated the poster-development effort, allowing Wizard to think he was in charge. Vida seemed to be everywhere, spreading enthusiasm and motivation as she cut cardboard and painted both peace signs and clenched fists on alternating posters, half-humming, half-singing lines from dozens of songs, "All You Need is Love," "I'd Like to Get to Know You," and especially, "Tommy, Can You Hear Me?" which she quickly edited to "Judy, can you hear me?" whenever a lesson was at hand. "Love conquers all . . . 'Judy, can you hear me?'"

Judy couldn't believe she actually said it with a straight face.

"Give me a single example when it doesn't?"

And of course, after Vida shot down a few, neither Judy nor any of the others could come up with any.

"We just need to pull out of Vietnam now, and everything will take care of itself," Vida said. "What are we afraid of? We *can* change the world. It's our responsibility."

"You just keep thinking; that's what you girls are good at," Fish teased her.

But to Judy, when Vida said it, it made perfect sense.

"Wil," she asked at one point. "The first day I met Vida she said I came to the Tune Room because I *know*. What did she mean by that?"

"Don't try to explain it," he said, continuing to color in the Os on a poster that read STUDENTS OF THE WORLD UNITE. "That's all wrong. That's like seeing a work of art and trying to say it looks like something when it simply *is*. To *know* is to not have to say you do. Just let it flow and be happy Vida sees it in you."

"I *know*," Judy said to herself. She smiled as she volunteered to take over cutting a bolt of black cloth into armband-length strips.

Around one in the morning, splinters of the group began to take brief trips out of the Union to get high.

"We have a lot to do here," Judy called after them. "I'll keep going." She hated to miss anything but could hardly risk getting caught with drugs. And they were definitely *not* part of her plan. In her situation, she needed to stay sharp, always.

Instead, she focused intently on her scissors as she sat on the floor, cutting the material into segments. She had triple-folded the cloth so she could get more done faster and found herself working her jaw in time to her scissor rhythm, opening and closing her mouth as she made each cut. She stopped once she realized what she was doing, hoping no one had seen her, but then looked up to see a gallery of fraternity guys in chairs turned toward her from the Greek side, as if they were watching a floor show. They started laughing as soon as she noticed them.

"I think it's a blowfish," one said.

"No, definitely a cow, chewing its cud."

She continued to cut, this time with her mouth consciously shut. Just ignore me like you all used to, she wanted to say.

She needed support but realized she was three-quarters of the way down the center aisle at the end of a line of drying posters by herself, the others still gone or all the way up past center stairs.

"Hey, Tank, I think we found you a date for homecoming," said a jock in a CIU jacket. He bent down and picked up one of the piles of black strips and started draping them along his arms and around his thick neck. "See," he said, twirling in front of the others. "She's cutting cloth for the dress she's going to wear."

"Give those back. They're for the Swanson support march." Judy tried to get up but had been sitting on her knees so long her feet were asleep.

"You mean, you're marching for that commie professor?"

"He has rights," she said.

"Yeah? Well, then take his pay out of your tuition, not mine."

"How about we just take those back?" Pete walked into the space between Judy and the jock, a taller, neater version of them all in his pressed khakis. He began pulling the strips of cloth off the guy and assembling them in one hand.

Judy was surprised to see him, then realized she had missed their regular study session tonight to go to the meeting.

"Nope," Pete said, shaking his head. "I really don't think black is your color. In fact, since you seem to like picking on women, I'd say you should consider something paler, like maybe powder blue."

The fraternity boys hooted with laughter.

The jock sputtered. He tore the remaining strips from his arms and threw them at Pete. "Go ahead, take 'em and give 'em to your hippie girlfriend."

Pete carefully laid the stack of cloth strips next to Judy, leaning in with his face close to hers. He raised his eyebrows at the line of posters. "I assume you'll have reviewed those redox reaction formulas by next week."

He straightened up and circled around her, walking out slowly in front of the tormenting Greeks who turned their chairs back to their tables as he passed them. She watched him walk down the long aisle, up to center stairs, where he looked back, but Vida, David, and the others were just coming in, and she lost sight of him.

Chapter 7

JUDY WATCHED THEM COME TOWARD HER DOWN THE center aisle, picking up markers and scissors as if they had never left. Once they got close enough for her to hear what they were talking about, she decided not to tell them what had just happened with the jocks. They were talking about something much more important—draft deferments.

Howie had joined them and wanted reassurance that if he did what it took to keep up his grades, his student deferment would be safe. He wasn't so sure, and it was clear the dope he'd just smoked was making him paranoid. Fish was telling him he was being a major buzzkill by harping about it all the time, but Vida and RoMo were trying to calm him down by saying they would never draft anyone before graduation.

"Are you kidding?" David said. "With the body count going up every week? Michael?"

"The count doesn't come out until Thursday," Michael said from behind his book. "Last week it was 135; that's a grand Killed in Action total of 38,599."

"See, with numbers like that it's just a matter of time before they get rid of all deferments," David said. "It's already happening. First, you could stay out if you were married; then you needed a kid. That's why that upperclassman Potter got married in the first place, remember? Now they have this kid while they're both still in school. Why do you think we don't see him anymore?" He paused, letting them remember the last time they saw Potter. "And he had to get a job. Her parents still pay tuition, but not his, and he still has to make grades or it's all over."

"Oh, wow," Vida said.

Marsha fumbled with her scissors.

"I heard MacNeal will flunk you, period, even if you show him your draft notice," Wizard said. "He did it to a guy on my floor."

"Asshole," Meldrich said. "Like he doesn't know the wrong grade could be a death sentence. He's probably on Nixon's Christmas list."

Judy inhaled sharply. She had actually seen what happened with the guy she now realized was Wizard's floormate. It was in her chemistry class with Pete. The student had begged for a B instead of a D, but MacNeal held firm, saying they had to stick to standards. She had felt sorry for both of them.

As if reading her mind, RoMo pointed out that teachers couldn't suddenly give everybody A's because Selective Service would probably figure that out.

"They're already watching every move we make," she said.

"You mean every move *we* make," Wizard said.

"What's that supposed to mean?" RoMo snapped.

"And what's your draft status exactly, honey? Not like you'll ever be in this situation. Guess you can afford to be sympathetic to the poor prof."

"And I thought cops were the only pigs around here," RoMo said, getting up to leave.

The lone security guard stepped out of the Tune Room and a joint was passed. When it came her way, Judy handed it on to Howie.

"Maybe you shouldn't," Marsha said to Howie.

"At this point, it's either in my head or it's not," he said. "Goddamn class. What the hell do I need to know about Appreciation of the Visual Arts? I'm a history major. Supposed to be an easy A. Fuck that."

"I'm taking that, too," Judy said, wondering how she could have missed Howie, even in the large survey class.

Both heads shot up.

"The class with the big exam tomorrow?"

"The eight o'clock in Anderson Hall?"

"Yes," Judy said.

"Did you study?" Howie asked.

"Of course, I did."

"Great," he said, moving his chair very close to hers. "Then you can help me." He ticked off instructions with the matter-of-factness of experience. "It's all multiple choice. I'll sit on your left, and you just keep your arm down so I can see your paper. Simple."

There was nothing simple about it, thought Judy. They would both be caught and he would be out and draft-ready for sure. She couldn't very well explain how bad it would be for her.

"It's foolproof if you do it right," he said. "Trust me."

She frowned, all her A-student, rule-following ethics flashing warnings through her head. "It's cheating." She said it with a tone she felt sure would remind him this would be an unconscionable breach, and he would reconsider on his own.

"Look," Howie said. "I'm not that smart, all right? I'm only here so I don't get killed in Vietnam. That plain enough for you?"

They were all staring at her, these people she had come to like so quickly and now, before she had a chance to even begin to think about it all, she was right in it with a choice to be made, one that could be fateful for both of them.

"I'm so sorry," Judy said, shaking herself as if he had thrown ice water in her face. "I'll help, of course." It was the least she could do, she told herself. And it wasn't like she would be the one cheating, right?

"God, that's great," Howie said. "Vida, you're right. She *knows*."

"Told ya."

Someone passed Judy the joint, and this time she took a hit.

❀ ❀ ❀

THEY stayed until the Tune Room closed at three in the morning and skipped out singing and laughing. Judy realized how much fun it was to chant "Power to the People," and they all rooted her on, even David. She would sing out the one line and they would answer with a quick, "Strike for Swanson." They repeated this sequence over and over until someone opened a window and told them to shut up. Then they separated and headed to their own dorms.

As she approached hers, she suddenly felt her arm being grabbed. It was Pete, pulling her off center. She floated, then landed hard on one of the iron benches that lined the path to the classroom buildings.

"Hey, that hurt! What's going on?"

"Just what I was going to ask you . . . again."

Judy stared up at all six feet of him, glaring down at her. Why was he here? It was dark, and the streetlight only lit parts of his face—the tip of his nose, patches of his forehead, chin, and ears. He was mad. Pete was never mad. She worked hard to focus. This *was* him, wasn't it?

"Attention, Talton." He snapped his fingers in front of her face.

"Stop doing that. And I'm not Talton anymore," she raised herself up and tossed her head. "I'm Judy Blue Eyes. You know, 'Dew do do dew do . . .'"

"Straighten up." He sat down and repositioned her so they were facing each other. Then he shook her.

"No," Judy grabbed his arms as her head tried to catch up with the motion. "That's making it worse." He stopped and she steadied herself.

"How long have you been here?"

"All night," he said. "When I found you at the Tune Room I wasn't about to leave you there alone with what was going on."

"There's nothing going on." She rubbed her forehead. "Can we talk tomorrow? My head is killing me."

"That's what you get for doing drugs. And I'm not leaving here until you explain yourself."

"And why should I do that?"

"Because you're playing with fire."

"Oh, come on."

With that he leapt up and started pacing, back and forth in front of the bench, first with fists shoved into his pockets, then punching one into the palm of the other hand and yet again raising them into the air. She thought she could literally see sweep marks behind his limbs as he swung his arms and pivoted back and forth in a pantomime of fury as he tried to control himself. She shrunk low on the bench, shocked and dizzy, bracing herself for when he blew.

Finally, he drew his shoulders back, raised his face to the sky, and let out a deep groan of frustration. Then he opened his fists and turned to her, letting it all out. He ticked off his points, finger to finger, as he hit her with a barrage about how she was a *member* of the United States Army who, like him, was at CIU on a full scholarship *paid for* by the United States Army, and who was now screwing around with a bunch of druggie radicals who, if they knew, would probably think she was *spying on them* for the United States Army.

His words cut through her with their rage but not their substance. It wasn't like she hadn't had this lecture repeatedly with herself over the past year. Finally, he seemed to run out of gas, plopping himself back on the bench.

"You're going to blow your entire future over . . ." He threw his hands up. "That's what I don't get. Over what? What could be more important?"

Judy burrowed her face into her collar, trying to quell the sensation of her head catapulting off her shoulders.

"How about my conscience?" she said quietly.

"Your what?

She concentrated to try to make sense, knowing she must be very high.

"I wanted to come to college to figure myself out, Pete. To learn what I think and what I'm good at and what I want to do with my life, not to be a soldier."

"We're only students, Judy."

"But we're not. We're not like other students. They only have to worry about passing tests and maybe what job they'll get when they graduate. I know what that job will be. I'll be in the army, and they'll expect me to think like them."

She turned to face him. "So I want to be sure I can actually believe in what they're doing—what I'll be doing. You see what I mean?"

"And what does that have to do with hanging out with hippies?"

"Maybe I think they've got a point . . . on some things. How can I figure out what I should think until I understand both sides?" She was trying to use some of Swanson's words about making decisions, but could hear herself slurring and had no idea if she was making any sense.

"Just remember that without the scholarship, you wouldn't be here thinking about anything," he said, standing up and dusting off his slacks. "You're lucky you were able to get it."

She pushed herself up to stand.

"I said it before and I'll say it again," he said, pointing a finger in her face. "Be careful. Don't do anything stupid. The army gets a whiff of something politically radical, and you'll be back home in Belmont Heights in a secretarial pool with all those greaser girls in a second."

Her head wouldn't stop spinning.

"And you'll have almost two years of tuition to pay back."

Chapter 8

THE ALARM WENT OFF AT SEVEN THE NEXT MORNING.
"You and your eight o'clocks," Maggie said, then buried her head under her pillow. Judy took a quick shower and grabbed a swallow of coffee at the cafeteria before heading off to Anderson Hall, mentally running through the exam topics. It was so simple, the basics of form and structure, but she was having trouble keeping it straight in her mind.

"I was getting worried," Howie said, stepping out from a group hanging around the entrance to the hall. "We were supposed to meet up fifteen minutes ago."

Judy was startled, then remembered her offer to help him cheat. She felt a tightness start to pull between her eyes.

"Sorry, I'm a little slow this morning."

"Just a little reefer," he laughed, then got stern. "You're all right, aren't you? I mean, I didn't study at all. You're all I've got."

The tightness turned to throbbing. She'd never felt this fuzzy. He took her by the shoulders and turned her to face him, holding on until she looked him in the eyes.

This was it, she knew. Pete was right. She was about to do something stupid that she might not be able to come back from. But it was too late now.

"I'm fine, Howie. I may have looked better, but I'm fine, really." She trusted she would be.

Anderson was one of the largest lecture halls on campus, with hundreds of seats set up theater-style in front of a proscenium stage. During major tests, a platoon of proctors would patrol the aisles. As she and Howie entered, the proctors were lined up on the stage, watching the students as they settled in. She kept her head down as Howie guided her to a seat in the middle of a row, with only two spots open, side by side. He lowered the writing table from the arm of his chair and patted it. Judy lowered hers. As she waited for the test papers to be passed, she tried to figure how this would work. She looked around and saw he had seated them well; in this mass of bodies, unless they did something blatant, they shouldn't be noticed. Looking away, Howie ran his pinky vertically down his writing table, cueing her as to where to place her paper. She hoped he would stop now. She got it. She just wanted it done and over. He did a final shift in his seat, inclining toward her as if this were a natural position.

"You have forty minutes," a proctor announced. "You may turn your papers over and begin . . . now."

She knew she had to keep her left arm down, not curled around the top of her paper as usual. She turned to the test. She zipped through the questions about mediums, forms, the interrelationship between positive and negative space. She paused at a question about perspective and skipped it, as was her practice. If she wasn't sure about a question, she would move on, answer all the easy ones first, then return to those that would take more thought. Finally, she did a last check to see if she wanted to change any answers. Howie made a movement, and she realized she hadn't told him about her system. Didn't everyone do this? She started to panic. If this didn't work . . . and he ended up drafted and killed in action . . . it would now be her fault. Calm down, she told herself. Focus on the test. He'll figure it out.

She drew her shoulder blades back and down so she could finish up without putting a shadow over her paper. Sitting like this, her peripheral vision didn't include a view of Howie's paper, so she couldn't tell where he was. Her nose itched, but she didn't want to scratch; you never knew what would draw a proctor's eye. She felt Howie go up and down and realized he was sitting back and staring up at the ceiling after he finished each answer, as if he was thinking about the next question. That was when he would look at her paper. How obvious, she wanted to scream. She couldn't believe he was moving so much. At any moment, she expected their papers to be ripped from their desks.

How had she allowed herself to get in this spot? What did she owe Howie, anyway? She barely knew him, and he had made it sound like he was so good at this cheating business. Foolproof, he said. She was sure that, in her place, Pete would just lean over and cover his paper.

Her hair was in her face and she wanted to tuck it behind her ear, but with all this shifting around she was afraid it would attract even more attention. She concentrated on the test, hair in front of her eyes, blowing it away when she couldn't stand it anymore.

She returned to the question she had skipped about perspective: option B, the vanishing point, yes, that was it. She filled in the dot next to the answer, completed the other open questions, and finished her final accuracy check.

"Ten minutes," a proctor's voice rang out. She moved back slightly to give Howie a better look, hoping he had kept up with her, but not sure. She decided to divide up the remaining time. She would keep one side of the answer sheet up for five minutes, then turn it over so he could see the remainder for the rest of the time. Surely, he would get it.

As she waited, she wondered what would happen if she got caught. They wouldn't send her to detention or anything. You didn't get black marks in college, after all. But could they kick her out? Oh, that would be just great, she thought, all that anguish over the scholarship and suddenly she would be booted over cheating on a stupid art test. Her mother would love that.

She wondered if they would let her out of the army then. Seven years was such a long time. She would be twenty-five before her tour was up.

When she asked her induction officer if anyone had ever changed her mind and left the program, she remembered how the officer narrowed her eyes at the question. "You do realize you can't just quit the army, don't you? Unless, of course, you get pregnant . . ."

"Five minutes."

She turned over the answer sheet. Getting pregnant was certainly way too drastic, but what if you got kicked out for cheating on a test? If she didn't finish school, her program wouldn't want her anyway, would they? It's not like they would put her on kitchen duty peeling potatoes for the six years she had left.

She raised her head high as she pondered, looking around the room. She stared directly at the proctor at the end of their aisle. It could be as easy as catching his eye. She could settle the whole thing right now. Might as well, she told herself; she had sunk to cheating, what would be next?

But then, lowering her head, she argued the other side. What were her personal standards next to what could happen to Howie? What would Swanson have said about this? She wished she could ask him. She felt he would have agreed it would have been selfish to refuse . . . and wrong. He was doing the same thing, right? Taking the same risk with his activism while his job was at stake? It was the damn war that had created their dilemma, she decided. It wasn't their fault. It wasn't her fault. It was the military. She could get out now, if she dared. She raised her head again. . . .

Just as the proctor began to turn her way, she felt Howie lean toward her.

"Pencils down."

"Jeeze," Howie said, when they exited the hall. "You freaked me out."

"Oh, I wouldn't really have . . ."

"Those questions you skipped."

"What?"

"Yeah, I had to check out the chick's paper on my left. It's fine, though. She had all the answers. Thanks, really."

Judy gaped at him. She wondered if she might still be high.

"No, seriously. Thanks, you saved my life." He patted her on the shoulder and sped off.

Chapter 9

JUDY WAS MISERABLE. SHE COULDN'T EAT THAT DAY OR sleep that night, the two sides of her conscience battling away. Was she a despicable cheater or an admirable lifesaver? Her plan had really only been to put her toe into the counterculture to help her figure things out, but now she wondered if she had passed the point of no return.

Then, suddenly the next day, people started giving her soul handshakes, and many nods and winks that came along with "right on," or "righteous." The word was out that she had helped Howie cheat, but that wasn't how they put it. "Judy *knows*," the news spread. Michael even told her, "The movement thanks you," and she was beside herself that he had finally acknowledged her. She came to realize she had done something good, even brave. She began to reconsider some things she had always taken for granted about what was right and what was wrong. At the same time, she had to admit she liked the attention, but hoped no one would ask her to do it again.

Activities for Swanson's support march accelerated through the next weekend, and she was caught up, exhibiting previously undiscovered skills, impressing herself along with her new friends. Giddy with her new status, she volunteered to author the leaflet that would blanket the campus:

FREE SPEECH MUST REIGN.
UNITE IN SUPPORT OF TEACHERS WHO SPEAK OUT.

She thought it a bit dramatic but added a last line based upon its positive reception: "The Man Must Hear Our Cry Against Oppression."

The morning of the strike, she felt a little silly standing outside the cafeteria in her dorm pushing leaflets on groggy students who ignored her or tossed them away right in front of her. Then Vida appeared, grabbed a stack, and began to hand them out, showing Judy the technique.

"Our finest teachers are being muzzled," she shouted. "We can't let them down. March today. Support Swanson."

Judy watched interest grow as more and more students took the leaflets, asking when and where the march would begin. Then she joined in.

"Support Swanson! Join the march."

She handed a leaflet to a guy who seemed like he would be receptive and noticed Maggie standing by the cafeteria door with another girl, watching her. They were laughing.

HER group had all agreed to meet at the Tune Room after dinner and go to the march together, but when Judy got there, she found everyone at a table way down the center aisle near the jukebox, with slumped shoulders and depressed faces.

"They settled," Wil said, answering her unspoken question. "Swanson stays and the teachers still get a raise out of it."

"But it's only half as much money as they asked for. Can you believe it?" David said. "If only they'd waited for us, the ungrateful fucks."

"Maybe they got what they wanted," Michael said.

"What's that supposed to mean?"

"We rushed in to help the poor oppressed. And now the poor oppressed have more than they had before."

"But Michael, it's half, *half* what they were after."

"Is it?" He formed a smoke ring and watched until it turned to haze. "I think they used the threat of a university shutdown to get what they were willing to settle for all along."

"But it was your idea."

"Yeah it was, wasn't it?" He blew three rings in slow succession.

They all sat quietly, listening to the steady click of Sheila's knitting needles.

"YOU know who they remind me of?" Marsha said later, as she pulled the cellophane off her last pack of cigarettes. "The football team after a game they just lost."

She, Vida, and Judy had retreated to Marsha's room, leaving the guys back at the Union, rehashing the protest. Judy and Vida had taken over the bottom bunk, perched on the edge, side by side. Marsha was folded into her desk chair, both feet up on the seat cushion, arms around her knees. They were eating stale potato chips Vida had bought from the vending machines with change she'd found in the bottom of her purse.

"I dated a guy on the varsity football team, and you'd have to listen to all that every week," Marsha said. "If they won it was great, but if not, there was just no end to it. He was going to be mad, stay mad, and get madder and madder by thinking about it more and more. I have to admit, that was one of the appeals about not dating a jock," she added.

"We should tell Howie that," Vida said, altering her voice into lecture mode. "Howie, you're acting like a defeated letterman, and it's not high school anymore. Get over it, and remember there's this little war going on that could use your attention. These are just a bunch of teachers."

"Those teachers were pretty important to you last week," Marsha said.

Vida waved her off.

"I do see where the guys are coming from, though, don't

you?" Judy said. She was excited about being asked to join them, especially since RoMo and Sheila hadn't been. "Remember what David said, 'Oppression is oppression.' If you're *against* the war, you have to be *for* the protest. You have to be consistent with the stands you take."

"That's true, of course," Vida said. "And I'm sure that gorgeous Gagliano did say it." Judy saw her wink at Marsha. "But let's also admit that Marsha's right; it got them in their testosterone. You teacher, me Abbie Hoffman." She beat her chest, and they laughed.

Gagliano, so that was David's last name. Judy rolled the syllables along her tongue as if she were speaking aloud with an Italian accent.

"It's not as if I like it any more than they do that we were played by a bunch of people we're supposed to look up to," Vida added, suddenly irritated, "but you can't beat it to death, and they aren't the issue. The lottery's coming. People are dying. There's no time to just whine."

Judy looked at Marsha, who shook her head. She felt guilty suddenly, but wasn't sure why. "Maybe we should work on ideas for the Moratorium ourselves," she said.

"No, screw that." Vida shook her head. "That's what the guys want, don't you get it? They want to hold court in the Tune Room and go on and on about the grand plan they had that was brought down by a conspiracy until someone else, one of us for example, points them in the next direction. Then they'll start all over again, getting the attention and the credit."

She dug a hand into her purse and thrashed around until she was up to an elbow and her grimace turned to a smile.

"Forget them. Let's get this party going," she said, pulling out a wax paper sandwich bag that contained one perfectly rolled joint, with sharp points on either end. She held it up so they could admire it. "It's a work of art. Wil is such a Renaissance Man."

Judy watched Vida go through the process of finding matches and an ashtray, racing around the tiny room, filling it with long limbs and flying hair. She pretended to examine the purple and orange psychedelic peace sign on Marsha's bulletin board but was really thinking about the dope, and how quickly Vida could change. Vida took a drag and handed it to her.

"Come on, girls."

There was no way Judy was going to break the mood. She tried to remember what David told her in the Tune Room about keeping the smoke in and pressing down. It was much harder than she thought, and Vida and the others had teased her. Now, she noticed Marsha didn't seem all that proficient, either, exhaling almost immediately. As they passed the joint, Marsha got up and put the Moody Blues on the stereo.

"I love this band," Judy said, after a few tracks. "But I have to admit, right now they're reminding me of the sound-track from *Bewitched*."

They exploded into giggles. Marsha pounded on her thigh to get back into control.

The loud ring of the phone startled them, then sent them shrieking again.

Marsha eventually picked up the receiver. "Yeah, we're here," she said, trying to catch her breath. "No. Can't. Yes, Vida and Judy. Bye." She hung up the phone. "Guess who? They're all still over there. They want us to come back."

"Fuck them," Vida said. "Jesus, why do we put up with them at all? I mean, really, Marsha, aside from not being a jock, what do you see in Howie, anyway?

"Well, he's cute. He's really cute. And he's, I don't know, easy."

"Meaning?" Vida said.

"You know how guys usually suck you into everything of

theirs, like sports and politics and stuff? But Howie doesn't really care . . ." She pulled at her hair. "But even then, I guess you always have to fit in with it all, you know, their friends . . ."

"Screw fitting in." Vida got up and marched over to Marsha, who braced herself slightly. She pulled a cigarette from the pack on the desk and returned to the bunk. She leaned back against a pillow propped along the wall, pulled her legs up on the bed and made a ceremony out of lighting the cigarette, holding the match till it was almost out, then puffing like mad to ignite it from the last ember.

"I have to ask," she said finally. "You're pretty straight. How did you two ever link up in the first place?"

Marsha stiffened at the insult. Then, sighing, she pulled her bangs back with the fingers of both hands and held them there as she started to speak. She told them how she had been at the Tune Room with a few sorority girls who were trying to rush her and saw this incredible-looking guy smiling at her from the freak side, motioning for her to come over.

"Well, I couldn't very well do that. But he kept at it, and as we walked out he put his hand on my arm and said, 'Sit down, prom queen,' and he gave me that grin of his, and well, here we are."

"Yeah, there's just nothing like a cute guy to make you want to change the world, right?" Vida said.

"What's that supposed to mean?"

"Face it. He sucked you in, just like the letterman. And now you're still just trying to fit in."

Marsha glared at her.

Judy wondered how much of David's appeal was his looks and if she was talking herself into the rest. Then she realized that Marsha and Vida were still staring each other down. The ash fell from Vida's cigarette.

Suddenly, Vida took off down the hall toward her room.

"What's going on?" Judy asked. "I thought you were friends."

"Oh, no," Marsha pulled at her hair. "I'm not radical enough for her. We all hang around together, but we both know I don't belong. Not like you."

"Me?"

Vida burst back into the room waving a yearbook. She threw herself on the bunk with the book in her lap, the other two joining her on either side, as it opened to a well-worn spot.

"I'll show you the last time I cared about fitting in. Somewhere on this page is me with roller hair. First one that finds it gets the rest of the chips."

They bent over the book, examining the rows of black-and-white photos. When she couldn't take it any longer, Vida pointed her finger, and Marsha and Judy leaned close to find something familiar in the tiny, two-by-two-inch headshot. They couldn't believe this was her, until she moved the book to catch the light, and they gazed at a formal portrait of a girl with a bouffant flip and bangs adorned with a small bow at their base. They looked at Vida, then at the photo, then back at Vida, repeating the process amid yelps and wild laughter.

"Tell me you don't have pictures like this."

"Oh, this is a story I have to hear," Judy said.

"I will if you will. Dare ya?"

Judy looked up into Vida's grin, and it seemed her teeth had gone all pointy and sharp. She was sure Vida was looking right through her and could see *US Army* branded on her chest. She was suddenly lightheaded.

"Fair's fair," Marsha said, turning to Vida instead of Judy.

Judy shook her herself until Vida seemed like Vida again.

"How should I begin?" Vida took over the desk chair, squeezing in another quick hit from the joint. She told them how she was raised to marry another Albanian and help run a restaurant, but she was interested in what was happening in the world and got herself a reputation for stirring things—from the right for girls to wear pants to school to a Hike for the Hungry to supporting both Eugene McCarthy *and* Bobby Kennedy at the same time. They were both antiwar, she reminded them.

"So, you organized even in high school?"

"That and I sang." They looked at her in disbelief.

Vida cleared her throat and sang along with the record. "Nights in White Satin . . ." She went through all three verses and the bridge, twice.

Judy and Marsha dropped their jaws.

"Yeah, it's something, huh? I was always in the choir, had all the leads and everything."

"Why aren't you a music major?" Judy asked. She thought Vida had a nice voice when she sang casually in the Tune Room, but this was spectacular. Or was she just really high?

Vida told them about how she wanted to focus on music, but then met her first freak boyfriend freshman year.

"He introduced me to smoking grass and screwing, and in our big moment we dropped out for a semester and hitchhiked to Greenwich Village and panhandled. It was great. He played the guitar, and I sang 'Nights in White Satin' and all the Joni Mitchell songs. People would throw us spare change and offer us crash pads, and we talked to all of them about the war."

Judy pictured rooms with paisley curtains and friendly intellectuals from New York universities all talking about exciting things and being free to do whatever they wanted. She watched Vida in awe. She wasn't a student pretender; she was the real thing.

"My boyfriend was a Teacher's Assistant in poli sci," Vida went on, "and I realized that was where my head was at, so when I got back, I switched majors."

"So, you became a radical because of him?" Marsha asked. "Bet he was cute."

"You really think I'd do it just for a guy?" Vida snapped. "Hell, I was adding up body counts back in high school."

"So, what happened to him?" Marsha asked.

"Oh, history, you know."

"Because of Wil?" Judy asked.

Vida sighed. "Wil just is. He writes me poetry and talks to me in song lyrics. Trouble is," she added, "he's after my soul."

"But that's great, isn't it?" Judy asked.

Vida shook off the question.

"It's certainly better than the wimps I ever dated," Judy said, with a laugh. "Not that I even dated *that* many wimps. Mainly, I dated friends of my girlfriends' boyfriends so we could all double and triple. I even went to the prom with my best friend's brother. Talk about hard up."

"Bet you kept a prom picture, didn't you?" Vida said, springing up. "I bet it's in your wallet right now all folded up and cracked." She grabbed Judy's purse and started hunting through it.

All Judy could think about was the army ID Vida would find. She grabbed the purse back in a reflex. She couldn't believe what she had done.

"What the fuck," Vida said, "it's not like I'm some guy who's gonna find your Tampax."

To Judy's relief, the phone rang. Marsha answered it, then handed it to Vida.

"No, Wil, we're not going to come back just to hear you all keep bitching. No, I don't give a shit. You're probably too fucked up to plan anything, anyway. No, this time you guys figure it out. Just keep thinking, that's what you're good at. Let us know when you come up with something."

"At least that got their attention," Vida said, hanging up.

"They want us to come back and help them start to plan the Moratorium. I swear the revolution would die on the vine if it weren't for the women. And then he calls me 'man.' I hate that. 'Come on, *man*, you gotta help us, *man*.' If I didn't know better, I'd say he's the one with the extra chromosome."

She stopped and smiled. "Though I *am* the one who knows how to mobilize." She looked at Judy. "And I know when someone *knows*."

"What about me?" Marsha asked.

"You don't need to know; you're the prom queen."

"Vida thinks we all should be like her and do big things," Marsha said to Judy.

"Yes, we have a responsibility, don't you think?" Vida also said to Judy, "With the war going on? If you *know*, you get that."

"I see what you mean," Judy said, thinking that she and Vida really understood each other to the core, more than she and Maggie ever had. She wished Marsha would just leave so the two of them could talk.

Marsha glared at Vida again. "Maybe I don't want to *know*, anyway. Did you ever think of that? Maybe I just want to be comfortable."

"So, how comfortable are you about Howie and the draft?" Vida asked. "He can't even cheat smart enough to stay in school. He only got a C on that art test Judy aced."

"It was enough . . . for now." Marsha took a long toke. "He has a plan. Haven't you noticed? He's stopped eating. Nothing but water, ice cubes, and chewing gum. He's six-two and thinks he can qualify for underweight if he gets down to 160."

"And you're comfortable with *that?*" Judy asked, as Vida tapped her forearm, passing the joint.

Marsha pulled at the sides of her hair and flattened her bangs, running her hands over her head, hard.

"You have a better idea?"

Judy halted the joint midair and ground it into the ashtray, realizing with every twist that she didn't. A few days before, Howie's life had been in her hands, and now it was back in Marsha's.

Chapter 10

THE NEXT TUESDAY. JUDY STOPPED COLD WHEN SHE SAW Pete at their table in the corner, under the clock in the library loft, where they met every week to go over their chemistry notes. He was wearing his fatigues. She wondered if he was trying to make some kind of a point after their last encounter.

She had seen him in them dozens of times, every Monday this semester, every Wednesday all through last year. He had to drill regularly with the other ROTC recruits on the Quad. Freshman year, it was comical, and she asked him if he was afraid CIU would be invaded, if the Quad would be occupied. She taunted him that she had no on-campus military obligation before she transferred to Walter Reed other than to carry her ID and cash her tuition checks. But now, seeing him dressed like this made her feel . . . what? She glanced around to see if anyone else she knew was near and joined him at their table.

"Since when is this a uniform day?"

Pete looked up and started laughing.

"I could ask you the same thing? What's with the getup?"

Judy was wearing the suede vest with the long fringe Vida had lent her when she told her the button-down shirt she had on was "straight enough to make your eyes water." Later, Judy gave the shirt to Maggie.

"Very funny. You don't like it?" she asked.

"You kidding? Love the look. Very age of Aquarius." He started to sing, "Aquarrriiiiius."

"Shush, we're in the library, remember. Oh, and by the way," she whispered. "Eat shit."

"I'm sorry, ma'am, but that's not regulation grub. And our women don't talk like that where I come from."

He grinned at her as she settled her books. She was relieved that he seemed back to his old self again.

"All right, peace," she said, waving two fingers in the V-sign. "I assume they changed your drill-day schedule."

"No, but you'll appreciate this. President Jones doesn't think we should wear our fatigues the day of the Moratorium. He thinks it'll be too 'provocative.' Our CO doesn't agree, so he's staging his own protest by making us wear them every day until then."

"And they call *us* kids." Judy laughed.

"Unless we're being drafted," he said. "Then we're plenty old enough, apparently." His face darkened.

"Hey, what happened to 'America, Love it or Leave it'?" she said.

He narrowed his eyes and didn't rise to the usual bait.

She tried to catch his eye, but he wouldn't look at her. "You're safe, aren't you?" she asked. "You don't have to worry about the lottery, right? Aren't you set through graduation?"

"Oh yes, set," he said, clipped, as if repeating an order. "They're not allowed to pull me out for any new Tet-type invasions before June of '72. Then, four years of Uncle Sam payback, just like you."

"I'll only have three."

He smiled at her thinly. "I'd say that's blatant inequality. Where are the women's libbers when you need them?" He opened his chemistry book.

"Pete, are you having second thoughts?" she asked.

"Is this where I'm supposed to say, 'I can't afford to,' so then I can tell you, 'You can't afford to, either'?"

She was taken aback. He was still mad.

"Don't be so righteous, Talton. Picking sides isn't all that clean. You do what you have to do. You should know that better than anyone."

JUDY was unsettled walking back to the dorm. Pete was getting irritated a lot lately. She felt guilty that sharing her own dilemma might be making him question what he was doing. He really couldn't change anything, and that wasn't fair. It also made her wonder why she felt she could change anything for herself.

She picked up her mail and caught her breath. The envelope was addressed in bold, black Magic Marker anyone could read a mile away: "PRIVATE FIRST CLASS JUDY TALTON."

Sometimes she could just kill her mother.

She shoved the letter into her shoulder bag and headed out of the dorm. She walked fast, pounding the ground with every step, past the Administration Building, down the hill in front of the Science Hall, around the house that had been converted for the CIU newspaper, farther and farther past other walkers until she was alone finally, on the far end of campus just before the highway that led into town, at the lagoon.

It was getting dark. She chose a spot firmly in the shadows with enough glow from a streetlight to read, and sat on the grass against a tree. She pulled the letter from her bag, but instead of opening it slapped it rhythmically against her thigh, like a metronome, and waited for her breathing to return to normal. She looked out over the silky surface of the water.

The lagoon's winding ribbon was all that had been left of the wild after they bulldozed the cornfields to build the college. From where Judy sat, she could see the original teachers' college building that could almost pass for Old Ivy, in contrast to the rest of the campus, filled with bland buildings hastily erected to accommodate thousands of baby boomers. The lagoon was a favorite place for students who wanted to get back to nature, to escape from the grind, or to just be. She had never needed it before.

When she couldn't put it off any longer, she broke the letter's seal and pulled out the familiar notebook paper, *her* notebook paper, her own letter. She unfolded the top third to see her mother's handwriting above the Dear Mom:

What's going on?

Her breathing sped up again, and she braced herself as she opened the letter fully and then recoiled, as if from a slap. Her original letter was written over with lines, circles, exclamation points, and question marks, a mosaic of clashing handwriting and violent annotations.

She couldn't tell where to start and turned the letter sideways to read a sentence written down the margin. She touched the script, feeling the indentations, and pictured her mother's long fingers strangling the ballpoint.

You're in your last year before transferring and now, you decide to send WRITTEN communications like this!

She could barely read the comments for all the markings, but it was pretty easy to find the offending sentence, circled heavily: "I haven't told anyone this semester about the army thing. It's getting a little uncomfortable, if you know what I mean?"

No, I don't know what you mean!

She felt what she had written had been pretty mild, actually. She had just tucked the two lines in, after the news about how Maggie was getting better about stretching the phone cord out into the hall and closing the door when Danny called after ten o'clock.

She had followed it with a diverting message about how she got a B+ on her chemistry exam though she felt she would have been lucky to get a C, and how much she liked her new dorm, which was co-ed with lots of students from the city.

She scanned the rest of the letter, seeing big circles around the words *co-ed* and *city*.

Watch yourself and who you're associating with!

So much for trying to soften her mother up. She should have known better. Judy moved down to the comments at the end.

You're questioning the very institution paying for your education? After all we went through? Am I going to have to listen to this all year?

"No, you won't have to listen to a damn thing," Judy answered out loud, vowing never to write again. What'll you do then, Mom, take out an ad in the *CIU Clarion* announcing my name, rank, and serial number? She ducked inadvertently, then shook herself, annoyed that even though she knew in advance the button her mother would push, she let it get to her anyway.

Judy was about to refold the letter when she noticed way down in the corner a scribbled *Mom*, as if her mother had nearly left it unsigned and then thought better of it.

She leaned back against the tree and watched the light flicker across the water leading back toward campus. She knew she would be expected to write something in return to acknowledge "message received." She toyed with two-word responses: "Got it!" Or even, "Roger that!" But then she thought she might just stay silent and let her mother twist. She stood up, brushed the damp autumn leaves from her butt, and followed the lights back up the hill to the dorm.

THAT next Sunday, after Vida returned from a weekend trip home for her brother's birthday, she put her finger to her lips and pulled Judy into the dorm study room. It was deserted, as usual: an airless, sterile room full of unmatched chairs and parts of desks that were stored in their last stop before being tossed. It was always too loud to study in, with clunky vents that broad-cast the heavy bass track of every song on any album playing in rooms along the corridor.

Vida unlooped a canvas bag from her shoulder and pulled out an American flag, regulation folded into a tight triangle. Judy felt her stomach turn over. It looked like her family flag, the one she had the job of carefully angling into the bottom drawer of the front hall armoire after major holidays, taking care not to scrunch its three sharp points. Her father was manic about the points, checking them when he took it out to display on Memorial Day or the Fourth of July, or take to his American Legion parades. The points on Vida's flag were perfect, sharp enough to stab someone.

"See this? My father bought it when he first came to this country. It only has forty-eight stars. I'd show you, but it's too hard to fold back." She sat in one of the shabby chairs, petting the flag in her lap. "When he finally bought a new flag with fifty stars, he gave this one to me as the oldest child. I had it in my hope chest with all my mother's doilies." She let out a single, dry hack. "I brought it here for the right moment."

"What do you mean?" Judy asked.

"At some point, it will be important for me to make my statement, and I'll use it for something worthy. Maybe I'll wrap myself up in it at a march, or give it to a soldier going to Vietnam. Or, maybe I'll even burn it to signal the start of the revolution."

"I'm pretty sure at least one of those ideas is illegal," Judy said, trying to joke her out of her mood.

"Good! It will be my moment of supreme protest to use this flag, my father's pride and joy. He thinks everything about this country is wonderful, because of where he came from, but it never occurs to him to try to make it better. He's willing to settle. If you say anything about it, it makes him mad. I can't talk politics with him at all, and I have to just stop going home to visit because I can't help myself. He threatened to take my flag back this weekend. That's why I brought it to school."

Marsha stuck her head in. "What's going on? I heard voices."

Vida quickly shoved the flag back into her bag. "Judy and I were about to finish that little get-to-know-you talk we were having last week. You remember, don't you, Marsha? You told us all about how you met Howie, and I told you the story of my life, and all we got from Judy was some pathetic little story about dating wimps. I don't think that's fair, do you?"

"Absolutely not." Marsha settled into a chair and patted one next to her with wheels.

"Yes, Judy," Vida said. "It's your turn in the hot seat. We want to know all about you."

Judy could suddenly feel each of her heartbeats.

"Come on, who's the one who made you crazy?" Vida asked. "The one who broke your heart? The one you still pant for, besides David of course?"

Judy knew Vida was trying to keep Marsha out of her own stuff, but still.

"There's no one really. I'm not all that interesting."

"Not good enough. Everyone has someone who tortures them." Vida spun Judy around in the chair and leaned close. "Whose face is on your dart board?"

Judy got it now. Vida was in the mood for a game. "Well, if you put it that way," Judy said, feigning nonchalance. "It's my mother."

"Oh, wow! I love this," Vida shrieked. "Mom! Of course! Mom! Move her over. Put her next to mine. Mama! Mama!

"Well, we all know this story," Vida went on. "Mama wants control, Mama wants grandchildren, yes?"

"Actually, in my case," Judy said, "Mama, which I would never call her, my *mother* is pretty obsessed with babies, but it's as in, don't bring any home for her to raise."

"Loving," Vida said.

"And, be clear on how you make them, so you don't bring them home." Judy was having fun with this now.

"Educational," Vida said. Marsha cracked up.

"And, understand they will get in the way of, as she puts it, the rest of your life."

"Bitter, yet somehow inspirational." They laughed. Vida lit a cigarette. "Is she a professor or something?"

"She's a nurse, an army nurse," Judy added, before thinking.

Vida was on the way to taking a drag but missed her lips.

"Oh, wow! You win," she said.

"Is she really in the army?" Marsha asked. "Your mother, not your father?"

"Not now, but she was during World War II," Judy said, rapidly calculating how she could divert and recover. "She was overseas for three years in Patton's army. She actually saw more action than my father."

"My mother saw more action than my father," Vida repeated. "That is a great statement."

They were silent, and Judy could feel her face heating up. Her mind spun various scenarios she could use to explain without implicating herself.

"I'm trying to picture my mother in a uniform," Vida said after a while, "hauling her pots and pans."

"I was just thinking that, too," Marsha said. "But my mother would be packing her tranquilizers."

"Well, it was a perfect match for my mother's personality," Judy said. "As far as I'm concerned, she's still in the army."

"Is she super strict and disciplined?" Marsha asked.

"Yeah, I guess. I never thought of it that way. She's just always shaking her head and tsk-tsking like she's eternally disappointed and, of course, irritated I'm not doing what she thinks I should be doing, not that she ever tells me what that is. I'm apparently supposed to read her mind. I learn what to do by doing it wrong. Maybe that's how drill sergeants do it. It's brutal."

"Moms are all the same, like football players," Marsha said.

"Well, at least she doesn't issue orders, or does she?" Vida asked.

"No, not orders exactly, but you spend a lot of time on your toes, trying to figure out the point you seem to keep missing. She assumes I emerged as a fully-formed and all-knowing adult presence, like Athena from the head of Zeus, and should just know everything I'm supposed to do to make her life easier."

"That's good." Vida said. "Are you sure you're not an English major?"

"No, not quite."

"So, what is it?" Marsha asked. "Your major? What is it?"

"Yeah, come on, Judy, what's your major really? And none of this science bullshit," Vida said.

Judy was cornered. "Nursing," she answered quietly.

"Reeeeally . . . ," Vida said, drawing it out, "interesting choice. Hard to see you as a mommy's girl, but at least it's not in the army."

Judy's heart jumped.

"I wouldn't have pegged you for it," Vida went on. "But I suppose it's kind of like going into the family business, yes?"

"Yeah," Judy agreed, with relief, though amazed that Vida had driven right to the core of her dilemma without even realizing it. "You're around it and get comfortable with it. We used to play with blood pressure cuffs and practice giving shots by shooting oranges with water."

"I wouldn't let any of the guys know that," Vida said. "It's all they'd need to hear if they decide they want to chip at something stronger than grass or acid. I don't suppose your mother knows everything you're doing these days?"

"I'd say she knows about as much as your father does?"

"Touché," Vida said, and raised her hand for Judy to slap.

Marsha looked back and forth at them.

"I never know what you two are talking about anymore."

Chapter 11

ONCE SWANSON'S TENURE WAS SECURE, HE CHANGED THE syllabus for Poli Sci 201. He started by using a full class to thank the students for their support and to underscore that they really did have power, after all. This should be a lesson to them about the need for activism moving forward, he told them, this time against the war.

There was a faction that thought that he had rolled over and somehow stopped both the teachers and students from striking, and that he was now being rewarded for keeping the campus from turning into one of those political hotbed universities. David and Meldrich were of that camp.

"Just assume from now on he's a spy for the administration," David said.

Judy agreed with Vida, who felt, if anything, his new curriculum was even more radical. In Tune Room debates they pointed to the new reading list, from *The Strawberry Statement* to *The Armies of the Night,* to show how he was paralleling past conflicts with the situation today in Vietnam. Michael wasn't sure.

"You never want to completely buy the argument of any side in authority," he warned them late one afternoon. "You think you have all the facts, but you really know only what they want you to know, and in a second you can become a pawn or a patsy with the best of intentions."

Judy headed back to her dorm, replaying all Swanson's actions in her head, wondering. She was thinking about going to see him during his student office hours.

"Hey, Judy Blue Eyes," David called to her, catching up. She was on the sidewalk, but he stayed in the street along the curb, matching her stride. She reached up to fluff her hair, exposing the title of the book she was carrying.

"*No Exit,* eh?" he said. "One of my favorites. That stuff about people making you feel like you're in hell. Couldn't agree more. You in Vorner's class?"

"Yeah, he's good."

"He's okay."

"I mean, so far this semester, that is."

They walked on for a few minutes while Judy tried to think of something intriguing to say. She hoped he would step up to the sidewalk next to her. If he did, it would mean he was interested.

"It's Sartre's relationship with Simone de Beauvoir that's the really fascinating thing," David said, after a while.

"How so?"

"Their connection."

"You mean intellectually?" she asked. "How they fed off each other's ideas?"

"Of course, that was the basis of it all," David said, now stepping off and on the curb as he walked. "But I'm talking about how they didn't need to be married, and even had other lovers, but their primary allegiance was to each other. They were always together but not . . . bound."

"Yes, it was something," Judy grasped for a response. She noticed that the color of his eyes nearly matched his coat, green with a circle of yellow. "But if it were me, I would have married the lover Nelson Algren."

"Ah, so you're a traditional girl at heart."

"You *have* seen photos of Sartre, haven't you?"

"Traditional and shallow," he teased. "I'm not surprised."

"Because I think Algren was better looking than Sartre?"

"Because traditional is what army brats usually are."

"What?" Judy's stomach clenched. How could he have heard that so soon? Was Vida broadcasting, or had Marsha told Howie, and David got it off the grapevine? . . .

"Isn't your mother in the army?" He stepped up on the sidewalk.

"*Was* in the army. She quit after the war. Now she works on an army base, but she's civil service."

"What's she doing on the base?"

"Nothing major, just average nurse stuff, physicals and shots."

"For guys going to Vietnam?"

"Well . . . yes, I guess . . . some of them."

"Same difference," he said. "Must be awkward for you."

"I don't think about it much," she said, though until now she hadn't thought about it at all. Her mother was so clearly associated with World War II, it never occurred to her that she was also involved in Vietnam, in a way.

"Yeah, right."

"Well, I try not to."

"Like I said, must be awkward." They slowed, approaching David's dorm.

"What does your mother do?" Judy asked.

"You know, cook, clean, nag. You going in to dinner?"

She nodded.

"Why don't you eat at my dorm? You've got your meal card, right? Come on, we can talk about how the other people in hell will probably include our mothers." He smiled and put his arm around her shoulders, pulling her his way.

THEY entered the cafeteria to the smells of detergent and boiled beef, the mixed-up hum of clanging silverware, banging trays, and voices.

They went through the line, and David loaded up: Salisbury steak, fruit salad, two rolls, and apple pie. Judy just took the steak and some salad; she didn't want him to think she was a big eater. They weaved their way through the crowded, cavernous room around the Black Power and various Greek tables, bringing their trays to a long, nearly full table of six guys and RoMo, all from the Tune Room crowd.

There was a spot open for each of them, but at opposite ends of the table. David motioned for Howie to move down, and there was a sliding of chairs as they shuffled so Judy and David could sit together. David ended up at the head of the table.

"Hey, how's the revolution going?" Meldrich asked.

"Why would I tell you?" David said. "You wouldn't know Nixon if he was in the rice paddy next to you."

"As long as the weed was good, what difference would it make?" He laughed. "Watch out, Judy Blue Eyes, this guy sounds all politically sincere, but he's just trying to impress you and get into your . . ."

"Meldrich!" RoMo warned him.

"What did I say?" Meldrich said. "I was just going to warn her she will soon be enlisted in one of Gagliano's causes. I'm right, aren't I?" He leaned toward Judy. "It starts innocently enough." He looked around the table. "Remember when he broke the *in loco parentis* rules that kept boys out of girls' dorm rooms? We liked that one. You may or may not thank him for it as you get to know him better."

"Knock it off, Meldrich," David said.

"My favorite was the 'All Night Our Right' campaign to keep the Union open after ten," Fish said. "I'm still not recovered from that one. Was it a two- or three-night sit-in?"

"Kiss my ass." David threw a bunched-up napkin at his head. "Listen to this," he said to Judy. "I do all the work and see

how I'm treated." He made the whistling sound again. *"Zeeze."*
Judy felt she should laugh but wasn't sure.

"Don't say I didn't warn you, Judy Blue Eyes," Meldrich said.
"Oh, and watch out for that 'come up to my room and see what
I've painted on my wall' routine."

"You know, this is about what I expect from you guys,"
David said, and Judy noticed a turn in his voice. "And what I
expect from this place."

It was uncomfortably quiet for a few minutes, then Wizard
asked about the latest on the Moratorium. "You guys met with
Swanson this afternoon, right?"

"It's the same bullshit." David stabbed at a carrot, then
dropped it back onto his plate. He told them they had decided on
a student strike for one day, where you either boycott classes or
teachers can turn their classrooms into forums to discuss the war.

"I can see the story now," Meldrich said, stretching his
hands out as if reading an imaginary newspaper, "Students Take
Wednesday Off to Pout While Soldiers Die."

David pushed his tray away and sat back. "I hate to say it,
but Meldrich's probably right. This won't do shit. It'd be different if this was a decent university. Then we'd know how to get
something done."

"Here we go," Fish said.

"You know damn well the Swanson protest would have
turned out a lot differently if we were at Madison, where they
really understand street action, or better yet, at Columbia," he said.
"They took over entire buildings and shut down part of the city
for days. Now that's activism." He sat back up and slapped his
palm against the table. "And what are we doing? A 24-hour student
strike! Woo. Yeah, that's sure to scare 'em right out of 'Nam. *Zeeze.*"

"You've heard Swanson talk about this before," RoMo said.
"It's just a first step. Give it a chance."

"A chance?" David said. "Maybe if we were somewhere like Berkeley. What can we do here in our cornfield in the Midwest that can have any real impact on anything? We have little meetings and little marches." He stabbed a grape with his fork. "Hell, we wouldn't know what a boycott was if Cesar Chavez himself came down to dig out every grape they're still serving in the cafeteria, like this little fucker right here in the fruit salad." He twisted his fork back and forth, examining the grape carefully.

He stopped talking, and other voices murmured indistinctly, mixing with the clicking of silverware into background noise. Judy picked at her food, watching David carefully and wondering what he had painted on his dorm-room wall.

"I've got it!" David said, suddenly. "Let's refuse to eat them."

"Come again?" Achilles said.

"We'll give 'em a boycott, all right," David said. "We'll join Chavez and boycott grapes. He's got it organization-wise way over our Student Mobilization Committee."

"How did we get from the war to grapes?" Fish said.

"Seriously," David said. "Let's work on something where we can make a real difference. Screw the day off classes."

Judy was trying to follow, certain David must be on to something, but not sure what. She wanted his green eyes to notice hers, so he would know she was with him, but instead they seemed to take in everyone at the table, without singling her out.

"Stay with me," David waved his fork still topped by the impaled grape. "Everyone knows Chavez has been leading a national boycott against grapes for his United Farm Workers. That's a real opportunity to fight against oppression."

"Of whom?" Achilles said.

"Migrant workers—you know—better pay, benefits, working conditions."

"Gee, workers' rights. Now that's something new," Howie

said. He was crunching on a cube from a large glass of ice that was all that was on his tray. "Bet they'll give a shit, just like those teachers."

"Broken record, Gagliano," Wizard said.

"No, no, come on," David said. "Listen." He explained that the student strike was only symbolic, and if it generated any attention at all the glory would be grabbed by NYU or one of the bigger national schools. Then, he pointed out that the grape boycott had been going on for five years, and he hadn't heard of any current action on it on any campus.

He pointed his fork. "This salad proves nothing's changed. So, we can fix that and do something that will put us on the map, maybe even get amplified by Chavez himself. Then we can plan something meaningful against the war."

"That's a stretch," Wizard said.

"It's how it's done," David said. "One step at a time. Make a point, get noticed, build your ranks, and then let it all out against the war. Trust me. We just haven't had the right issue. Till now, that is."

Judy noticed how his voice revved up the more he got into it, like when he had argued with Swanson at the protest meeting.

"Okay, so we don't eat the grapes, that it?" Howie said.

"More than that," David said. "We have to be sure they *know* we didn't eat them."

"How?"

"Like this." David took a mouthful of salad, swished it around for a few seconds, made a sucking sound and spit a grape onto his spoon clean of sour cream, coconut pieces, and bits of mandarin orange. Everyone at the table stared at him as he repeated the motion with a second mouthful, then a third, depositing each nude grape at the edge of his plate.

"Well, that took care of my appetite," Fish said.

"I'm getting more." David got up, grabbed his plate and headed toward the serving counter. When he realized no one was following he turned back. "You're not going to tell me you won't support rights for workers just because you're afraid of a little spit, are you?"

"He's doing it again," Meldrich said to Judy. "And we're going to follow him again. See how it happens." He spit a grape onto RoMo's plate as he stood up to follow David. "Sucked in every time."

They returned to the table, each carrying huge mounds of fruit salad and a few extra plates. David transferred his cleaned off grapes onto one of the empty plates and placed the others down the middle of the table. The guys got into it quickly and began spitting their grapes at the plates at ever longer angles, missing and letting them roll more often than hitting the mark.

"Come on," David said. "Pick them up and keep them on the plates, spit or not, that's the whole point."

"Hey man, you're making me gag," Meldrich said. "Get it, GAGliano?"

"Yeah, back off, GagMan," Fish said, cracking up.

"Yeah, your ideas are so out there, you elicit a gag reflex," Wizard said, clutching his throat.

"GagMan, Gagliano!" Achilles said. "That's the name. We finally got one for *you*."

They all repeated it amidst shrieks of laughter that made heads turn throughout the cafeteria.

"It's perfect," Achilles said. "In virtually every way."

"I think I'll just call him Reflex," Howie said, licking sour cream off his lips.

Judy made a mental note to tell Marsha that he was getting at least a few calories.

RoMo and Judy looked at each other cautiously as they each

took a small mouthful of salad, then delicately laid a single grape out onto their fork, like an olive pit. Other diners, intrigued by the goings on, joined in. Soon the stock of fruit salad was depleted. Just before the cafeteria closed, they returned their trays to the conveyor belt and exited. Left behind, on each table, were mounds of shiny purple orbs, speaking for themselves.

Chapter 12

THAT NIGHT, WHEN DAVID WALKED JUDY BACK TO HER dorm, he was bursting with ideas about how so many movements shared the same fundamentals. "Oppressed teachers and grape pickers have a lot in common with unwilling draftees," he said. "We should all be reinforcing each other."

He hung around in the common room, and they talked for hours. She asked him how he ended up at CIU, and he told her how even with straight A's he couldn't get into a better school without a lot more money than his family was ever going to have. She was glad he didn't ask her how she came to CIU. When they cleared the room at two in the morning, he lingered at the door awkwardly, then gave her a quick hug and took off.

After that, he quickly picked up on her class schedule and usually appeared somewhere along her walk back to the dorm to engage her in long talks about his new ideas or what they were both studying. She was delighted to notice that though David always talked with great energy and gestures, he walked as slowly as possible, to make their encounters last longer, she fancied. The topics were more interesting than what anyone else wanted to talk about. He had come back to Sartre and Simone just the night before.

"You think Sartre was more admired because he was a man, right?" he said.

"No. Even if you agree with de Beauvoir, you have to admit she wasn't a very elegant writer," Judy said. "She kind of hits you over the head with her ideas. You just want to say 'Stop. I get it.'"

"I swear, you're the first woman who's ever admitted that," David said.

"Don't get carried away, now. I still think de Beauvoir's ideas are all over Sartre's work, and she hasn't had her due as a result, but he had the greater literary talent."

"It's debatable, but you've got a point."

Judy was always prepared with a new topic to discuss. Tonight, when he called up from the lobby, she grabbed a book off her desk as she headed for the elevator. She checked her hair in the reflective glass of the bulletin case as she rounded the corner to find him in the vestibule, leaning against the wall. They grabbed two seats in a corner of the common room.

She showed him the cover of the book, *The Fountainhead*. "I'm having a hard time getting through this for Vorner's class," she said. "I don't know if it's really a literary novel, or more like a polemic."

"Maybe the Trots should write their own novel; it would have as much appeal," he said.

She laughed and teased that he wasn't helping at all. Even if she didn't buy it, she had to write a paper and make it work.

"Make it work?"

"Yeah, Vorner says we need to build a case. You have to pick a point of view and support it with evidence from the book. It doesn't have to be the author's strict intention, but you have to be able to make it work logically, so it makes sense and could be possible."

"Interesting," David said. "I should try that with the Student Mobilization Committee."

He went on about the need to get more attention for the SMC, so it wouldn't be preempted by the Trots or even the Students for a Democratic Society, which promised action at any cost. The SDS had started to grow in prominence on campus. He was getting frustrated about all of them.

"We really need to accomplish something soon or everyone will start to bail."

"What if you had a strong central event during the Moratorium that was clearly sponsored by the SMC?" Judy suggested.

"Yeah, we'd run the march, of course. But something else, you're right, something really memorable."

They continued to talk for hours before he left, leaving her puzzled as usual.

She felt they were connecting on all levels and was surprised he would never try to kiss her. She was beginning to be afraid he considered her just a friend, like she did Pete.

JUDY spent the entire next evening at the library. She had to cram on the redox equations Pete had walked her through, as well as the rest of her homework and class reading, including analyzing at least a dozen poems by Sylvia Plath before Vorner's class in the morning.

Her new life was exciting, but it took up most of her time, and she certainly couldn't risk her grades or she would lose her scholarship. When she wasn't with her new friends until three in the morning, when the Tune Room closed, she was invited night after night as they assembled in one dorm room or another, supposedly to study, but they always ended up just lying around on the bunks or on the floor listening to music. The guys, other than Wil, would dig deep into the albums—not the lyrics, which she thought was the best part, but the riffs. They would imitate Eric Clapton or Led Zeppelin's Robert Plant by seeing how fast they could play their imaginary guitars, often down the spine of whatever girl was lying next to them.

Judy tried to get as interested in the music as they were, but to do that she needed to be high, and she couldn't keep up both sides of her life if she was wasted every night. She started to smoke cigarettes so it wouldn't be so obvious that she was passing on most of the joints going around.

"It's more important to experience life, not books," Achilles would say of an evening. "To hear this fucking incredible music. I mean, 'Come Together,' what else needs to be said? That's what's real, man. There can be no war if we think like that."

As Judy walked back from the library, Achilles's words came back to her. She was starting to feel there was an incredible groundswell everywhere she looked and in everything she listened to about love and understanding and a common agreement that there was no longer any need for war. The army was wrong and Vida was right. She felt the world had started to turn a corner, and was convinced she didn't want to be left out of it.

When she opened the door to her room she was stunned to see a USMC sticker covering the face of David Crosby on her Crosby, Stills & Nash poster.

It was true that as the semester progressed, Judy had transformed the room, covering the walls with posters and copies of the leaflets she had authored, crowding Maggie's many pictures of Danny and her family. She turned to the space above her desk, where there was a huge drawing by Wil, along with his own poem that started with the line "All I can give you is peace and a promise that tomorrow will be a better day." He gave it to her after a long night of talking, when he became her second guy friend. Now, the drawing was covered by a photo of Maggie's brother in full marine dress pinned with her own MAKE LOVE NOT WAR button.

She sat on the edge of her bed and tried to remember when things first started changing with Maggie. She was still there when Maggie walked in a half-hour later. She looked momentarily surprised, then turned defiant, throwing herself on the bed and scooting up to sit against her study pillow.

"I've had it," Maggie said, angling her head toward the wall so she didn't have to look at her. "It's one thing for you to be hanging with all your hippie friends instead of me, and I have to listen to all this peace/love stuff, but now you're crowding me. I *am* from a marine family, you know? Like *you* are from an army one, remember? Jesus, Judy, Rick is over there."

Judy took in Maggie's folded arms and the clench of her jaw. "I'm sorry," she said. "But you're so tied up with Danny that you're hardly ever here, so I figured it didn't matter . . ."

"That we're not best friends anymore?"

Judy started to object, then thought of Vida and realized Maggie was right.

"I heard you the other day. I heard everything you said."

"What are you talking about?"

"When you were in the study room. I heard all that stuff about how Vida's going to burn a flag and how awful you made your mother sound? That vent comes right into our rooms, remember? I'm sure everyone on the floor knows that Vida's planning a political crime and that you're . . . a . . . a terrible daughter."

"You don't like my mother, remember?"

Maggie hissed out a long sigh in frustration.

"All you ever do is whine about her," Maggie said, furiously twisting a hunk of her hair. "If she hadn't found that scholarship, you'd be back home learning shorthand. Hell, I wish *my* mom was that interested in my future."

Judy was speechless.

"It's because of Rick, isn't it?" Maggie said, finally looking at her.

Judy sank back on her elbows. She was so tired of hearing about Rick. He was two years older and an inch shorter, a quiet, tiny guy who had been good at track and nothing else. He had always had a crush on her. Maggie kept trying to push them together throughout high school. Judy reluctantly went from time to time, feeling sorry for him, until she realized these pity dates were just encouraging him.

"Why would you say that?" she asked.

"Because he's like one of those ROTC guys all of you are trying to get off campus."

"Maggie, you know I don't have anything against Rick," Judy said. "And I'm hardly in a position to be anti-ROTC, given my situation. It's practically the same program as mine. I want the war to end for everyone, him too. Don't you want him home safe?"

"Someone has to be over there."

"Why?" Judy asked, remembering Vida's words about just pulling out of Vietnam and everything would take care of itself. "I'm really starting to wonder, aren't you?"

"Well, it's not like he can come home now. He's over there and we should support him."

"Of course, Maggie."

"It's because he's short, isn't it? This new guy, David, is tall, I bet." She moved toward Judy, eagerly. "It just would have been so great if you and Rick had gone together, especially now that Danny and I are talking about getting married."

Judy couldn't believe Maggie's rapid topic-switch to something so trivial and imagined how deep a conversation she could have had with Vida about supporting troops, if she would be able to explain why she was interested, that is.

"Come on," Judy said. "You've had Rick and me paired off since we were fourteen, and I know you'll keep trying till we're forty." She leaned over and tickled Maggie's side. "We're still friends, aren't we?"

Judy went through the motions of their familiar banter about boys and let Maggie criticize her new taste in rock music, comparing it to her preferred—and relentlessly played—Monkees. She even instigated a pillow fight to get Maggie back to giggling. But she knew she was just buying time.

Chapter 13

SHORTLY AFTER THE GRAPE INCIDENT, AS THE TEMPERATURE slid into sweater weather, Michael clucked behind the newspaper, turned a page, and clucked again.

"What are you reading?" Judy asked. She was wary of talking to Michael directly, but the others had left for classes, and they found themselves alone at their table in the Tune Room. Even his shadow, Sheila, wasn't there.

He looked over the top of the paper and seemed surprised to see only her. "Journalism of the absurd. Observe." He snapped the paper. "The front page of the *CIU Clarion* tells us that the upcoming Moratorium has turned into a veritable potpourri of educational events, both inspirational and ridiculous, from sit-ins to seminars, something for everyone. There is even a handy schedule. I can tear it out for you, if you like."

Judy smiled because he seemed to expect it, but she wasn't sure why he was being so sarcastic.

"However, an even larger graphic shows young David. My God, this must be his freshman photo, hard to know him without that hat. Listen to this caption, 'GagMan Scores with Grape Spit-Out.'" Michael went on to half-read and half-paraphrase. "In the accompanying story, we learn the administration has removed Fiesta Fruit Salad permanently from the menu in support of the National Farm Workers boycott. 'Sometimes,' David is quoted with stunning originality, 'actions speak louder than words.' Well, what do you know. He'll be so pleased with himself."

Judy smiled again, rearranging herself in her chair.

"Sorry, I know you're currently under his spell, Judy Blue Eyes. But the day's news is not done," he said, turning back to the paper. "It is Thursday, after all, the day of the week when we get the body count. Let's see. Today it's ninety-six, a total of 38,735 KIA." He stopped reading and looked at her. "Do be sure to go to all the Moratorium events, those little carnival activities need all the fresh meat they can get."

Judy opened her mouth to respond, but Michael put up his hand.

"I know, I'm a jaded son of a bitch, worse than your David, I'm afraid."

She tried to think of something to say, but he started reading the paper again.

"Here," he continued, "in a much shorter story, we learn that progress continues on our national game of chance."

Judy watched his face fall into deep creases as he scanned the story. "Incredible. A lottery. Can you believe it's come to this?" He stared blankly over the top of the paper for so long, Judy started to wonder if maybe she should leave, but then he closed it and started to reassemble it carefully, caressing each fold. "They've turned it into a game, a game of death."

"Just like the story," Judy said.

Michael frowned.

"Remember 'The Lottery'?" Judy asked. "You know, an entire town draws lots, and the one who gets the black mark is killed by the others."

"You're right!" Michael's face opened up. "You're absolutely right. That's a great story. I read it in school years ago."

"They're forced to choose, yes," Michael continued, "I remember. It's sanctioned murder, like war. That's it exactly."

Judy was excited they were connecting. Michael hadn't accepted her like the others, and she felt she had to prove herself to him. Somehow, she felt whatever Michael, as their leader, knew about the war would be key to her own decision. This was the second time she had impressed him, after helping Howie cheat. Maybe soon they would be able to talk.

David came to the table with Achilles and Wizard. He put a hand on Judy's shoulder as he sat down.

"Why, it's GagMan!" Michael said. "Have you seen your publicity?" He tossed the paper to David. "Right on the front page. Charming photo. Too bad it wasn't an actual spit shot; might have made the front page of the *Chicago Tribune*."

David sat down as he read.

"Seriously, man, you pulled it off," Michael said. "Have to hand it to you."

David didn't appear to hear Michael. He studied the article with his mouth hanging open, soon stretching it into a broad grin.

"Not bad," he said, reading it a second time. "I knew it'd work."

"Yeah," Achilles said, joining them, "It was right out of the radical playbook. Chapter three, wasn't it? How to change the world by playing with your food?"

"You're just pissed you didn't think of it first, man," David said. "Go ahead and make fun. You can't bring me down."

Achilles slapped him affectionately on the back.

"Listen to this," David read from the story. "'The stunning swiftness of the campus response to the protest was driven by the cafeteria workers who were upset about having to clean up all the grapes.' Don't you love it? Workers of the world, unite with your migrant brothers."

"A few extra bucks, a few pieces of fruit to chase across the room, seems fair to me," Michael said. "Perhaps we can progress to a real cause soon, like the war?"

"Where are you going?" David said, when Judy started gathering her belongings.

"To class. Don't you have a three o'clock, too?"

"I think I'll just hang around," David said, looking past her to someone who was giving him a thumbs-up.

"Go get 'em, GagMan," said the guy, approaching the table with a group of four others. One gripped his hand, thumbs crossed in a soul handshake, another gently punched his fist against David's shoulder. As Judy picked up her books, still others were coming to the table. She heard many new voices calling "Gag-Man," then a familiar one.

"Hey, Reflex," Howie said.

Judy turned to leave for her biology class nodding to Michael, who didn't see her. He was watching the scene with an amused grin.

THAT evening David called her. "We're having a victory party. It's in Meldrich's room on the seventh floor. Can you come over? Oh, and Michael's here. He wants to know if you have a copy of that story you were talking about."

She found the story and headed for Meldrich's dorm, where she followed the music and knocked on a door with a piece of notebook paper taped to it—a drawing of a spittoon filled with grapes.

After a bit of scuffling, she was let in. The door opened only enough for her to squeeze through before it was slammed shut. Towels were quickly stuffed back under the doorjamb. The air was thick with smoke and the smell of grass and sulfur. It took her a while before faces emerged out of the haze. She was pleasantly surprised when David came up and kissed her on the cheek.

"Did you bring that story?" Michael asked.

She pulled out her *Understanding Fiction* textbook marked to the page. Vida and a few others huddled around him.

"It's exactly what's going on, a perfect metaphor for the Draft Lottery," he said. He flicked his lighter and started to read the story aloud.

"Come on," David said, "we know it. We don't need to listen to it again." He pulled her out of the room and directed her down the hall. "I'm too keyed up to sit still. I'm just so . . . do you believe they actually pulled the salad? It didn't take long. They were spitting grapes all across campus. It was so great. Of course, they couldn't let me know directly or anything. I didn't even hear about it until the *Clarion* called. In here."

A few steps and they were in David's room. She sat on one of the beds and looked at what was painted on the opposite wall in bright red.

IF IT WASN'T FOR BAD LUCK, I WOULDN'T HAVE NO LUCK AT ALL.

"Your Resident Advisor see this?"

"Like I care," he said. He sat down beside her. "It's just tempera. I'll wash it off at the end of the semester. Don't tell anyone. It's better for my image if they feel it's etched indelibly." He snickered. "It kind of is, though. The lyrics are from the Cream song, 'Born Under a Bad Sign.' I always thought it summed up my life."

"Come on, after the Great Grape Spit-Out triumph? I wouldn't call that bad luck," Judy said.

"It's something, I guess, but like Michael says, it's not really about the war. I seem to be able to start things, but they don't get anywhere. I feel like I could really be leading all this, you know? At CIU at least, or maybe even nationally, if I could just get a break."

He put the song on and they listened for a while.

"But there's always the chance my luck could change." He moved a strand of hair that had fallen over her face. "You don't want anything covering those up, Judy Blue Eyes," he said, and leaned down to kiss her.

As much as she liked him, she couldn't help notice that it didn't feel much different than the high school wimp kisses, Rick's in particular. It was better when he moved to her neck, and then ran his fingers up the back of her head, holding her firmly before he kissed her again, deep, French. Yes, she could feel the difference now. They made out for a long time, David's lips traveling around her face, her ears, then returning to her mouth while he looked into her eyes before finding another spot along her hairline or her throat.

Eventually, he got bold enough to run his hands down her spine and lean her back, rubbing the thigh of the leg she kept firmly bent, so he couldn't roll on top of her. He nuzzled his forehead down the front of her chest, and her alarm went off. She knew the next step would be under the sweater, up her back, and then around to the front and higher, very slowly, as if she wouldn't notice. She pulled his face toward her and kissed him hard, then eased up, taking her time with her tongue like she had read about in the Harold Robbins book they passed around in eighth grade. She had always wanted to try it and was delighted it worked, surprising him enough that she felt him let go and was able to roll on top herself. She put her tongue in his ear, for the sure giggle and shrink back. Close, she thought. There was a pounding on the door.

"Hey, GagMan, Fish has new weed, come on back."

"Get lost." The banging continued, and David went to the door and opened it.

"Do you mind?" she heard him say low and firm, closing the door to laughter. "*Zeeze.*"

"What is that?" Judy asked, welcoming the opportunity to slow things down. "That whistle you do?" He smiled and pulled something from his desk drawer and blew into it. It was a kazoo.

"Pretty close, don't you think?" He changed the record to the Grateful Dead's "Truckin'" and played the kazoo to accompany the song. She laughed, surprised at this side of him.

"There was this group of guys I used to hang out with in high school, and we'd play this over and over. It's a great marching song." He demonstrated by high-stepping up and down the small room playing the kazoo in time to the music. "Pretty soon, we could all imitate the sound and used it as a secret code in class. It drove the teachers crazy. I guess it became part of my language."

"Sounds like fun."

"It was, for a while. Seems pretty silly now."

"What do you mean? There's nothing wrong with fun."

"It's not a fun world anymore, Judy. You know Michael's down there reading about drawing lots for the draft, for chrissake. We have no control over our lives at all."

It still surprised Judy how quickly everyone changed, jumping from silly to serious, first Vida, then Michael, and now David. The two sat side by side on the edge of the bed, facing the Cream lyrics. Judy tried to think of something politically serious to say.

"Is that why you don't like Swanson? Because you don't think he cares enough?"

"He calls himself a radical, but all he ever does is shut everyone down, like at the protest meeting. I had a real movement going on last semester about getting ROTC off campus, and he killed it over some legal bit—as if war is legal." He shook his head slowly. "I guess that's the issue, isn't it. War *is* legal and we can't do shit about it."

Judy didn't know what to do, so she took his hand. He closed his fingers over hers.

"I'm thinking about going for a CO," David said.

"CO?"

"Conscientious Objector, to stay out of the military."

"Oh, right. Of course. Do you think you can get one?"

"I've got something in the works. A guy in my dorm is a Baha'i, and he's been talking to me about becoming one."

"Baha'i?"

"It's a religion that began in the Middle East, but now it's in every country. They have this incredible temple just north of the city. I've been there." He paused. "It's a guarantee, really. If you're a Baha'i, you get automatic Conscientious Objector status, no questions. This guy thinks I should do more, like start a worship group here on campus to show I'm serious, or something, but I don't think I have to go that far."

"Will they take you?"

"They'll take me if I want it."

"Sounds almost too good to be true."

"You don't think it sounds like a cop-out?"

She cradled his chin in her palm. This time, when his hand moved down the front of her sweater, she just let it go.

Chapter 14

"SIX O'CLOCK IN FRONT OF THE UNION," VIDA SAID, ON THE morning of October fifteenth. "You can still change your mind, you know. We need you for the Lottery Performance." She stood up and pulled on her jacket.

"Got it," Judy said.

"No, you don't get it, Judy. No one understands why you won't be part of the Performance. I don't get it. Marsha doesn't get it. Michael wants to talk to you about it. He'll be in the Tune Room all day setting up, so you'd better find him there before six. And, you know David's pissed. You're the one who told him to do an SMC-sponsored event, after all." She threw her bag over her arm, grabbed what was portable off her breakfast plate, and shook a piece of bacon at Judy as she turned to leave the cafeteria. "You'll be there."

Judy was almost sorry she ever mentioned the "The Lottery" story. She had only come down to breakfast to get away from Maggie, who had been at her about all the horrible things that could happen if she went to the Moratorium. Now Vida was on her case.

She needed to find a place to be alone. This was going to be her day. She wanted to plot it out carefully, without interference. She ducked into the TV room. Though it was empty at this hour, she still took a seat in the far corner. She reached into her pocket and pulled the article Michael had given her from the *Clarion* with the schedule of activities and reviewed it, wondering where to start. She wanted to attend as many activities as she could, certain it was her best chance to catch up to the others in their understanding of the war.

"Yeah, that's the biggest lie since the Gulf of Tonkin," David said to Fish just the day before when he said he found a piece of actual meat in his vegetable beef soup. Even Howie seemed to know what he meant. She always confused the Gulf of Tonkin with the *Pueblo* incident. Weren't they both submarines, boats? She hadn't paid that much attention. She had always been a good student, but now she felt as if she had come into a class midterm and was trying to piece it all together without being able to let on about what she didn't know.

She looked down the list of lectures and discussions led by what had to be every group on campus. The topics covered the gamut: "The Real Roots of the War: How We Got Involved and How We Can Get Out," "The Deception of the Domino Theory," "Countdown to the Revolution." There were also multiple protest activities, including sit-ins at each of the administrative buildings, group signings of petitions to be sent to Washington, and sessions to express feelings about the war where you could participate in writing an epic poem like the *Iliad*, painting a giant banner like *Guernica*, or writing a protest song. The day would end with a candlelight march at dusk across campus, through town and back to a final rally at the Union.

The performance of "The Lottery" was to be held just before the march. They were going to read the entire story out loud, and she knew they would need a large cast.

As much as she wanted to participate, she couldn't risk the exposure. It was one thing to hand out leaflets in her dorm, but this was different. She was pretty sure CIU was low enough on the radar not to have government spies infiltrating the student movement, but she couldn't risk showing up in a *Clarion* photo.

She ticked off a list of the sessions she wanted to attend but felt she should start by at least making the gesture of attending a class just to see what would happen, especially MacNeal's, given how he had shut down Wizard's friend about his grade.

Today, class attendance was spotty, and MacNeal motioned for everyone to come down and fill from the front rather than stay spread out. That made it easier for Judy to avoid sitting in her usual spot, next to Pete. MacNeal paced as they rearranged themselves, then settled with his hands gripping the podium, staring at them until they began to shift and whisper.

"I know I'm supposed to be talking about the war today," he said finally. "But what do I know about it? I'm a chemistry teacher."

The room waited to see what he would say next. They began to fidget.

"So, here it is," MacNeal said, at last. "If you want to talk about the war, go ahead." He gestured toward the door. "There are all kinds of people out there to do so with you. But if you stay here, we're going to talk about chemistry." He turned to the board, picked up a piece of chalk, and began to write out the equation for a redox reaction.

The students responded unevenly, some packing up immediately, sneering at how he could ignore an issue as important as the war, but most looking around to see what everyone else would do.

Judy felt she had to leave. She couldn't focus on chemistry and was anxious to get out and see what else was going on, but she felt odd about it. As she walked up the stairs and took a final look back, MacNeal was continuing to lecture to five students as if the room were full. He asked Pete a question about the equation. Judy knew the answer but kept walking.

ONCE out the door, it was as if a bell had rung and the entire school population had bolted outdoors. They were playful, like kids on a snow day, or the beginning of spring when classes moved outside to the lawn. Students were sharing schedules, bent over sidewalk tables full of literature, wandering over to hear music, or gathered around a speaker. It was as if permanently gray CIU had suddenly become ignited with energy; even the sun had come out, shining on the many colors of the fall leaves.

She wandered from forum to forum, staying for an entire presentation or leaving early if she got the premise right away and could move on to check out something else.

Throughout the day she felt both liberated to be able to just listen and learn, and uneasy as a double agent, hiding from two camps. She was careful to avoid *Clarion* cameras and made sure to hang at the edges, sitting in the last row or leaning against a wall in the back, apart from what had now become her group of friends. She would acknowledge people she knew with a nod if they spotted her and then turn quickly to the speaker as if rapt with attention.

Judy came into the packed Watson Auditorium for "The Real Roots of the War" session as they were finishing up about the French involvement in Indochina. On the stage, the speaker concluded, and Swanson took over, unbuttoning his tweed coat and hanging his thumbs from the loops of his jeans.

"The real flashpoint," he said, "was the incident at the Gulf of Tonkin in 1964." Judy perked up. No wonder she didn't know. She had been in eighth grade. She listened carefully as Swanson detailed the attacks by North Vietnam on US destroyers.

"That can be viewed as the real start of the war," he said. "President Johnson went on television on the fourth of August to announce air strikes against North Vietnam, a huge escalation."

It was the summer. She was fourteen. She would have been at the beach, not watching the news.

"But was it really an attack, or an excuse? Was Johnson just itching for this fight? How much was true and how much was an arrogant charade for a country that prides itself on the fact that we have never lost a war?

"These are not rhetorical questions, people," he went on. "We need to know the answers. Do you know if Tonkin was real or a setup?" He pointed to a girl in the third row wearing a yellow paisley tunic.

She sunk in her seat.

Judy was glad she blended in, in her denim and olive drab.

"How are we supposed to know what really happened, if the government is lying to us?" Heads turned toward a female voice on the side of the auditorium.

Judy recognized her as one of the Trots. Wil was sitting next to her.

"Exactly," Swanson said. "We don't know what to believe. We don't have the facts, or know if the facts are true. We need to question: question authority, question everything." He let them shout their agreement.

Judy felt he was talking directly to her. Hadn't she just blindly accepted this scholarship, caring only about herself, without questioning anything?

"There is, however, something we absolutely all know is true," Swanson said, raising his voice. "There's a lottery coming. They're dusting off an old Selective Service tool that hasn't been used since World War II. A draft lottery can wipe out the lives of half the men in this room, men who are considered too young to vote but not too young to die."

"So, what do we do?" a voice said from the middle of the room.

"Get informed. I know you all hate hearing this, but you're in a bubble here on campus. It's the first time a war is on television every night, and you're not tuning in. I bet you never thought a teacher would tell you to watch TV, and I know there are only a few sets on campus, but you have to get involved and work harder to realize what's going on. Then you can better decide what you want to do.

"And, that's what today is all about," he continued. "It's a moratorium. Do you know what that means?" He went on to explain that a moratorium was a delay, a postponement, to give time to reflect, to question, so the country didn't stumble blindly ahead in a direction that might be wrong. It would be a series— one day in October, two days in November, three days in December—until the end of the war.

Swanson took off his jacket, laid it across the podium, and wiped the sweat from his receding hairline. He moved dead center on the stage. "How many of you are going to Washington for the next one on November fifteenth? We need a million marchers to make our point."

"I am," scattered voices said, accompanied by a few raised hands.

"That's it? I see." He slowly turned his head and scanned the room. "You think you don't have power because you're kids? Because you don't think anyone will listen?

"Don't underestimate yourselves. Each of you has a choice, a decision to make, a conscience to deal with." He pointed a finger in a half circle across the width of the auditorium. Judy was sure he was looking right into her soul. "What will you tell your children you did right here at this decisive moment? Your actions today will define who you are . . . and who you will ever hope to become.

"There are thousands listening to us today, there will be a million on November fifteenth when the whole world truly will be watching." He paused. "Now, let me ask again. Are you going to Washington?"

"Yes!" yelled the crowd. Judy had to catch herself to keep from joining them.

"And you're going because . . ."

"The whole world is watching."

Swanson nodded, picking up his jacket as the crowd chanted in obedience, arms pumping with clenched fists.

"The whole world is watching. The whole world is watching." The chanting went on for a while, then dribbled down, first softer, then with fewer voices.

Swanson would be going to Washington himself, people whispered around her.

Judy watched a plump woman in tight jeans confidently stride across the stage to shake Swanson's hand. Judy recognized her as one of the student senators. She lowered the rostrum microphone.

"We're sending at least two buses from CIU to Washington, but we can rent more," she said. "So, sign up by October thirty-first. Registration forms are in the back. You can turn them in at the Tune Room or any of the dorms."

Judy took one of the orange slips being passed out at the exits. She stared at it, then at all the students filing out of the auditorium, envying them their freedom. Any one of them could go to Washington as easily as filling out this form.

Chapter 15

JUDY HEADED ACROSS CAMPUS, THE FOLDED REGISTRATION slip in her pocket, passing in front of the Quad where a few musicians were singing, "Be the first one on your block to have your son come home in a box."

She saw David's hat and duster and was about to skirt the area when she realized he had his arm around a small blonde. A zip of pain, like an electric charge, shot through her. It was Sally, a girl she had only seen once before, passing in front of David.

"What a body," she had overheard him say to Achilles, as she watched Sally walk ahead of them early in the semester, wondering at the appeal of her hipless, breastless, little pencil shape. He probably called her Mustang Sally. Now, she turned quickly and headed to the lagoon as the musicians' chorus echoed in her ears, "Whoopee! We're all going to die."

The wind was up, and it was really too cold to sit on the grass, but she did it anyway, clutching her knees and covering her face, until she settled down enough to look up.

She watched red and gold leaves detach and seem to remain at bay, suspended, waiting to be thrown across the water by a gust or just land at random on the soft, browning grass. She picked one up, then tossed it, choosing another that still had some green, yellow green like David's eyes. She carefully took it apart, separating the smooth leaf material from the veins until there was nothing left but the skeleton.

"He loves me not," she said out loud, as she held out her palm, letting the wind take away the remains.

It was because she had stopped him. She knew it, even though she assumed they were just playing around. She let him unhook her bra, but not unzip her pants. He talked about how they didn't need to play games, and she said games could be fun and teased him about his wandering hand trouble, WHT they called it in high school. She had lost more than one second date to WHT in her time but never with anyone she really liked. David was different. How many guys who looked like he did knew about Sartre or could lead something like the grape boycott?

Acronyms scrambled in her head: WHT, SMC, ROTC. She was in WRAIN, the Walter Reed Army Institute of Nursing program. ROTC . . . WRAIN . . . different letters, same thing. No one knew what WRAIN was, thank God. There were no slurs like ROT-ZEE. What could they say?   She's WRAIN? WRAIN, rain, everywhere but not a drop . . .

She was tired of feeling so stupid—stupid about David, stupid about being trapped into this army thing. She should have been smarter about both and thought there was a time when she would have been. She had even been kind of excited about the army at first, once she'd accepted it. As a kid, she had nearly memorized every image in her mother's scrapbooks: pictures of London and the south of France, ticket stubs and playbills of events enjoyed on leave when the cities were in blackout, and photos of clowning GIs and captured German soldiers huddled together at a train station. Interspersed had been clippings about casualties, veiny snapshots of the rubble after bombings, and liberated POWs with dead gazes, not believing they were now free.

From time to time throughout her childhood, her mother had gone through some of the photos with her, talking about range-of-motion triage for prisoners who were frozen in the fetal position, the maggots used to eat the dead tissue off the burn victims, and how severed limbs were thrown on the cots with their wounded owners, to keep all the parts together. Judy had even pictured herself in the scenes, working alongside her mother, imagining the smell of prisoners who hadn't washed in years, the fat white worms, what it would be like to wake up next to your own detached arm. She felt amazed at what her mother had been able to do and wanted to do it, too, until she was grown and realized her mother had already lived that life. Her future needed to be all her own, with no comparisons and no obligations. And, above all, *this* war wasn't anything like *that* war, as she was understanding more sharply by the day.

She wished there was someone she could level with. It wasn't the same, talking with Pete. After all, as he said, he *had* to do something about his military service, WRAIN had been her choice, even if it didn't really feel that way to Judy. There had only been one other girl at CIU in the program. Her name was Anna or Anita or something. Her recruiting officer had encouraged Judy to look her up, and she had seemed nice enough, a tall, plain person with efficient edges you could spot as a nurse a mile off, but she had never heard from her after the brief hello her first week on campus. Anita was a year older and would have transferred to Walter Reed by now. She wondered how all this was coming down out there. No student strike, that's for sure. Anita probably had no qualms at all, or maybe she had been knocked up by some handsome radical and kicked out of the program.

Judy shook herself out of it and headed back to campus. The sun was gone, the gray back, and she felt lonely now, the excitement over. She wandered among all the activity, here and there adding buttons to her jacket: BRING THE TROOPS HOME NOW and WAR IS UNHEALTHY FOR CHILDREN AND

OTHER LIVING THINGS. She passed on FREE HUEY NEWTON, because she didn't want to have to ask anyone who he was, and was afraid if she wore the button someone might ask her. She picked up leaflets offering everything from the "real" story behind President Johnson's refusal to seek a second term to a be-in on the fourth floor of Stevenson North: Leave Your Clothes, Bring Your Grass. She walked among the musical events, keeping an eye out for David's hat. There were bands, trios, combos, and soloists, with and without instruments, playing every type of protest song. The phrases rang out, "Give Peace a Chance," "Got to Revolution, Got to Revolution." She even heard Vida's clear soprano from the Quad: "Where have all the flowers gone?"

She came over and stood next to Wil to listen to Vida's calming voice.

"I really need this," she said to him. "It's soothing."

"That's not the point," he said. "Didn't you hear Swanson? There's a war on. People are dying. Today's about getting angry and doing something about it."

She couldn't believe this was coming from gentle Wil and felt like bursting into tears. She melted back into the crowd as Vida finished her song.

She looked for an open spot so she could escape, but the campus was mobbed. She needed her own moratorium, a postponement so she could figure things out. She finally found a corner on a stone bench next to Anderson Hall and sat down. What was she going to do now? She wanted to go to Washington, but how could she? She knew she should probably dump David, but . . .

"You just sitting here, Judy? With so much going on?"

She looked up, ready to smack whomever it was.

"Come on," Achilles said with a big grin, pulling her up by

the elbow. "There are only two sessions left that are worth anything, and they're both at the same time. You go to one, and I'll go to the other. We can compare notes later."

The moderator turned out to be her teaching assistant from American history. He always said he had gone to school with Jerry Rubin, one of the eight alleged instigators of protests at the 1968 Democratic Convention now being judged at the Chicago Conspiracy Trial. He even looked something like him: chunky, with a full beard and reddish, straggly hair that just missed his shoulders. He always wore the same clothes, jeans with a purple patch on one knee and a fatigue jacket he never took off, even when the room was warm. In her mind, he was also named Jerry.

He was sitting askew on one of the chairs with its attached writing table talking to a group of twenty or so students about the role of guerilla theater at the trial of the Chicago Eight: the defendants blowing kisses to the jury, Abbie Hoffman baring his chest, the North Vietnamese flag on the defense table, the day they all came to court in judges' robes.

"You get why they did that, right?" he asked.

He didn't actually answer the question. No one ever did, Judy realized. You were made to feel like you should already know, so there was really no way to ever find out for sure without making a fool of yourself. Did anyone really know anything?

"I still think they're working against us," said a bold guy in the back row. "They're so outrageous everyone thinks they're nuts, and so everyone against the war must be nuts, too."

"Think back to your American history," Jerry said. "Remember the Boston Tea Party? Taxation without representation? How many of you feel that was justified? Come on, hands up or down."

Nearly everyone raised their hands.

"Well, it might surprise you to know the patriots who threw that party were the Chicago Eight of their time, and that many people thought throwing all that tea in the harbor was the guerilla theater of 1776," Jerry said. "Think of it this way, Rubin and crew are pointing out the absurdity of the war's aggression without representation."

"But we have representation," the same guy said.

"Do you? You voting? You don't look twenty-one. And yet the lottery could send you off to Vietnam. I call that at the very least conscription without representation."

Judy hadn't thought of it that way. She was impressed at how good a teacher he was under all the attitude.

"Here's a fact that should get your attention," Jerry said. "The life expectancy of an infantryman under fire in Vietnam is six seconds. That's what the war has come down to, six seconds."

He looked out at the stunned room.

"I thought it was more like fifteen minutes," the bold guy spoke up again.

"You looking for all the caveats?" Jerry barked back. "You think fourteen minutes and change is going to matter?

"None of you gets it, you know. You can go to all the sessions today and talk about whether enlisting or joining ROTC might give you a safer deal, or teaching or going to law school might extend your deferment for a while. But it all boils down to the same thing.

"Read my lips—six seconds. It's that simple. You get six seconds, you're outta here. The next guy gets six seconds, and he's gone and on and on. What difference does it make if you delay it with a deferment? At some point, you'll be on the line, and you'll get six fucking seconds. A six-second life doesn't mean shit. Get it now?"

Jerry stood up, pulling his papers together. He was angry,

like Michael and David tried to be. "You can go to all the marches, hear all the speeches, and sing all the songs you want today, but the lottery's coming, and if your name is drawn, they're going to give you six seconds to live a life." He paused, giving them a sinister smile, then threw a finger in the face of a pale guy in the front row who hadn't yet said a word.

"And if your number is under a hundred, you can kiss it."

The guy reeled back.

Jerry turned to another one, jabbing his chest.

"Six seconds. Tick tock. So, what the hell are you doing *here?*" Then he was out the door.

"Fucking Jesus!" someone said.

"Holy shit."

"Goddamn asshole," someone else said, and Judy noted how God's name taken in vain always made it through when there was nothing left to say.

Chapter 16

JUDY APPROACHED THE QUAD CAUTIOUSLY, HOPING NOT to be seen, but didn't notice anyone she knew. A huge crowd was milling around, and there were calls that they were moving the Lottery Performance to the lagoon. The sun was low. Golden streaks mixed with shadow limbs, making the crowd appear to be moving as a giant spider, lots of little legs walking quickly, but the overall body advancing at a slow crawl. By the time they arrived at the north edge of the largest finger of the lagoon, darkness had settled in.

The scene they came upon made them hush. On the opposite shore were a dozen people with tall, thick candles. They were standing tall and still, the candles placed just below their chins, lighting their faces with a ghostly glow. The water's reflection magnified their impact, like footlights.

The crowd disassembled, tentacles of dark figures lined up all along the edge of the lagoon, dozens deep. When they were settled, Michael raised a megaphone with his good hand and began to read "The Lottery," by the light of his candle, from Judy's book. The beginning of the story set the scene in an anonymous town gathering for an annual ritual.

After a few minutes of reading, Michael handed the book and the megaphone to Wizard, who took over, read several paragraphs, then passed them on to David, who read about how the children were gathering stones and piling them in the town square.

They progressed through the story, relaying how each of the dutiful townsfolk stuck their hand into a black box and pulled out a piece of paper, one of which would be revealed to have a black mark.

Judy knew all the performers: Vida, Marsha, Achilles, RoMo, Fish, Wil, Sheila, Wizard, and Howie, even Meldrich. They handed the megaphone back and forth again and again among the readers. They *had* needed her.

The crowd listened in respectful silence, the wind sometimes taking the words away when Marsha or RoMo spoke. Then Michael or Meldrich would bring them back with force.

The sentences piled up with horror as the story revealed that this lottery was not for a prize that anyone would want to win.

As they approached the end of the story, the readers signaled their final lines by turning their candles upside down and snuffing them out, disappearing into the dark.

Michael took the megaphone and recited the last paragraph of the story that makes it clear that the one who has drawn the paper with the black mark is to be stoned to death. His broad, clear baritone echoed the length of the lagoon.

Wil reached over to reverse Michael's candle, and the final reflection was sucked into the water as they all stared into darkness. The crowd stood silent in the black, the only illumination from headlights on the highway and high above them from the distant Union Tower.

LATER that night, all of the performers were packed into Wizard's room, draped over the bunks, chairs, and most of the floor, passing joints and alternating spoonfuls from a jar of chunky peanut butter with swigs from a half bottle of Southern Comfort. A towel, shoved under the door, kept the smoke from escaping. It was dark except for the glow from an orange lava light on one of the room's two desks and the periodic flick of lighters.

David sat on the other desk, going on about how significant it was that he had jockeyed the Trots out of leadership of the march. "They'd have blown it," he was saying for at least the third time. "They never would have been able to get all those kids from the Lottery Performance back to the Quad in time for the march."

Fish was flipping through albums next to Meldrich, who was doing a spastic, goofy dance while playing with the stopwatch Achilles had used to time the march so they wouldn't exceed the two-hour permit. Judy had ignored David and was sitting cross-legged on the floor between Vida and Michael.

"That was brilliant, Michael," Judy said—yelled actually, because the stereo was playing an extended scream from a song on one of the Pink Floyd albums. "Where did you get the idea for using the candles like that?"

"Turn it down," Michael said, waiting until he was obeyed before facing Judy. "It's part of the excommunication ceremony the church performed in the Middle Ages. The priests would hold these long, thick candles high as their waists and when the ceremony was over, they'd say the condemned's name, turn the candles over, and snuff them out, damning him forever. I saw it in the movie *Becket*. It hit me as so . . . final. I thought it was appropriate."

He leaned closer to Judy.

"The idea for the candles I got from the movies. But you know the idea for the whole thing I got from you." He gave her a wink, then turned toward Meldrich, who was calling for their attention.

Judy noticed David watching them; so did Vida.

"So, what's going on with David? Did you finally sleep with him?" Vida whispered in her ear.

"Let's just say Sally beat me to it." She started to say more but felt her voice begin to shake.

"The blonde? Big surprise."

"Yeah, how stupid am I?"

"He's not worth it," Vida said and passed her a joint. "Besides, look at him. He's dying. No one cares about his march; all they're talking about is your Lottery Performance. I love it."

"*My* performance?"

Judy was glad when everyone's attention turned to Meldrich.

"Guess how long?" he cried, waving the stopwatch. "I just timed the scream, guess how long?"

"Four fucking hours," Fish said.

"I know it seems like that," Meldrich said, laughing. "But it was only 5.4 minutes, do you believe it, out of an 8.5-minute cut? I know I'm high, but Jesus!" He began giggling uncontrollably.

"Here, I'm gonna hold this hit; time me," Howie said and inhaled. Marsha rolled her eyes as Meldrich counted.

"Five . . . seven."

Howie let go, coughing and spitting smoke.

"Let me try," Achilles said.

"Eight . . . nine. You're turning blue, man." Achilles let it out, choking.

"No fair, you made me laugh."

"I can do better than that. Check me out," Vida said. She inhaled and exhaled a few times, then sang out a pure clear note.

"Ten . . . twelve. You're gonna break the record. Keep going. Keep going." Vida's eyes got big. She started to pound her thigh and finally ran out of breath.

"Twenty-four seconds. Yes! What else can we time?" Meldrich looked around.

Michael leaned toward Judy again. "Why weren't you with us at the performance?"

"I'm not much of an out-front person," she said. "Shy, you know." She cursed herself for not knowing what to say. She had been waiting for Michael's attention all this time and now just sounded like an idiot.

"Hmm." He took a drag of his cigarette and gave her a skeptical look.

"Michael," Meldrich said, "give me something to time."

"I'll pass."

"Come on, everyone's got to do something."

"I've got one," David interrupted. "Let's time the length of the chorus in 'Judy Blue Eyes.' You know, the 'dew do dew do dew do' part."

Judy refused to look at him.

"You got it!" Wizard said, reaching for the album.

When the song began, David came over to sit between Judy and Michael.

"Where were you all day?" he asked. "You just disappeared."

"At the sessions."

"All day?"

"There were a lot of them."

"Swanson do the usual bullshit about how the war started again? You think he'd progress."

"It doesn't sound like bullshit yet to me," Judy said.

David snorted.

She watched him take a long drag off a disappearing roach. He had removed his hat, and his hair kept falling in front of his eyes. Periodically, he flung his head in that way he had. Why did it have to be true that all the cute ones were jerks, especially the cute smart ones?

"Besides," she added, testing him, "listening to Swanson warmed me up for the march. You really had them tonight."

He smiled as he held his hit.

She resisted the urge to hum "Mustang Sally."

"Okay, Judy Blue Eyes," Meldrich said, "you're up."

"No," she said. "I can't think of anything."

"Sure, you can, something with time, seconds."

She remembered what the TA said earlier in the day, and struggled for an alternative. "How about a Beatles song?"

"No, sick of music," Meldrich said. "Something else."

They were all staring at her.

"All I can think about is something I heard today. It's nothing. I don't want to be a downer."

"No, tell us," Wil said.

She hesitated. "All right. Did you know that your life expectancy under fire in Vietnam is only six seconds?"

The room went quiet.

"Finally, something worth timing," Michael said. He grabbed the stopwatch from Meldrich, told Wil to bring the lava light to the center of the floor, then rubbed his hands and spread his arms out like the maharishi.

"Listen carefully," he said. "Close your eyes. Come on, do it. Picture this. You're in a jungle, wading through mud, carrying a heavy backpack and a rifle. Suddenly, you hear gunfire. It's coming at you and you're done for. This is it, six seconds left to your life. What will you do with it? Go." He clicked the watch button.

"One second."

Judy was already there, out of the jungle into a field hospital from one of her mother's scrapbook photos. A cot was rushed alongside the narrow table. Giant eyes fixed on her above sinking shock-white cheeks. His own foot was in his face. The soldier lifted his head to where his nose nearly touched the sole of his boot.

"Is that my foot?" he screamed.

Judy pushed aside his severed leg and pulled the heavy blanket, saturated scarlet, up to the top of the soldier's chin. "It's just your boot," she said. "They knew you'd need it later."

"Jesus," he said, "For a second I thought . . ." His head fell back and he sighed.

"I know."

He locked all the fingers of his right hand around one of hers.

"Better move him on," a corpsman said. "We need the space."

"A second." Judy put up her free hand.

"You can't . . ."

She kept her hand up for another second.

"Okay, now."

The corpsman pulled off the blanket as she disengaged her finger. She rearranged the leg on the cot, putting it back where it belonged. She lifted the soldier's arms by the elbows and angled her head to motion for the blanket to be returned. She placed the soldier's arms on top of the blanket and folded his hands high over his chest.

"Six seconds," Michael said.

She was able to close the soldier's eyelids just before the explosion.

"Stop."

Judy came to attention in a room full of faces staring at Michael holding the watch by the orange glow of the light. She was sure he had been observing them, eyes open, the whole time.

"Now tell us, what were you thinking?" he asked. They looked at each other, wondering who would go first. "Meldrich, you."

"I was thinking about the instant the bullet hit. Splatter, eh?"

No one laughed, and he immediately got serious.

"Do you think it hurts when you're being blown apart, or does it just . . . happen? You know, do you think you see your own guts flying out of you?"

Judy saw Marsha shake herself.

"Wil?"

"I was watching the lava light," he said. "It took six seconds for one drop to separate from the blob and move on. It's like a microcosm. Your life is just the process of being extracted from the collective goo and then drifting off."

"It was weird," Wizard said. "I saw the bullet and watched it open up, and then all this shit was coming at me. And then I saw the face of the guy who shot me. It was Swanson, do you believe that? Maybe he really is a spy for the administration."

"I think it would just be ordinary," Vida said. "You'd be thinking it should be a big deal, and then it wouldn't be. It would be about ducking and running, and one second it would just stop."

"Yeah," David said. "Just gone."

"I couldn't think of a damn thing," Howie said. "I was waiting for my life to flash before my eyes, but it wouldn't come. It was nothing. Over, done, nada."

"Judy, what about you?" Michael asked.

She was still in the tent. She pictured the young soldier's green eyes, the irises ringed with yellow, rings that had begun to glow so bright the light filled the tent and, in a second, incinerated her life.

"Nothing," she answered, skirting Michael's gaze.

"It was like Howie said, nada."

Chapter 17

JUDY LEFT SHORTLY AFTER. ALONE. IT HAD RAINED WHILE they were in Wizard's room. The lights that lined the ring road winding from the dorms down to the Union were reflected in the wet blacktop. She watched the mist, lingering over the shiny spots, and remembered how scary it had been to walk up this road her first week of freshman year, when she had been so worried something would go wrong and she would find herself back in Belmont Heights with a steno pad. She thought of that calculated first visit to the freak side of the Tune Room. It seemed a lifetime ago.

She squinted to follow the lights all the way to the highway, next to the black expanse of the lagoon. She was shaken by her six-second reverie. She shook herself and inhaled deeply to clear her mind. She wanted to enjoy the moment. The Lottery Performance had been a great idea, and it had been hers, and Michael had told them so. Judy didn't care who David slept with.

When she reached her dorm, she picked up her mail, stopping abruptly when she saw the familiar note card. She turned it over and over as she took the elevator to her floor and walked down the hall. Rather than wake Maggie, she stayed just outside her door and slid down the wall to sit in the dim hallway.

The address was just normal, no rank or any other signal about her mother's message this time. She broke the seal and unfolded the card. There was just one word:

Well?

She heard the phone ring and for an instant was sure it was her mother, knowing somehow that she had just read her message. She jumped up and rushed to get it before it woke Maggie.

Danny never called later than midnight, and it was now after one.

"Yes?"

"You disappeared again," David said.

"Did I?"

"I'm in your lobby. Come down, I want to talk."

"Not now, David," she whispered. "It's late. I'm tired."

"No way, we're all too keyed up after today to even try sleeping."

"Really, I'm not in the mood."

"Why? Something's wrong, isn't it? I can hear it in your voice. Come on down and talk about it."

"I don't need to talk. If you do, I'm sure you can find someone else. Michael, Vida . . . Sally."

"What the—ah . . . *zeeze.* I get it," he said. "That's why you're pissed. You come down or I'm coming up." The phone clicked.

"Fuck!"

"Go rinse your mouth out with soap and let me sleep," said Maggie, pulling the covers over her head.

She stuffed the card into her desk drawer and hurried to the elevator to head him off. But once downstairs she walked right past him, and he trailed her out the door. Puddles reflected the sidewalk lights, offering a bright path between the dorms. They followed it automatically, walking slowly, hands in their pockets, without a destination.

Judy breathed in the wet dampness and prepared herself as much as she could, half wishing she was alone and could figure out what to do about her mother and half happy David had been so insistent.

"So, what's up?" David asked.

Judy told him about getting the card, and how it was a reply to her earlier letter where she had tried to share some of her feelings.

"So, what did it say?"

"It just said, 'Well?'"

"'Well?'"

"It's an attack question," Judy said. "I didn't respond to her last letter, and now no matter what I answer, I can't win. She'll either say she knew all along I was going to screw up, or she just won't believe me."

"Why doesn't she just call?"

"And spend money?"

David nodded. "It has to do with the antiwar stuff we're doing, doesn't it?"

Judy stopped walking. "How did you know that?"

"What is it Vida says, 'Maybe I'm clairvoyant'? Or maybe I know you better than you give me credit for. You were practically doing backflips to stay out of the Lottery Performance. What do you think, your mother has her military spies here?"

"No, it just feels that way sometimes. Under surveillance, you know."

They laughed, but it died quickly. They followed the puddles among the dorms, passing David's, doubling back to hers, and halfway back to his again.

"Why not level with her?" David said. "Just tell her what you're doing and get it over with. You say you can't win anyway, so be honest and be done with it."

Judy stopped midstep. He had no idea.

"Or don't answer at all," he put his arm around her shoulder. "There are really only two alternatives. I'm here to help." He reached in his pocket and smiled. "I'm sure I have a coin here somewhere. Want to flip it?"

No idea at all.

They ended up in his room. She sat on the bed and watched as he paged through albums. "Looking for something specific?"

she asked, tempted to say "Mustang Sally." If he played "Judy Blue Eyes" she was going to get up and leave.

"Yes, as a matter of fact, I am. Listen."

> I said you'd be free, didn't I?
> I said you'd climb high, didn't I?
> Took you out to the sky,
> I told you one day you'd fly.

"It's Argent, he was lead singer for the Zombies. This song reminds me of you."

He sat next to her, pushing her hair off her forehead. "I see you as this beautiful bird who always seems to be holding herself back and not able to take off. It's like you're afraid of what you could be." She frowned as he put his arms around her. She was still too mad at him to want him to be understanding, and it annoyed her that he was sounding a little like Wil.

"It's not bad; it's good." He put his hand under her chin so she would look at him. "You come up with mind-blowing stuff like 'The Lottery' story. That's what I like about you. I'd just like to see you not give a fuck about what anyone else says—your mother, even me—and just fly."

"Not even you?"

"Not even me, except when I'm right, like now." He kissed her, then lit a joint and handed it to her.

She let herself go, and the rest of the night was a haze of talk and sensation. She listened to the words of the song, feeling David's arms around her, pushing away thoughts of obligations and mothers. He kept lighting joints, and after a while they didn't even need words.

"Yes, that's it exactly," she knew they were both thinking. The yellow circles in his eyes danced every time he smiled. Whenever she felt like she was starting to come down, he ran his fingers along the back of her neck and she soared up again and really did feel like she could fly, that she was flying.

At one point their mouths were so dry from the grass their tongues stuck together, and they had to separate for water.

"It would have been great if they'd played more stuff like this today," David said, using the break to get up and adjust the stereo. "It beats all that Peter, Paul and Mary sappy shit." Judy remembered Vida singing "Where Have All the Flowers Gone?" and flashed on the image of David's arm around Sally in the Quad. She was straight in a second.

"So, what's with you and Sally?" she asked.

He snapped his head toward her. "Whoa. Talk about left field."

"I saw you two today. You looked pretty tight."

"What's the big deal? You know her; I know her." He held out alternating hands as if he was weighing the information.

"No, I don't know her, actually."

David shrugged and went back to the stereo.

"It's because I won't go all the way with you, isn't it?" she said.

The arm of the stereo skittered across the record, a sure scratch. He caught it and reset it back to the same song, then sat on the opposite bed, the "Born Under a Bad Sign" lyrics framing him in screaming red.

"Well . . . maybe if you . . ." He stood up, then sat down again, fumbling with a cigarette. "Besides, we're like Sartre and de Beauvoir, aren't we? Connected, but no strings?"

"Yeah, just like that. I'm pretty sure they had separate bedrooms." Judy grabbed her jacket.

"Whatever you say," David said, lighting the cigarette. "But de Beauvoir never shrank from a fight. And she wouldn't have been afraid of her mother."

Judy gave him the finger and ran out of the room.

Chapter 18

IT TOOK EVERY BIT OF CONTROL JUDY HAD TO STAY OUT of the Tune Room the next day. She was anxious to be part of the post-Moratorium momentum and knew Vida would be planning something, but she absolutely didn't want to see David and hoped it would make him crazy she wasn't there.

Instead, she came back to the dorm between classes, hanging around in the third-floor study room, avoiding the co-ed floors. If David showed up, they would never let him up here. She wandered the halls and dropped in on floormates she had barely said hello to all semester, feeling as disconnected from their sorority concerns as she did now from David.

That evening she talked Maggie into ordering from Pizza Villa instead of going down to dinner and risk running into David in the lobby. She desperately wanted to talk about what had happened with him, but she hesitated. They had always shared everything, including the blow-by-blow of Maggie's first time with Danny ages ago, but now they rarely talked like they used to. She decided to warm her up first, and as they ate she let Maggie catch her up on what was going on with Danny.

They were already getting pretty specific about the wedding, Maggie told her, and where they would get their first apartment back in Belmont Heights, even though they had miles to go before they graduated. As she went on about details, Judy was amazed she would think they could make plans like this with the lottery coming up. Had it even crossed Maggie's mind? When she started in on the job Danny wanted to get as a supervisor at his father's factory, Judy couldn't stand it anymore.

"Maggie, what if Danny gets drafted?"

She stopped midsentence.

"Have you even thought about it?"

Maggie looked at her with cold eyes. "Thought about it? What makes you assume I don't think about things just because we don't talk about them anymore? Why don't you just ask me if I think about him going over there and getting killed? That's what you really want to know, isn't it?"

"You obviously do."

"It's hard not to, isn't it? With all this stuff around," she pointed to one of Judy's posters, "and watching you run all over the place masquerading as a protestor. If only they knew."

"I'm not masquerading."

"Then what *are* you doing?"

"I'm trying to figure it out. No one seems to have a good reason why we're in a little country that has nothing to do with us, other than we can't leave because we never lost a war. So, kids our age will die over some old guy's pride. And we don't even have a say in what happens to us because we can't vote."

"You sound just like all the demonstrators."

"Ever think they might be right? I can't believe you're not into this. Look what Rick's going through, even if he did enlist."

"You know why he did that. He knew he'd get drafted, so he enlisted to get a better assignment. It didn't exactly work out, I don't think." Maggie looked away.

"Oh," Judy said. "I didn't know that. I thought he was trying to be an officer or something."

"It doesn't matter why he enlisted," Maggie said. "What matters is he's doing something really dangerous. He writes my father about it, but no one tells me anything."

Judy thought about six seconds, and tried to picture little Rick under fire with a heavy rifle, but she could only see him running in his track shorts. Maggie was twisting her hair, and she felt guilty about upsetting her, but felt she had to make her understand.

"To be honest, I'm hoping I can keep my scholarship and stay in school but still be involved in this antiwar movement," Judy said. "I think they're both important. I think the only way this war will end is if people in the military say it should. Maybe I could be one of those."

"Get real, Judy," Maggie snapped, then reached over to cover Judy's hand with her own. "Seriously. Give it up before you get caught and lose it all."

"I don't know if I can."

"Try. I want to stay in Belmont Heights, but all you ever wanted was to leave. Even your mother wants to help you get out, don't you get *that*?"

AT breakfast the next morning, all Judy could think of to say when Vida and Marsha asked her where she went after she left Meldrich's room the night before was to tell them she received a mean letter from her mother.

"David says I should just tell it like it is or don't write back at all," she said.

"That sounds like him," Marsha said. "He probably hasn't communicated with his parents since he left high school. He does have parents, right?"

"It's a rumor, but I don't believe it," Vida said, picking at her toast and powdered eggs. "Parents and how to bring them along. Yes, it's a dilemma."

"Just be boring," Marsha said. "When my mother calls and asks me how I am, I tell her 'I'm fine.' She asks how classes are, I tell her 'fine.' She asks if I'm dating, I say 'not really.' Then I ask what's going on with her. At the end of the call she tells me she can hear I'm still smoking and I say, 'Yes, Mom, I'll quit. Goodbye.' She's done her motherly job, and I haven't revealed anything except my continuing nicotine habit."

"I don't think 'fine' would work with my mother," Judy said. "She's military, remember. We're talking interrogation. I made the mistake of writing something that made her suspicious, and now she's zeroed in and won't rest until she thinks I've pulled myself back in line."

"So, fudge. Give her what she wants and let it go," Marsha said.

"What did you tell her, anyway?" Vida said.

"Nothing, really. It was barely more than a sentence, you know, about the protest, but she freaked out."

Vida laughed.

"What's funny?"

"I'm just thinking, when I met you that first day in the Tune Room you were the last person I would ever have thought would say something like 'freaked out.' Hearing you say it is kind of like watching you smoke dope the first time. You couldn't even hold it in. Mom's right." She gave Judy a playful nudge. "We *have* had an evil influence on you."

Judy balled up her napkin and threw it at Vida's head. She threatened Judy back with her fork. Marsha and Judy picked up theirs, and they playfully tussled back and forth with each other, laughing.

"But seriously," Vida said, when they'd tired of the game. "Much as I hate to appear even vaguely to agree with David, maybe this is an opportunity, and you should just go with it. Give your mom the benefit of the doubt. How do you know she won't buy it?"

"Trust me," Judy said.

"Yeah, yeah," Vida brushed away her own smoke. "So, you and David are back together? What happened to Mustang Sally? She gallop off into the sunset?"

"Ask *him*," Judy said.

"Come on, what happened?"

"Apparently, the liberated woman is supposed to share."

"You buy that?" Marsha asked.

"Please."

"And did this come up before or . . . it was after, wasn't it?" Vida stretched her arms over her head and yelled. "You did go all the way with him, didn't you?"

"Keep it down," Judy whispered. "I did not go *all* the way."

"Bet Sally did."

"You're probably right," Judy said, leaning down to pick up her bag.

"Don't leave. I was just teasing."

"He's not worth it," Marsha said.

"I know, I know," Judy grabbed a napkin to blot her eyes. "So, why do I keep? . . ."

"I get it," Vida said. "There *is* something about David." She put her arm around Judy's shoulder. "And then, of course, there's also the gag factor."

Judy laughed in the middle of a sniff.

"You're just pissed, not heartbroken," she said, putting her arm around Judy and shaking her gently. "Trust me on this one."

"Think so?"

"I know so. How do you think I got the name In-A-Gadda-Da-VIDA?"

Judy's bag slid off her lap and hit the floor.

"Time to clear out," said a white uniform throwing a wet rag in the middle of the table.

Chapter 19

"MICHAEL TOLD ME TO SHOW THIS TO YOU." ACHILLES said later at the Tune Room, laying a poster in front of Judy. "We're setting up a registration table for the bus to Washington right inside the door over there, and this will go above it. I think it's pretty catchy."

Judy stood up to give herself a better view. It was a drawing of a purple bus with three cartoon figures sitting on the roof, their hands arranged, no-evil-wise, over eyes, ears, and mouth. Above it, giant letters drawn as mock love beads spelled out YOU CAN'T HIDE. SIGN UP TO RIDE.

"Michael said to show it to *me?*" Judy said.

"Yep. Sheila says he's not going to be around today and to run it by you. So, what do you think?"

"It's great, man," David said, inserting his head between Judy and the artwork. "Like the double meaning with the beads."

"I see what you're trying to do," Judy said, ignoring David, "but it might be hard to read if you're too close. I'd put it over there," she pointed to a wall opposite the Tune Room entrance. "For the registration table, I think you need something short and direct, like what Swanson and Michael say about the whole world watching. What about 'Dare to Change the World'? I could see that on a banner on the bus, couldn't you?"

"Yeah, got it, like it." Achilles grabbed the poster and was off.

"Wow, great idea," Vida said.

Judy looked away.

"I still like the first one," David said, pulling up a chair next to Judy. "What are they charging for this tea party, anyway?"

She had planned to be gone before he came in after his two o'clock. He must have skipped it. She moved her chair to angle away from him.

"Forty bucks for the bus," RoMo said, "but you're on your own for food."

"*Zeeze.* Second semester tuition's $167, and it's due at the end of December," David said. "I've only got $110 and my pathetic paycheck at Pizza Villa will barely put me over the top by then."

"Time to call home and ask for an early Christmas present," Fish said.

"Yeah, that works," Meldrich said. "Daddy, can I borrow some money to go protest against everything you stand for?"

"That's what I did," Wil said. "I told my mother I needed a new winter jacket before it got really cold. She sent me fifty bucks."

"Good going!" Vida clapped him on the back.

"Check with Fish," Wizard said. "He's usually looking for help unloading his hash."

"But he only pays in product," David said.

"So, sell your cut."

Judy watched David mulling over the proposition out of the corner of her eye. After what she heard earlier, she couldn't look at David or Vida without wondering if he had run his hands up the back of her long neck, and if she had liked it.

"Not going there. No. Fuck it," David said. "The revolution is out of my price range."

"What's this?" Michael said, joining the table.

Judy thought he looked odd; his skin seemed to match the yellow of his hair, and his eyes looked enormous.

"I didn't think we were going to see you today," Wizard said.

"Well, obviously you do," Michael said. "What's up?"

"They just released the price tag for the trip to Washington," RoMo said. "It's pretty steep, forty bucks."

Michael whistled. "Does anyone have it?"

"Wil got it through some excellent subterfuge," Achilles said.

"Wizard says he's working the registration desk, and he's obligated to go even if he has to rob a bank," Vida said. "And I'm in. I'm going to sell the Who tickets I bought with my birthday money."

"You're going, right, Judy?" Vida asked. "You can afford it. Scholarship kids always have walking-around money."

Judy shrank back, dumbfounded. "How do you know I have a scholarship?"

"Well, let's see. You're smart, always studying. Your family doesn't have any money, and yet you seem to have enough. I saw you put a whole buck into the hat at the rally for the Chicago Eight guy, Rennie Davis, when the rest of us were giving quarters. It doesn't take a genius to figure it out . . . or even a clairvoyant." She laughed.

"But I never said I was going to Washington."

"Too late, I already put your name on the list for the Steering Committee."

Judy opened her mouth to object, but thought of the Lottery Performance, and didn't see how she could justify refusing this, too.

"Four people? That's it?" Michael said. "How lame."

"It's a big chunk o' change," Meldrich said. "I'm on a pretty tight leash. My parents cover tuition and room and board, but beyond that I'm on my own. Maybe if it was ten or twenty."

Heads nodded around the table.

"David, you're the head of our SMC chapter; you have to go," Vida said. "I hear every Trot's signed up."

"Maybe the next revolution."

"You guys figure this out. I've gotta run," Vida said. "Swanson's doing all his pre-March-on-Washington classes on populist revolutions, and I don't want to miss anything. Judy, come to my room after dinner, and we can work on that letter to your mother," she called over her shoulder.

"What letter?" Wil asked.

"Nothing, she's just fooling around," Judy said.

"Come on," he said, pulling her slightly by the arm. "We need to escape. Let's hit the golden arches. I could use a burger."

They hunched against the wind as they walked down the main drag through campus toward the highway, jumping up on the sidewalk as a car came by, then stepping back when they got caught behind a slow-moving student. Wil chatted on about some writing he was doing, poetry or philosophy, he hadn't yet decided which, but was convinced it could be the secret to life. Judy leaned into him so she could hear his soft voice under the howls among the leafless trees.

"We keep trying to figure things out when we should just let them happen," he said. "We're powerless, really, against the forces of destiny. So, rather than make ourselves crazy, we should just let it flow and know that we'll end up where we're supposed to."

"I don't know if I could do that," Judy said. "It would make me pretty nervous to just—"

"Trust?"

They pooled their change, bought a single cheeseburger and an order of fries to split, and took a booth in the back corner, against the wall.

"It's a little like Zen," Wil said. "You see what you're doing right now, sitting in this booth, tapping your fingers on the table, putting ketchup on this fry? You know your body is here, but your mind is burning up about all this other stuff like how are you going to get an English paper done by Wednesday, and what you're going to say to David next time you see him, and how you're going to deal with your mother, not just in that letter you think you have to write but for the rest of your life. I'm right, aren't I?"

Judy lifted one arm in a lazy shrug.

"Now if you were a Zen master you'd be doing the same thing, but you'd be content with the universe that is this booth, and you'd be enjoying how the surface of the table feels as your fingers touch it, and how the salt on this fry mixes with this sweet ketchup to create this wonderful taste. You wouldn't be thinking about the rest because you'd know it will all take care of itself in its own way at its own time."

"Can *you* do that?"

"We all should be able to. I do admit you have to work to get your head around it." He smiled. "But why spend all our energy trying to control things we can't, and for what? What's going to happen is going to happen."

She wondered if Wil was also going to tell her he was clairvoyant. He had lined up a few of the fries on the table as if they were Michael's cigarettes, and was arranging them by length.

"So, are you saying we shouldn't even try to influence things, like study for a test? Should I just show up and hope for the best?"

"No, no. A test isn't beyond your control. You can study and change how that turns out, but you can't, you know, change people. Your mom, for example. Do you really think this letter is going to make a difference? She's going to think what she's going to think. So, take your best shot, then let it go, or don't. However it ends up is probably what was supposed to happen all along."

"I was raised the exact opposite, by her, you know, to always try to figure everything out."

"No shit."

She threw a fry at him.

"I'm just saying things happen for a reason, and we don't always know what that is, so just go with your gut and do your best and let the rest just . . . be."

She watched him pull the pickle off the burger and lay it aside.

"Are you trying to tell me something specific here?"

"You and I can't change Vida or David, for example. They are who they are. I might wonder what you see in David, but it's your destiny. He's obviously going to teach you something you need to know." He paused. "Or rather, the experience with David is going to teach you."

"Think so?" she said. "I do keep feeling there's got to be some reason I put up with his shit."

"A reason that may not be apparent to the rest of us," Wil said, with a grin.

"I knew you were up to something," Judy said, wagging her finger at him. "Oh, I don't know how to explain it." She put her back against the wall and stretched her legs the length of the booth. "There's the obvious stuff. He *is* cute, you know."

Wil mirrored her lazy shrug from a few minutes earlier.

"And it's exciting to watch how he gets people to follow him . . . ," Judy continued, "and then it's embarrassing to see how he blows it. And there are times when I think he understands me better than anyone has ever understood me, and other times when he acts like the worst type of jerk that everyone always warns you about. I really believe when he works it all out he'll be a great guy, so great sometimes I wonder what he sees in me."

"Maybe that's it," Wil said. "If you think he's special and he sees something in you, then you are special."

"Could be." She sat back up.

"Or you need his approval."

"Kind of sick, when you look at it that way, isn't it?"

"Just let it flow." He squeezed the ketchup bottle. "What happens, happens."

The ketchup belched out a huge glob, drowning the fries, and splashing Wil's shirt. They laughed at the punctuation of the moment, as Judy pointed to ketchup beads in his hair and on his glasses.

"Flow? That's what you do with Vida, right?"

"Of course." He smiled, cleaning his glasses on a napkin.

They headed back to campus, talking about Vida and David the whole way.

"Enough about them," Judy said, as they reached the Union. "Maybe you're right and we can't change people, but I wonder if we can change anything. Like the war. Do you think it's something we can really change with what we're doing?"

Wil stared up at the stars in the night sky.

"We have to."

JUDY left Wil at the front door of the Union. With all this going on, she was way behind on studying and needed a quiet place where no one would find her. She ended up in a perfect spot, the last chair at a long table on the second floor of the library. It was full of Greeks. In her jeans and psychedelic T-shirt, she thought certainly no one would talk to her, and in fact they skirted her, leaving her half the table.

As she tried to concentrate on biology, she kept thinking about David and Vida. She knew it wasn't fair to hold it against Vida, but she couldn't help herself and kept picturing them in bed together. When she moved on to the dreaded chemistry, it reminded her of Pete and then ROTC, which was a direct line to her mother. Well, that was one project she could eliminate. She didn't care how many cryptic notes she got; she just wasn't going to write back and give her mother any more ammunition. It might be easy for David and Vida to tell her what to do on a lot of things, but on that subject, she had to go with Wil. It would be what it would be.

Hours later, when she felt like she could make it through the coming week of classes, at least, she came back from the library and found David sitting on the steps in front of her dorm. He rose when he saw her coming. She was excited in spite of herself.

"I don't mean to be such an ass," he said. "Sometimes I just can't help myself."

"That's quite an apology," Judy said, and before she knew it, he had cradled the back of her head in his hand and was kissing her deeply.

"No PDA!" someone yelled, and they broke apart.

"No Public Display of Affection?"

"You know, dorm rules."

"How about a little WHT?"

"I'm not that easy," she said.

"Judy, if there's anything I know for sure, it's that neither one of us is easy."

Judy stared up at him. "You're not going to give me that Sartre/de Beauvoir shit again, are you?"

"No way." He put his hands up in surrender, and she let him stay that way until he started to get nervous.

"Because I'm not going to be just another notch on your belt."

"Absolutely not." He unbuckled his belt and took it off. "Here, it's yours."

"What am I supposed to do with you?" she asked.

"Anything you want," he said, taking her hand.

They sat on the steps. He held her in a loose hug with one arm around her shoulder, nuzzling her neck. She was happy, but glad they weren't in his room.

"You know," she said, looking up into his eyes, "sometimes I'm not sure who's the real David and who's the one I have in my head."

"You're outta your mind. I'm real. I'm right here," he said, and kissed her again.

Are you? She wondered as she gave herself into his kiss. Are you?

Chapter 20

"I HAVE A JOB FOR YOU," VIDA SAID, PULSING HER FINGER in Judy's face. "Listen, here's what you do. Lori Mueller is one of the head Trots, and she's called a meeting for all the women from SMC, YSA, anyone who's going to Washington, the whole female contingent."

"But I'm not going to Washington," Judy said. "I told you that."

Vida had cornered her over breakfast in the cafeteria.

"Yeah, yeah, well, they don't have to know that now," Vida said. "You need to be at that meeting to make sure she doesn't get carried away and take over the whole thing."

"What? Vida, you can't just throw me into this. I didn't ask to be on the Steering Committee, remember? I don't even know her."

What Judy had seen of Lori was alarming. She was always the first up with an in-your-face comment in any class or lecture, going on and on with elaborate gestures, wearing everyone out. Few could stand her, let alone take her on.

"Why don't you do it?"

"It's better if there's a new face challenging her," Vida said. "She won't expect it."

"But what am I supposed to do, exactly?"

"Just put her in her place. You'll know."

Judy wasn't so sure. There were only six people sitting around a small conference table in one of the Union's common rooms. She recognized a squat woman who was the girlfriend of the head of the CIU chapter of Students for a Democratic Society. There was at least one other Trot she remembered from the Swanson protest meeting and a few other girls Judy had never seen before. They looked up when she came in, but no one introduced themselves. If this was the whole female contingent, it wasn't impressive.

Lori was at the head of the table, drawing something, and the others were leaning over her, watching. Close up she was tiny, for someone who had a reputation for making a big impression, with dark, stick-straight hair that fell to her waist and a beautiful face marred by flame-red acne she did nothing to camouflage.

"Tah-Dah! Our new symbol," Lori said, holding up a piece of paper for all to see. It was the universal symbol for the female, with a fist in place of the plus sign. "We'll put this on the banner of the women's bus."

"The women's bus?" Judy asked of the girl next to her.

"Yes," Lori said, answering for her. "It looks like we'll be sending three buses to Washington, so we can reserve one just for the women."

Not the one I'd be on, Judy thought. Solidarity's fine, but if she went to DC she certainly wouldn't want to be separated from the guys and stuck with this bunch of losers for twelve hours.

She listened to Lori go on rapid-fire with plans for the trip. They were each to recruit two others, and make at least one more contribution. That was fine, even impressive organizing, but it was all presented in over-the-top radical-speak. They were to "force the unthinking masses into revolutionary action" by signing up for the march. They were to "guilt" the local food co-op into donating lunchmeat and bread for meals on the bus by telling them if they didn't they were supporting the war. If necessary, they were even to "liberate" the required supplies.

Each act would be an important political statement that step by step would lead to "a permanent revolution to oppose the hypocrisy of the capitalist system supporting the war." It grated on Judy how Lori was clouding the issue with her own socialist agenda. This must have been what Vida had meant.

"A question," Judy said.

Lori seemed surprised at the interruption.

"Why do we need to label everything about the antiwar movement as political? Wouldn't it be better to just focus on bringing the troops home and ending the war, and not the entire underlying political system? Isn't that what gets everything so complicated?" She looked around for a sympathetic face and found none. "I mean, technically, you could even be in the military and against the war. It doesn't mean you want to bring down the country. It's a difference of opinion; it's not political."

"Of course, it's political," Lori said. "Aside from the flaws in your example—being in the military and against the war is such an obvious oxymoron—can you think of anything that *isn't* political?"

Judy wondered if calling Lori a "moron," like that Greek had called David that first day in the Tune Room, was more of what Vida might have had in mind. Without waiting for a response, Lori let loose with a litany of verbal punches that sounded well rehearsed.

"Food? Chickens were tortured for your dinner. Clothing? Workers were exploited for those jeans."

"But—" Judy tried to interject.

"May I finish?" said Lori. "Education? You're at this school on the backs of those who didn't have the right doors opened to them. Love? Do you really want to get into the second-class citizenship of marriage? Can you give me even one example?"

It was dismissive: the subject settled and the agenda moved

on with split-second swiftness before Judy had even been able to think. She sat with her mouth open but speechless.

Judy was furious as she told Vida later at the dorm. "She even called me a fascist as I left."

"Yeah, she does that. I was hoping you'd surprise her and knock her off her game."

"You might have warned me," Judy said. "I felt like a peasant arguing with Trotsky."

"That's good. I'm going to use that."

"You're welcome to it. Just don't pull something like that again."

"Got it, let you hide in the crowd and make sure you don't have to take any personal risks for the movement, that right?"

"Vida!"

"You just broke your Trot cherry, that's all," Vida said. "You think this is confrontation, wait till you get to Washington."

"I told you I'm not going."

"Oh yeah, I forgot."

"VIDA set me up," Judy said later, in the Tune Room, throwing her books on the table in front of Michael and Sheila. "She absolutely set me up, just because she was too chicken to do it herself. She threw me at Lori Mueller, with no warning at all. I'm beginning to see why you all hate the Trots so much." She was humiliated and near tears. Just when she thought she was beginning to be taken seriously.

"Hate?" Michael pretended to be horrified. "Hate would imply a depth of feeling I wouldn't waste on Trots. They are supremely annoying, and act like they all went through the same little radical finishing school where they apparently learned to talk endlessly, but I wouldn't say I hate them. I would certainly like for them to

shut up and realize that socialism is not the answer to everything. Knitting, for example." He fingered part of Sheila's white
fabric. "Socialism means nothing to knitting, but I'm sure Lori
could find some reason why a good communist should . . . or
absolutely should not . . . knit."

Judy and Sheila cracked up.

"See," Michael said. "Better already. Don't let them get under
your skin. That's the danger of going to all those meetings."

"How else will I learn?"

"Learn? The master of the Lottery Performance?"

"Seriously, Michael. I still feel so far behind. At least at the
Moratorium I caught up on some things I was never clear about.
The Gulf of Tonkin, for example. I'm sure you think it's in-
credible I didn't know, but . . ."

"There's really only one thing to remember here, Judy. People
are dying. Every minute, people are dying. Every week, they
confess to more and more of them. This week another ninety-
five, for a grand total of 38,830. Every minute we take, debating
about what to do to stop it or which political system wouldn't
have supported it in the first place, is another dozen dead. So do
what's necessary to get comfortable and then cut to the quick
and make something happen."

"Like what?"

"Like march, or blow something up, or use that brain of
yours to think of something that will be even better."

"Well, it's not like anyone in the movement really listens to
us women."

"No? Why do you think Vida sent you to Lori?"

Judy let that spin around in her head for a while. She played
with the corner of her book while Michael lit another cigarette.
He seemed to understand just when to pause, once he got your
wheels turning. He was right, people certainly did listen to Lori,

or at least they heard her. She thought about it as Vida walked over to the table with Fish and Wizard and took a seat directly across from her. She still couldn't look at her without imagining her with David.

"Did you hear Judy stood up to Lori Mueller?" Michael said. "That's got to be a first, don't you think?"

"Motormouth Mueller?" Wizard said, "I don't believe it. Did she call you a fascist?"

"Of course."

"There's no blood on the floor. How'd you pull that off?" Fish asked.

"I just asked her a question. You know how she is," Judy said, more boldly than she felt. "She didn't like it. Not one bit."

"Hey, anyone who makes a Trot stop for a breath is a hero in my book," Wizard said. "Wil, did you hear Judy shut down Mueller?"

"Of course," Vida answered instead. "That's why I sent her there in the first place."

"Watch yourself," Wizard said. "I hear she has an enemies list."

Shortly after, once the others dispersed off to their afternoon classes, Judy found herself alone at the table with Michael. She asked him about David.

"What do you really think of him? You know, as a leader in all this?"

"GagMan?" He laughed. "He'll either end up on the top or the bottom. Let's see if all that bluster has legs."

"Are you rivals?"

"Life's too short."

Judy felt proud to be accepted by Michael. Just a few weeks ago he scared her to death, and now he seemed to feel they were the same, though it seemed to her that little had happened to make him feel that way, just the idea about the "Lottery" story.

"What on earth could be responsible for that facial expression?" Michael suddenly asked. "If you concentrate any harder, your features will merge."

Judy blushed. "I'm having my own private moratorium."

"Yeah?" Michael said. "Interesting."

"A moratorium on my life. I love that word. I may use it forever. I'm reflecting, pausing to think and assimilate before I move on." She used some of Vida's sweeping hand gestures to take the edge off, but Michael took her seriously.

"We're not just talking about David here, are we?"

"Oh, no. I mean, I suppose he's part of it. But think about this. I met you all less than two months ago and look at everything that's happened. It's really life changing, but it's less than eight weeks. That's nuts."

"Maybe not. Eight weeks can be a lifetime. As you have pointed out, six seconds can be a lifetime."

"Now you sound like Wil," she said.

"Our Wil is pretty wise under all that metaphysical bullshit, you know," Michael said. "He doesn't make it up. He really believes that life is pretty clear and doesn't get himself all tied up in nuance."

"And predestined."

"Yeah?"

"As in let it flow, let it be, and what happens is supposed to happen."

"No shit," Michael said. "Hell, let's make him our guru."

"You're hardly the let-it-flow type."

He looked at her with a half smile, as if trying to decide how much he would reveal. Then he leaned back with his good arm wrapped around the chair top behind him and straightened his legs. In this position, she had to turn all the way around to see his face.

"Look, there are a lot of people making a lot of noise and claiming they have some special insight. And you're listening to them all, and that's fine. But again, don't take too long."

"To do what?"

"I think you came looking for something and you found it, but you don't realize it yet."

"And what is that?"

"That's all you're getting from me. You came here an outsider, and you get it better than most, period."

"Get what?"

"You know."

"No, I don't."

"Yes, you do. You *know*. Vida was right about that."

Chapter 21

MICHAEL CALLED A WAR COUNCIL AT HIS APARTMENT FOR the next night, which caused great excitement because only Sheila and a few others had ever been there. It was rumored he had a $600 stereo and a legendary blues collection, which no one could figure out how he was able to afford.

It turned out to be a single basement room with a twin bed along one wall, and a worn couch along another under a pass-through window to the kitchen. In front of the bed was a coffee table assembled from concrete blocks and a board, covered with candles of all sizes and colors, hardened drippings cementing them in place. On the wall next to the couch was a giant poster of a lean figure with a guitar under the words CLAPTON IS GOD. Beneath the poster was a single brick, topped with a *Wheels of Fire* album cover, a few more candles, and an incense burner, like a shrine. There were lime-green lights flickering across the ceiling from a revolving lamp, with cut-outs in the shade. The whole place smelled like grass, beer, and old laundry.

Michael stood in the kitchen, leaning against the counter of the pass-through, as if he were about to serve dinner.

The guys headed straight for the stereo, a sleek silver flash of knobs and panels, and plunged into his blues albums, shouting out "Siegel-Schwall" . . . "Paul Butterfield" . . . "Lightnin' Hopkins."

"Just choose something and put it on low," Michael said. "We have strategy to discuss."

When they had all sat down, he said it was critical they show up for the March on Washington in force or they would be shut out of the plans the National SMC would be making at a key summit to be held onsite, as well as lose leadership of the CIU movement to the Trots, who he had learned were all attending. Above all, it was their responsibility, he told them, with the body count up to 38,925, to be part of this last action before the lottery.

At his suggestion, they pooled their money to see how many they could afford to send. Judy kicked in the full forty dollars, getting secret satisfaction that her army pay would be supporting this subversive action. They could afford to send five representatives. Michael decided who would go: David and Vida, of course, since they were the SMC leaders; Wizard, because he was the ace organizer; and Wil, of all people, because he was a true believer who wouldn't let any anger or emotion steer him wrong. That choice surprised everyone, including Judy, but she knew it was because of what she had told Michael about him earlier that day.

They all assumed Michael would be the fifth, but he said he wouldn't be going—he couldn't very well choose himself— though Judy noticed he was leaning heavily against the counter and wondered if that was the only reason. Those who went would need to observe everything and report back very thoroughly, he told them.

Judy couldn't believe it. The Michael she knew would kill to go. She looked at Sheila, who kept her head down. Everyone else was stunned, and then it got worse.

"So, who's the last person going?" Achilles asked.

"Judy," Michael said.

The room went dead quiet.

Judy was shocked. "No, I'm not going," she said. "I told you, I was never going to go."

"She doesn't even want to go," said Meldrich, who led an

explosion of anger from Achilles, Fish, and Howie: "What's she gonna do?" . . . "Hold up posters?" . . . "Help Wil write poetry?" . . . "What kind of contingent is this?"

"I can't go," Judy said. She was on her feet now.

"You have to," Michael said.

"Why?"

"Because you'll notice everything. You'll be our eyes and ears," Michael said. "You'll be *my* eyes and ears."

He scowled at the others, shaming them into silence.

"Okay," Achilles said. "I surrender."

"No, really, I can't," Judy said.

"Too late," Michael said, "you've been chosen."

JUDY tossed and turned all night, trying to figure out how to get out of the trip without saying too much. She could get sick at the last minute, and they could send Fish. Or she could pretend there was an emergency at home. But then she would have to actually go there or at least figure a way to be off campus without anyone finding out.

Still, she couldn't help rehearsing the entire journey. She would wear her bulky sweater because it would be extra warm and it was soft and would be easy to sleep in on the bus. She would take her paisley bag. It was big and would carry a lot. She could wear some kind of disguise. She could put her hair in a ponytail, claiming she wouldn't have time to fuss with it. Her green knit hat would cover it completely. She could wear sunglasses and say she needed them because the glare would be too much with her contacts. How likely was it to be a sunny day in mid-November? But she would really only need the disguise when they were marching. Who would see her among a million people? She would just blend in with the crowd the rest of the time. She could leave her ID here, and no one would ever know.

Why had Michael singled her out? she wondered. Meldrich and the others had been so angry. But Wil had been positively gleeful.

"This'll be the biggest protest yet, and we'll be there," Wil had said to her, walking back from Michael's. "And Swanson's right. I do want to be able to tell my kids I was there on the front line of the struggle."

When would she ever have another chance like this? She wondered if there would be a way to sneak onto the bus without anyone finding out.

Finally, she drifted off into a doze, waking fully only when Maggie returned from an early class the next morning, startled to see her still in bed.

"You sick?" she asked.

"No," Judy sighed. "I'm trying to decide if I'm going to Washington for the Moratorium."

"What?" Maggie said. "You . . . wouldn't . . . dare."

"I feel I have to be there, you know?"

Maggie started to fool with her books.

"And what about all your new friends?" she said. "If you get caught, how do you think they'll take to finding out some PFC was in their private meetings, planning their protests, and sharing their drugs? Get real, they'll think you're undercover or something."

"Please," Judy said, with a huff.

Maggie raised her eyebrows.

"They wouldn't believe that," Judy said.

"If you say so," Maggie said, in her singsong voice.

Judy let her head fall back on the pillow.

"Rick's home, by the way," Maggie said.

"He is?"

"This is the only leave he'll get. He wants to see you over Thanksgiving. It's the least you can do. So don't get yourself arrested or anything before then." She went over to the record player and set the arm on the album that was already teed up.

Here it goes again, Judy thought, the Monkees, over and over for the rest of the day and night, until she leaves for the weekend.

MONDAY night the phone rang at eight o'clock. Judy was lying on her bed, trying to finish the Brobdingnagian part of *Gulliver's Travels* for her morning class, and didn't stir.

"Hi, baby," Maggie said, poised to cuddle the receiver. "Oh, hello, Mrs. Talton."

Judy looked up into Maggie's horror-struck face and reached for the phone. Maggie put her hand over the mouthpiece.

"I forgot to tell you, I saw her at the Dairy Queen over the weekend. I think I might have said something about Washington. I didn't mean to, but . . ." She handed her the phone as if it were hot to the touch.

"Hello?" Judy said into the receiver. "Is something wrong?" Long distance calls were for emergencies only.

"You tell me." Judy took the phone into the hall and slid down the wall, taking care not to sigh audibly. "What do you mean, you're going to march on Washington? You can't do that. You're a member of the United States Army."

"I'd be going as a student, Mom, not as a member of the armed forces."

"You can't pick and choose like that. Once you enlisted you became Judith Talton, PFC US Army. You can't just decide to go back to plain Judy Talton whenever you want. You made a commitment."

A deal with the devil, Judy thought, and listened to her mother's voice getting deeper and louder with each sentence, a giant sound booming out of giant lips attached to a giant Brobdingnagian face that swelled ever larger as she bellowed into the tiny Lilliputian receiver.

"Yes . . . but—"

"There are no 'buts.' I can't be wondering if your face is going to show up on the evening news. If I can see you, they can see you. Think!"

"I am thinking . . . but . . . no." Judy couldn't get in more than a word or two when her mother took a breath. She couldn't remember her ever talking so fast or so violently. She could barely follow, though the drift was clear, and certain words would emerge out of the harangue with extra emphasis . . . ramifications . . . AWOL . . . tuition payback. She felt she was being slapped silly with words, one cheek and then another, with no opportunity to respond.

"So that's it," her mother said. "You're not going, and that's the end of it! . . . Judy?"

"Yes."

"You hear me?"

"Loud and clear."

"It's settled, then. If we have to continue this discussion, it will be when you're home for Thanksgiving. Goodbye."

"Yeah, bye," she said, after she heard the click. "Love you, too."

"Thanks a lot," Judy said to Maggie, who was cowering against her study pillow.

"She got it out of me. You know how she is," Maggie said.

"I would never have done that to you."

Maggie hardened. "So what. She needed to know."

"That was *not* your call." Judy tore down the USMC sticker

and unpinned the photo of Rick from Wil's poem. She smacked them down loudly on Maggie's desk and took pleasure in watching her jump.

"Just stay out of my life, will you?"

Chapter 22

RIGHT NOW THERE WAS ONLY ONE PERSON'S OPINION Judy was interested in. She half ran to the Tune Room.

The line for bus registration was blocking the entrance, and she had to squeeze her way through the press of bodies to get to center stairs. The place was crackling with activity. There were new banners up along all the walls: YOUR VOICE IS YOUR VOTE. GET TO DC AND BRING THE TROOPS HOME NOW. On the center floor, there was a group with arms linked, line dancing to the chorus of "Golden Slumbers." Vida was table-hopping with her clipboard. Everyone was smiling, excited.

"I was beginning to think I'd have to come looking for you," Michael said, from somewhere behind her.

"What's going on here, anyway?" she turned and asked.

"They just finished a rally. Swanson, Lori, David. Whipped 'em into a frenzy, as you can see from the length of the registration line. We even signed up some of the Black Panthers."

"Michael, this is serious. There's a lot at . . . I have to ask you one more time, why me?"

He rested his good hand on her shoulder and grinned, "You *know.*"

Judy nodded and went over to join the line at the registration desk. Take that! She pictured her mother as she signed the attendance sheet with a flourish.

❀ ❀ ❀

"I'M in," she said later that night to the group making posters for the march in the Lutheran church basement. "I'll do anything except sit next to Lori Mueller in her women's bus."

RoMo handed her a marker. They drew until they ran out of poster board, when Judy suggested they pull the want ads from a stack of newspapers next to the wastebasket. They were printed dense enough to draw over, she explained. She had once used them as background for current events announcements in high school. To demonstrate, she took a broadsheet and drew the octagon of a stop sign, ringing it with black barbed wire. Inside the outline she wrote STOP THE WAR in block letters, then filled in the background with a colored marker, blood red against the black and white of the newsprint.

"Oh, wow," Vida said. "Isn't that the Chicago Eight 'Stop the Trial' logo? Great work."

"It's the Chicago Seven now." Judy was still too annoyed with Vida to give her an inch. "I thought everyone heard about Bobby Seale. He's going to have his own trial." It was the only time she ever one-upped Vida.

They duplicated the design until the papers ran out and set off to hang the posters across campus.

"Your roommate home tonight?" Judy asked David, as he juggled an armful of posters.

"No. He's essentially living with his girl in University Apartments, the room is just his address."

"Then I guess this is your night," Judy said, enjoying the look of shock on his face. "Let's go."

They tacked posters on every bulletin board along the way to David's dorm. He started putting up two and even three posters with the same thumbtacks. In the elevator on the way up to his room he grabbed her, sticking his tongue deep into her mouth and cupping her rear end with both hands. The doors opened on a lower floor and she heard people enter but didn't pull away. When they got to his floor, she ran ahead of him as he fumbled for his keys, and leaned against his door, waiting with hip cocked, waving the end of her scarf as he hurried toward her.

"Argent," she said as she slipped past him into the room, and soon the song was playing:

> If you're gonna sweep the sky
> And feel the wind come rushing by,
> Remember that I told you to be free.

Judy didn't stop David at all this time. She let him unhook her bra and unzip her jeans. She helped him pull his T-shirt over his head.

"Why are you laughing?" he said at one point.

"You keep looking at me like I'm going to shut you down."

"But you're not, are you?" Without changing position, he reached one of his long arms into his desk drawer and pulled out a cellophane packet.

"No, I'm not." She winced when she saw him rip the corner open with his teeth. "Just be careful."

"We don't need to use this. Is it a good day?"

"No, we need it. Just be careful."

"Careful? Why?"

"Why do you think?"

David stopped moving, and looked down at her.

"No way?"

"No way, what?"

"You're not . . . Jesus!" David rolled over and sat on the side of the bed.

"What is it?"

"You're not going to tell me you're a virgin, are you?"

Judy just stared at him.

"Why didn't you tell me before?"

"What difference does it make? You know now."

"I'd be the first?"

Judy couldn't believe what she was hearing.

"In some primitive societies, that would be considered an honor," she said, pulling the sheet around her. "And as you always say, what's the big deal?"

"This is too heavy, way too heavy." He got up and started to pace, back and forth, between the beds, stark naked.

"Let me get this straight," Judy said. "You want to sleep with me. You've been after me for almost the entire semester, telling me I need to be open like de Beauvoir, and now, when I finally say yes, it's too heavy?"

He sat down on the opposite bed and lit a cigarette. She wanted to scream that they should trade places. Surely the bad-luck lyrics on the wall above his head applied to her at this point. She had heard all her life about this moment, about giving, even throwing it away, but never had she imagined it would be rejected.

"Well, of course I still want you, who wouldn't? I mean . . . I just never thought it would have this much . . ." He waved his hands, searching for the word.

"Significance? You mean, like I might remember it the rest of my life? . . . Or *you* might."

"Well, yeah."

"Turn the music off." She tried to get up, but he had moved over to the bed and was sitting on the end of the sheet. "Now!"

She scrambled out from the bedclothes as he leaned toward the stereo. She pulled on her jeans and jacket, picked up the rest of her things, and made for the door.

"Judy?"

"Don't say a word," she said, without turning back. "Not a fucking word!"

She ran all the way back to the dorm, without socks or underwear, the seams of her jeans and her desert boots chafing with every step. She burst into her room, thankful that it was a Saturday and Maggie was home in the suburbs with Danny. She changed into a T-shirt and pajama bottoms and curled up under the covers. She felt beaten up and exhausted, as if she had gone ten rounds with David and her mother simultaneously. She pictured them coming at her, one knocking her down, the other coming in with the second punch. Then they would start over, switching places.

JUDY woke up the next morning, exhausted from her combative dreams but knowing she had one more encounter ahead of her. She had to tell Pete about her decision to go to Washington. She felt like he was the final person, after her mother, Maggie, and even David, who was trying to distract her from her purpose. She had to get herself up for it.

He had grown increasingly frustrated with her during their regular tutoring sessions. He had a way of judging without saying anything, like when he persisted in flattening out the peeled-up edge of the BRING THE TROOPS HOME NOW sticker she had pasted to her notebook, or when he focused a second too long on the SMC button that she had been wearing since she joined the Steering Committee. He almost lost it the day she was rummaging for a pen in her bag and a pack of cigarettes fell out. He did say he hoped it was only tobacco. But aside from that, he had been holding his tongue. She was pretty sure this news would loosen it. She could almost script what he would say, but she did need his advice, or rather—and she would have to make this clear—she wanted to verify her facts. Still, she postponed it until the last tutoring session before the trip.

As usual, Pete was early, already waiting for her in the library loft with papers spread and assignments ready. Fortunately, he wasn't wearing his fatigues. That would have been too much for this conversation, she was sure.

"I need your help with something," she said. "You're not going to like it."

He leaned back. "Okay."

"I'm going to Washington for the march against the war."

He crossed his arms.

"We leave on Monday. I'll only be gone for about forty-eight hours, so no one will know that I'm there, but I want to be sure of my standing just in case . . ."

"In case you get arrested?" He made a sound, not quite David's *zeeze,* but close.

"I knew you were going to . . ."

Pete put his hand up to stop her. "I won't judge. Just the facts."

"Thank you."

"The facts are, you'll be AWOL," he said.

"AWOL is pretty strong, Pete. I'm just a student."

"No, you're not. You're enlisted in the United States Army, and if you're thirty miles past your CIU duty station without permission, you are Absent Without Leave, and that's a military crime. I won't even mention the bigger issue about how you shouldn't be anywhere near the antiwar movement."

She explained that the army hadn't given her any hard and fast rules. She had checked her manual and there was just this general "code of conduct," nothing specific to this situation. As far as she could tell, she could do anything as long as she did not say, "I, Judy Talton of the United States Army, think this way." The AWOL issue was a problem, but there wasn't anyone at CIU who had the power to give her a pass anyway, so what else could she do but go without it? That only made sense, didn't it? Even Dr. Vorner would have agreed it was an argument that worked.

"It's pretty easy to find someone on campus with military authority, you know," Pete said. "Who do you think keeps all us ROTC guys in line?"

"But that's *your* program. We both know there's no one on campus with authority over *my* program. And since that other girl transferred to Walter Reed this year, I'm the only one."

Pete shook his head. "Well, that's an amazing piece of logic for someone who has trouble following the physics of a redox reaction. Maybe if science would let you be this creative, you'd be doing better in chemistry. You should be a lawyer, not a nurse."

There are lots of things I should be besides a nurse, she wanted to tell him.

"What do you want me to say, exactly?"

She sighed. "That it's not as bad as I think it is."

"Only if you don't get caught." He put a hand on one of her shoulders. "If they find you, your friends could be arrested, too. If they catch guys protesting in the wrong kind of demonstration, they can be immediately classified as 1-A and sent off to 'Nam in a heartbeat, lottery or not."

She thought of David being shipped off. Wil.

"I never heard that before," she said.

"It happened to some SDS guy from Oklahoma, and they're looking at it more closely now because of this thing you're going to."

"What's the wrong kind of demonstration?"

"Whatever they decide at the time, apparently. Look, your presence makes them vulnerable. Do you really think that's fair?"

PART TWO

November 1969

Chapter 23

ON MONDAY, NOVEMBER 14, AFTER A WEEKEND OF PRE-Moratorium rallies, a frenzy of banner painting and poster making, and a giant send-off in the Tune Room, Judy arrived at the bus boarding location at 4:45 p.m., cutting it as close as possible to the 5:00 p.m. departure time.

Still, Vida was standing by the door of the lead bus, flapping her hands.

"Hurry," she yelled. "Wil's lying across two seats, and he needs help saving places."

Judy refused to speed up.

"Guess what," she stage-whispered as Judy approached, "the Trots are splitting themselves among the three buses, so I told David we had to do the same. He and Wizard are taking the other two buses, so you won't have to see him."

Judy stopped cold.

Vida grinned. "Still hate me?"

"Do we end up with Lori, or is there a woman's bus after all?" Judy asked, ignoring her question.

"No to both, but we get Bill Donnell." Vida smiled.

Donnell, Judy had learned, was the black-haired, chalky-skinned guy David had gone after and Vida had flirted with at the Swanson support meeting back in September. He was head Trot on campus, with a student membership in the Socialist Workers Party.

Vida's eyes shifted over Judy's shoulder, and her face lit up.

Judy watched her rush to Donnell as he approached the bus. He was a striking guy with black Irish looks, penetrating gray-blue eyes, and a mission. He was friendly to all and personal to none. Judy didn't see the appeal. He seemed more like a symbol than a person.

She joined Wil in the bus. He was watching Vida out the window. She felt bad he had to see Vida with Donnell.

To divert him, she asked about the final count.

"Two hundred," he said. "Three buses with two hundred people. That should make an impact."

She gave some of her stuff to Wil so he could use it to save the seat next to him, then staked out her own place in the seat ahead, by the window. She heard a bang on the side of the bus below, slid the glass down, and stuck out her head.

"Here," Marsha said, holding up a paper sack. "Sandwiches for the road. Be sure to call me the minute you're back. I want to hear everything first."

The engine of the bus started up, and Vida was the last to come down the aisle, settling behind her next to Wil. "Swanson bolted," she announced. "Do you believe it? He's not coming."

"Everyone sit down *now*, or we aren't going anywhere," the bus driver yelled.

They obeyed like schoolchildren. Judy looked back at Marsha waving them off. RoMo and Sheila were with her, even the guys, sullen, hands in their pockets.

"Where's Michael?" she turned back to ask Wil.

"Don't know. I haven't seen him in a week," he said. "It's 38,989, by the way. The body count."

The second bus aligned next to them, and she saw Wizard's profile. A guy next to him turned slightly. Who was he? She thought she knew everyone who was coming. His hair was a little too short. Her heart started to pound as she remembered what Pete had said about putting her friends in danger. Then the buses accelerated, and she lost her view.

Vida sang behind her as they pulled away: "Last night I had the strangest dream I'd ever dreamed before."

By the time they turned onto the highway, everyone had joined in: "I dreamed the world had all agreed to put an end to war."

THE bus had been made for short trips. The green vinyl seats were cracked at the corners, and it was easy to see what passed for padding was no more than a half-inch of compressed, fibrous white stuff. Judy slid down to give her butt some relief. After a few hours of driving along the flat boring highway, singing songs, and making far too much progress into two days' worth of food, activity had fallen off, voices were down to individual mutterings, and the scenery was gone. The orange and pink streaks of the sunset had long ago left the sky, which was barely hanging onto a bit of midnight blue.

The driver flipped on a light that glowed from dim fluorescent coils above the windows on either side of the bus, but it wasn't enough to read by. At least the Greyhound buses from CIU to Belmont Heights had reading lights. These were school buses, intended for daytime. She put aside the novel she was reading for Vorner's class, *The Bell Jar*. It was about a nervous breakdown, and she didn't want anything messing with her head right now. She lay back against the seat, arms folded, steadying herself to absorb the constant bouncing as much as she could. It was going to be a long ride, two hours minimum to the first rest stop.

Judy was beat. From the moment she had begun to think about coming on this trip, she had been constantly busy, plotting how to get around Maggie, planning her camouflage, packing, being involved in all the poster making, and listening in on the political planning among Michael, David, and Vida.

She thought she would be more excited but was too upset now that she couldn't trust Vida and had been humiliated beyond belief by David. It wasn't at all how she should be feeling; she knew that. She needed to get past this personal stuff and focus on the event. She was going to be part of making history. And she was pretty clever, even brave, about how she was pulling it off, if she did say so herself, regardless of Pete's opinion.

She turned to the window and started to draw a big *J* in the dust with her finger and then moved on to a small *u*. She heard a cackle up front and saw that Vida had moved from beside Wil and was trying to get Donnell to sing.

"Come on," she said, squealing with laughter. "You can do it. Just repeat after me. 'We shall overcome. We shall overcooome.'"

"'We-shall-over-come-some-day,'" Donnell joined her in a flat, talk-sing voice, with no intonation up or down. "That's enough," he said. "It's the most boring song in the world, and I sound like an idiot."

"Then let's change it." She began to sing "Give Peace a Chance."

"That's just as boring. We might as well be singing '100 Bottles of Beer on the Wall.'" They giggled and sank down in their seats. She heard Wil shift behind her. She moved back to sit next to him.

"How are you doing?"

"Fine," Wil sighed, with his face toward the window.

Judy slouched back, wondering what David was doing at this minute in the other bus. Knowing him, he was probably hitting on someone, just like Vida. She looked at Wil carefully, running her eyes down his small, curled-up frame. Such a nice guy. She wondered if she could ever make herself be attracted to him. It would be so much easier. And it would serve David and Vida right.

Eventually, everyone settled down and tried to sleep. Judy couldn't find a good position and kept waking up, wondering why Michael hadn't come to see them off and why Swanson wasn't coming with them.

"Five minutes to the rest stop," the driver announced later. "No one stands up until the bus comes to a complete stop." They rushed for the restrooms. Judy got in line and noticed Lori was already at one of the sinks. She had taken a cake of soap out of a plastic container. She gathered her long hair to one side, rolled and knotted it, then tucked it under her collar. She carefully washed and dried her face, replaced the cake of soap in the container, and put it into her pocket. Judy tried not to stare as she watched Lori examine her ravaged cheeks in the mirror, tilting her head from right to left. If it had been anyone else, Judy would have offered her some of her cover-up cream, but Lori would probably have attacked her.

"How bourgeois," she could just hear her say.

When they returned to the buses, Vida and Donnell were gone. Judy went back to sit by Wil again. She opened the package of HoHos she had bought and offered him one.

"Where's Vida?" she asked. "Did she switch buses?"

"It's a free country," he said. "She can do what she wants, hell if I care." He slouched back toward the window, then sat up again. "And I guess I have to stop being such a dumb shit and get used to it or get lost. What do you think I should do?"

"Seriously?"

"Seriously. I mean, I look at it one way and it's just how Vida's always been. She wants to experience everything and be completely free. And that's part of what I like about her." He lit a cigarette and sat back with a bent leg up on the seat so he could face Judy.

"But then I look at it another way and ask myself if I'm not the biggest doormat in the world. It's like the more I take it, the more she does it. So, level with me. What am I, a huge joke? Am I at least decent comic relief?"

"Come on, Wil."

"No, really. I've decided I have no ability to figure this out, so help me."

"I'm hardly Miss Lonelyhearts, you know. I'm doing the same thing with David."

"No, you don't let him walk all over you."

"In my head I do," she confessed. "But it makes no difference now. We're off, very very off."

"Yeah, right." The bus lurched.

"Everyone sit down," the driver said. He turned on the night-light.

Judy moved back to her original seat so they could both stretch out, but she still couldn't rest. Instead, she kept her face to the window as the bus progressed, hoping to make out some of the scenery. All she could see was the partial signature she had written in the dust with her finger and the moving blackness behind the *J*. She heard someone say they were passing through Pennsylvania. She had never been to Pennsylvania. From now on, she could say she had been, and that it was flat and black. She finished the edge of the *u* she began earlier but didn't move on to the *d*.

Several hours later, when the lights came up again and everyone began to shift, Judy realized she must have fallen asleep. She got up and shook Wil.

"Rest stop."

They dragged themselves up and met outside the bathrooms. Wil bought devil's food cupcakes. They grabbed an empty table and performed the childhood ritual, scooping out the filling with their tongues and leaving the icing for last. She gave him her cake part, and they headed back toward the buses ahead of the crowd to get some air and shake off the smoke. They stopped at the top of the stairs leading down to the parking lot and could see their three buses lined up under the moonlight, so bright they could read their signs: DARE TO CHANGE THE WORLD. CIU MARCH ON WASHINGTON NOVEMBER 15, 1969.

"I need to stretch," Wil said, arching his back and lifting his arms in an exaggerated V. As he came upright, he froze, arms still up in the air like he was being held up.

"What?" Judy asked. She followed his gaze to the parking lot and saw two couples darting from the center bus. It was David and Lori and Vida and Donnell.

They were creeping around the side of the bus, as if no one could see them. They watched them hug, kiss, and separate back into different buses.

"Looks like we're all off," Wil said.

Chapter 24

A FEW HOURS LATER, THEY WERE LET OUT IN A PARKING lot in Washington.

"Listen up," the driver said. "We're at the corner of Fourteenth and Constitution, just across from the National Museum of American History. See it? I'm leaving from this precise spot at six o'clock. That's exactly seven hours. So be here or stay here."

They filed out, amped up with excitement and sleep deprivation, carrying bulky signs and milling around Wizard, who had taken charge. He herded them all like little kids to make sure everyone had a hold of a portion of banner, a poster, or handfuls of leaflets, ready to hand out to the crowds. Judy declined a high-profile spot with the banner and reached for the leaflets.

"Hurry up," he called to everyone, as most of the CIU group merged into the larger swarm of people surging toward what they assumed was the march origination site. Half-thrilled, half-terrified, Judy pictured her mother watching television and catching maybe the edge of her sleeve or an inch of her hair, and she would know. She probably already knew. Maggie probably told her. Or she just sensed it. She wouldn't be surprised to see her on the grandstand watching the parade, pointing Judy out to the military police, telling them she deserved to be thrown in prison.

David clutched the sign he had carefully selected as the one most likely to end up on camera, the one she designed with the barbed wire around a stop sign, STOP THE WAR: CIU. He kept craning his neck in every direction. She knew he was looking for Lori, or even Donnell, but she didn't see either of them. As a group, they continued to follow the crowd and waited for Wizard and David to tell them what to do. They knew it had to be happening soon. It was freezing. Judy put on her hat and sunglasses even though there wasn't a camera in sight. Soon, they stopped moving.

"What's going on?"

"Why did we stop?"

"Is this where we're supposed to be?"

"Don't know."

"Who does?"

There were shrugs all around. They started to jump up and down to keep warm. One of the guys lifted Vida onto his shoulders so she could get a better look.

"I just see people, miles of people. I don't see any line or starting point or anything."

"You call this organization?" Wizard whined. "Hell, where are the march marshals? The signs? *Something!* We're just standing here."

David was pacing. "I'm going to find out what's going on." He didn't want to give up his sign but couldn't get through the crowd with it. He finally gave it to Wil, demanding assurance that he would get it back as soon as he returned.

"Listen," Wil said, cocking his ear. There was a faint noise of loudspeakers, though they couldn't hear any actual words.

"Wait here," David said. "Vida, stay up there as long as you can so I'll be able to find you." He and Wizard headed for the sound.

They stood around and hugged each other to keep warm in the November damp. Judy wished she had worn her heavy coat and not this thin jacket. The guy set Vida down every so often to rest but then lifted her right back up again. Judy kept moving so he wouldn't ask her to take a turn, a sure photo-op on the evening news.

Slowly the dense wall of people began to loosen up a bit. They picked up the signs they were resting against their legs. The banner holders got in position, one team on one side, one on the other, carefully trying not to tear the paper as they turned.

"Keep it rolled," Wil said, clinging to one of the corners. "Don't open it till we get in position."

They waited longer. Their arms started to ache, but they didn't want to put anything down, sure they would be on the move in a minute. Judy was chilled to her core. At one point, they began to realize the crowd was spreading out and on the move, but heading in the wrong direction. People pushed past them, knocking them off their ground.

Suddenly, David broke through the crowd.

"It's over. We fucking missed it," he said, beet-red and fuming.

Wizard came around behind him. "The permit ran out before even half of us could march."

"What do you mean, ran out?" Vida asked.

"There was only a three-hour permit. After that, the DC pigs wouldn't let it keep going, even with so many people who obviously had yet to march," Wizard explained.

"Fuck. All this way and we can't even march?" Wil said.

Judy was disappointed and relieved at the same time.

Someone bumped into David, and he pushed back at him vigorously.

"Watch it."

"Watch it yourself, asshole."

David grabbed the guy by his jacket and was about to punch him. Wizard took David by his arm and spun him back around.

"What the hell?" He aimed his fist at Wizard but caught himself.

"Fuck. Fuck." He threw the punch into his own left palm. "Let's find the SMC Summit." He grabbed his poster from Wil and headed off into the crowd, Wizard right behind him, struggling to keep up.

Without the need to hold their ground, the rest of them were propelled along with the crowd. Judy tried to hang on to Wil's sleeve so they wouldn't get separated, but it was useless. She kept her eye on his familiar jacket, so she would have some sense of her bearings, glad he hadn't bought that new winter coat. She saw Vida and headed toward her, but the crowd swallowed her up. They slowed but kept moving steadily away from the march site, she wasn't sure where. They were sometimes on the sidewalk, sometimes on the grass or the street.

"How many people do you think there are?" she finally asked someone next to her.

"It's a million, easy," one voice said.

"No, it's at least two," another said.

Judy felt tremendously excited, at last. She wasn't sure how much of it was because—with the march over—she was now safe from cameras, and how much was the sheer force of numbers in the city. They passed one famous white building after another—the Capitol, the Lincoln Memorial—like a series of postcards of sights she had seen all her life. When they came to a cross street, she looked sideways and caught her breath. There were thousands of bodies, packed wall to wall, building to building, the width and length of the street, all moving in the same direction. She had never seen so many people. Not on television, not anywhere. Where was Wil? He had to see this.

"Trade ya?" a cute blond guy said.

"What?"

"Your button." He pointed to the blue-and-white CIU/SMC button on her chest.

"How about this one?" He unpinned a green SMC button with a white reverse-out of the state of Texas.

"Hurry," he said, as she fumbled pinning it on her jacket. "We don't want to miss the rally." He pointed down a long thoroughfare, covered with bobbing heads, all walking toward the Washington Monument. "Can't you hear it?"

She could, slightly, and looked around for Wil's jacket, or anyone she knew. She didn't see a familiar face, but it didn't matter. Everyone was her friend now. They called to her to follow them.

"Where are you from?"

"Chicago," she found was easiest to answer. CIU's little cornfield town didn't register. "You?"

"Boston."

"California."

"Did you get to march?" asked a girl walking beside her.

"No," she said.

"I missed it, too," said a guy on her other side.

"Doesn't matter," said yet another girl. "Didn't you hear? We shut the city down, proved we're stronger and more powerful than they are. Running out that permit was the best thing that could have happened. Who knew?"

Judy hadn't thought of it that way, but of course they were right. She wondered if David would buy that. It was the biggest protest march in American history, people were saying. At the same time, no one would ever know she was there. It was the best of both worlds she'd been hoping for. There was no reason to worry. She took off her glasses and hat and put them in her pocket.

The crowd slowed as they started up the hill to the Washington Monument, and eventually she sat down with everyone around her to listen to the music. She hugged her knees and knew she would never have forgiven herself if she hadn't come.

"Oh, wow. Do you believe this?" Vida suddenly appeared, plopped herself on the grass and was joined by Wizard and about a dozen others from the bus. The blond guy with the buttons sat down next to her.

"Your friend tells me you're Judy Blue Eyes," he said.

She lowered her eyes but was pleased. Who needed David? They huddled against each other in the cold, flashing peace signs and waving to everyone. They couldn't exactly hear any music or see anything, but people were saying Peter, Paul and Mary, Country Joe and the Fish, and other big acts were there. The button guy offered her some of the peanut butter cheese crackers he had in his pocket and told her he was a psych major and a Pisces. She told him she was science and a Virgo. She didn't tell him she wasn't particularly attracted to blonds but what the hell, David had slept with someone covered in zits.

"The scientific and the cerebral, compatible signs," he said. "Solid." He bumped his fist against hers, and she tried not to laugh. She had seen it done on *Mod Squad* but not in real life. But it didn't matter, nothing mattered right now other than what they were there for.

A wave of sound came over them, and they realized everyone was singing: "Give peace a chance."

They joined in and sang it over and over, soon swaying in unison from side to side, smiling from ear to ear. She wondered if Donnell was bored with it, somewhere.

"This is how a movement begins, people," a voice said from a megaphone, "and how a war ends." People started cheering and singing, and singing and cheering, and even crying. Judy found herself choking up but didn't want the button guy to laugh at her, so she held it in until she noticed tears in his eyes. She used her scarf to wipe his cheeks, and he kissed her, first slightly and then deep. He was a much better kisser than David.

He sat behind her so he could wrap both his arms and his legs around hers. They kept each other warm until Vida tugged at Judy's arm.

"I have to pee," she said. "Come on. The Smithsonian's open. We can go there."

But before they had gone far, Vida saw Donnell.

"I'll catch up with you later," she said and ran to him.

Chapter 25

JUDY KEPT ON TOWARD THE MUSEUM. SHE WAS ANXIOUS for a mirror and a sink. She realized she had kissed the button guy even though she hadn't brushed her teeth since she left CIU, and she felt a sore bump next to her nose and was worried she was beginning to look like Lori.

Entering the Smithsonian, she found herself under the Wright brothers' *Flyer*, a small fragile airplane suspended from the ceiling. It looked like a toy.

She joined a long line of girls and settled in for a wait, grateful for the warmth of the museum's heat reaching deep into her chilled bones. A guy got in line behind her. She pointed out that it was the line to the ladies' room.

"I know," he said. "They turned all the downstairs restrooms into women's and moved the men's upstairs. See the signs?" Judy followed his pointing finger and saw that one door had a metal plate with the word LADIES, and the second had a hand-lettered paper sign taped over what was obviously the men's plate that also spelled out LADIES.

"But the line's too long up there, and you've got urinals down here that aren't being used." He pointed to the door with the makeshift sign. "I don't care who sees me."

His long hair was clumped behind his ears, but he had eyes like James Taylor.

Guy after guy got in line behind them, everyone thinking it was tremendously funny.

"Can you believe the security in here?" one of them said.

"Museum guards, DC police, even the military. What do they think? We're going to trash the Star-Spangled Banner or maybe take off in the Wright brothers' plane and fly down the mall and crash the Capitol dome?"

Judy looked up the full expanse of the multistory atrium, past the wings of the plane, and saw them patrolling every level, with many stationed along the railings, scanning the crowd.

She teased "James" about how embarrassed he would be if he had made it all the way to Washington to march against the war only to get arrested for using the ladies' restroom, but he pointed out that they would both be in there, so she would probably get arrested, too. She hadn't thought of that.

"Don't worry, though," he said. "We might get hassled, but so far they aren't arresting anyone. Just checking IDs to be sure you aren't an instigator like at the Democratic Convention."

"That's no problem for me," Judy said, "I left my ID at home, even my driver's license."

"Bad move," he said. "You draw more attention to yourself if you don't have it. Then they *have* to take you in and check you out."

Judy froze. She looked up at all the uniforms, watching as the restroom line snaked through the lobby, changing sexes as it went like some exotic reptile. At some point, it was sure to attract their attention.

Part of her knew she should leave and not take a chance. But it was almost her turn, and now she really did have to go.

She was glad to finally get into the bathroom, but just as she was about to sit down she heard an authoritarian male voice yelling, "Any women in here, get out *now*."

Any women? Surely, he meant any men, Judy thought.

"I said out. There are cops out here. Any women not out by the time I count to three will get arrested." She stopped mid-pee, and pulled up her pants. They were tight and didn't come up easily.

"One . . ."

She kept at it, and then her scarf got caught in her zipper. She couldn't believe it. She had just joked with James about how he could be arrested and now here she was, with her pants down, her scholarship at stake, her mother waiting to say I told you so—

"Two . . ."

She fumbled with the scarf. Two seconds! Her future passed before her eyes: dishonorable discharge, a lifetime as a secretary. Would the army put her in jail for being AWOL? She should have listened to what Pete was trying to tell her about that.

Finally, the threads of her scarf broke loose. She zipped up her pants, swung open the stall door, and ran for the door, noticing it no longer had the paper sign, just the metal plate that said, very clearly, GENTLEMEN.

She pushed past the guys in line and made it to the exit just as the voice said, "Three."

She felt a vice clench over her arm. She spun around and stopped dead in front of a cop whose huge hand was holding her entire bicep like it was her wrist.

"I believe the man said 'Three' before you cleared that door."

Next thing she knew, she was in and out of a paddy wagon, marched down a long brightly lit hall, and sitting in a tiny, windowless room at a table next to a sobbing girl of about her age. Another demonstrator, she assumed. She was about to ask, when in one continuous motion, a cop burst in, took two long steps to the table they were sitting behind, threw down a yellow legal pad, and barked at the girl.

"Name."

He issued the order with pencil poised, expecting immediate obedience.

Judy was glad she didn't have her ID after all. She didn't think you actually had to give them your name. That would be like incriminating yourself, wouldn't it? Or did you have to give them your name, and it was the rest you didn't have to say anything about? Even without the army situation, she had rights, didn't she?

What was this girl going to do? Judy wondered, turning to her. Right now, all she was doing was gurgling.

"Eyes straight ahead," he said to Judy.

"Name." He said it again louder to the girl, who flinched from its force but didn't move from her protective position, crouched low in her metal chair, arms below the table top, one hand cupping an elbow, supporting it as she clenched a chunk of hair just below her ear. She pulled at it, just like Marsha.

She was going to crack. Judy could see it coming, and then it would be harder for Judy, too. We both plead the fifth, she imagined saying. Could you do that in a police station, or do you have to wait until you're in court? Shouldn't they be offered a lawyer? A phone call? Who would she call? She certainly couldn't call home. Pete?

Whack. The cop slammed one hand down on the pad, the other still hovering with the pen. Name, rank, serial number, Judy thought. She could do it. That would blow his mind.

The girl flinched again. How much smaller could she get?

The cop's move altered the way the light hit him, harsh overhead fluorescents flashing on silver everywhere—badge, belt, pen, gun. It was blinding. Judy bet it was all on purpose as an interrogation technique. She couldn't believe it. Not any of it. How could she have been this stupid? Spending all this effort trying not to call attention to herself and now getting busted and facing a federal crime for using the wrong bathroom.

She could tell the cop wouldn't wait much longer. He wasn't angry, just expressionless. How did they do that? Judy swore his eyelids weren't even moving. The girl made a stifled noise, and Judy hoped she wouldn't cry. He didn't look like that would work on him at all.

She wondered where they put everyone else? The paddy wagon had been full. The first thing they did was grab IDs. That's how they had isolated her. The girl must not have one, either.

"No," Judy said, a little surprised at the sound of her own voice.

"What did you say?" He immediately switched his attention to her. His eyes were gray, silver-gray, like everything else. For the first time he was mad, kind of shocked, too, she thought, but definitely angry.

"We don't have to tell you our names."

The girl sat up, fearful but alert.

The cop stared at Judy. She felt sweat raining down her sides and brought her elbows in close to sop it up. She waited for him to quote regulations or the Constitution—or *something*. That's when she would ask for the lawyer. Yes, that's what she would do.

But he slammed down his pen, picked it up with the pad in another single motion, and was out the door. They were sealed up again, the stale air seeming to reel around them as if a locomotive had just zoomed through. The girl grabbed Judy's hand. It was dry as a bone; Judy's was hot and wet.

"Thank you," she said. "Just so you know. I would have told him my name. If it weren't for you, I would have, and my parents would have yanked me out of school and thrown away the key."

"I wouldn't get too excited. This isn't over yet."

"What do you think is going to happen now?"

"No idea, but I don't think it's going to be good."

Judy felt like she had been trapped in the room for hours. Or did it just seem like that? No clock. Her shirt was soaked. She had a bus to catch.

After way too long a time, the door opened again and a short female officer entered. She said she had to search them. She was as nice as the other cop was hard. It wasn't much of a search, waistbands and tight spots. Judy was so relieved, she actually smiled at the policewoman as she ran her finger under the elastic of her soaking-wet bra explaining that they just have to do this sort of thing.

"Okay," she said when she was finished and held the door open.

"Okay?" Judy asked.

"Okay. You can go."

"Go?"

"You're free to go."

The girl was already up and moving toward the door.

"I'm sorry you had to wait so long," the officer said. "I was off duty, and they needed a female officer to search you."

Judy wanted to say, "That's it?" but didn't dare.

Once outside the station, the girl was suddenly assertive. "They were just giving us a hard time, the pigs," she said. "I bet they would have arrested us if they could have. God bless the Fifth Amendment."

She and Judy hugged, as if they actually knew each other, and separated as quickly as possible.

Judy checked her watch. It was 5:40. She had twenty minutes to get to the bus. She asked for directions to Fourteenth and Constitution, put her sunglasses back on, and pulled the hat out of her pocket. She was fairly certain no one was following her, but she couldn't take a chance or lead the cops to her friends. She ran for the bus.

She was one of the first back and was glad not to have to talk to anyone. She sat in a corner of the bumper seat at the very back of the bus, sank down with her feet on the top of the seat in front of her, and tried to calm her breathing. Too close, much too close a call. She couldn't take another one. At this point she wondered if she might even want to be a nurse, maybe in the army, and was just being a jerk fighting her mother about it because it had been her idea, or if she genuinely wanted to give it all away. It would be comforting, in a way, just to go with it. No money worries, all of school worked out, no decisions until she was twenty-five. Right now, that sounded good.

Look what she did when she had to make decisions on her own. Her mother was right. She was an immature, ungrateful little punk who was biting the hand that fed her. What was she thinking? She just had to keep her head down now, and figure it out later. All she wanted was to get back to CIU as fast as possible.

Chapter 26

THE LAST PERSON JUDY WANTED TO DEAL WITH WAS
David, but he sat beside her in the back of the bus and refused to
talk to anyone. At first, she thought he must have done something and was afraid the cops would be checking the buses. She
could now certainly relate to that. But he paid no attention to
anyone getting on or off and hardly noticed when they finally
pulled away. It was something else.

He was staring blankly at the floor in front of him, tightly
gripping his folded arms, one leg bobbing as fast as it could go.
Eventually he made a fist and started gently punching the back
of the seat in front of him, slowly and deliberately, as he appeared to calm down.

Wil motioned for her to come up front and join them,
throwing his hands up like it was obvious they had to talk.

Judy didn't think she could leave David in his condition. She
assumed he was upset about the march and tested it.

"David, everyone is saying that running the permit out was
a great thing. It shows we overwhelmed the city." He didn't say
anything, so she kept at it. "The story is it's the biggest protest
in US history.

"There were a million people here," she went on. "All their
systems shut down. We choked the city. There's no way this
won't hit the airwaves all around the world."

"No shit, really?" he said, finally.

"See, we were part of it just by being here." She saw him
relax. "Just like Michael said."

David closed down again; for a moment, she thought he was going to cry.

"I'm a total dick," he said. "I mean really. I don't know why I'm here . . . why they sent me . . . why you have anything to do with me. You have no idea . . ."

"Just let it go," Judy said. "We have to get together on this story . . ."

"Some things you can't just let go, you have to—"

"No, you don't. You really don't have to," she said. She wouldn't be able to stand to hear Lori's name.

"I swear you're the only one who really understands, who *knows.*"

She turned away and looked out the bus window. It was getting dark, and she could see his reflection clearly as he waited for her to turn her head back toward him. He seemed surprised, as if he believed what he was saying.

"Yeah, I probably am," she said.

Wizard, Wil, and Vida eventually came back to sit with them.

"We've got to figure out how we are going to tell the others about what happened," Vida said.

"What didn't happen, you mean," Wizard said.

"That's the tricky part," Judy said. "They need to understand it was a victory, not a defeat."

They talked on and off throughout the journey home, trying out various scenarios. Eventually, David warmed up and started to weigh in.

"Let me lead it, and the rest of you can jump in," David said. "I think that's what Michael expects. And it's my responsibility," he added.

The others exchanged puzzled looks, but Vida signaled they should just let it alone.

❅ ❅ ❅

WHEN the group gathered to head for Michael's apartment the evening after they returned, it was clear something was going on, but no one was talking. Even Marsha had blown off Vida and Judy when they called her, as promised, as soon as they got off the bus.

"So? Did you see us on TV?" Wil couldn't help asking.

"Yeah," Howie said. "I told RoMo I was sure you were that gray speck in the corner of the screen, didn't I? Good work, Wil, making an impact."

They walked the rest of the mile out to University Apartments in silence, the wind off the fields hitting them full in the face once they cleared the dorm buildings. Judy ended up behind Howie and noticed how baggy his pants were as they flapped against his legs.

When they got to Michael's, Sheila opened the door to the dark, close apartment. It still smelled like grass and incense, but now there were new odors, sharp astringent and sweet, old-people's camphor. The overhead lights were off, and the room was lit only by candles and the lime-green lamp, which was stationary, the shade's revolving mechanism off. Fish put on the first *Super Session* album, and they each found a place to sit, those who had not gone to Washington opposite those who had, on either side of Michael.

He was sitting on the couch, supported with pillows, covered by one of Sheila's hand-knit afghans. His fine face had sunken in on itself. His complexion was dull, eyes watery, and his blond hair was now pasted against his head as if he hadn't combed it since they had left. She tried to remember how long it had been since she had seen him. They had been busy getting ready, but maybe it had been over a week, or more.

"Ah, my little red-scarfed volunteers," he said. "You're back with your reports. They better be good."

"What's going on, Michael?" Vida asked.

Sheila shook her head to warn her off, but she persisted. "We're not blind, Michael. You're sick. You've been sick."

"Just a little setback, a few days in the hospital, but not to worry. I'm assured I'm not contagious."

"Hospital?" Vida said. "Why didn't anybody tell us?" She looked around the room, stopping at Marsha, who looked down.

"And yet, here you are, and you know all you need to know," Michael said.

"Is there anything we can do?" Judy asked.

"Yes. Tell me about this march."

"Absolutely, Michael," David said, jumping up. "First thing we did was fry some Trot ass." Michael smiled. "We found out they were splitting their forces among the three buses, so we did the same."

He set the scene carefully, as they had discussed, making sure everyone knew how important it had been to take control, even on the bus.

"Lori Mueller ended up on my bus. I saw her send a few of her minions to fan out and spread the word, and I could tell she was keeping the seat next to her open for a potential convert. So, I sat myself down, and asked her how many guys did she figure she had banged into little Trots. She was so pissed, she folded her arms in a hissy fit and called me a . . . come on, everyone, what did she call me?"

"A fascist!" They answered him in unison.

Judy was curious as to why he was talking this way about Lori and wondered if they had a fight. She also wondered if he would be telling the story the same way if he had been aware she knew about the two of them.

She watched Michael's face and tried to ignore the green cast to his skin from the lamp reflection. He seemed to be working hard to stay focused. Sheila responded to his every movement with quiet attention, a shift of the afghan, a shuffling of the pillows. At one point, Judy saw him give Sheila a glance and watched her take a pill from her pocket and give it to him with a cup of water. Judy looked away and noticed the others were doing the same.

Vida told the story about how she got Donnell to join the rest of them in singing every protest song they could think of. But of course, since Trotsky didn't write any songs, he actually suggested "The Battle Hymn of the Republic."

"I told him it was too bad he didn't know it in Russian," David said.

"Maybe you should try this story in Russian," Achilles said. "It might go faster."

"Yeah," Howie said. "Can we get off the bus, please?"

"Anytime," David said. "You know what Timothy Leary says, 'You're either on the bus or you're off the bus.'"

"We didn't actually get off the bus, ourselves," Wizard said, oblivious to David's sarcastic reference. "It was more like we were dumped."

They laughed at that, and Wizard told them how the bus driver had been like their worst grade-school nightmare. Then he started complaining about the lack of organization and how he would have had decent signage, or something, to tell people where to go and what was going on. He told them how they followed everyone else, dragging their banners, and how they were freezing while they just stood around waiting for the march to begin and then, without any setup or anything, he just slid right into how they heard the permit ran out and they weren't going to be marching at all.

It wasn't how they had agreed to tell the story.

"You didn't march?" RoMo asked.

Michael sat up, his entire face in a deep scowl.

"No, we didn't get to march, but the fact that we didn't shows how successful we were," David said, fumbling back to their plan.

Fish made a *pffft* sound.

"Wasn't the march the whole fucking point?" Meldrich said.

"There were literally so many people, we'd still be marching now," David continued. "They had to cut it off."

He told them what Judy had explained to him on the bus.

"They didn't expect anywhere near a million people," David said. "It was an overwhelming show of force, get it?"

"Yeah, we get it. The question is, do you?" Fish said.

"What happened at the Pentagon?" Howie asked. "That's what hit the news."

"We heard about that later," David said. "A bunch of kids ran up the stairs there, just like they were all over the stairs at the Lincoln Memorial and everywhere else in town, but the police freaked and tear-gassed them."

"You weren't at the Pentagon yourself?" Michael asked.

"No, Michael, I wasn't," he said apologetically. "It was hard to get where things were happening because there were so many people. We didn't even know what happened at the Pentagon until it was over, and after that, they cracked down so much you couldn't get there at all."

"But you were at least *at* the SMC Summit, right?" Fish asked.

"It was the same kind of thing," David said. "Wizard and I kept asking, and someone would say they thought the meeting was going to be in front of the Capitol Building, and then we'd make our way over there and hear, no, it was by the Washington Monument, and then we'd hear all this bullshit about whether there was going to be a meeting at all. Eventually we just gave it up and went to the rally."

"Do I understand this correctly?" Fish asked. "We set you up to go all the way to Washington on our money, and there's no march and no meeting?"

"I just explained," David said.

"Any coordination for the next moratorium?" Achilles asked. "Anything on the lottery? Anything at all?"

"We tried, *zeeze*," David said. "It's hard to understand if you weren't there."

"So, you guys just ended up going cross country to a concert, right?" Howie said.

"It wasn't just a concert," Vida took over. "It was more like an exchange. You couldn't see anything, and you could only hear a little bit, but it was absolutely incredible, all these people were singing and trading buttons.

"See." She pointed to her vest. "This orange one is from the Georgia SMC. Here's my favorite." She pointed to another: I'M AN EFFETE SNOB. "It's Spiro Agnew's favorite name for us."

"No shit," Meldrich said.

"I brought it for Michael," Vida said, with a snap. He tilted his head up with effort to look into her face while she pinned the button to his sweater. "Because I know he's such an Agnew fan." They both tried to laugh at the joke.

"I was almost arrested," Judy said. She hadn't told anyone, and she certainly wasn't about to share all the details, but now she could see that the story could be funny and might calm things down.

David, Wil, Vida, and Wizard all looked up at once, startled.

"Did you get arrested at the Pentagon?" RoMo asked.

"No, in the bathroom at the Smithsonian."

They laughed again and the tension broke. Meldrich took the opportunity to change the music to *Fresh Cream*, Howie lit a few joints and started them around the room, and Wizard grabbed a six-pack out of Michael's refrigerator.

"Truth is," Judy said. "We might have been there to change the world, but half the time we were trying to find a bathroom."

"Revolutions have been lost over such details," Michael said, amused. "I think Napoleon could empathize."

She recounted the details about how crowded it was and how the guy had joined the line to the ladies' bathroom behind her.

"I was a little surprised," she said. "But it was pretty funny, and he was very entertaining. He looked like James Taylor." She was hoping David was listening, but he and Vida had their heads together.

"So, here I was," she said, "standing in a line under police surveillance that any moment could get me thrown in the clink, and I couldn't just bolt because I had to go so bad." She finished the story as a comedy, about her zipper getting stuck, and the asshole guard grabbing her as she ran out.

"And the cops?" Meldrich asked.

"I have no idea, I don't think I stopped running until I was halfway to Pennsylvania." She started laughing and they applauded her.

"For that story, you deserve the first hit," Wil said, handing her a hash pipe.

"And for saying the word *asshole* out loud without blushing," RoMo said.

Michael was watching her so intently, she had to look away.

Suddenly, Meldrich stood up and began to clap loudly. "Congratulations, Judy. I think your little pissing story about sums up the situation." His clapping slowed to hard regular slaps. Wil still had his hand on the arm of the turntable, so it was the only sound in the room, piercing the air like thunderclaps.

"As I see it, you all pissed away our forty bucks, you pissed away our chance to get involved in the national movement, and you pissed away CIU's last hope for an impact on the lottery. You have my congratulations. Come on, everyone, let's give our Washington contingent a big hand."

His clapping sped up as he was joined by Achilles, Fish, and Howie. The two factions glared at each other across Michael's couch.

"This is serious," David said. "She could have been arrested."

They shouted him down.

"Yeah, well, if you'd been there, Meldrich," he said, "we'd probably all be in jail, the buses impounded, and CIU the joke of the country."

"And you don't think you are now?"

The shouting continued with both sides going back and forth.

Michael motioned to Judy. She was sitting on the floor and crawled over to him.

"You didn't tell us everything, did you?"

"I can't really explain," she whispered. "But my scholarship . . ."

The angry voices drowned her out, and Michael struggled to hear.

". . . shouldn't have been there," she continued. "It was stupid. I was almost caught."

"Caught for what?"

"I was AWOL," she whispered.

Michael frowned, puzzled.

"I'm in the army." She couldn't believe she said it, and that she said it at that particular time.

The shouting suddenly elevated, and Michael nudged her away, pointing to the scene in front of them. David and Meldrich were red faced, with Fish and Achilles taunting on one side, and Vida, Wil, and Wizard on the other.

"I want my money back."

"Now who's being a fascist?"

"That's enough," Michael said.

They quieted down, but continued to sputter here and there. Michael held up his hand for silence as David and Meldrich tried to start up again. He kept his hand up for what felt like a full five minutes.

"What's this about, anyway?" David asked. "We're supposed to be in this together. Our victory is your victory, too."

"Show him the newspaper," Meldrich said.

RoMo pulled the crumpled front page of the *Chicago Tribune* from her shoulder bag and handed it to David.

"You say there were a million people in DC," Meldrich said. "This says there were only a couple hundred thousand. Why should we believe what you say about anything?"

"That's impossible, man. You didn't see it," Wil said, joining Vida and Wizard, who had gathered around David. Judy stood behind to read over his shoulder.

The headline read "250,000 Demonstrate in DC." A single photo showing some freaks throwing something toward uniforms made it look like there had been a riot at the Pentagon.

"There's got to be more here," David said, scanning the articles.

"They must have only counted the ones who actually marched," Judy said, remembering how every thoroughfare and side street had been packed with people. "Maybe they couldn't figure how to count the rest. It's the only explanation."

"Or they did it on purpose," Michael said. "It's easier for them to say the movement called for a million protestors, and all we could deliver was a quarter of that. And they threw in the Pentagon action to show we were violent. Do we ever really know what's going on?"

"Either way, it was fucking useless," Meldrich said. "We knew before you even got back, it was a bust. It's been all over the news."

"I don't know about the numbers, but if you'd been there you'd know Nixon had to be sweating bullets over the public pressure, the tension," David said.

"I don't think he was too tense," Achilles said, grabbing the paper and holding the page up to David's face. "According to this caption, he was watching a football game on television."

David crumpled into Michael's only chair.

"All in all, a pretty effete effort, I'd say," Achilles said.

David sprung up and tried to punch him in the face. Both sides jumped back up, ready to fight.

"Out!" Michael said. "And don't come back until you stop squabbling and are ready to make a serious plan for the lottery action."

Chapter 27

THEY TOOK OVER TWO TABLES IN THE TUNE ROOM.
keeping their factions, pissed off and a little ashamed of themselves. They were too wound up to go back to the dorms to
sleep, but they had nothing to do or say, other than to bitch
about the lack of availability of enough grass, now that they
needed it more than ever.

Vida tried to get them talking again.

"Do you guys know what's wrong with Michael?"

"If he doesn't want us to know, then I say we keep out of it,"
Fish said.

"Thanks, just like a guy," Vida said. She turned to Marsha.
"Did Sheila tell you anything?"

"It's hard to get her alone, so we haven't been able to talk to
her. We don't know, really. And you see how he answered you.
He doesn't want us to know."

"Yeah, respect that, at least," Achilles said.

"At least?"

"Just give it a rest," David said.

Meldrich was rolling around on the moldy carpet that bordered the shiny wood of the central aisle, making out with a
blonde, semi-straight girl he had been sleeping with for most of
the semester. He called her Patches, after the teenage death
song, for no apparent reason. They were watching simply because it was in front of them, and because Patches was wearing a
skirt that would ride up higher every time they turned over.

Judy was getting grossed out by the cigarette butts that attached themselves to her thighs with every roll.

She pulled Wil's sleeve and put her finger to her lips. "Come on," she whispered. "Let's get out of here." She was frustrated that she couldn't talk to Michael about her situation, and wasn't even sure he had heard what she said. She had to talk to someone, alone, and Wil was the only one left she could trust.

"I'm so bummed," Wil said, following her out, pushing against the double glass doors covered in notices and stickers. "I really thought Washington was going to mean something."

"At least we tried, Wil. At least we were there, and we're not the only ones who know how many people were on those streets. Maybe the other papers will report it accurately."

"Yeah, while fucking Nixon was watching football. Makes you wonder why we should try anything."

They headed up to the Browsing Room on the second floor of the Union, a large study room, full of plush chairs and couches, used by students as an alternative to studying in the library. It was empty now, and Wil rushed to try out all the chairs and lie on all the couches.

"I always wanted to do that," he said, when they finally settled on a couch. "What's up? I'm not really in the mood for any more politics."

"I was just sick of watching Meldrich and Patches," Judy said.

"Hard to believe they're both involved with other people."

Judy screwed up her face.

"You didn't know?" Wil said. "Oh, yeah. He's got a girlfriend who's still in high school back home, and she's engaged to some guy up at Madison."

So, it's everyone, Judy thought.

"We never talked about what happened on the bus," she said.

"What's to say? David and Vida are who they are."

"I guess. Vida once told me that all Lori had to do was crook her finger, and she could have any guy she wanted."

"I guess it takes one to know one."

"Be honest. Do you think Lori's that good looking? I mean, David makes it sound like he hates her, and yet . . ." This isn't what she had intended to talk about, but it wouldn't hurt to get a man's perspective.

"Jeeze, I don't know. She's okay. I mean, if she shuts up, she's okay. I think she's kind of scary myself, but come on, she puts out. She practically advertises it as part of her women's lib rap."

"I knew it," Judy said. "David's . . ."

Wil didn't ask her to finish.

"You want me to weigh in on Donnell?"

"Doesn't matter. It's obvious. He doesn't really give a shit about anyone but his socialist self, so Vida doesn't have to, either."

They both lit cigarettes. There were no ashtrays, so Wil transferred his remaining cigarettes to his shirt pocket and propped the empty pack against a table lamp to hold their ashes.

"I feel like I'm the world's oldest virgin," Judy said, barely realizing she had said it out loud, and then just deciding to go with it. "It's so bad that when I hear stories about a teenager getting pregnant, all I can think about is that at least she got it over with. It's like I have this disease." She shrank down into the couch. "Don't you dare laugh at me."

"I wouldn't laugh. I know this is serious. I know David won't sleep with you because he doesn't want to be first."

"He told you?"

Wil shrugged off her question. "I know you think nothing's worse, but I can top it. Vida won't sleep with me unless I promise not to fall in love with her."

"Too late."

"No shit," he said. "The point is, our situations are equally absurd, but it's the same problem. They don't want to be involved, and we do."

"So, what do we do about it?"

"I guess we just have to become better flower children and be more into free love. I mean, they must be onto something, like everyone else, apparently. Besides, with what's happening in the world today, why stand on ceremony? I could be dead by spring."

"Don't joke about that," Judy said. "Even if your number is low, worst case is you're safe till you graduate."

"Yeah, Wil, the graduate." He stood up and bowed, flipping his scarf as if it were a tassel on a mortarboard and he was accepting his diploma. "Or Wil, the graduate, as intellectual professor." He sat in a chair opposite her, folded his arms, and pretended to smoke a pipe.

Judy laughed.

"Wil, the graduate, military version." He puffed himself up like a little toy soldier and goose-stepped around one of the couches. "And of course, Wil, the last graduate." He threw himself length-wise on the floor with his arms folded over his chest as if he were dead.

He lay there for a moment then opened one eye. "There will be no Wil, the graduate, get it?" He sat up. "I'm on probation. Have been all semester. I'm a set of finals away from a first-class draft ticket to Saigon, regardless of my number."

Judy moved to his side.

"Why didn't you tell me?" she asked, shocked. "I thought Howie was the only one in danger from his grades."

"My grade point has been eroding in direct proportion to the changes in the draft. At least Howie has the smarts to cheat. I can't concentrate on anything except what's going on in this insane world."

He picked himself up off the floor. "So, I'm pretty fucked . . . I pretty much fucked myself, I know."

"The semester isn't over, Wil. You can study, and besides you could still get a high number."

"I won't."

Judy moved to touch his arm. "That's what everyone says." Wil started rolling one of his cigarettes around until the tobacco started to come out the end. "I'm pretty sure I should just let it be what it's going to be."

"You're the one who told me that destiny and tests aren't connected. That's just a lazy excuse for not studying. I can help. I'm good at tests."

"I heard."

"So, show me what you've got."

Judy went through his book bag, found the syllabus for each of his classes and explained how he could catch up. When he pushed back, she reminded him how many CIU students crammed ninety percent of their studying into the night before a test and still passed.

"It's not like we're Harvard. You can do it," she said. "When's your first midterm?"

"Wednesday, sociology. That's what I was going to study for tonight. I dropped some speed, so I can stay up all night. You know, I have another tab. You could take it and help me."

Judy realized that's why he was acting so oddly.

"I could really use your help."

"I'll just stay up with you without the speed."

"But we won't be on the same wavelength. It makes a difference. My mind is going really fast now. You could drill me."

Judy reluctantly agreed. Wil gave her the tab, explaining how to peel it off the foil then swallow it like an aspirin. She left to find a drinking fountain. As she brought it toward her mouth, she wondered how she had come to this. But Wil needed her, and he had always been there for her.

"What the hell," she said to herself, and swallowed the tab.

By the time she returned, the Browsing Room had begun to fill with students who had settled in and spread their study materials, surrounding Wil, who seemed on a little island. He was angling his head to and fro as if he was having a conversation with himself.

"All right, let's look at these chapter headings," she whispered, as she opened his sociology book to straddle both their laps. She took some time to scan the material. "Is this what the test is on? It's all about prison chaplains."

"That's what this professor is writing a book about. See why I fail to understand the relevancy?"

He started to laugh, and the others in the room shushed him.

"But at least the next time I'm in prison and need spiritual advice, I'll know the pressures the chaplain is under," he laughed again, trying to keep it down, ". . . especially if I end up on death row for breaking the sound barrier in the Browsing Room."

Judy lost it, and neither one of them could stop laughing.

"I'm sorry," she said to the others between breaths, as they grabbed their things and made their way out of the room.

"Boy, that stuff hits fast," she said, and they both shrieked. "We can't do this all night; we have to study. I didn't know speed made you laugh so much."

"Um. Actually, it's acid," he said. "Orange Sunshine."

"LSD?" She stopped in the middle of the corridor.

"Don't worry. I took it before, and it's weak, mostly speed."

"Weak acid? Is there such a thing?"

"I don't know why everyone's so afraid of it," he said. "Like it'll make you lose your mind. If it's good, it opens you up and—"

THE FOURTEENTH OF SEPTEMBER

"But you should have told me," Judy said. "What about birth defects?"

"Oh, that stuff's not true. It was just made up so people wouldn't take it."

"You're sure?"

"So I've heard," he said. "Besides, I'm not gonna have kids anyway."

"I thought you wanted to be able to tell them about the March on Washington."

"That was before I knew I'd be dead."

Judy stopped short, but then Wil started to laugh as if this was extremely funny, and so did she. They practically crawled down the stairs to the lower level of the Union, gripping the hand rails, and stopping to sit on every other step as they fought for breath. By the time they got back to the Tune Room, they felt they had been walking for miles and were so exhausted they sat on the floor just inside the entrance, people skirting them as they came in and out.

Judy listened as Wil chattered nonstop about his love for Vida, his philosophy, his name.

"Are you really related to Wilfred Owen?"

"I think so . . . I want to be," he screwed up his face, concentrating. "I like his poetry. If only I had the talent. I'd like to be, you know, John Lennon." He started to sing in a thin voice, "'The fool on the hill,' something, something, he sees the world spinning round, something, something. Anyway, it's just beautiful. If I could write like that and Vida could sing . . ."

As the hours went by, this all became hugely funny, and they were giggling themselves silly.

At one point, Judy heard the sound of an engine. She had never been on an airplane, but now she was. Whirling, grinding sounds were coming out of the jukebox, whipping her around:

Burrrrr . . . whOOOOle lot of love . . . *grrrrrrr . . .* whole lotta love . . . *grrrrrrrrrr.*

The zoom and roar of the guitars were the engines revving, and she was flying. She wanted to tell David she got it now; she knew how to fly. She flew for days.

Later, she made her way to the ladies' room and stared at herself in the mirror, appalled as she examined the cavernous pores in her skin, much worse than Lori Mueller's. She got sidetracked marveling at how her contact lenses rippled over her black pupils and her deep irises turned into fish eyes. They were teal fish eyes, but then they changed colors and turned green like David's duster, green like army fatigues. She had told Wil about the army, hadn't she? Or maybe not. The face in the mirror turned into her mother, and she made for the door as fast as she could, laboring through each step in the heavy syrup of the linoleum.

Still later, they were moving outside. Wil led her to the Tower, a huge structure next to the Student Union. At the top was the beacon that both lit up and loomed over the campus. Judy was surprised the door was open and they could just go up. Wil explained that you could get in anytime except during finals. Apparently, some kid had jumped when the pressure was too intense, so they locked it down at test time to prevent further suicides. Otherwise it was open, and Wil said he came up here a lot. In the daytime, even though you could see nearly twenty miles beyond the campus, it was just cornfields, but at night, he said, the sky was all yours.

They climbed the stairs for hours and finally emerged through a heavy door onto a shallow balcony, its edge loosely protected by a gesture of a railing—no more than a few feet high—with widely spaced supporting bars. Wil immediately made for the center of the balcony, stuck his feet through the spaces, wrapped his arms around the metal bars and rested his chin on the railing. Judy took some time aligning herself in the same posture. She moved slowly, sure she was going to go right over the edge.

"I'm afraid of heights," she said. "I think I have vertigo."

"You're just tripping. Look at this," he said, sweeping his arm. "All of the stars are laughing, just like it says in *The Little Prince.*" He went on to recite from memory.

In one of the stars I shall be living,
In one of them I shall be laughing,
And so it will be as if all the stars are laughing when you look at the sky at night.

And, in fact, Judy was now sure she could hear them. Wil started to laugh, and the stars started to twinkle. Then they both laughed, and they twinkled brighter. The more they laughed, the more the stars glittered. They watched it, for days and days, before it started to slow down.

"There was something important I was going to tell you," Judy said, "but I can't remember what it was."

"About the test?"

She thought for a moment but didn't think that was right.

"I think I hate David," she said, after what must have been another hour. "Do you hate Vida?"

"Probably not."

"So, we should just not care so much either way, huh?" Judy said.

"Something like that."

"So what about the rest of our lives?"

They decided Judy would transfer to the English program and get a new roommate next semester. Check.

Wil kept trying to guess what his lottery number would be,

weighing the options for what he would do about it. Maybe he would study harder and get his grade point up, maybe even try to lose weight like Howie, and if neither of those worked and he was drafted, he would become a medic.

"I wouldn't have to kill anyone," he said. "And they wouldn't kill me. Maybe I could even save a life." Check.

"Vida?" Judy asked.

"At some point I have to sleep with her. I swear if I did that, I could die anytime, happy."

"I don't think I'll go quite that far for David," Judy said. "I think I'll just settle for getting someone else to go first and get it out of the way."

"Think that would work with Vida, too?" Wil asked seriously.

"Don't tell me . . . ," Judy said. "First we have the same birthday, and now this. All I can say is . . . oh, wow."

That sent them into another fit of giggles.

"So," Wil said. "Let's just do it and get it over with, you and me."

"Oh, be still my heart. This is the most romantic proposition I've ever heard."

"I'm serious. That's the beauty of it. We won't get romantically involved. We need to know what it's like. It's an important part of our education."

Wil made it all sound very logical, something they owed themselves. And Judy knew she could trust him. It would be their secret, they decided, and after, they would both be free to engage in insignificant sex with whomever they chose. They could make it work. Check.

Wil helped her disengage her arms from the bars. She stamped her feet so they would wake up, and they headed for his room. He was so sweet, really, offering to do this for her. Or was she doing it for him?

❋ ❋ ❋

HIS room looked like he hadn't cleaned or picked anything up in months. There were clothes strewn everywhere, along with overflowing ashtrays, a bowl of what looked like rotting oatmeal, and at least two pizza boxes, one of which had been stepped on. Wil quickly cleared a path to the bed.

"I'll go out and give you a few minutes. Let me turn on the desk light."

"No, don't, please," Judy said. "Just wait in the hall for a minute."

She was wearing a big loose shirt under her sweater and decided to keep it on, suddenly very worried about all the details. She pulled the dishtowel from under the oatmeal bowl and put it under her. She pulled Kleenex from her purse and put it next to the mattress, fluffed up and ready to grab. She had just finished *The Bell Jar* and wondered if, like Sylvia Plath, she would bleed and bleed and have to be hospitalized. How would she get to a hospital from here down the elevator and through the lobby?

She lay for what seemed like forever, staring at the ceiling. He had covered it with stars, little gold stickers like you get on your A tests in grade school.

Wil came in and took off his shirt. She knew he was thin and pale, but now she saw how absolutely twig-like his arms were and wondered about the rest of him. She probably outweighed him. He awkwardly pulled off his pants while sitting on the edge of the mattress, both under and outerwear together, the former getting stuck on one foot. She turned her head away until he got under the blanket. He made sure they were both completely covered. There was no top sheet, and the wool was rough against her skin.

He lay down next to her and started to kiss her neck. It felt like a rodent, nibbling. She went through all the same motions as with David, but they were an effort.

She kissed him, but it felt like nothing but the physical touching of two sets of lips, his tongue merely a place for hers to lie. She searched his small eyes and thin lips for a response. David had deep eyes she could fall into, full lips that knew how to hang on and press. She redoubled her efforts. He didn't make any sounds at all. She ran her hands down his back and felt the long bone, uneven and bumpy, and tried not to compare it with David's muscled back. He did the same, unhooking her bra more deftly than David, but then keeping his hands on her back, not moving to her now freed breasts. She felt enormous next to him. She was no longer high at all.

She tried not to picture David, feeling guilty until she realized that Wil was probably thinking about Vida, adventurous Vida. I must be like a nun to him, she thought.

When the pushing began, she was surprised at the pain. She had always relied on her high threshold. Her mother had seen to that, forcing her as a child to watch without flinching when she got her shots. To this day, she could coolly offer advice about preferable veins to technicians drawing blood. But this was completely different, a vulnerable kind of pain she couldn't steel herself against. She heard herself gasp, but kept from crying out. Up and up he went, to the point where she wondered if it might not work. Would she be one of those whose hymen wouldn't break, and she would have to have it surgically cut? How did you know when that was the case? Did you just keep at it until you couldn't stand it anymore? Did you give it a certain amount of time? Five thrusts? Ten? Wil was huffing with the effort. She realized her attempt to stay silent was in her head, and she was hissing through her clenched teeth with each try.

"Are you sure you want me to keep going?" he asked.

"Yes," she said, not having to add, "let's just get it over with."

Then a quick rip, and Wil was out. She reached for the towel, stuffed it between her legs, and was up, heading for the bathroom.

She locked herself in a stall for a long time, surprised there was so little blood, waiting for more. She then crept out and, once sure she was alone, examined her face in the mirror as if she was a deflowered Victorian heroine wondering if she looked any different. She didn't but was flushed from all the effort with her hair all over, in what she felt David would think was sexy disarray.

When she came back, Wil was sitting on the bed fully dressed and looking guilty.

"Are you all right?" he asked.

She nodded, knowing that if she tried to talk she would cry. He insisted on walking her back to her dorm, though she really wanted to be alone.

"Thank you," she said, startling him when they were still a good hundred yards from the front door, and ran inside. Thank God, Maggie was home again for the weekend. She crawled in bed, put the covers over her head and sobbed until her chest hurt, thinking of how she would remember this the rest of her life.

Chapter 28

NO ONE HAD HEARD FROM MICHAEL FOR NEARLY A WEEK after the meeting at his apartment. They agreed he must still be angry at them. But when Vida called, hoping to make amends, Sheila told her he was gone.

"Vanished," Vida told Judy, afterward, on the phone. "His stuff's still here, but otherwise no trace."

"Is he in the hospital?"

"Not the one he was in while we were in Washington, apparently. Sheila's pretty freaked out. She caught him mixing his meds with grass and acid and was so mad she took off for a while, thinking she'd teach him a lesson. She left in the morning while he was still asleep, and when she went back later he was gone. She's staying in the apartment, hoping he'll turn up, or call, or something."

"You don't think he's—"

"No. Seems like we'd know more if he was. He used to always drop out of sight for a while and then come back. We assumed he just got sick of us and wanted some time to himself. That's kind of funny, isn't it? Sick of us. And now he's sick. Anyway, he hasn't taken off like that lately, not since Sheila."

"Shouldn't we do something?" Judy asked.

"Not for Michael. He does what he does. But maybe we should go out there and keep Sheila company."

Judy, Vida, and Marsha went to Michael's apartment later that day with pizza, four bottles of the super-sweet Ripple wine

Sheila always drank while the rest of them smoked dope, and a box of Salerno butter cookies, which, when you put them on your finger and nibbled them down to where the ring finally broke, always gave you something to focus on and made you feel better. They found the door open. Sheila was propped up on the bed, knitting furiously. The apartment was dark, curtains closed, only the green flickering light on. It was amazing Sheila could see to knit in this cave.

Vida arranged the food on the coffee table amid the candles. Marsha tried to coax Sheila out of the bed.

Judy felt useless; all she could do was stare at the couch and picture Michael in the chaos of that post-Washington screaming match and how she had tried to tell him her secret. She had gone over it a million times in her head. Had he heard her actually say the word *army?* She wasn't sure. If he had, and Maggie was right, he might be off somewhere now thinking she was an undercover military spy. She wondered if that might even be why he had disappeared so suddenly.

Marsha put a record on the stereo. No one cared what it was, just that there was background noise and it wasn't too loud. They gathered, sitting cross-legged around the coffee table, cheeks shining in the candlelight. Sheila eventually came over, dragging her yarn.

"You're knitting in red?" Marsha said. "I've only seen you with white yarn."

"Fish gave me a commission," Sheila said. "He said he'd give me fifty dollars to knit him an American flag afghan."

She looped off a red stripe and started a white one. Judy wondered what she had done with her wedding dress.

"We let Michael down. I think that's why he left," Judy said. "Sick or not, he sent us to Washington in his place, and we disappointed him. I'm just so sad."

"I'm not sad," Vida said. "I'm angry, which is what Michael would be if he felt better. Fuck Nixon and his football game. I can't believe it."

"David's the only one who disappointed him," Sheila said. "He promised to write 'DARE TO STRUGGLE, DARE TO WIN' with a name on one of the outside walls of the Pentagon. The name was really important," Sheila said.

"If he couldn't get to the Pentagon, he was supposed to try the Lincoln Memorial or any really public building," Sheila continued. "He was supposed to use a red marker."

"Poor David," Vida said. "That really would have been impossible to pull off with all that security."

Judy realized now why David had been so upset on the bus.

"But it wasn't *his* name," Sheila continued.

"What do you mean?"

"He was supposed to write 'DARE TO STRUGGLE, DARE TO WIN. MAREK '69.'"

"Who's Marek?" Judy asked.

"I don't know."

"You didn't ask?"

"Michael doesn't tell you what he doesn't want you to know." She was knitting faster.

"What's wrong with him, anyway?" Marsha asked.

"I don't know," Sheila whined in her tiny voice.

Marsha, Vida, and Judy exchanged glances.

"I've been with him through all this, and I ask about his arm, and he puts the other one around me. I ask about his pills, and he tells me to just have them handy. I know you don't believe me." She dropped her needles in her lap and started to shake in dry sobs.

Judy put her arm around Sheila, and Marsha came over and put her arms around both of them. Vida watched, and they caught each other's eyes over Sheila's head as they rocked for a while until she seemed to calm down.

Vida reached for a cigarette, and they watched her go through the whole process, picking up the pack, tapping one out, striking the match, lighting the end, and flipping the match until the flame was out, dropping it into the ashtray until the glow slowly ate up the matchstick and it crumbled into ash. She looked at them and laughed.

"I just noticed that we're circled around this table with all this light, like Girl Scouts around a fire," she said. "I feel like we should be telling ghost stories or something."

"Great idea," Marsha stretched her arms out to command attention and took her voice down low. "Jooooohnnny, I want my liiiiiiver. I'm on the first step. I'm on the second step. Gottcha!"

She grabbed Sheila, who shrieked in spite of herself.

"See, I knew we could cheer you up."

"Vida, your turn," Marsha said.

Vida leaned forward and touched the end of her cigarette to an area of congealed wax on the table until it liquefied into a little pool.

"I've got something scarier than a ghost story," Vida said. "It's true. It's about the tunnels."

"Vida," Judy warned, cocking her head toward Sheila.

Vida went on. "Apparently, the Viet Cong have these miles of tunnels they've dug all over the country that they disappear into whenever they're being chased. When one of our patrols finds a tunnel, they send down the smallest man they have to check it out. Imagine being that guy? You could be shot on the way down, or impaled on those pongee sticks, or hacked by machetes in the dark. Sometimes they never come up and no one knows what happens to them."

Marsha broke the silence. "Right, where'd you hear that one?"

"Washington."

They listened to a faint blues whine from the stereo, the radiator hissing, and the eternal *click, click* of Sheila's knitting needles, faster now than before.

Rick, little Rick, might be one of the tunnel guys, Judy thought. She remembered Maggie telling her he was doing something dangerous.

There was a sudden clang from the radiator and they all jumped, checking each other's expressions in the candlelight.

"Judy?" Vida said.

"I have nothing."

"That's what you said before you told us about the six seconds," Marsha said. "Of course, if nothing scares you."

"Nothing scares me?" Judy said. "If you only knew."

"Knew what?" Vida asked. "Come on, the candles are burning down, and all the ghosts are out. What scares you?"

They crouched closer toward her.

"The truth?" Judy said. "You scare me. All of you."

"Yeah, sure, *you* scared of *us*," Marsha said.

"What's going on, Judy?" asked Vida. "This isn't you."

"Not me?" Judy laughed. "You don't even know who I am. Hell, I don't even know who I am." She breathed deeply to regain control and then started again, very slowly.

"I'm scared, really scared, that you'll think I lied to you, that I put you in danger, even that I betrayed you."

"What are you talking about?" Vida asked.

Judy rubbed her fists against her temples.

"You can tell us anything," Marsha said.

Could she really? Should she? She had been ready to tell Michael and then Wil, and now here she was with her closest friends. She would feel so much better if she could let it out, wouldn't she?

They stared at her.

Judy heard a high-pitched wail but couldn't tell if it was the music or if she was screaming.

"What was that?" Marsha said, and looked toward the door. There was the sound of a key trying the lock.

"Michael," Sheila shrieked.

They scrambled up and ran toward the opening door. The woman on the threshold jumped, startled to see them there.

"Who are you?" she asked. "What are you doing here?"

"Who are *you*?" Sheila said. "Why do you have a key? Michael's going to have a fit when he hears this."

"No . . . no, he won't," the woman said softly, and sighed. "I'm Michael's sister, Susan Morgan."

Judy felt sick.

They stepped back slightly, and she moved among them, deeper into the room, looking around, stopping her gaze at the table with the dying candles and disheveled groceries, then at the Clapton altar, and the stereo. She then turned very slowly, a full 360 degrees, as if to drink it all in.

She didn't look anything like Michael, Judy thought. A thick, thirtyish woman in a sacky, beige granny dress, dark hair pulled back in a heavy ponytail, low against her neck. She wore gigantic round eyeglasses that magnified her eyes, making her inspection both creepy and strangely comic. She settled hard into the couch, in exactly Michael's spot. Judy had to stop herself from yelling no.

"Which one of you is Stephanie?" Susan asked, looking from face to face.

"It's Sheila," she answered in a small, cracking voice. "Where's Michael?"

"The helicopter transfer just finished him off, I'm afraid. I told him he should have been at the University of Chicago months ago, but he was still worried they'd figure out the name change/draft problem, like it would matter at this point. But the CIU health center didn't want the responsibility, and then the organ donation would be easier from there and . . ."

"What are you talking about?" Vida yelled.

The sister stopped, confused.

"Yes, it's upsetting," she said, looking at Sheila. "But, you know, he was already almost a year past the prognosis for his type of lymphoma . . . and his poor heart just couldn't take it anymore." Her voice trailed away.

Sheila sank to the floor in the puddle of her red-and-white yarn stripes.

I knew it, Judy thought. She looked at the wide eyes and open mouths of the others and felt her face, realizing she must look the same. "When?" she asked, managing only a whisper.

"Three days ago. I'm sure that it was tough on you all that he did this on his own, but it was a smart move so you wouldn't get mixed up if there was any fallout." Judy, Vida, and Marsha now joined Sheila on the floor, staring at each other as if in a terrible dream.

"I can't pretend to be sentimental about this," Susan said. "Michael and I barely knew each other. We didn't even have the same fathers."

"But you have the same last name," Vida said.

"Only since he went underground."

Judy's head felt like it would explode.

"It wouldn't have been my choice, and I can't believe they never caught him, running like he did, virtually the second before he was to get on the plane to Vietnam."

"Was his name Marek?" Judy asked.

She stared at them. "He told me he didn't tell anyone that— ever. I'd keep it quiet if I were you. It's bad enough that you helped hide him, but there's no reason for the authorities to know any more. It was hard enough to process the body under Morgan."

Sidelong glances flashed among them.

"He didn't tell us much," Judy said.

"That was smart."

"Can't you tell us more? Anything?" Sheila asked.

Susan had been eyeing the contents of the apartment. Now she began running her fingers along the top of Michael's stereo.

"How he could afford that, for example?" Vida said.

Susan pulled her hand back.

"Oh, he had some money. I made sure of that."

"He never mentioned you," Sheila said.

"I said we weren't close. I don't know any more than he chose to share."

"We loved him," Judy said.

Susan closed her eyes, the glasses amplifying the two crescents of her lids, as if they had been drawn on her face by a cartoonist. She sighed as she opened them again, now softening her tone.

"I'm glad," she said.

With that she was up and out the door, returning in a few minutes with an unidentified man, and the two of them began to clear out Michael's possessions.

No one moved from where they had been sitting.

"We didn't know him at all," Marsha said.

I did, Judy thought. He was the bravest man I've ever known.

Chapter 29

ONCE THEY FOUND THEIR VOICES AFTER THE SHOCK, they pieced together the situation the best they could for the others, recounting what little they had been able to pull out of Susan Morgan before she left, taking every trace of Michael with her except the few things they squirreled away as she packed. There were dead parents, half relations, a borrowed last name, a trust fund. Michael had deserted three years earlier. He wanted to lead the revolution, then came cancer. He told his sister his friends were his family. She had assumed they all knew everything.

The Tune Room group marked Michael's passing with a private service of their own in a corner of the lagoon the next evening just before twilight. They dressed up, out of respect, in the old high school clothes they had last worn before jeans became their daily uniform. Wil even had a tie, though he just looped it without a knot. Wizard was wearing a gray sport coat over his jeans with sleeves that were too short; Vida, a purple miniskirt that clashed with her red canvas tote; Howie, an old sport coat so big it might have belonged to his father; and Marsha, a perfect black suit and her gold chain. Judy had squeezed into a herringbone wool skirt that now was way too tight.

They were wearing the black armbands Vida had passed out that morning. She and Marsha had appropriated them from the SMC office. When reversed, you couldn't see the peace signs on the other side. David took two, one for each arm.

Sheila spread her unfinished wedding dress on the grass and

arranged some of Michael's favorite things over it, his jean jacket with the blue peace sign, his little red Mao book, his Bic lighter, his dog-eared copy of Dostoyevsky, and the Clapton poster. There were also a few albums Susan hadn't taken. They watched Sheila position each piece just so and weren't quite sure what to do once she finished.

They stood a long time, quiet and still.

"The body count was eighty-three yesterday, total 39,232 KIA," Wil said. "I think Michael would want us to keep track."

He would be so angry, Judy thought. He had missed the March on Washington, and he was going to miss the lottery. What were they supposed to do now? Would they stay together without him? Who would they be if they weren't living up to what Michael expected of them? And she had needed him herself, someone wise she could level with. Now who would it be?

"So what kind of cancer was it, anyway?" Fish asked. "Anybody know?"

"What difference does it make?" Meldrich said. "It was fucking arm cancer, okay?"

"He could have told us," Wil said.

"It was none of our goddamn business. Don't you get that by now?" Meldrich said.

"It was lymphoma," Judy told them. She had looked it up in the nursing school library and explained to them how the enlarged lymph nodes in the underarm can cause injury to the brachial plexus, the trunk of nerves traveling from the neck to the arm. If the pressure is severe enough, there can be reduced strength and feeling or even paralysis in that limb.

"So that's why his arm was the way it was," she said.

"This is shit," David said. He picked up Michael's jean jacket, put it on, and headed back toward the Union.

Then Howie went up and took the Clapton poster, rolling it

tightly. Wizard took the red book; Meldrich, a Lightnin' Hopkins album. Achilles and Marsha each took an album. Fish picked up the last one, smiled at Paul Butterfield's photo and then the book, which he handed to Judy. She ran her fingers across the title, *Notes from the Underground.* Inside was a loose piece of paper with a KIA list going back to 1967.

All of a sudden, Vida threw aside her canvas bag and walked ceremoniously over to the wedding dress, laid something down, and turned to address them.

"This should be a military funeral," she said. She stepped aside, and Judy saw that Vida's father's flag, still trefoil folded, was in the center of the white yarn. "In honor of Michael Marek, a soldier who dared to struggle. Just like Michael is gone, without a trace, so should this war be gone, without a trace." With that she pulled a matchbook from the pocket of her skirt, lit a match, and tipped the flame to one of the sharp-folded points. It didn't take. She unfolded the tightly packed flag slightly to get a thinner piece and lit another match, lighting the flag in three places until it caught fire.

"Ashes to ashes," she said, and began to sing: "Day is done. Gone the sun . . ."

They listened to the clear, bell-like tones of her voice. It was painfully hard for Judy not to cry: "God is nigh."

They watched for a while as bright orange lines threaded along the edges of the flag and faded to black. Then they filed away, one by one. Judy had her arm around Sheila's shoulders. Once they got to the ring road, Sheila turned to her and burst into great sobs against her shoulder, as if her birdlike frame would crack. Hanging tight, Judy maneuvered them to sit down on the curb, over a damp gutter clogged with dead leaves, in their little skirts, exposing their underwear. Judy cried, too, missing Michael and knowing he died thinking she might have betrayed him. After a long while, Howie and Achilles gently guided them up by their elbows.

"Michael, a vet. I can't fucking believe it," Fish said, as they started back toward the Union. "Why wouldn't he have told us? He couldn't think we would have ratted him out."

Judy felt she understood perfectly, but didn't have the energy to explain.

They heard David's voice before they saw him cross the ring road, pass them, and head back toward the scene of the ceremony. They watched him kick at the folded flag, stomping on the remaining embers. He picked it up and half ran to the Administration Building. They followed him, trying to match his pace. He slowed as he noticed a campus cop making a round and gestured behind for them to stay low and quiet.

When the cop was gone, David went to the center of the circle-shaped plaza in front of the building, where the university seal was rendered in painted stone. He put the ragged flag in the center. He then threw Michael's lighter on the stone, crushed it with his boot, and drizzled the lighter fluid over the flag. He motioned for them to step back and threw a match at the wet cloth, which immediately burst into flames. He started to run, and they followed him again until they could safely watch the fire from the Union steps along with everyone else, as if they had nothing to do with it.

A spark from the fire reached the shrubbery at the edge of the plaza, and the dried twigs lapped it up, spreading flames around the edges of the stone in a full circle, a perfect glowing tribute. Sirens approached, getting progressively louder, screaming, like the *wha-wha* note from Clapton's guitar.

"Now this is what Michael deserved," David said.

"What's all over your clothes?" Marsha asked. "Is that paint? What did you do this time?"

He smiled like he had after the Grape Spit-Out.

"I've got to take off and change before anyone else notices. Why don't you all head back to the dorms. Take the scenic route along the north side of the Union. The lights should be up by now."

With that he was gone, and they did as they were told. Once they turned north, they stopped in awe. Along what was previously a pure white expanse was painted, large and in bright red:

DARE TO STRUGGLE. DARE TO WIN.
MICHAEL MAREK '69

When they got back to the dorms, Judy went right to David's room and knocked on his door. She didn't know what to expect.

He pulled her into the room and kissed her hard. They held each other and moved without questions into silent, needy lovemaking before falling into deep, satisfied sleep.

When she woke in the middle of the night, he was sitting up as if he'd been poised there for a long time, looking down at her with an expression she couldn't place. She braced herself for the inevitable question, reviewing the responses she had rehearsed about who had been first. "Isn't this what you wanted?" "It doesn't matter who it was." She had even decided to hit far below the belt by answering, "Michael," if he pressed. That would have shut him up and more than settled the war about Sartre and Sally, even Lori.

"I've made a decision," he said. "I'm not going after my CO."

She was shocked. His conscientious objector status was his lifeline, and he was going to throw it away? She felt guilty that she had been thinking he would even notice something as minor as what had happened to her virginity at a time like this.

"You're upset. This is no time for decisions."

"It doesn't have anything to do with being upset. I can't in all conscience be out there in the movement if I'm protected and others aren't."

"I thought you had it already."

"Not yet. I'm just waiting for final word. So I figure I can cut it off before it comes through."

"But maybe it's good if you're protected," she said, spinning. "You can be very high profile, and no one will be coming after you."

"No, it's decided. It's done."

"Are you sure?"

"I think Michael would have done the same thing in my shoes, don't you?"

She wanted to tell him that Michael would have done anything to stay alive, but she was no longer sure that was true. David continued to smoke and nod his head with assurance, as if he had concluded a long debate with himself and was satisfied.

"Yeah, that's what I'm going to do."

She knew she couldn't push it any more right now. She felt small and cowardly. If David was willing to give up his CO, how could she justify staying in the army and supporting the war effort? She might be giving up her future, but he could be giving up his life. As much as she knew this was the wrong thing for him to do, she admired him for having the courage to even consider it.

But his thoughts had progressed to other things. He was rubbing her back and working his way under the sheet so he could get his hands on her skin. He was tender and surprising, and she decided to consider this night her first time, wiping out memories of her encounter with Wil. This was more like it, she thought, as she felt along his smooth backbone, reassured by the sounds he made and delighted at his confidence as he worked his way around her body, moving into it slowly and surely like they had already done it a hundred times.

In the morning she watched him sleep. The frown was off his face, and she could see what he must have looked like when he was a boy. Was the angry David gone now? Would the night-time David remain? She snuggled down beside him and kissed his back, ever so slightly. She wasn't sure which David would wake up.

"There's no reason to rush on that CO," she said, once he stirred.

He shook his head for a moment, waking, confused. Then it appeared to all come back.

"Maybe you're right."

He pulled her toward him.

Chapter 30

THE FIRST THING JUDY NOTICED WHEN HER RIDE DROPPED her off at home for Thanksgiving vacation was the flagpole in the front yard. A new addition, blowing robustly in the November wind. Another signal, she felt, that her mother could read her mind.

She took a deep breath, walked through the front door, and called from the landing.

"Hello? Anyone home?"

Nobody answered. She would have time to gather herself, one thing to be thankful for, she thought.

She took her overnight bag downstairs, past the rec room to the converted den they had turned into a bedroom for her when her brother and sister became too old to share one of the two upstairs rooms. She had trouble opening the door. There was stuff everywhere. Her brother's coronet and music stand, her sister's old dressing table, the cage that had been home for Picasso, the hamster, before he squeezed his boneless body behind the dryer and perished there, unable to flatten out again and get free. She cleared a path to the bed to drop her bag and went to the closet to hang up her coat. It was full of summer clothes. She washed her hands in the small powder room, looking into the mirror where she first put on makeup, inspected her complexion nightly, and practiced inserting her contact lenses.

When they sat down to supper that evening, Judy, searching for a topic of conversation at the strangely silent table, just blurted out what was on her mind. "What's with the flagpole?"

"Is it necessary," her mother said, "to bring your political views into mealtime?"

Judy was taken aback by her attitude.

"It's your flagpole, so it's your political view, not mine. I was just asking."

She was sitting across from her brother and sister. Her father was at the head of the table. She watched her sister's eyes as they darted nervously from one parent to another. Her brother slumped down and took a bite of green beans from the edge of his plate.

Both of her parents scowled at her. Clearly, she and her views had been discussed in her absence.

"Fine, don't tell me," she said, then bolted down the rest of her food in silence and went back downstairs, thankful for the design of their home—split, like their lives.

She went into the powder room, directly under the kitchen, where through the pipes she had always been able to hear what was said above.

"Who the hell does she think she is?" her father said.

"She's going to lose that scholarship," her mother said. "That, or she's going to be stupid enough to give it up and then come begging us for tuition."

"She had her chance. I'm not giving her any money."

There was silence, then mumbling. Chairs squeaked against the floor, and Judy waited for the footsteps downstairs. They never came. Much later, after she stopped standing by the door, listening, she heard hard steps that turned into the rec room and television noise. Her father had settled in for the evening.

She turned her clock radio to a heavy-metal station, switched off the lights, and lay on the bed smoking, one of her father's ashtrays next to her. She started humming to the music: "See Me. Feel Me."

Feel me. She wrapped her arms around herself and realized how much she wanted to touch David. It was all she had been able to think about since they had "done it," as Vida would have said.

By the time she heard the third repetition of the phrase and its segue into touching and healing, she decided the song was speaking to her. That's what she needed right now, healing. She let the music play until she was so depressed she could hardly stand it. It was too much. Michael dying, losing her virginity to Wil, sleeping with David, trying to figure out what to do about the army, her parents.

She was sure Michael would have known what she should do now. She would have been able to reason it out with him.

She noticed *The Sonnets of Gerard Manley Hopkins* on her old bookshelf. It had been assigned reading her junior year in high school at a time when her mother was particularly down on her about college, and she found out the guy she had a crush on was interested in another girl. It was her favorite depression book. She reread the introduction, where Hopkins described the dark night of the soul. It was a transition, a period of suffering from which you would get a clearer path. It sounded something like a moratorium. That's what she was in now, her own dark night, and she couldn't see her way out.

"Send my roots rain," Hopkins wrote. Yes, that's what she needed. "See me, feel me," send my roots rain. And in her mind's eye, Hopkins had yellow-blond hair cut straight to his jaw, with a matching moustache.

THE next day, Maggie called for her to come and see Rick, and she thought even that would be better than staying at home, but her mother got to her before she could grab her coat and leave.

She came in and sat on the bed. Judy braced herself for a confrontation.

"You know I'm having trouble trusting you now, don't you?" her mother said. "I don't hear from you. I have to find things out through Maggie, who told me that you did go to Washington, after all."

Judy reeled. She would kill Maggie, no hesitation.

"What am I supposed to think?" her mother continued. "I actually watched all the news coverage of that march, so sure I'd see you, maybe even being arrested. I shouldn't have to go through that. I thought we understood each other about all this."

She seemed genuinely perplexed, which surprised Judy.

"I'm just trying to figure things out," Judy said. "You know most people at school change their major at least once. I'm the only one who seems to be stuck with my decision."

"This is not about changing majors," her mother said. "You can use your degree for anything. It doesn't have to be only for nursing, like mine. That's all we could do with an RN. But you'll have a BS. Don't you see? You can always do something else, later."

"You mean six years from now?" Judy said.

"You think that's a long time, but it will go by fast, and you'll have all these experiences that others won't."

"But I'll spend it being part of the same institution that's sending people my age off to die. How do you think that makes me feel?"

"Don't be melodramatic. The army isn't a death sentence."

"Not for me, maybe. But it is for a lot of people. The life expectancy under fire in Vietnam is only six seconds, you know."

"Well," her mother said. "If that's what you're so worried about, I would think you'd be anxious to help as a nurse . . . and proud that you could." She sighed, putting her hands on her knees and pushing herself up heavily, as if she were elderly and not just fifty-two.

Now who was being melodramatic. Judy was sure she was exaggerating for effect.

She was so angry with Maggie she decided not to go over to her house, after all. She knew Maggie would call, wondering where she was. If she had been at school, she would have let the phone just ring and ring and torture Maggie but knew that here at home someone would keep picking it up, and then she would have to explain.

So when the phone rang, she answered on the first ring.

"Where are you?" Maggie asked.

"I'm not coming. I just had a fight with my mom because you told her I went to Washington for the march. I can't believe you did that, Maggie."

"Well, she asked me directly, and you know I can't lie."

"You could have at least warned me."

"I knew you'd be mad."

"You were right about that," Judy said. "And I'm not coming over."

"What will I tell Rick?"

"Whatever you usually tell him when you talk about me, I imagine," Judy said. "This is a fantasy relationship you've cooked up. He's probably no more interested than I am. Goodbye."

Judy left the house as quietly as she could, hoping no one would hear the opening and closing of the door. She walked and walked, all over the neighborhood, and down the street she had taken back and forth from school each day of her four years in high school.

She ended up at the Dairy Queen, her old hangout, and ordered coffee. Later, she ordered a Brazier burger and a coke. She looked out the window, across the football field toward her old school, remembering how much time she spent in this glossy white oasis after classes. She shifted her seat throughout the evening, changing her view while remembering countless incidents as they had occurred at this table or that, with this girlfriend or that group of kids. Gossip and fights and secrets.

Part of her wished she could go back to that easier time. Part of her wished she could leave now and never come back to Belmont Heights as long as she lived.

That night she had a dream about Rick and the tunnels. She pictured herself being lowered into the narrow space, descending into darkness, not knowing what horror lay below. She felt Rick letting her down into the tunnel slowly, his arms giving her more reach until he had to . . . let go. But then he wouldn't let her back up.

"You had your chance," he said, cutting off the light and shutting her in.

THANKSGIVING dinner was tense. No one said anything, the only sound the clinking of silverware. They kept their eyes on their plates. When they were done and half the family moved downstairs to watch television, Judy's mother called her into the living room.

She was sitting in her reading chair. Because there was no chair opposite, Judy settled on the floor, cross-legged, not too close.

"I have something to say, and I just want you to let me say it without interruption." Her mother looked down, and Judy saw she had index cards in her lap.

"I know you'll probably laugh about this with all your friends, but I want to make sure I say everything I have to."

Judy realized she must have won the last round. She was

surprised and sat back obediently, prepared to listen and be as open as she could to what her mother had to say.

"If you give up this scholarship, you won't graduate," her mother said, virtually reading from the cards. "If you don't, you can't expect help from us. We don't have the money to give you. We have other children to take care of. We shouldn't even be living here . . ."

Judy disengaged then, hearing her mother repeat the monologues she'd heard her whole life, relentless as a Trot. Money. Always money.

After half-listening for a while, she noticed a tone change. Her mother had stopped referring to the index cards.

"You hated it when I made you save half of what you made babysitting," her mother said. "And you were embarrassed that someone thought you looked like a nurse. How do you think that made me feel? Here I am helping you as hard as I know how, and you're ashamed of what I do and never even . . ." She broke off, her voice trembling.

Judy couldn't imagine her mother being hurt. She sat up to speak but stopped at the hand raised in warning.

"You think I never had dreams about other things I wanted to do?" she went on. "I could draw. I could act. But I had to be practical. I know you don't believe me now, but all that pushing I did. It will make you stronger. You'll be able to do more than I did, to have a different life, a better one."

It feels the same, Judy wanted to say.

The index cards resurfaced. "If you want to stay in this family, you need to do your part . . . I can only do so much for each of you. Your sister's only five years behind you. She needs the attention now, and then your brother . . ."

"Mom," Judy said, breaking in. She really had no new words to explain what she felt they had gone over again and again, but she wanted her to stop. "Like I told you, other students don't support the war just by graduating. I do. I'm taking army money, so I *do*. That's the problem."

Her mother dropped the cards. "How can you say that to me? What do you think I did?"

"You're right. This scholarship makes me feel like I'm doing just what you did. But that was a different time and a different war. This is nothing like that."

They were talking at odds with each other, making separate points and arguing firmly but unable to stay on the same page. Judy didn't know how to get back, and she could tell from her mother's strained expression, a mixture of pain and fury, that she didn't know, either.

"I don't know if you want me to be like you, or not be like you," she said.

Her mother looked at her in frustration.

"To be honest," she answered. "Right now, you're making it hard to even like you."

Judy was shocked.

She spent the night alone in her room, letting the knowledge that her own mother did not like her move across her and penetrate into every cell. She knew deep down inside that her mother didn't mean it, that she was just hitting back, but it hurt just the same. It upset her far more than she would have imagined, but it gave her a perfect excuse for whatever she decided to do next. By morning, she felt she had grown her own layer of armor, one even her mother couldn't penetrate.

She lied and told her mother she had to get back to campus the next day because she was behind in her studying. It had been a distracting time with the death of her friend, she said, wanting to make her feel guilty for not asking about it, and now the lottery was coming up.

She called Vida, who said she'd also had enough of her family and came to pick her up in the beater she had borrowed from Wizard.

As they pulled away, darkness started to move in. Judy looked back at the house and strained to see if her mother had even come to the front window where she usually waved goodbye. The lights weren't on yet. She wondered if her mother was there, standing back behind the curtain, watching.

Vida drove through the suburb, past Judy's elementary school, her junior high, her high school, down the street she had walked along with her friends to Wonderland Burger when she was twelve, past the many houses where she babysat, the rectory where she went for confession when the church was under construction, along the park with the pool where she learned to swim. She allowed herself a final pang and then detached, leaving the world of her childhood behind. Once they hit the interstate, Judy exhaled audibly. She felt like she had crossed the border into Canada. She knew there was no coming back.

Chapter 31

THE SUNDAY AFTER THANKSGIVING, EVERYBODY IN HER group had returned and gathered in Wizard's room, worried about the next night's lottery drawing. There had been so many questions, Vida brought a clipping from the *Chicago Tribune* that explained how the lottery would work and was reading it out loud, throwing her own slant on it.

The government had decided to allow people to get on with their lives, she had read, adding "however short or long." They were going to turn the draft into "a game of chance," to choose who would go next. Slips of paper with birth dates for the pool of nineteen-year-olds and up would be put into little capsules that were to be dropped into a large plastic drum and mixed up "really well." The 366 capsules, "to allow for those February 29 babies," were to be drawn, one by one, and assigned a number. You would report for induction in orderly sequence: the higher the number, "the better for you." There would be a second lottery in six months, and "then another after that and another after that."

"I just want to know if my student deferment is still in effect," Howie said. "Just read that part."

"Let me find it," Vida said, scanning the article. "Wait, here's something really interesting." She read: "'The government admits that employers are shaky about hiring potential draftees. They can tell by the number of ads that call for returning vets or men with draft exemptions.' Wow, helluva recruitment tool."

"Would you just tell him what he wants to know, not what *you* think is interesting," David said.

"I understand," Vida said. "I'm getting to it."

"No, you don't understand. You need to get to it *now*. This is life and death shit. Don't put all this cutesy stuff into it."

They all turned to David, shocked.

"They're drawing lots, just like in that story we read at the Moratorium. The lower your number, the sooner you die. It's that simple. How many times do you have to hear it? Give it to me. I'll answer your question, Howie." He grabbed the newspaper out of Vida's hands.

"'Full-time college students are eligible for deferments through graduation if their records are satisfactory.' There, was that so hard?" He threw the paper back at Vida. They glared at each other. "What? You don't understand. Women just don't get it. That's all there is to it. Am I wrong?" He looked at Achilles and Wil for approval.

"Excuse me," Vida said. "I've been running antiwar activities since high school, and you're saying I don't understand?"

"It doesn't have anything to do with that," he said. "It's not your fault you're a chick." Vida stood up, and Judy thought she was going to slap him.

"What the hell do you think you're talking about?"

"What I'm talking about is . . . just don't say you understand." He pointed his cigarette toward her and then to Judy and RoMo and Marsha, "Don't ever say you understand. You might think you do, but you can't."

"Who do you think you are?" Vida said.

"I'm a guy. A guy who's going to get a number tomorrow, and that number will determine if I'm going to live or die. Something like that happening in your life soon?"

Vida sat down.

"I'm sick of all this empathy," David said. "Remember, we're the ones who might get killed. We're the ones who are going to have to decide if we can pull that trigger. There is nothing, nothing in the entire experience of your sex that can prepare you for how to understand what that feels like."

He looked around the room, and everyone except Vida was looking down.

"All right, so I'm an ass," he said. "I can't help it. I can take anything, but I can't take a woman telling me she understands."

"Easy," Howie said.

"Like you don't feel the same? Like all of you don't feel the same?"

"Well, maybe," Achilles said. "But let up, man."

Vida had a look of pure hatred in her eyes. "You are an ass, but I'm going to chalk it up to lottery nerves." She picked up her jacket. "Come on, girls. They need to be alone. We may not understand, but we get it."

Judy followed, but later felt like she needed to go see David. He had just done to the group what he had done with her so often since Washington. They would be talking pleasantly, or even deep into a seduction, and somehow something would set him off and he would go on the attack.

Usually it meant something was weighing on him, but she couldn't understand why he was lashing out about the lottery since he was virtually safe with his CO. It must still be about Michael, she thought.

"Go ahead, hit me with it," he said, when he opened his door.

"I'm not here to give you a hard time," Judy said. "I just thought you might like some company."

The room was stale with the smell of smoke and something pungent that was familiar, but she didn't recognize it immediately. She noticed two beer cans left on the plastic ring set of a six-pack on the floor by the bed, empties in the wastebasket. David didn't usually drink, preferring grass.

"Good, because I'm not in the mood for a mea culpa."

She sat next to him on the bed and took his hand, wrapping her arm around his at the elbow. They sat like that, not speaking, then lay down. She curled her arms around him and ran her fingers through the hair at the back of his neck.

"It's about Michael, isn't it?" she asked.

"Don't say that. It's just another way of you trying to say you understand. You're so transparent. And no, it's not about Michael. How do you know it's not about you?"

"Me?"

"Yeah." He sprang up and began pacing. "Who was it, anyway? Achilles? I know you like all his talk."

"I know you're on edge."

"See," he said. "That's another way. 'I know you're on edge.' It's about this. It's about that. 'I understand.' Well, you don't fucking understand. And you can't just come in and think you can shake your tail at me and everything will be all right."

"I'm not shaking my tail at you," Judy said. "I care about you."

He settled down a bit and lay next to her again. He took her hand, fitting his fingers over hers. "I'm sorry. They denied my CO," he said. "The letter was waiting for me when I got home for Thanksgiving."

"No," she said, putting her free hand over his, squeezing as hard as she could to make it not be true.

"I thought it was in the bag. I didn't follow that Baha'i's advice. They saw right through me." He shook his head back and forth slowly for some time. Then suddenly straightened up with a violent shake and let go of Judy's hand.

"Don't worry," he said. "I have a plan. My kazoo-band buddies came back with me to set it up. The military machine will be hearing from me."

He leapt up and faced her.

"I can't just be dismissed with a letter, Judy, or even with a lottery number. You'll see." He pointed a finger in her face. "Tomorrow night. More than minds will blow."

Chapter 32

"DRAFT LOTTERY TONIGHT!"

Judy folded the paper to cover the headline and threw it on one of the piles scattered across the table. Like the other surfaces in the Tune Room, it was covered with newspapers, sampled and tossed. It used to be only journalism majors who read the papers for class assignments, but for the past month the news had been checked by virtually everyone daily, stories compared to rumors and reports from the TV rooms, everyone adding it up.

"Vietnam is all a numbers game," Achilles had said during one of the endless dorm-room nights. "Body counts, birthdays." She thought about it now and realized he was right. Everything was reduced to numbers. Wil had taken over Michael's weekly tabulation of the body count. They hadn't released it the previous Thursday, in honor of the holiday, but Friday's news said there would be another 130 for the week or 39,262 KIA. Fish kept making crude jokes about the fact that it was '69 after all, so of course everything was upside down. It seemed that everyone was nineteen, but you still couldn't vote unless you were twenty-one. And now today, on December 1, your birth date was to become your destiny.

She could hear snatches of conversations at other tables. A lot of it was about Canada. Who really knew anything about that? It was cutting yourself off from family, from everything. But you'd be alive. That was the point, right? She tried to think about what to say to David or anyone who got a low number. He wanted to be alone today, which was making her climb the walls. Wil had practically convinced her he would be in the top ten. She couldn't picture any of them in combat. Achilles would be pissing everyone off with his talk, and Wizard would go berserk with all the chaos.

She felt totally at bay, wondering at the absurdity of why people her own age were expected to work this all out by themselves. She needed answers. She needed Michael. She had even finally gone to see Swanson, catching him before office hours as he was eating lunch at his desk.

"Can I ask you something?" she said, peeking around the ajar door.

"Of course." He invited her in, and she took one of the chairs facing his desk.

She faltered suddenly, realizing she wasn't sure she should trust him. She thought he was on their side, but he hadn't actually been around for a while.

"I was at your session at the Moratorium back in October when you got everyone excited about going to Washington," she said. "You were going to come with us. And then you didn't."

Swanson sighed and sat back. He pushed his food away and wiped his hands on several paper napkins.

"So you heard that I didn't go because I was afraid I'd lose my job, right?"

Judy nodded.

"Yeah, that story's out there. I suppose I should have tried to correct it, but . . . truth is, I was never going to go. That was an inaccurate assumption."

"There are people who say you felt your job was more important than your conscience." She couldn't believe she just blurted that out.

He nodded, as if he had been expecting the question. "I did a lot of soul searching, Judy, on just that subject. I looked at who I was in my life, the roles I had, and where I had influence. I'm Tom Swanson, an individual who has made a decision to be against the war. But I'm also a teacher in a position to open the eyes of students so *they* can make better decisions. That's what I do best. If I'm not in this job, then there's a gap. I don't mean that I'm irreplaceable, but I considered carefully where I could do the most good."

"Ever feel like a hypocrite?" She couldn't stop herself.

"Sometimes," he said after a long pause. "Don't get me wrong, I'm angry as hell about what's going on, but there's a lot of knee-jerk reactive hot air out there, and I see my job as helping my students see through it all. I certainly hope they agree with me, but that's not the point. It's important we do the right thing in the right way and don't trample what we're trying to protect."

"So, that's why you shot down the attempt to get ROTC off campus last semester?"

"Exactly. If we squash some rights to get others, even if we think it will save lives, it gets very precarious from a legal standpoint. I have to make sure we're all working within the right lines. And I have to be trusted by everyone on all sides."

"Has anyone actually *in* ROTC talked to you?" She was thinking about the military freaks. They had to be conflicted, like she was.

"Lots of people talk to me, Judy, like you're doing now." She didn't know what to believe. It's true, he could be an agent of the administration, working to keep things calm, which was fine unless some of them landed in jail. Or he could really believe there were two sides, like she was trying to do. She couldn't risk it.

Swanson seemed to have that quality Michael did, of knowing what she was thinking without her saying it. But thinking about herself now was not the point.

"But what are you saying to them about the lottery? About what they should do now, go to Canada or take their chances in Vietnam?"

"They want to know what I'd do, and I can't tell them or they'll think I'm telling them what *they* should do."

"What would you—"

"I can't tell you either, Judy."

"So what do you say?"

"That it's the hardest question they'll ever face."

Judy left, frustrated. If Swanson didn't have answers, how could she expect herself to have them? How could anyone else expect her to have them?

THEY had decided they would all watch the lottery drawing at David's dorm, since that's where most of them lived. However, after his outburst about women, Vida suggested the girls stay together, and they all agreed, except Marsha. Howie wanted her to be with him. So Judy, Vida, RoMo, Sheila, and a few other women took places early, along the wall in the back of the north TV room. Judy watched David and the others take over the front row as the rest of the ecumenical crowd gathered, letterman jackets and army-surplus fatigues. Greeks and freaks together, everyone in jeans. Denim and the war, she thought, the great levelers. As the room began to fill, the guys practically walked over the women, pressing them toward the last-row seats, then taking over the standing room.

"What about space in the back?" an irritated voice called out.

"That's girls," someone said.

Judy felt a wave of shame and grabbed Vida, pulling her by the sleeve.

A blonde she didn't even know looked up as they left. Judy

jerked her head, motioning her to follow as a look of recognition and guilt came over her.

"I didn't think," the blonde said, once they were out of the TV room.

"It's all right," Judy said, "me neither."

"Wait up," Marsha called. "I told Howie I couldn't take up a seat. He's sitting with David. I think he'll be fine."

They joined a crowd of women in exile in the adjacent student lounge. They waited.

"Ron's been a mess," one girl said, furiously twisting her ring. "He looks at me, and it's like he wants me to say something, but I don't know what."

"Al, too," another said. "And no matter what I say, it's not what he wants to hear. He can get real mad." She bowed her head. "It scares me."

"I'm going to leave," Marsha said. "I can't take this."

"Stay," Judy said, holding her by the arm. Marsha sat down as Judy continued in a whisper, "Later won't be any better."

"What if—" Marsha began.

"No, don't," Judy said, "not yet."

They waited in silence, prayer, and concentration. Hair was twisted, lips bitten; fingernails wouldn't make it through the night. They smoked, even if they didn't. They played with their pieces of paper that had birth dates of brothers and cousins and boyfriends at other schools. Even RoMo knew that Wizard's birthday was January 30.

"I want to scream," Marsha said, grabbing her hair with her hands and holding her head between her knees. The smell of fear, something like sulfur, thickened the air.

Sounds filtered through from the TV room like little pockets of pressure, exploding as they called each number. Sometimes hoots of relief. Sometimes the hiss of a loud, disbelieving expulsion of air. Snap, crackle, pop, dud, silence. They couldn't figure the code for the noises. No one came out.

At one point, Judy could no longer sit still. She went to stand just outside the TV room. The guys had turned off the lights, and she could see the strobe effect over them as the images changed on the television screen. A flicker, and she saw baby faces so tender she wanted to fold them in her arms and take them home to be safe. Another flicker, and she saw hollow eyes prematurely aged with fear. She shrunk down, lost her balance, and backed off.

Suddenly, Fish was running to her. He picked her up and spun her around, as if it were VE Day on the Champs-Élysées, then planted big kisses, wet as hell, all over her face. "I'm 327!" He fell to his knees with a beatific look on his face and a huge smile. "I love you! You know how much I love you?" He stretched his long arms wide. "I love you this much."

Judy laughed nervously as he turned to RoMo and called out, stretching his arms even wider.

"I love you this much," he repeated, "on the map!"

She was confused. If Fish was 327, they must be almost done. Could it mean that everyone she knew had a high number? Could they possibly be that lucky?

Achilles walked out somberly, and she held her breath.

"Ninety-six," he said.

"That's almost a hundred, Achilles. You'll be safe."

"Yeah, great." He walked past her toward the elevators. "I'd rather it was just nine. At least I'd know. Now I'm in no-man's-land." He stepped into the elevator, and she heard his voice die as the doors closed. "Fucking no-man's-land."

She heard Marsha shriek and turned to watch Howie come out, skinny and smiling.

"Take me to McDonald's," he said, then engulfed her in a

bear hug. "Three forty-three," he yelled with a clenched fist in the air and his old guitar-playing grin on his face.

David walked out slowly but deliberately, his gaze fixed at a spot on the floor, about three feet ahead of him. Judy could feel her fear rising, her heartbeat so intense it seemed to be coming out of the top of her head. She wasn't breathing. She would not cry. She could not cry. She touched his arm and he stopped his march.

"Two thirty."

She burst into tears and moved to hug him, but he pulled back.

"But David, that's nearly halfway. You'll be safe."

"Yeah, lucky me," he said and headed to the elevator.

"Don't follow me," he called back at her.

"But . . ."

"Don't."

Judy turned in circles as others walked out of the room, not sure what had just happened with David. She strained her neck looking for Wil, Wizard, Meldrich.

"We have a Number One!" she heard someone say, followed by a chorus of disembodied voices.

"Number One. September fourteenth."

Judy sat down in the middle of the floor, jelly legs giving up. "My birthday, too," she said out loud to people who weren't listening.

The post-lottery pandemonium went on above and around her. Someone just walked over my grave, she thought, and then had the sensation of dropping, like a heavy stone, accelerating. She tried to steady herself with her hands on the floor. In my family I was supposed to be a boy, she thought. It was to be a boy first and only then a girl.

"September fourteenth is my birthday, too," she said out loud again to stop her fall.

Judy felt she should find the Number One and tell him that

were it not for a flip of the chromosome coin—one extra more or less—she would be in his place, random, just like the lottery. She really could understand.

She tried to picture herself in a uniform, a helmet, but the closest she could get was to see her little brother, the same hair, blue eyes, and freckles. She tried to envision him older, so she would know what a male version of herself would look like. She couldn't make it work. All she could conjure up was the image of a small man in fatigues with the familiar face of a seven-year-old. This face and figure froze in her mind as she felt the digit *1* burning into her forehead like a private scarlet letter. This had to mean something.

She wandered outside. It was December. The cold hurt. She took her hands out of her pockets and forced them down at her sides as the icy air coated them, penetrating in daggers of pain to the bone. It was the least she could do. If only she could talk to Wil.

And then she remembered.

They had the same birthday. Wil was the Number One.

She rushed to find him. Surely, he had been in the TV room, but now she couldn't remember specifically if he had been sitting with the others. The room was empty. He must have slipped past her when she was with David, or when she was having her own breakdown. How could she have been so selfish? How could she not immediately have realized that if it was her, it was also him?

The elevators were crammed with people throwing numbers around. The counting had begun again. People who used to ask each other what was their sign, were now asking who had what number. How many days before induction notices arrive? How much time would they have? How much, how many, which one, who was the Number One? If they only knew.

She maneuvered through the crowded halls on the way to

Meldrich's room and entered through a deep, smoky haze to the pounding rhythm of "I Want You": "So . . . HEAVVVVVY."

She froze when she saw Meldrich. He was standing among a mass of bodies sitting and lying everywhere, on bunks, desks, and floor. He had drawn three sixes on his forehead, two in black magic marker, one in red lipstick.

He laughed at her reaction. "I'm sixty-six. Might as well be 666, the devil sign," he said. "Wouldn't that be perfect, sending the devil to Vietnam? I could really screw it up for them."

She imagined him high, going into his goofy act, jumping all around the jungle, drawing enemy attention or stepping on a landmine.

"There's a guy on the tenth floor," Meldrich said to the room. "For a hundred bucks he knows a way to break your arm so they can't fix it enough for you to go." He tried to demonstrate. "It has something to do with the doorjamb, you either put your arm into the edge like this as it opens and then he slams it, or . . ."

Judy looked at Meldrich's beefy arm, picturing what it would take to snap it. RoMo's mouth dropped open.

"Come on, Meldrich," Wizard said, offering him a joint. He had 196 on his forehead. "It's not like you're the Number One."

"Wil is," Judy said in a whisper, not being able to find her voice. She scanned the room desperately looking for him.

Someone grabbed her to stop her turning. It was David. He tapped his watch.

"Soon now."

What was he doing? What about Wil? Nothing was making sense.

She felt an arm on hers and a pull back out the door into the hallway. It was Vida. She hadn't seen her in the haze.

"Wil?" she said. "I keep trying to get to him. Don't they realize . . ."

"Never mind," Vida said. "They don't know Wil's number. He wasn't there. He stayed in his room. His mother called the minute they pulled his number. He said he had known it all along."

"I need to find him."

"Later. He dropped two Quaaludes. He's out cold, for now. But he'll be fine. I have a plan for Canada, remember? He'll finally listen when he wakes up."

She leaned against the wall and slid down, sitting on the floor. Judy slid down next to her.

"What did you say to him?"

"I didn't have to say much. I went to his room when I realized he'd never made it to the TV room. I fucked him, gave him his drugs, and stayed with him till he crashed."

"You slept with him? I thought—"

"What else could I do?"

Judy was in flight toward Wil's room without realizing how she got up, Vida right behind her.

"Wait," Vida yelled.

Judy dodged over and around the figures that crowded the hallways, down the stairs, and back up to Wil's room. The door was open, and the room was empty.

"Don't worry," Vida said. "We'll get him to Canada. For now, just do what he always says and let him be."

"Vida!" Judy whipped around in terror. "He's walking around with Quaaludes *in* him, a death sentence *over* him, and that stupid fatalistic philosophy. And now you've slept with him. I know it sounds ridiculous, but it was one of the goals that was keeping him going. You really want to believe he didn't slip into the lagoon or that he isn't walking through the highway headlights."

"Oh, shit," Vida said.

They raced back to Meldrich's room.

"Wil's the Number One," Judy yelled. David dropped his roach. "He's on downers, and he's missing."

The room sprang into action.

"David and Fish, hit the lagoon," Wizard called out, on the run. "Achilles, the highway. The rest of you, check the dorm lobbies, outside, whatever you can think of. Meet up in the Tune Room in an hour or when you find him. One hour."

They scrambled out the door, barking orders at each other, as excited as they were scared, Judy thought, as thankful to be diverted from their own fear as they were worried about Wil.

Judy turned to follow them and tripped, kicking over an ashtray as big as a dinner plate that was left on the floor. Cigarette butts, roaches, and black soot shot through Meldrich's empty room. She stood in the middle of the rubble, looked out the window at the light high above campus and suddenly knew where Wil was—and she knew she had to go to him by herself.

Chapter 33

THE LATCH TO THE DOOR LEADING TO THE UNION TOWER opened easily, and Judy felt a pang in her chest. It had been too much to hope for, that the administration might have considered the lottery as much of a suicide hazard as midterms. She climbed the stairs slowly, then opened the door to the balcony and saw Wil. His back was to her, on the wrong side of the railing. He had crawled over it and was sitting with his skinny ass on its narrow, unprotected lip, one arm looped back around one of the bars. He was singing softly: "The fool on the hill . . . I'm the fool, the fool on the hill."

She closed the door behind her as quietly as she could.

"Told ya," Wil said, as if he had been waiting for her. "Number One. If you go, go all the way." He took a toke on a joint he was shielding from the wind in the cup of his free hand.

"This is still the best place to see the stars, Judy Blue Eyes," he said, staring at the sky. "Which one do you think is Michael? I think it's the one over there by itself, just waiting." He pointed, leaning at a dangerous angle.

"I see it, Wil. Why don't you come back here? You know me and heights." It didn't look like where he was sitting was much wider than a foot.

He didn't move.

"I already told Vida I'm not going to Canada," he said. "So don't bother. I think she's the one who wants to go to Canada. I think she'd like to be Number One and go to Canada."

"She's already figured it out, Wil. Her birthday's June twelfth. She'd have been number 321."

"I bet she's pissed."

Judy crouched down near him, but not too close, still on the safe side of the railing. She firmly clutched two of the bars. Wil's legs were dangling. She tried to calculate if the bars were far enough apart for her to reach through to grab him back, tight against the railing. She would hold him there until . . . she could talk him down? . . . help came? She hadn't told anyone she was coming up here. Wil was humming and drawing in the air with his smoking hand. She was sure he had taken more than two Quaaludes.

"It's all working out the way it's supposed to, you know," he said, after a long while. "That's why I didn't study for those tests. Somehow, I just knew it wasn't going to matter."

She saw that if she yanked him back suddenly his butt would probably slide off the ledge, and she wouldn't be able to hold him. "What did your mother say?" she asked.

"The woman who named me after Wilfred Owen? She's totally freaking out," he went on. "Like Vida. They all want me to tell them I'm fine, that I have a plan, that I'll go, that I won't go, that I'll jump off this balcony."

Judy moved her hand to the bar next to his.

He shot a look at her arm. "You, too."

"But, like I keep telling you, Judy Blue Eyes, you've just got to let it be. It will all become clear. The fool on the hill, he knows it all. He's just waiting for it to play out."

"Let's just watch the lights," she said.

"After all, I'm done," Wil said, with a laugh. "Got Vida to sleep with me."

"I'm getting dizzy, Wil. Why don't you come back here with me so we can talk?"

"I don't want to talk. I just want to disappear." He took a long drag off the joint, then swiveled it back and forth, and 'round and 'round, watching its light tracking against the sky. "I could disappear like Michael and become a star, or the Fool on the Hill. I could just be up here and watch everyone down there. I'd like that. You could come up here and we'd talk, and I'd be wise. It could be our secret."

"I have a secret, too, Wil. I told Michael. I've wanted to tell you for a long time, since that night we tripped."

"What?"

"Come back on the balcony and I'll tell you."

"Tell me here."

"No. It's big. And it's going to blow your mind. I need to see your full face when I tell you."

"You told Michael, and he died."

"Yes. I needed his help, and now I need yours. We're linked, remember? Same birthday. One chromosome, and I'd be a Number One, too."

He shook his head slightly, as if trying to compute the information. She was worried that even this slight movement might set him off balance.

"I guess you're right," he chuckled. "If I were Vida I'd say, 'Oh, wow.'"

"So maybe I'll come with you."

"Come with me? What do you mean?"

"To Vietnam, if you go. You know I have a scholarship for nursing, but what you don't know is that it's military. I'm already in the army. So I'm going to go anyway."

Wil gave her an uncomprehending look. "But . . ."

"Come back first. I'll show you."

She moved away from the railing, pulled her army ID out of her wallet and held it up, faraway enough so he could see that it was official but not read it.

"It's a trick, Judy. Don't do that."

"It's not, Wil, I swear. I'm a Private First Class in the United States Army, and my duty station is Central Illinois University until I go to Walter Reed next year."

Wil looked confused, like Howie. He pulled one leg back up under himself. "What did Michael say?"

"I didn't get a chance to talk to him about it."

"Wow, he was a deserter and you're in the army, and now I probably will be. What do you think he'd say about that?" He pulled the other leg up.

"He'd say we *know*, and we'll figure out what we're supposed to do." She moved closer to him.

Wil turned back to the stars. "I don't think I know anything, Judy."

Suddenly the sky lit up with a long series of sparks and what sounded like gunshots. Wil leapt up and Judy grabbed for him, sure he'd fall. She got him by the waist and pulled back with all her strength. She clenched her eyes shut, bracing for a long fall and a hard landing. Her hands lost their grip.

Shots continued to ring in the air.

When she opened her eyes, Wil was lying on her side of the railing, safe on the balcony, looking up at her. His eyes caught the reflection from the beacon on top of the tower, like two stars.

"What was that?" he asked, as Judy rolled off him.

They both sprang up and leaned back over the railing. They saw small explosions going off around a building near the Quad. It was the ROTC office. Suddenly, rockets started spewing red, white, and blue smoke, sparkling bursts shot up, and they ducked, thinking the balcony might be hit. The sparks continued in multiple spurts as if from a repeating rifle. Judy couldn't keep track of the streams of flickering light shooting out from around the building.

Wil pointed to a tree that caught fire. They watched the flames spread to all the surrounding foliage, full of dried autumn bark and leaves. It spread like lava, covering all the ground around the building, and the one next to it, heading throughout an entire block. They listened to the sirens and followed the firefighters as they manned the hoses.

Judy looked at her watch.

"David," she said.

PART THREE

January 1970

Chapter 34

THE SCORCHED BLOCK AROUND THE ROTC OFFICE SMOLDERED for a day, mirroring the aftershock that everyone felt after the lottery. Fast as the fire spread through the dried ground cover, it could have been worse, according to CIU officials quoted in the *Clarion*. The two-story house that had served as the headquarters for the Special Education Department was burnt to the ground and, although a storage building survived, all the books were ruined. The ROTC building, covered in flagstone, still stood, though the interior was shot and the stone covered in soot. The fire department had been able to stop the fire at the sidewalk line. Miraculously, aside from a firefighter who had been overcome with smoke and recovered the next day, no one had been hurt.

There was nothing miraculous about it, according to David, who knew the buildings wouldn't be occupied. "It's just property." He was gleeful, if a bit astonished that what he thought would be a fireworks show around the ROTC building had eaten up the whole block. He didn't want to hear anything about what could have happened.

He had brought Judy, Vida, Wizard, and Achilles up to the balcony of the Union Tower for the best view of the carnage, and to meet his kazoo buddies from Chicago. They had access to a leftover stash of Fourth of July fireworks that had been easy to get legally just over the Indiana border and had brought them to CIU, at David's command, a plan they had hatched over the Thanksgiving weekend. None of them were in school, "total draft bait" as David called them, and were more than happy to help. As it turned out, one of them was eighty-nine and the others had numbers over 250.

To top it off, they smuggled a live chicken into the Liberal Arts College and locked it in Swanson's office as punishment for his cowardice in not going to the March on Washington.

They had been up all night, drinking and smoking grass, and were laughing hysterically at their own comments as they watched groups of people in various uniforms huddling and picking through the smoking remains of the burnt buildings, taking pictures and notes.

"They should get the whole ROTC contingent, including those military freaks, out here to clean it up," David said, thinking that was so witty.

Judy watched the investigation underway and felt the kazoo guys, at least, should get out of town and back to Chicago, but she had to pick her moment. David didn't seem to understand the trouble he could be in. She even wondered about the fate of the poor chicken, pretty sure Swanson wouldn't be holding office hours anytime soon.

According to the *Clarion,* the assault on the ROTC office was the worst of a series of "provocative elements in the environment" both on campus and off. Apparently, maintenance had to deal with an alarming number of campus-owned television sets that had been maimed in various ways during or after the lottery telecast, and the health center had a record number of overdoses and stitches.

There had also been violent activity on campuses across the country, much of it worse than CIU, if you didn't count the fire that pushed it into the top five in the overall campus destruction ranking. On top of all this, the day after the lottery the Chicago police raided a Black Panther house and killed Fred Hampton and Mark Clark, and on Saturday the Hell's Angels stabbed a spectator at the Rolling Stones concert at Altamont. Many were spooked, thinking the revolution the radicals had promised was suddenly a possibility.

So it was on that Monday, one week after Lottery Night, CIU joined many universities across the country and closed the campus. It was determined that an early and extended holiday break would be useful in cooling things down before students came back the first week in January, in the hope they would be ready to buckle down for finals at the end of the month.

David claimed his "work" was what shut the campus down. He couldn't have been more pleased with himself, though it killed him that he couldn't take credit or he would end up expelled, or worse.

"I'm not worried," he told everyone who asked. "Like I said, it's only property. In Vietnam, it's lives."

Waves of students used the break as a chance to drop out or switch schools. There were those with high draft numbers like Howie and Fish, who were only in school to avoid the draft in the first place, who became the "poster boys," as Meldrich put it, to justify to Washington that the lottery "worked," and would now forget about all this protesting and get on with their lives. David was incensed.

"The body count just hit 39,398. You can't give up the fight just because you're personally out of it," David said to Fish and the others. But they couldn't leave fast enough.

Judy was gratified David at least agreed to join them in packing Howie's stuff and helping load his parents' car. Even he could see that Howie hadn't been able to revive his appetite or focus. Howie's mother seemed glad to be taking him home, but at one point Judy noticed she clutched the back of his shirt with one hand, gauging his thinness, and covered her mouth with the other, appalled.

"He's safe," Vida said to her softly, touching her shoulder. "That's what's important."

His mother turned to her, confused, and Marsha stepped between them before Vida went on.

"He could have just as easily been forty-three as 343," Vida said to the others. "It was the right thing for him to do, and now he'll be alive to recover from it." They all nodded as they watched the car pull away, everyone but Wil, who stood apart—there but not there.

Others used the campus turmoil as an excuse. Maggie leapt at the news.

"If the administration thinks it's too dangerous to be here, then I'm sure my family would agree. I'll finish up the year at Danny's junior college and then decide what to do next. I'll see you when you come home to visit," she said.

Judy thought she would be at least a little sad to have Maggie gone but instead was relieved, no more pipeline to her mother and sneaking around hiding her double life. Now the only person on campus who knew she was in the army was Pete . . . and Wil, of course.

She was afraid that telling him her secret had been a mistake. She thought at first everything would be all right. Her focus had been on making sure Wil didn't jump after all, and the ROTC explosions seemed to have shaken him out of that. As she guided him down the stairway of the Union Tower, he had even warmed to a plan.

"If they make me a medic, we could both go and take care of people instead of kill them," Wil said.

"So it's settled," Judy said, "you and me, together, right?"

But the talk they had about her army status when he came down from his high later left her feeling unsettled about his understanding of her situation, and the need for absolute secrecy.

They ended up in one of the newly remodeled study lounges on his floor. He was curled up in a Day-Glo orange chair surrounded by lime-green walls and wild Pucci prints framed as art. "I'm tracking off all these colors," he said, fanning his fingers. Once she had his attention, she told him the story as she imagined she would have told Michael.

"How do you rationalize it to yourself?" he asked.

She explained about the need for someone to be taking care of the soldiers.

"I think I'd buy this better if I felt you really wanted to be a nurse," he said. "Do you?"

She shrugged. "This is the scholarship I got, so this is what I'll be. At least I'll have a degree. And it's not like you can just leave the army, though they'd be happy to toss you out if you got pregnant. I did enlist for seven years."

"Are you asking me to knock you up?"

"No, Wil. Absolutely not."

He whistled. "What does Vida have to say about all this?"

"She doesn't know, Wil. No one else can know, remember?"

He pretty much checked out after Lottery Night. He was smoking a lot of dope, and Vida and Judy agreed to watch over him so he wouldn't do anything stupid. The more out of it he got, the more Judy worried about him sharing her secret, not on purpose, just letting it slip during pillow talk with Vida or in the pauses between the Beatles songs he was half humming, half singing almost all the time.

Everyone in the Tune Room group but Judy left campus for the long break, which upset her. After all they had gone through, she assumed they would want to stay together to plan for the next phase of the antiwar protest, certainly to support Wil, but even he was heading home. Vida was driving him, to make sure he got there, and had talked herself into staying with his family for a week. Marsha seemed to evaporate somewhere as soon as Howie left, and David was anxious to return and spend the time with his kazoo buddies, who were all living in a house they had rented in the city, which hurt Judy's feelings.

"No one seems to realize we've had a major victory with the ROTC fireworks, and now there's so much more we can do," David told her. "I want to celebrate, and everyone here's being such a downer. At least my friends in the city get it. . . .You can come with me if you want," he offered half-heartedly while they were lying in bed the night before he left.

But she begged off, knowing she was one of the downers he was referring to. She couldn't understand his excitement over what he had done, when what happened overall was, in her mind, so funereal.

She didn't know what to do with herself. After the tortured Thanksgiving visit, there was no way she could go home for nearly a month. She already decided she would only make an appearance for the fewest possible obligatory days around the holiday. RoMo said she would love it if Judy could spend the week between Christmas and New Year's with her and save her from total boredom with her family. But she had a lot of thinking to do, and also figured it would be a good time to get a jump on studying for finals. She decided to stay on campus, even though the dorms were closed.

Once her December army paycheck arrived, she rented a room in a student boarding house on a side street parallel to the lagoon and looked forward to the quiet. Instead, she found she couldn't concentrate on anything and spent the long, chilly days sitting by her window, looking out over the deserted campus, now permanently sunless and dirty-snow gray, the stillness interrupted only by the banging of doors, warped with time, responding to winter drafts.

❋ ❋ ❋

THINGS picked up when the administration, stunned that so many students were not returning after the break, announced they were relaxing the rules requiring dorm residency through sophomore year. Judy made arrangements for all the girls to move in to her house. Vida wanted to bury the hatchet. After all, David had slept with a lot of women before he met Judy, and none of them took it any more seriously than they did him. Certainly, on that they could agree, she explained. And now that Vida was safely with Wil and Judy at least officially with David, they were both excited to get their friendship back on track, though Judy was still too wary about trusting her with her secret.

Not yet.

Judy's room on the top floor was snug, so she convinced the housemother to switch out the twin beds for bunks from another room to make it work for both her and Vida. There was a closet-sized room next door for Marsha and another double downstairs that would accommodate RoMo and Sheila.

When Vida moved in, bright and early on January second, she immediately made the small area her own, spilling her stuff over into most of the single closet and one of Judy's dresser drawers. She accomplished this all while bringing Judy up to speed with great energy, talking nonstop as she pulled books out of boxes and filled her shelves with information she had accumulated about Canada: history, maps, industries most popular for employment. She was brimming with research and plans for getting Wil up there, taking him on as more of a cause than a boyfriend.

Yet, she was frustrated with him. She couldn't understand his reluctance. Even his family was against Canada. They were not enthusiastic about him being a draft dodger, even less that they might never see him again. She couldn't believe they didn't see what was at stake. She said she had to make quite a scene during her visit over break right in their living room, to try to scare them into realizing he could die. But, of course, it backfired because they just shut down, which was too bad because they were lovely, really, all thin and quiet, like Wil.

Vida had even considered going to Canada with Wil, if that's what it took, until she read an article about Joan Baez and David Harris and realized she could do more for him, like raise money, if she stayed in the States. She was full of enthusiasm, making plans for campus fundraisers, speeches, and publicity. She was confident she would ultimately convince him. Whenever Wil balked, Vida had sex with him. It worked like a charm, she said.

Sheila moved her boxes in, but never exactly unpacked, using them as cardboard end tables to hold everything from dirty dishes to her laundry. She had been too busy. Every guy on campus was looking for sympathy. So, throughout Lottery Week, when Sheila had started sleeping with as many as she could, it wasn't quite as shocking as it might have been any other time. She started with Fish, which made sense since it was an easy segue from negotiations about the afghan, though in the middle of it he decided she was taking way too long and his fifty-dollar commission was maybe too much. They all figured it was his lottery nerves that were making him act like such an imbecile. He certainly wasn't the only one these days. When she heard he was dropping out, Sheila got pissed and kept both the money and the nearly finished afghan.

Even when Sheila moved on to Wizard and Achilles, it had seemed somehow acceptable since they didn't have girlfriends, and according to her everyone needed comforting.

But it was still going on. Over the break she had been shacking up with some guy no one even knew out at University

Apartments near Michael's old place, screwing and knitting, as she put it. He was number thirty-two.

RoMo was strangely upset that Sheila had slept with Wizard but not so much that she would consider doing it herself, she told them. She wasn't happy to have to room with Sheila and was hoping Marsha would be back soon so they could switch rooms.

But Marsha didn't come back. When there was no sign of her by the day before classes started, Judy called her parents' house and started talking to her mother before she realized it wasn't Marsha. They shared the same soft, nervous voice.

"I can't take it anymore," Marsha said, once she was on the phone and before Judy had been able to say a word.

"What about Howie?"

"You know, he couldn't even eat that McDonald's I got for him on Lottery Night. He just sat and stared at it while his eyes teared up. He's really made himself sick, Judy. I honestly don't know if he'll recover. I . . . can't. I just can't."

She drifted off rather than hung up.

"She was never one of us anyway," Vida said. "She'll probably end up with one of the football players."

Judy had to agree, but felt guilty that Marsha hadn't been able to fit in. She was noting their numbers dwindling: Michael, Fish, Howie, Marsha, and soon Wil.

Every day she became more worried about him. He continued to talk about going to Vietnam as a medic, but medics could get killed, too. She was having a hard time picturing him in the military. He wasn't crazy like Meldrich, but he was so . . . breakable. How could he defend or take care of himself, let alone anyone else? She felt like the bargain she had offered to keep him from jumping off the Union Tower almost made sense, that they would need to go together so she could protect him. She was pretty sure he wouldn't make it to Canada, but didn't say anything to Vida.

Her worry about Wil seemed to take over concern about her own situation, especially since she wasn't reminded all the time by seeing Pete. It was probably just as well they weren't going to be sharing a class in the new semester, since he had virtually cut himself off in their last encounter after Lottery Night. He showed up at her dorm saying he needed to talk, and they grabbed two chairs in one of the alcoves in the lobby.

"I'm here to tell you to be careful. You know we hear things," he said, pulling his chair close. He looked around to make sure no one was listening. "You know they're investigating that fire on Lottery Night as arson, don't you?"

Judy nodded. David and others in her group had considered it a protest, so she hadn't thought of it as a crime, exactly, but of course it was.

"You'll see a lot more activity as soon as everyone returns from break and they can start questioning people. But there's more, Judy. If you screw with a federal military office, they have a tendency to take it very seriously."

"What do you mean?" She was thinking about David.

"I don't know specifically, but there are new faces on campus. I'd say people could be watching."

"You mean undercover?" she asked. Now she was thinking about herself.

Pete gave her one of his looks.

"What you've all been doing is too risky, Judy. You have to stop. Now."

"I'm not doing anything destructive, Pete. Don't worry."

"Everything you're doing is destructive, to yourself. Don't you understand? Just walk away from it all while you still can."

"One of my friends is a Number One in the lottery, Pete.

And it doesn't look like he's going to make grades. I can't desert him."

Pete stood up suddenly and took three quick strides to the window. Judy could see his facial muscles throb along his profile. His fists were clenched.

"If we don't keep it up, this war will go on and on," she said. "I believe that."

"Fine. If you feel that strongly, maybe you should just get out." He turned from the window. "Quit. Give up the scholarship, drop out, go home, and do whatever."

"Now you're just being mean."

"No, I'm stating the facts. What's so awful about being a nurse, anyway?" he asked. "You sure seem like you're always taking care of people. What else will you do? In Belmont Heights? Have you even thought about it? What will be the point of the point you'll be making then?"

She made a sound, not a word. She didn't have one.

He put his coat on in rapid, jerky movements and pulled out his gloves. He calmed down as he fitted them carefully to each finger as if they were delicate fabric that might rip.

He came over to stand right in front of her. "Just keep your nose clean. And I'm sorry, but if anything goes down, the last person you want to be talking to about it is me."

He kissed the top of her head.

"Good luck, Judy Blue Eyes."

He turned and walked out of the dorm.

Chapter 35

THOSE FIRST FEW WEEKS AFTER BREAK, JUDY FELT THE world had turned inside out. The cooling off the administration had hoped for didn't apply to the returning students who had to deal with the reality of their lottery numbers. Violent words kept occurring to her as she watched the guys coming back to campus: wired, ripped, frayed, wasted. They were needy and defensive, sympathetic and angry. She understood Sheila's need to help them forget it all for a few hours. What she worried about most was the drugs. They had progressed from the kind that made you laugh and discover yourself into harder stuff, the kind junkies did. Sharp, the drug dealer, whose name was really Greg Shapiro, was everywhere.

The gloom wrapped around Judy, and she felt as if she had to harness it or she would explode. She felt responsible. She knew it wasn't rational, really, but the fact that she could have been a Number One, that she and Wil shared this fateful September 14 birth date, made her believe Wil was right about destiny after all. Maybe somewhere in all this was hers. She just had to figure out what it all meant, but there was no one she could discuss it with now that Pete was out of the picture. More than once, she'd talked herself out of confiding in Vida. The only one who could begin to understand was Wil, but she feared he had just given up. She was relieved to see him the day after classes began and spirited him off to McDonald's as soon as she could. He seemed smaller, quieter.

"Just study to get decent grades on your finals, then at least you can stay in school while you figure things out," Judy said, back in their usual booth. She had paid for the hamburger and fries, asking them to remove the pickle.

"It's too late, Judy. Let it go."

"No. You've got three weeks. I'll help."

"We tried that, remember?" he said, with his little smile. "Not tonight, anyway. Vida's coming over."

"Yes, I understand you're together now," Judy said, cautiously.

"A sympathy fuck. I know that's all it is. But I'll take it. And you and David? He hasn't come over and challenged me yet."

"I didn't tell him . . . who."

"Did it have the desired effect?"

"In that respect, yes, surprisingly."

Wil raised his eyebrows.

Judy felt her cheeks glow.

He ate a handful of fries.

She calculated their calorie count. "You should give serious thought to going for underweight," she said. "It would be so much easier for you than Howie, maybe only fifteen or twenty pounds. You could do it."

"You just want my fries."

She didn't feel she could bring up anything about her own circumstance. His was always going to be more pressing, even if she did feel they were linked. Somehow, though she knew it didn't make sense, she felt like she had to make sure he would be all right, and then she would be, too.

"You've got to straighten up."

"Really? Why exactly?"

When the phone rang late the next night, Judy had to take a moment to process that Vida was on the line and not in the bunk above her. Then she remembered that she and Wil were spending the weekend off campus in a house rented by friends of Vida. They were off to Chicago for the Who concert with the tickets she had sold them to finance her trip to Washington.

"Can you get over here right now?" Vida said. "Something's wrong. Bring RoMo. I need all the help I can get. And hurry."

When they arrived, they made their way through the main room of the now-deserted house, past party detritus and silent stereo components, to the sound of voices in a back room. Judy parted strands of glassy beads that functioned as a door and entered a dark room with a mattress on the floor, a small dresser with a tiny lamp, and books in sloppy stacks around the perimeter. The room smelled of old cigarettes and rotting leftovers.

At the edge of the mattress, Wil was falling out of Vida's lap like a noodle. He couldn't sit up and kept sliding when she tried to steady him against a wall.

"What did he take?" Judy asked.

"I can't get a coherent word out of him," Vida answered. "He won't look at me. He says I have kaleidoscope eyes and I'm freaking him out."

RoMo helped Vida prop him up.

"Wil, what did you take?" Judy asked. "We have to know."

"Just working my way through the color wheel," he said, tittering. "You remember, first we did a little orange sunshine . . ."

"And now? What is it now, Wil?"

"Now it's green, green slime, I mean green smear. Smear? Yeah, I think it's smearing, or sliming." He faded off.

"You imbecile!" Vida yelled and dropped him on RoMo. "It's just acid. Here I thought it was smack or something. I've never seen him so out of it."

"I thought you were just partying. Did something happen?"

"I'll say," Vida said. "He got his notice. See?" She pointed to a partially burnt piece of paper in an ashtray. "He has to report for his physical on January eighteenth—next week."

Judy felt an icy blast of dread shoot through her.

"Don't they wait until you actually flunk out?" Judy asked. "Maybe it's a mistake."

"They have to get the physicals in, regardless," RoMo said. "Then they call you later, when your number's up, if you don't have a deferment."

"I think I'm bad tripping," Wil said, then started rubbing his head violently. "I'm bad tripping, man."

Vida grabbed his hand, and he pulled it away quickly, feeling his arm up and down with his opposite hand, as if he didn't recognize it as a limb.

"There's something wrong with Vida's eyes," he said to RoMo. "Her eyes are broken. Did someone drop her? Nooooooo . . . ," he screamed.

They sprang into action like an emergency medical team.

"Get Sharp," Vida ordered, and RoMo grabbed the phone to call Meldrich for his number. "I hate that drug-dealing son of a bitch, but at least he'll know what to do. We can't take Wil to the health center or they'll report it."

"Maybe we should try to make him walk," Judy said, but he was back to being a noodle. He kept collapsing on them, his yelling settling into a constant murmur.

"Nooooo . . ."

Soon there was loud pounding on the door, and in a flash RoMo was back with Sharp.

He was just what Judy had expected, a lanky, creepy guy. He moved through the rooms with presence, carrying a white bag and a carton of liquid. What surprised Judy was his caring attitude.

"Having a rough time, are you?" he said to Wil. "You know

it's just the drug, don't you, buddy? It's not you. I've got the orange juice and the sugar. You'll be fine."

He talked to Wil with what seemed to be genuine concern and confident knowledge. They deferred to him immediately. RoMo handed him a glass.

"Look at me, man," Sharp said. "Come on, you've got to drink this. It'll bring you down."

"Get behind him and hold him up," Sharp said to Vida.

But Wil shrank back at the sight of her, and Judy took over. She climbed behind him on the mattress, wrapping her legs around him, just the way the guy with the buttons had kept her warm in Washington. Judy stabilized herself against the back wall and put her arms around Wil, holding his head up by the chin.

"Drink this. Remember it's just the drug, Wil," Sharp said. "It's not you. That acid's playing tricks on you. It's fun, but it can get pretty weird." Sharp looked up at them. "Anyone know what he took?"

"He said it was green acid," Vida said.

"Yeah, that green smear stuff can be nasty, Wil. Gotta watch it. That's it, yes," Sharp said, when Wil finally started drinking.

"Thanks, man," Wil said, in between sips.

Judy thought he looked vaguely embarrassed that Sharp had been called, as if it was now public that he couldn't handle his drugs. She took that as a sign the orange juice was working.

Suddenly, Wil noticed Vida behind Sharp and pushed back against Judy.

"She's going to make me disappear," Wil shrieked.

"Get her outta here," Sharp said.

"What the fuck?" Vida said. "I'm the one who . . ."

RoMo pulled Vida out of Wil's sight.

"Keep drinking, now." Sharp's voice was soothing.

He and Judy worked as a team to get a mouthful in, then let him rest his chin and breathe, then do it again, until the carton of juice was empty.

"He should be all right unless he throws it up," Sharp said to Judy. "If he does, load up another glass of OJ with a ton of sugar and just keep at it." He watched Wil carefully. "I think he's gonna keep it down."

"It's not real," Judy said to Wil, taking over as Sharp left. "Nothing that's happening is real."

"It's two worlds!" Wil suddenly cried, sweating and panicky. "Two worlds! It's this one, and then everything's the same but scary and . . . and Vida's this monster with broken eyes . . ."

Judy started to shake him. She kept shaking him to pull him back to this safe world. "See, Wil, I'm bringing you back. Is it working? Can you feel it?"

"Yeah," he said. "Keep doing it."

It was like CPR, every few seconds another shake until he no longer felt the terror world would grab him. Wil rhythmically beat the back of his head against her chest. It went on for most of the night.

Judy didn't know exactly what Wil's second world looked like, but she could imagine. She remembered her dream about Rick not letting her out of the tunnel.

In her mind's eye, she would hit bottom, then light a match. What would come at her out of the blackness? She started to scream and realized the sound was coming from Wil. Her mind dropped the match. "It's only the drug . . . it seems real, but it's only my imagination . . . your imagination. It's just a physical . . . It doesn't mean you're going . . . I know I can't really understand," she told him as she talked both of them down.

Chapter 36

THE MORNING DAVID RETURNED FROM BREAK, A WEEK late, he showed up unannounced at Judy's house, grabbed her in the entryway, and overwhelmed her with one of his soul kisses before she could speak. They snuck upstairs to her room. David hung his bandana on the doorknob in place of a tie, and they barely left her lower bunk until dark when she came down to the kitchen to forage for food. She was happy as she heated up noodles and tomato soup, filled two bowls, then dumped them quickly into a single larger one as she heard her housemother descend the stairs. She snuck a second spoon in her robe pocket and nodded with embarrassment as she was chided about the amount of food she was about to consume.

She scampered up the stairs, delighted at what she was sure this day would mean for their relationship. He had obviously missed her. And her excitement convinced her she must care for him more than she had admitted. Things would be changing.

When she opened her door, she realized their moment had passed. David was fully dressed and at the desk with his head resting on his chin, deeply into what had to be Vida's copy of *Soul on Ice*. He stretched his arm out for the bowl without even looking up.

He read excerpts aloud to her with his mouth full until he'd obviously had enough of both. He snapped the book shut, gave her the bowl, and told her to hustle and get dressed. They had to get to the Tune Room for a major confab in a half hour.

Judy reeled but obeyed, too stunned to absorb the whiplash of another of David's mood swings. As she pulled on jeans and a sweater and tried to make sense of her bed hair, he leaned against the windowsill, smoking, and explained that he had decided over break that it was essential the movement didn't lose its momentum now that the lottery was over, and it was obvious he should be in charge of what would happen next. He was certain the meeting called for tonight was what he had been waiting for, and everyone wanted him to take over and lead. Vida joined them as they left the house.

When they walked into the Tune Room, they noticed a noisy crowd at one of the tables down by the jukebox and made their way through, hearing snippets of what was going on as they progressed. A group of Trots had been assaulted the night before at the YSA house on campus. Apparently, a pack of unidentified assailants broke in, trashed the place, and beat them with fists and baseball bats.

"Sure, they're obnoxious, but who would have done that?" Judy heard Meldrich say under his breath.

"And why now?" Wizard added.

When they got to the table, they were shocked at what they saw. Lori was sitting with her back against the wall, surrounded by Donnell and the other Trots, including Sorsa, their first black recruit, all bandaged but oddly energized. Donnell had a gauze patch on his head, with peeling tape. Vida's eyes were examining it carefully, and Judy knew she was dying to reach out and comfort him. Lori had fared the worst. Her right eye was swollen shut; a huge pink crescent of flesh bulged out of the socket, distorting half her face and stretching the red acne spots so she looked like some kind of spotted puffer fish.

David did nothing to mask his disgust at the sight of her face. He didn't seem to know what to do.

Judy tried to cover. "Were you scared?" she asked.

"I can take care of myself, obviously," Lori snarled. "The movement doesn't need anyone who scares easily."

"Bastards," Achilles said. "Did they catch them yet?"

"They'll never be caught," Lori said, seemingly unconcerned. She was playing to new faces who had joined the gathering, now spilling onto the center floor. "It's up to us."

"We're planning a press conference," Lori said through her swollen lips. "It will be in the auditorium on Monday. We have the ombudsman, the security chief, and we're hoping to get President Jones. He should speak out when his students are attacked."

"And we can talk about how to avoid the draft," Vida said, moving to share a seat with Donnell. "We're already researching Canada. Why can't we do a whole day on it, like we did at the Moratorium?"

"Not about Canada, not if you're trying to get Jones," David said, snapping back into it and taking over a chair that one of the Trots had vacated. "He can't come out as if he's supporting people trying to skirt the law. I know you like things public." He looked at Lori. "But this will have to be underground, probably off campus."

"We can use the Trot house," Sorsa said. "It will attract people to the scene of the crime."

They went back and forth, as excited as they had been before the March on Washington. Judy watched David's face beam as the plans progressed and his idea prevailed about Jones, then darken as he lost it when he suggested another march and Lori shot him down. She wondered if it was a turn-on for him to tussle with Lori like this.

THE press conference was a success, and the Trots leveraged their assault into a campaign that wiped out memory of the

ROTC fireworks on Lottery Night. Judy thought the timing was strangely convenient, but the viciousness of the attack meant it had to be genuine, she said to Vida, who was highly suspicious of anything involving Lori, even if Donnell was included. David and Vida were both doubtful that even the Trots could have organized this degree of follow-up and watched it all unfold, aghast.

Whereas previously the Trots had always just popped up to insert themselves whenever anything was brewing, now they functioned as a single, multiheaded unit, like a hydra. They fanned out to host education sessions and make presentations about draft avoidance at events all over the campus.

They also took over leadership of the movement, just because they were better at it, it seemed to Judy, though she would never say that out loud. Running meetings was their forte, as if they had been trained in it or, as Vida said, "were all born with little gavels up their butts." They had always all been great speakers, but now they seemed to thrive on their ability to beat their opposition with superior debating skills, their rhetorical serpent heads reproducing when they were cut off, only to come back with greater force. David regularly lost it whenever they used the phrase "may I finish," which always allowed them to keep the floor.

He started referring to Lori as "Lori, may I finish, Mueller." It was hard for Judy to hear him say that without picturing if she had said it to him during sex in the bus that night on the way to Washington.

David was beside himself. He kept trying to use the SMC to gain the upper hand, but after the lottery, many of the guys had lost focus, and it was difficult to organize. And it was near the end of January; finals were approaching. Diverted as they were, everyone knew that grades had to be made or those with low numbers would be called up immediately.

For their part, David and Vida were finally able to assemble a group to organize a series of activities that would be held surreptitiously on and off campus, spread by word of mouth. Vida already had RoMo working on the CO stuff, and David was able to speak with authority on how it wasn't enough just to be a member of a pacifist group anymore, you really had to demonstrate you were a believer. His own story got more elaborate with the telling.

YSA retaliated by taking over the subject of medical deferments. The medical aspects were tricky and they couldn't pin them down, so information was shared informally on how over or underweight you would need to be and how to raise your blood pressure. Anyone who flunked a physical was an instant celebrity, and the YSA "trotted" them out, as Achilles said, to tell their stories, though there weren't many, and some of them were a little sad, Judy thought, like the guy who was discovered to have some kind of heart issue. Though, by this time, even something serious was considered a blessing. "Better that than a sniper shot in a jungle," it was said and repeated, over and over.

The Trots attracted a standing-room-only crowd, including most of fraternity row, when they invited the guy from Meldrich's dorm with the surefire system for breaking your arm. RoMo questioned how many of those they could actually get away with, from a single university. "Selective Service would definitely figure that one out," she said to jeers from the audience.

Sheila worked on the curriculum part of the deferment issue, since it was so important to so many of the upperclassmen with low numbers that she was still having sex with. She made calls to find out what degrees would protect you from the draft, and there was a distinct switch in majors to medicine and dentistry, as well as new interest in graduate programs in optometry and veterinary medicine. Judy wondered if she should tell Pete he probably would have been safe without ROTC, but then remembered he had signed up for the scholarship money. How could she have forgotten that, she chided herself. But with all this fear about getting killed, scholarships versus defer-ments seemed to pale in comparison, and her dilemma with it.

Vida was mostly interested in Canada, but it had been virtu-ally impossible to find out what you really had to do. "Apparently you can get across the border through upper Minnesota and other non-checkpoints," she told them. "It helps if you know someone up there."

No one did.

She ended up making speeches about how pathetic it was that those already in Canada weren't sending back information to what she started calling "The Lottery Class."

She kept pressing Wil to consider it. The harder she pushed, the more dope he smoked and the less Judy could con-vince him to study. Judy felt it was the only viable alternative, but he considered it a Hail Mary, not worth the effort.

"I never said I was going to Canada," Wil said again and again in a smaller and smaller voice.

"Vida, this is turning out to be more about you than about Wil," Judy said.

"No," Vida snapped. "It's about life. His life."

EVERYONE Judy cared about kept bouncing their issues off her, as if she were the one they needed to convince of the veracity of their position. To Vida, it was Wil's life or death; to Wil, it was the inertia of not resisting what he felt was his karma. And to David, it was the increasing mania over who would be in charge of the movement on campus. He was getting paranoid.

"I think they did it to themselves," David said, from their

regular table in the Tune Room, glaring at all the posters and notices covering the walls for competing events. "The YSA beating. I think they staged it all."

"How can you say that?" Judy asked. "Even they wouldn't have beat each other."

Vida thought it might be possible in a stretch, but even Wil chimed in to say David was getting carried away.

"Come on," David said. "Like you wouldn't put it past them?"

Later that night, after he and Judy had sex at what was becoming an increasingly thank-you-ma'am pace, he started in again, all fired up from another of a series of daily insults by the Trots.

"David," she said, "you're losing all perspective here. You have to give people a reason to follow you."

"What do you mean, give them a reason? I'm giving them tons of reasons every day."

"If you want to lead this, you can't just try to one-up Lori every time she does something," she said. "You have to have something bold of your own."

"Of my own? I'm the one who blew up the ROTC office, for godssake. What more am I supposed to do?"

"Well, all your anti-ROTC efforts were focused. They were clear; people got it. Right now, they don't see a difference between the YSA and the SMC—and you have to give them one."

He wrinkled his brow and lit a cigarette, exhaling violently, then brushed the smoke away with his free hand like it was keeping him from seeing clearly.

"I'm just saying that you need something distinctively SMC," she said.

"Like 'The Lottery' performance," he said. "I get it."

JUDY was still trying to keep Wil in line and suggested he get a makeup pass for his sociology final that was to take place on

January 18, the same day as his physical. It would give him more time to study, or rather give Judy more time to help him figure out the minimum he had to commit to memory to get a C.

The day of the physical, she offered to take the bus trip into the city with him.

"Not necessary," he said. "Don't worry. It's all going to turn out the way it's supposed to."

After he left, everyone but David gathered in the Tune Room as if being together would reduce their anxiety about Wil's fate. Vida had taken her headband off and was picking at the stitching, and Achilles, Meldrich, and Wizard were brooding, sharing what they had heard about the mass medical examinations and how they were increasingly letting in those who previously would have been cut.

"At this point, if you can stand up without falling and make out the side of a truck in front of you, you're in, even if you're essentially crippled, blind, deaf, and dumb," Achilles whined.

"This is it," David announced suddenly from center stairs, his arms spread wide. Their heads whipped around. Once all eyes were on him, he raised his voice. "VOTE ROTC OFF." He pumped his fists with each word, then opened them, full fingered, for a final flourish. Then he hopped down the stairs and over to their table.

"What are you talking about?" Judy asked, her pulse quickening.

"Fuck all these little sessions about how to postpone getting drafted; the Trots can have them. The SMC needs to focus on one, clear objective, and I've got it: ROTC."

"What do you mean?"

He looked at her as if he couldn't believe she didn't immediately understand.

"ROTC? The war machine on campus? We'll get rid of it, finally. That will be our platform."

"Swanson killed that already, remember?" Meldrich said. "Give it up, GagMan, you're just going in circles."

"Screw Swanson. He's gone to ground anyway, too scared to lose his job to take a stand. He won't interfere this time."

David threw down a piece of paper with copy for a leaflet. Vida grabbed it, and they rearranged themselves to read it over her head. David watched with a shit-eating grin.

"'Forget the vote we don't have,'" Vida read. "'Take action on the one we do. VOTE ROTC OFF.' Actually . . . ," she tapped her finger on the end of her nose. "This just might be an idea whose time has finally come. I mean, free speech or not, what else can we actually *do*?"

"Exactly," David said. "Take the focus off what we can't change and turn it on something we can. And we can do it quickly, as a response to the lottery. They're both about getting students into the war, get it?"

She and David batted the concept around with the others who all agreed, too easily, it seemed to Judy, that this would be the ticket to rally around versus the Trots, who were trying to change the social order.

"No one wants to be a socialist," Achilles said. "We just want the war to end so we don't have to die."

Judy listened with increasing panic. It was the step she had been able to skirt to date but feared the most. "But isn't ROTC really just a scholarship program?" she asked, choosing her words carefully. "If someone wants to be in it, they should be able to, right? They might even really need to be in it, David. Who are we to judge?"

"That was the argument before the lottery," Wizard said, suddenly excited. "I think it's pretty clear things have changed." He turned to David. "I'm with you."

"You participate, you're complicit," David said. "Like I always say, those ROTC recruits need to know they can't have it both ways."

The words hit Judy like punches.

"But, David," she said. "ROTC is so narrow, there are only a few guys here in the program. Is this really worth our time? Don't you want to make a greater impact?"

"You're forgetting the lesson of the grapes," he said, with a smile. "You start small, then leverage. Besides, you're the one who told me to focus. Remember?"

"Let's call a meeting and get the planning going," RoMo said. "As Michael would have said, the body count is escalating every day. We don't have a minute to lose."

They made for the door.

Judy made an appearance of taking a long time to pack up her things.

As David approached center stairs he looked back and called after her.

"Aren't you coming?"

"I've got some things to do first," she said. "I'll get there."

"I know you will." He smiled at her, then turned to race toward his latest brilliant idea.

Chapter 37

"THEY JUST PLAYED ROULETTE WITH YOUR LIFE, MAN," David repeated over and over. "This is the only power we have to send a message that we're off limits. They can't recruit here."

The new, improved VOTE ROTC OFF message resounded immediately. The petitions that had been rejected earlier last year were now resurrected with a new pitch, echoed by legions of SMC members across campus taking over the Trot playbook.

Plans were made for polling kiosks to be set up at the dorms, throughout the Union, even on Greek row. Like a formal national election, ballots would be collected and student senators would vote per the consensus of their student constituents at the Senate meeting coming up at the end of May.

For Judy, it was hard to tell if they really believed it or if everyone was just desperate for something, anything, they could do. And now with finals behind them and the new semester under way, they were ripe for action.

Meanwhile, the Trots were undeterred and picked up the opposing message.

"ROTC numbers are already way down. There are only twenty-six members on campus, anyway. We have a whole war to end."

The new effort made it a contest between them, and David's leadership soared. Vida refocused all her energies into it, especially since Wil was not budging on Canada and she was getting exasperated. She stopped sleeping with him, which was sad because it was all he had to look forward to, as Judy tried to point out to her.

Judy had to tread very carefully and spent as much time as possible at the library. For the first time, her studies were able to keep her mind off what was going on, and she remembered how much she actually enjoyed learning. Escaping a secretarial fate had never been her only motivation, just the important one that would lead to something she was better suited for. She even longed for a really challenging redox equation, but her classes this semester were mostly Gen Ed humanities that she had to get out of the way before next year, when she would be deep into her nursing major far away at Walter Reed. She often studied in the library loft, which somehow made her feel like Pete was still around. There was a comfort there that she couldn't quite put her finger on, and a hole in her life that surprised her.

By the end of January, it was clear that Wil had failed his finals and passed his physical. He was just waiting, and the boom was finally lowered in early February when he learned he was to report for basic training somewhere in Texas on March 28.

"How do you feel?" Judy asked. She had pulled him off, alone, to PePe's, a Mexican joint between campus and the highway.

"Everyone wants to know that," he said, peeling the hardened bulbs of yellow mustard off the side of a plastic squirt container. "My parents, the entire Tune Room. But they don't just come right out and ask it, like you did. Mostly they just treat me as if I've been diagnosed with a terminal disease. Everyone's patting me on the back like we're old friends, offering their seats, their cigarettes, their dope. Buying me cokes . . . and tacos. I feel like I'm already dead."

"I'm so sorry," Judy said. "I didn't realize."

"No, it's fine, really. I know everyone's trying to do the right thing, but it makes me think of my grandma's funeral, where everyone kept going up to my grandpa and telling him they didn't know what to say."

Judy squirmed in the booth, noticing how her pink pullover clashed violently with the brilliant reds and oranges in the vivid, festival upholstery. The discord seemed to exemplify what she was feeling.

"Seriously, Judy." He reached for her hand. "I know there isn't anything to say, and now I understand that just saying that . . . is all there is, and that it's . . . enough."

"I know," she said.

"We both *know*. Hasn't that always been the point?"

She blinked rapidly, and they released their hands as the waiter brought their food.

"It's really spicy," Wil said to him. "I can already feel those jalapeños." He sniffed.

The waiter left and they both started giggling. It escalated as if they were high, and every time they caught each other's eyes, they would howl even louder. They were attracting the attention of the entire restaurant. Every time someone looked their way, it sparked even more laughter to where they were barely breathing.

"I needed that," Judy said when her air returned.

"I think laughing with you will be what I'll remember most," Wil said, biting into his taco. "It even beats sex with Vida."

Judy tried to stifle her tears.

"Go ahead," Wil said. "It's okay."

DAVID turned Wil's going-away party into a rally. "BRING THE TROOPS HOME" became "BRING WIL HOME," giving the movement the personal touch it needed to get the campus re-energized. Even the Trots came, looking truly devastated, though whether that was because one of CIU's own was going to Vietnam or David was running the show was unclear.

"Don't worry, buddy. We're going to get you back as soon as we can," David said, clapping him on the shoulder right at center stairs. "And," he couldn't resist, "we're going to keep as many as we can from joining you. VOTE ROTC OFF, VOTE ROTC OFF."

He started a chant that made Judy furious. David would use anyone for his purposes. Wil stood beside him, vacant. Judy motioned for him to come over to their table. He hesitated a bit because Vida was there, and they had essentially broken up because she was so angry about his decision.

"For God's sake, sit down," Vida said. "I won't stuff you in the trunk and take you to Canada, okay?"

He took a seat beside her.

"There's nothing easy about this, Vida. But it's been coming a long time, just let it be."

"You are so full of shit."

She was crying now. Judy had never seen her do that before. Wil took her hand, and Judy left the table, elbowing Achilles to join her and leave them alone. Achilles was livid.

"Of all the people to be Number One. That guy wouldn't hurt an insect." He paused. "Do you think he'll make it?"

"If he's supposed to, I guess. That's what he'd say." She started crying herself, silently, and Achilles put his arm around her.

"I wish there was someone I could punch," he said. "I'd want to hurt them really bad."

As she left the Tune Room, she walked past Vida and Wil one final time, overhearing them.

"You just have to understand," Wil said.

"I can't. You're right. I just can't," Vida said, covering her face with her hands.

There was a loud crash. Judy looked behind her. Achilles had thrown a chair against the wall.

Chapter 38

ONCE WIL LEFT, JUDY HAD TO TURN HER ATTENTION TO schoolwork. For the first time, her grades had fallen. She'd worked so hard on Wil's subjects, she'd neglected her own. Her poor showing on finals had pulled her grade point average down dangerously close to a B-, not the caliber of the WRAIN program, according to a letter sent by its administrator to her parents that she would be expected to answer for, even if they weren't speaking.

Her escapes to the library became more frequent as Vida and David continued their activities. This left her out of a lot, but David and Vida made sure she was where she needed to be. David, of course, had aced everything after a few all-nighters, and Vida was fine with her usual Cs.

She missed Wil but had comforted herself that she didn't have to worry about him as long as he was still stateside. And she had coached him carefully on making his intentions about being a medic clear from the moment he started basic training.

She got a letter from him in early April. It didn't say anything about what he was doing, other than to describe his rock-hard mattress, but he wanted her to know that even though the Beatles had just released a song called "Let It Be," he had written the words first.

No one else had heard from him, not even Vida, whose feelings were hurt but not so badly that she didn't encourage Judy to take the letter to the Tune Room and read it aloud to everyone from center stairs. They made sure the song got on the jukebox right away and inserted their quarters over and over to play it continuously. It became a ritual. Every night they gathered at the Tune Room, played "Let It Be," and repeated the rally chanting to "BRING WIL HOME." The whole thing made them feel like he was still part of them.

Judy wrote back to his training base address immediately, sending him the full "Let It Be" lyrics, in case he had only heard it on the radio. She smiled as she noted how the Beatles had been wise enough to add "whisper words of wisdom" to "his" words, and said that if he was going to claim royalties, she would testify that he absolutely came up with "Let it be" before anyone else on the planet. And that Vida, David, RoMo, Sheila, Wizard, Meldrich, and Achilles had volunteered to back her up.

She eagerly looked forward to what she knew would be a witty reply, maybe even a song lyric. When she hadn't heard in a few weeks, she worried that she had gotten the address wrong, or maybe he had been transferred, and called his mother.

She identified herself as a friend of Wil's from CIU, and for a moment thought Wil's mother had hung up on her. Then she heard soft, wet noises, which filled her with the same icy dread she had felt when she heard about Wil's draft notice.

"I'm so sorry," Wil's mother said, when she collected herself. "I should have let someone there know. But . . ."

And Judy knew.

It had been a stupid accident. Wil was on an obstacle course, hanging on to a rope, about to climb a rappelling wall with two other guys, when he yanked too hard and out of sequence. The other two weren't ready, and he crashed into the wall, hitting it so hard that, despite his helmet, something essential had cracked. They had taken him to the infirmary, where at first he'd seemed only dazed. But over the next few days he lost the ability to talk, to move. In the end, he was conscious but could only communicate with his eyes until the brain hemorrhage finished off that final sense, and he was gone . . . dead before the end of his first week in the service. What kind of a contribution was that, she wanted to ask Pete.

No one could believe it. Vida nearly totaled Wizard's beater, driving it right into a restraining wall and then kicking it as she left it smoking. The guys were all shocked into incomprehension, not even able to smoke grass. They wouldn't look at each other. Meldrich kept doodling his number—66—on a piece of notebook paper at a table in the Union. At one point, Achilles burst into uncontrollable tears.

"This . . . this feeling . . . is what you mean when you say there must be a reason your birthday is September fourteenth, right?" David said to Judy.

All anyone could do was nod.

Judy sent Wil's mother the lyrics of "Let It Be" with a note indicating they were words of brilliance, and Wil had written them first.

At the beginning of May, David, Vida, and the rest all had a commemorative event in Wil's honor, as the first CIU student to actually die because of the war. Judy couldn't bring herself to go, she just couldn't.

"Wait until you see Wil's picture in the Tune Room," RoMo said, when she called with a report. "It's huge. And Sheila finished the American flag afghan. We're going to hang it next to Wil's photo, but Vida wants you to see it first. She's on her way over."

Judy didn't want to see Vida. She didn't want to share her memories of Wil with anyone. She crawled into the bottom bunk, and put "Let It Be" on the stereo, lifting the arm off the cut and setting it back to start over, again and again, so that it would never end.

When Vida arrived, she put the afghan on her desk, sat in

her chair, and listened to the song play all the way through, twice. Then she started talking.

"It's funny, you know. I used to joke about being clairvoyant, because I could pretty much spot people who *know*. But this time I really was. I always knew Wil couldn't go to Vietnam. I knew he couldn't help himself from being drafted, and I knew he'd never make it. Well," she said, "maybe there wasn't anything all that mystical about that. Anyone could see it. That's why I pushed so hard for him to go to Canada. I knew that was the only way. I even made that scene in his living room with his parents." She put her head down and shook it. "They must have thought I was this crazy hippie who was just looking for a cause. . . . I couldn't just come out and say that he was going to die."

Judy nodded.

"I loved him, you know, I really loved him, but not like he wanted me to. And then he was always so moon faced around me. Hardly my type, you know." She let out a soft "*Ha* . . . But I had to sleep with him eventually. You know that too, right? Especially after he got his Number One. I mean it would have been cruel not to. Sheila gets it. Do you?"

"I know he was glad it happened."

Vida gave her a weak smile, a Wil smile.

"His mother is really very nice," Vida said. "Just like him. They're all very nice. His father and sister. They all kind of look alike. Pale and . . ."

"Fragile?"

"Yes, fragile, that's a good word for it. She didn't really name him after Wilfred Owen, you know. That was his own trip, thank God. Can you imagine how she'd feel now? Like she'd doomed him."

"I think he was a bit doomed," Judy said. "He was always off somewhere in his own head, as if he'd always been more of a spirit than a person."

"You think so? I like that." Tears were starting to roll silently down Vida's cheeks. "I'm so sorry I didn't love him."

Judy beckoned her to join her on the bed and put her arm around her. "Vida, come on, no guilt. It was a freak accident."

"But you aren't really surprised, are you?"

"No, I wasn't," Judy said. "I made a pact with him, and I didn't . . ."

"Was that before or after you slept together?"

"He told you?"

"I thought it was sweet. Two virgins. I guess we gave him what we could, Judy."

"But it wasn't enough."

Vida lay down next to Judy and covered them both with the afghan. She hadn't been able to stop him, and Judy hadn't been able to save him, so they held each other, crying. Judy sniffed the wool and wished that Wil had actually touched it himself. Then she focused on one of the stars, one single star.

JUDY felt so raw and exposed that the next day she even wrote her mother a letter about Wil and how the fact that they shared the same birthday must mean something. She got carried away and also wrote about the tension on campus and how she felt things were ready to erupt, but decided she'd better stop before she got her mother going again. She knew she should reread it, or rewrite it, or even not send it, but she just went ahead. Let it be.

Later, she let Vida talk her into going to the Tune Room to see Wil's photo on the wall. Sheila would meet them to hang the afghan. Everyone would be there. But as they entered the Union, along with David and RoMo, Achilles's voice rang out from the upper level.

"They're shooting us," he screamed. "They're shooting us."

He was still screaming when they reached him at the bottom of the stairs, spewing great arcs of spit with every word, so red Judy thought he would spontaneously combust.

"What the fuck?" David said.

"Students! Dead! By the National Guard."

"Right here, on the news." Achilles pointed to the lounge with the only operable television set left in the Union after Lottery Night. "They're fucking mowing us down."

Then he ran past them down to the Tune Room.

"They're shooting us. They're shooting us. The revolution has begun."

Chapter 39

MAYBE THE REVOLUTION HAD BEGUN, JUDY SAID TO HERSELF the next day. For the first time, she was considering taking seriously what previously seemed like so much radical fantasy. "Revolution Now!" was a phrase that had been as over the top as "Off the Pig!" a great blood-rushing rallying cry, but no one was going to really kill a policeman. This was Central Illinois University, not Watts.

But now it could be true. It really could be true. She worked at the corner of the binding of her Western Civ book, pulling out strings of fabric. Students were dead at Kent State. Dead! Four of them shot by the National Guard. She still couldn't get her head around it. She drew the threads out one by one, pulling them up the full length of the book, separating the spine. This was too much, way, way too much. She hadn't even been able to cope with Wil being gone, let alone dead, so soon after Michael, and now this. What would they have thought of this? she wondered. What could any rational person think of this?

The pounding rhythm of "I Want You" boomed out of the jukebox. Couldn't anyone play another song? Her head started to throb in time with the song's ominous, endless chorus, blotting out other sounds in the Tune Room as more and more people gathered to fill every table, lean against every wall space, and sit on every inch of the hard, wooden central aisle and the once-green carpet, now virtually tuftless with cigarette burns. She continued to play with the fabric, balling up the strands into makeshift worry beads.

"Revolution Now!" Achilles pounded the table, and the book shook. She lost her thread. Before she could react, he ran to another table, repeating the gesture with the cry: "We can't stand for this!"

Judy watched him, amazed as he went from table to table with his fist pumped, knocking over books, kicking chairs, even punching arms—hard—for emphasis.

"What are we waiting for?" he shouted.

This laid-back guy who preferred talking to action was now the celebrity who had broken the news about Kent State and run, like Paul Revere, from the Union to the dorms to spread the word.

"They're Shooting Us! They're Shooting Us!"

The vein on his neck bulged. His face had darkened dangerously and contorted into a fierce scowl. If you could radicalize Achilles, Judy thought, anyone could turn.

Rage rose in waves around the packed room. People jumped in and out of positions from standing to sitting and back again, pacing up and down the center aisle, like lions in a cage. Banner paper had been hastily tacked on the walls with a scorecard: KENT STATE 4, CIU? She felt the room bubble and pop, knowing that at some point something would boil up and take form or burst. She knew she should absolutely be here, and absolutely not.

She turned back to her book to try to get a grip on her runaway mind but couldn't. The music continued. So . . . HEAVVVVY. They shot students! Kids! It was surreal. A bad trip. Initially, she assumed it was an absurd rumor. Surely, they had fired over their heads. Worst case, it had to have been an accident. When she realized it was really true, she felt responsible. The soldiers who had shot the kids were in the military, just as she was.

Her imaginary conversations justifying her position were no

longer only with Michael or Wil. Now they were also with David.

"Don't you see that just by being in the army you're endorsing the war, like ROTC?" David would say, if she told him the truth. "Get pregnant to get out if you have to. A baby's a bummer, yeah, but people are dying, and you're tacitly saying it's acceptable, right?"

She felt he was an agent of her conscience, like a lurking beast flapping about her, an angel of either white liberation or black destruction.

She heard a rustle and looked up to see David staring down at her from center stairs, as if he were reading her mind. When he was sure he'd caught her eye, he stepped up on a chair and stood with his arms wide.

"We have a plan," he announced to the room. "There's going to be an emergency session of the Student Senate tonight, right now."

"A goddamn meeting?"

"We should be in the streets!"

"It's for the only thing we can do," David said loudly but calmly.

Push-back continued to sputter at him.

"Kids are dead, and you want a meeting?"

"This is bull. We need an explosion. Match violence with violence."

"It *is* a statement," David answered. "Listen, I get it. You're mad; you're infuriated. But do you know why?"

"Because they're fucking shooting at us."

"Yes, and that's bad. That's unbelievable. But that happened yesterday. Do you know why you're mad right now, this second?"

He let it sit for a minute. She watched him use the power of his full height as he stood stick straight, arms still out and raised above them all.

"You're mad because you don't have any power. You're mad because you're too young to vote but not to be drafted."

"Yeah," responded a few weak voices.

"You're mad because you fought back, and they answered you with the lottery."

"Yeah," answered many more voices.

"You're mad because now they are gunning us down, and you don't think there's a damn thing you can do about it."

"Yeah!" The crowd bellowed back, and David watched as the match he lit took fire.

"You're wrong," he said. "You've got more power than you think. We are going to unite against the only thing we can. You've heard the calls to vote the war machine off campus. We're going to get rid of ROTC, right now, once and for all. Tonight! We've tallied all the ballots and moved up the Student Senate meeting. We'll show them we have a voice and we know how to use it."

Judy's heart sank.

Responses sailed back, half supporting and half incredulous.

"Is it *really* all we can do?" Achilles asked, a genuine question.

"All? What do you want, a riot?" David shot back. "More dead students?"

The two of them stared each other down in a moment of tight silence.

David then returned to the crowd and spoke again. "You don't think this can be a movement that can spread, campus to campus, across the country? Don't you see it can be a message to Washington that we aren't going to allow them to continue to pull from our ranks for their dirty war? They Can Shoot Us, But They Can't Recruit Us!"

"Come on," he beckoned. "Say it! They Can Shoot Us, But They Can't Recruit Us!" The crowd joined in. "They Can Shoot Us, But They Can't Recruit Us!"

"We can do it." He looked at Achilles, who had started nodding. "We have to do it."

Judy realized she was nodding as well. Vida was right, the timing had caught up with the concept. Yes, David would use anything, but this time it made sense. The killing, all the killing had to stop, and this is where they could make that start to happen.

"Yes, we *have* to do it," Achilles shouted back

Cheers of agreement drowned out the boom, boom beat of the song.

"Yeah!"

"Right on!"

"Let's do it!"

David let it run for a while.

"Listen," he waved his hands. "They moved the meeting to the ballroom so we can all get in. Quick, get up there."

They followed Achilles, streaming up the stairs to the second-floor ballroom. David slowly stepped down from the chair and held his hand out to Judy. She took it and looked up into his eyes.

Her head was still pounding so loudly she couldn't even hear the lyrics. There was nothing but the throbbing bass along the floor, pulsing up the length of her body and settling right behind her eyes, louder and louder. If ROTC went, WRAIN would be next. Her life, as she'd planned it, would be over. But when David pulled her hand slightly, she stepped over the line with him and headed up the stairs.

❀ ❀ ❀

THE Union ballroom had been reconfigured to accommodate the crowd, with tables arranged in a large U. The student senators sat ready for action. Student spectators jammed around them in every chair, in all the aisles. It was as if the whole school wanted, needed, to be part of it. Their previous factions were all mixed up: the Greeks, the Trots, the Blacks, her group. Kent State had made them one.

"We have a vote at last," Wizard said, once the meeting had been called to order.

As the newest senator, he jockeyed for the honor to call for the motion: ROTC was to be eliminated from the CIU campus as a symbol of the "aggression without representation" of the war in Vietnam. Various senators, including Donnell, stood up to speak of the government that was now murdering the very students it was recruiting to fight that war.

"It might only be a token victory," Wizard said, "since there are only twenty-six students enrolled in ROTC at CIU, but still, it's twenty-six fewer body bags. This is our statement."

"We've got the ballots! We *do* have a voice, we *do* have a vote, after all. All those who agree, say 'aye.'"

"Aye!" came the response, loud and forceful. The crowd cheered. David, Vida, and even Lori, were cheering. Everyone. Judy started to cheer. It felt great.

"It's our hope," Donnell said, standing up, "that this will be the beginning of a movement that will spread across the country, a meaningful rebellion and a message to Washington."

"Yes!" David yelled, raising his fist. He didn't even seem to care that Donnell had taken his line.

The cheers that joined him were deafening, the release of tension palpable. Judy felt tears brimming over. They were all tired, she realized, of feeling like victims passively sitting as kids their age were being selected for service—or now, gunned down.

For the first time, it seemed they all really believed they could make something happen.

She thought about Wil and September fourteenth and Michael and Howie and everyone else who had brought her to this moment and understood that, yes, it just had to all stop, now. There was nothing that wasn't worth making it stop. No one else could die. She started clapping like crazy.

Taylor Adams, the president of the Student Senate, called for order. An Alpha Delta business major, handsome and polished in his pressed slacks and shiny loafers, he had always been respected for his ability to handle the fractionalized Student Senate meetings, with a proven knack for being able to override even Donnell at his most obnoxious.

He paused for a long time scanning the crowd, then down at the table before him, and finally straight ahead, seeming to encompass the entire room.

"I'm sorry," he said. "I feel to join ROTC is an individual's choice. Anyone should be allowed to make it. I'm going to have to veto this."

The ballroom shrank into stunned silence. The crowd stood with their mouths gaping open, the senators' heads whipped anxiously from side to side, trying to figure out what had just happened. Swanson stood in the back. It was hard to know what side he was on.

"No," Wizard said, standing up. "Taylor, I'm sorry. But what may have seemed logical at some point is no longer viable. The stakes have changed. They're shooting us. You talk about choice? The draft offers no choice."

"If there was no choice *not* to go, why should there still be a choice *to* go?" Donnell chimed in.

Judy thought that made perfect sense.

"We just voted. Don't you see that vetoing this takes away

the only voice we have?" Wizard said. "How are you any different from the government not letting us vote at all?"

"I'm sorry," Taylor said, as if he really meant it. "It's done." He slammed the gavel on the table.

Screaming and shouting merged into a loud, agonized wail. Judy felt the pressure rush back, and was afraid nothing would contain it now. Hundreds of students ran from the ballroom yelling, every fist clenched in defiance. And then, as they passed through the doors and filed down the stairs in front of the Union, Judy heard it—the sound of that first window breaking, a sound as terrifying as a rifle shot, a chilling signal that all bets were off, all order gone.

The breaking glass stopped many. Judy was paralyzed. The crowd stepped over the shards in front of the Union and split up, confused. A contingent headed toward town, but she was terrified of being in the middle of a fractured mob. Repelled and emboldened at the same time, and very, very frightened, she joined the group running for the dorms.

What was left of the ROTC office was being guarded by two rows of men in fatigues standing at attention, probably the entire ROTC cohort. She slowed as she passed, looking for Pete, and lost a step. She couldn't make out which one he was. She was bumped into then drawn violently back into the crowd just as she saw his head turn toward her. There was no stopping as she was propelled forward.

Hundreds of them ended up in front of the electrical building, two stories of soaring glass windows through which you could see pipes and grid work, all the bones of what was needed to keep the campus illuminated. A nearby pile of construction debris from a new garden feature meant to soften the building's appearance was irresistible. The first stone didn't break the glass. The second was bigger, more of a rock. It made a clean round pocket of a hole, edges white with splinters. After that, a shower of projectiles assaulted the building.

"Here's my vote," said someone, who threw a piece of metal that hit the building's façade with a huge screech. Others followed, "Mine, too!" "ROTC off the goddamn campus!" "Stop the War with THIS!" "Remember Kent State."

Judy saw David, Wizard, Lori, and Achilles pick up stones from the garden and hurl them, again and again, their rage escalating with each loud *thwack*. Three guys pulled the bowl of a birdbath off its pedestal and smashed it to the ground, then threw the pieces and the pedestal itself against the building to inflict greater damage. Huge sheets of glass hit the ground, shattering as students ran for cover. A street sign was knocked over and its pole and plates were used to finish off the remaining glass. Students were hanging out of the windows of the nearby dorms encouraging them with cheers, many rushing down to join them. It was a bona fide riot, out of control. Judy was appalled by the twisted, triumphant looks on the faces of people she knew, Meldrich, Donnell, even RoMo.

But there were no police, no sirens. It was as if they were letting this part of campus be sacrificed.

Judy and Vida made their way to Wizard's dorm room, climbing in and out of his first-floor window to monitor what was going on. They heard a series of small, erratic explosions and watched as the electrical building went dark, their lights went off, and the eerie night descended like a heavy, opaque curtain over the campus. They stared out the window at the blackness, until their eyes adjusted, and they could make out shapes and forms by the light of the nearly full moon. They heard shouts, thuds, and the scrape of metal against stone. People were running, yelling—no longer slogans—just to each other for safety.

Their entire group eventually made it to Wizard's room.

They sent alternating sets of scouts to check out the source of shouts and unidentified sounds. RoMo began to scream hysterically when they heard a series of pops while Wizard was out. Vida took her by the shoulders and shook her. "Get it together," she said. "We've all got to keep it together." Then RoMo hugged her, holding on tight for longer than Judy thought possible. Sheila was in the corner, huddled with her yarn, knitting furiously like Madame Defarge, while the guys paced in frustration and to keep sharp.

"If this is the revolution," Meldrich said, "we need to be ready."

Chapter 40

THE STUDENTS UPENDED THE CAMPUS AND SURROUNDING community overnight. The group that headed to town broke every window they could find. Elsewhere, they pulled out shrubs, overturned benches, opened fire hydrants, and set cars on fire. Someone sprayed ROTC OFF CAMPUS and BRING THE TROOPS HOME NOW across storefronts in bright paint that seeped into historic concrete along the street in the century-old town square. The police followed this group, rather than the one that stayed on campus. The bandana guy from the strike meeting back in September was arrested as the ringleader with a dozen others, but it all happened so fast that most of the crowd had outrun the police and dispersed into the woods of the lagoon before capture.

The *Clarion* documented it all in a special edition the next day, labeling it "Riot Nite," and quoting Swanson in an editorial: "Your actions these days will say who you are . . . or who you aren't . . . and could ever hope to become . . . the character that college builds."

Swanson protested by indicating it was out of context, that he had said it about something different back during the Moratorium, but to most it still rang true.

The Trots didn't waste a minute. They went to President Jones and proposed a peaceful event with security to honor the Kent State dead. The resulting Solidarity March the next night was an ineffectual delight only the administration could love. It was covered by local media to demonstrate that order had been restored. Greeks joined freaks in a parade around the dorms.

Dozens of frat boys and sorority girls, tired of being told they were apathetic, donned white headbands and served as overly zealous marshals, practically holding hands to keep marchers stuck to the sidewalks while filing past the riot-trashed electrical building. They walked slowly, four abreast.

"What an embarrassment," Meldrich said.

"Be sure to keep off the grass," David yelled, as he and Vida led a breakout group running and cheering down the middle of the streets, taunting the obedient marchers, and drawing more recruits by the minute. "Kent State will really appreciate the support!"

Judy participated as if in a dream, trying not to think, just aware she had to be there.

The protest continued into a third night when an informal group staged a spontaneous sit-in on the highway bridge just over the creek that fed the lagoon, the main artery from town before the turnoff into campus. Word came back to the Tune Room that it was calm; they were singing and smoking grass.

Wizard checked it out and reported back that it was so tame that President Jones was to be joining the demonstrators.

"Just as I thought," David said. "It's a PR move."

Achilles said he didn't care how calm it was, anything done in the name of the Kent State fallen was something they should be part of. Judy agreed. They argued back and forth.

"I don't care. I'm not going for another walk-around-the-block demonstration or pansy sit-in," Meldrich said. "Imagine what Michael would have thought of those bozos."

"In the spirit of Michael Marek," David, Vida, and Wizard joined him, bumping their fists.

"I hope that's for solidarity and not violence," said a voice from behind them.

They turned to see Swanson approaching their table. He

walked over to them and bent down, leaning his forearm next to David's. "Listen," he said quietly but firmly. "I can tell where you're going with all this, and I just want you to know that things need to settle down, way down."

"What do you mean?" David said. "You don't think Kent State deserves a response?"

"A response, yes, but any more violence and you guys can be up on that poster wall." He pointed to the banner that said KENT STATE 4, CIU?

David started to stand up. "Did someone send you, or do you think you can scare us?"

Swanson put a hand on his shoulder and pushed him down, bending lower and looking around the table, directing his words to each of them.

"Pay attention. This is very serious. Laws are being trampled that have nothing to do with the message you're trying to send. Those shopkeepers who got their windows broken and their stores vandalized don't understand why you took it out on them, and they aren't going to risk any more. That fire after Lottery Night brought a lot of new attention to CIU, and Riot Nite capped it."

David started to stand up again, and Swanson pushed down harder.

"No one knows who did it. Just like they don't know who trashed the windows downtown or in the electrical building, or set the cars on fire. But you were all in that renegade group that broke off after the Solidarity March, and that was noticed.

"My advice to you is just to let things calm down. Kent State was a step too far; the entire country knows that. Give things a chance to work themselves out before something worse happens." He gave David's shoulder a final shake, looking right into his eyes.

"*Zeeze,*" David said. "Ease up."

"You don't know what's happened, do you?" Swanson said, stepping back, surprised. "That bridge being blocked is on a state road. The National Guard is here."

THEY headed for the bridge as fast as they could run, following David, not sure what they would do when they got there. When they arrived, they came to a halt. The bridge was packed with hundreds of seated, seemingly happy figures bordered by about two dozen uniformed and armed guards blocking the way to town. They saw President Jones, in his CIU baseball cap, sharing the peace sign and chatting with students as if they were at a picnic. There were flowers in the barrels of some of the guns. They had done that at Kent State, too, Judy had heard. She shivered.

They couldn't understand what was going on and stood by the lagoon watching the calm, unchanging scene in front of them for the longest time. Then, Achilles walked onto the bridge and stepped around people, angling for a place to sit. Judy followed. One by one, cautiously, the others joined them. They were about fifty yards from Jones. It had to be safe. But what was it, exactly? Judy wondered.

They got comfortable and asked about what was happening. The Guard had come and everyone had been spooked at first, but Jones was with them. He wasn't going to let anything bad happen on his campus was the story.

They relaxed and settled in with the others. It was cool, everyone was saying. Eventually Meldrich and some of the others even started smoking the joints that were being passed in full view of the president and the Guard.

Suddenly there was a human ripple, bodies leaping up. Judy

couldn't see a thing, but Achilles was tall and could see over most of the heads.

"Shit," he said, grabbing her hand. "They're charging. With guns! Run!"

He pulled her along one of the grassy berms bordering the lagoon. They sped past others, jumping over those who hadn't yet had time to stand, heading toward the Union for safety. There was screaming and splashing, and Judy realized many of the protestors had actually jumped into the lagoon to get out of the Guard's way.

She had never been so frightened. She couldn't breathe.

Someone yelled "Tear gas!" and she pushed herself to go faster. She had heard tear gas would melt contact lenses, right against your eyeballs. When she thought her lungs would explode, she wrenched her hand from Achilles and watched him speed ahead on his long legs, through the water at the edge of the lagoon. A guy in front of her turned, and the color drained from his face. The Guard must have been seconds behind them. There was no time to turn and look. She ran faster, way past adrenaline. If she made it, she told herself, she would never smoke again. She kept moving toward the light of the Union Tower, up the hill to the Administration Building, past the Science Building, the house where the ombudsman had his office, and finally up the Union steps. The noise was barely human—like animals screaming—wailing and shouting. But no shots . . . not yet.

JUDY finally reached the Union door, joining the stream into the Tune Room, where she collapsed on the dirty carpet. Dozens—maybe a hundred people—were on the floor, trying to catch their breath. She heard whispered voices, David's and Vida's, even Lori's among them.

"Sit up, like you've been here all night."

"Mix in."

"If you're on the floor, cross your legs."

Someone handed her a lit cigarette.

It was a few minutes before the National Guard stormed in. They hadn't been as close behind as she'd feared. The soldiers were taken aback. They halted and looked around fiercely at the seated students. At a signal from the leader, they huddled for an instant, then started grabbing students. It took Judy a few seconds to realize they were targeting anyone who was wet, knowing that they had been through the lagoon on their way from the bridge. People moved silently to hide anyone still damp, but the soldiers yanked them by their coats and collars, pulling them out from under tables, from back along the wall.

There was a huge scramble. Judy saw David and Vida rearranging their chairs, obviously hiding someone.

All of a sudden, Achilles walked slowly and deliberately out to the center of the room, his Hush Puppies squishing, his jeans so heavy with damp, they were falling from his hips. Evidence was dripping from the edges of his shoulder-length hair and moustache. Judy threw her hands over her mouth to keep from yelling out.

"Why?" he cried to the Guard soldiers. "Why are you doing this?"

He repeated it again and again, as two of them took him by the arms and dragged him out, his voice echoing as they pulled him up the stairs.

"Why are you doing this? Why?"

One of his shoes fell off. Judy and the others stood, looking up the staircase until they could no longer hear his voice.

The story was that President Jones had given the signal for the Guard to advance as soon as he left the bridge. He had been in on it.

"Why?"

Chapter 41

DAVID'S DESIRE FOR RECOGNITION WAS FINALLY FULFILLED when CIU hit the news. The media was following the National Guard closely after Kent State, and the events of their charge and Riot Nite were all over the papers, from the local shopper in their small university town, to the *Chicago Tribune* and the *Chicago Sun-Times*, where CIU was featured along with their great rival, the University of Illinois, and finally to the *New York Times* and the *Washington Post.*

The coverage pointed out that there had actually been three times the number of National Guard visible on the bridge. The main force was in formation at the other end of town with the retailers, who assumed they would be facing another onslaught of vandalism. President Jones, by letting the smaller force charge, had actually saved the day, it said.

"Jones, a hero? Tell that to Achilles and the other students in jail. There's not a single student on campus who can support what the government did at Kent State, or who doesn't understand what we tried to do to answer it responsibly with our ROTC vote," David said to the *Clarion*. He was careful not to take personal ownership for Riot Nite but instead made it more of a "what did you expect?" after the ROTC veto. "We're not kids. It's important we take a stand on what will happen to our lives."

He even mentioned Wil, and they ran his photo again alongside David's, as he pledged to carry on. His last quote was, "It's not over yet. Dare to Struggle. Dare to Win."

The campus was effectively a ghost town. It was only officially closed again for a week, but most students had left on their own, been picked up by worried parents, or were secluded in various enclaves around town.

Judy didn't know where RoMo was, maybe at Wizard's. Sheila was no doubt shacked up with someone, so Vida moved into her room. She was out most of the time, though, liaising from place to place to ferret out remaining radicals and keep everyone in touch, stopping in now and then to provide updates about what she had learned.

"The national SMC is pretty spooked," she said.

"You've heard about the spies?"

Word was that several members of the Student Senate were being followed. One, the heavy-set woman Judy remembered seeing in the Swanson lecture at the Moratorium, had gone underground. There was a rumor that a janitor at Southern Illinois University had found a list of state SMC members in a wastepaper basket in a student's room and had shared it with the FBI. For Judy, it was one more step into panic. Not only would she be on the list, but as part of the Steering Committee, she would be considered one of the instigators. This was way beyond losing her army scholarship; she could be arrested, just like Abbie Hoffman and the others at the Democratic Convention.

David had moved in with her. He hadn't been invited exactly, but when the dorms closed, he didn't have anywhere else to go. He'd brought his stereo and his speakers. The small room was already crammed tight with two of everything: beds, desks, bookshelves. When he sat on the bottom bunk, his long arms could reach half the room, from the stereo to anything on her desk, and he could cover the room's length in three strides when the coast was clear and he sneaked out to the john in the hall. Even now, she could get evicted if she was caught with a boy upstairs.

The phone rang at regular intervals ever since the news hit. Judy would listen to it ring four times, five times, knowing it would stop after six. Her mother calling. It must be making her crazy that she couldn't pump Maggie for information anymore.

In midafternoon of the third day after the National Guard charge, there was a commotion on the landing, the signal for David to bolt into Vida's room, and the sound of determined feet coming up the stairs.

Judy didn't even wait for the knock before opening the door.

"Hi, Mom," she said, surprising her slightly, the only edge she knew she would have.

Her mother recovered immediately and strode into the room, her eyes resting on the makeshift coffee table David had fashioned from one of his boxes. It held a wide, homemade pottery ashtray, filled with a backlog of cigarette butts, ashes, and roaches. Judy was pretty sure her mother had never seen a roach but, nonetheless, stepped in front of the box to cut off her view as casually as she could.

Her mother pulled out one of the desk chairs and sat down, surveying every inch of the room. Judy followed her gaze for anything that would obviously scream it belonged to David, or any man.

"You think this is better than the dorm?" she said.

Judy made a face as if to say, "Maybe?"

"I've been calling."

"I'm sorry, I haven't been here much. It's been a crazy time. My friend Wil died, you know, just before this all hit."

"I thought that was back before Thanksgiving?"

"That was Michael. Wil was another friend," she said, realizing how odd this must sound. She wondered if her mother even believed her. "He was a Number One in the lottery and died in basic training, a total waste. We had the same birthday. I told you about it in a letter."

"Ah yes, the letter." Her mother sighed and put the large purse she had on her lap on the floor, then sat back with her elbows on the chair arms, her hands tightly clenched.

"Of course, it's too bad about your friend, and I'm sorry." She paused, sucking back her chin and recalibrating. Judy could tell she was thrown off her game by this need for compassion, and noticed, momentarily, the saddest look in her eyes. For a second, she felt they both wished that they could just talk about Wil right now.

Her mother shook her head, slightly. "But it's not why I've come. I want to know what's going on. You've totally cut off communication, and your school is all over the news. I suppose I don't have to ask what you've been doing."

Judy didn't answer.

"At least I didn't see your face on the front page of the newspaper, though I don't doubt you were in the middle of it."

Judy wanted to sigh, but stopped herself. "Don't sigh to me, young lady" was not something she could stand to hear right now.

"Your letter came on Tuesday," her mother said. "It was hardly what I needed to read in the middle of all this."

Judy had to rewind mentally and remember that Tuesday had been the worst of it. She had written the letter just before they'd heard about Kent State. It seemed like years ago.

"And then I can't get through to you."

"As you can see, I'm perfectly fine," Judy said.

"Don't be snotty. And this letter?" Her mother pulled it out of her purse as an exhibit.

Judy sighed, after all.

"You have nerve being impatient with *me*. Do you think I'm

happy about having to drive up here two hours in the middle of a workday? Would you rather I sent your father?"

There was a creak, then footsteps in the hall. David, Judy knew. He was outside the door, listening.

"You've only got a semester to go before you're off to Walter Reed." Judy's mother waved the letter at her. "And what's this about a conscience? Like no one else has one? You don't even realize what you're saying."

She was getting louder as she got angrier, and Judy was sure that David could hear. She didn't know what to do. She gave up her vigil in front of the ashtray and moved to the window opposite the door, hoping that if her mother turned to face her, he wouldn't be able to make out her words.

"Well?" her mother demanded.

"It's not like I knew what was going to happen when I sent that."

"I doubt that." Her mother opened the letter and shook the pages in Judy's face. "You say right here that something big is bound to happen. You even say it *needs* to happen."

"I didn't mean murder."

"Why do you always have to be so melodramatic?"

"I'm not," Judy said. "They shot students at Kent State. They could have shot us, too."

"They weren't going to shoot you, Judy."

"There were rifles pointed at us here, Mom. I was there. You weren't. After this week, I think I know better what the National Guard is capable of. It could have been just like at Kent State. . . . We all thought it would be."

Her mother drummed her hands on the chair arms and inhaled and exhaled deeply. Judy had thrown her again. She wondered if her mother was picturing her dead, or just wounded.

"The one thing that is certain is that if you keep this up,

you'll put your scholarship in jeopardy." She said it like she was reading it from her note cards. "The army isn't going to tolerate this point of view, you know."

The floor creaked again.

"What was that?"

"I didn't hear anything," Judy said. "And I don't need a lecture."

"Well, I think you do, given what's at stake and the things you've already done," she said. "I honestly don't know what's worse, getting a letter like this or not hearing from you at all."

"It's how I see things, Mom."

She was so tired. She tried to focus on something visual that would not be her mother's face or the imagined expression on David's, and sighted a curl in the wallpaper where it was peeling around the doorjamb, yellow flowers under blue stripes.

The squeal of a guitar cut the air: "I said you'd be free, didn't I?"

Judy jumped. Her mother swirled around in the desk chair. The familiar lyrics poured out of the tinny stereo in Vida's room.

"What is—"

"It's next door," Judy said. "These walls are pretty thin." She banged her fist on the wall. "Turn it down," she yelled, as if to her housemate. The volume went down slightly, but the song continued to play: "I told you one day you'd fly."

She banged again, and the volume inched lower.

"What's going on here?" her mother asked.

"Turn it off!" Judy screamed. Her mother gave her an alarmed look.

David obeyed this time.

"Why aren't you all in classes?"

"They were suspended when they called in the National Guard."

"Suspended? Is everyone gone?"

"Mostly."

"So what are *you* doing here?" her mother hissed.

She heard another noise through the wall, *zeeze.*

She considered just stepping out of the way.

"I'm just here," Judy said, worn out. "I just need to be here."

"There's no reason."

"After this week, I can't think of a bigger reason."

"You need to stay out of politics or you'll be sorry. This is temporary. That scholarship is your life, Judy," her mother said, with an uncharacteristic catch in her voice. "Please, I'm just trying to . . . just tone it down," she continued. "Be smart. Tell me you'll do that."

"Aren't I always smart?" Judy said, her own voice halting. "Didn't you teach me that?"

There was a moment when things might have been better between the two of them. But at the sound of clattering and a male voice swearing in the hall, her mother's eyes narrowed, and she turned toward the door.

"You have a man up here, don't you?" she said. "Of all things."

"Maybe you should just go, Mom."

She looked at Judy, shocked, then threw open the door and, at the sight of David, let out a disgusted huff.

She turned back to Judy. "Don't tell me *this* is your plan."

Judy didn't have time to respond.

"Well, that's final," her mother said, pushing past David and heading down the stairs.

"Thanks a lot," Judy said when he came in.

"Fuck that," he said, poised for a fight.

"I can't do round two, right now. I really can't," she said.

He grabbed her arm, holding her back so she had to twist away and didn't make it downstairs until her mother's car was out the drive, making the turn by the lagoon that led to the highway.

JUDY kept walking to the lagoon and then around it, up and down the berms, along the ring road, right through the reeds at the edge of the water. Going in one direction, she mapped out a plan to leave the army. She would call the head of her program and let the chips fall where they may. She could always get a job on campus and maybe reapply for that first scholarship she didn't get after a year or so. Maybe then she could find a teaching job somewhere other than Belmont Heights. That would work. That would be fine. She tried to remember if she had left anything at home that she would really need and decided she could make it on her own, as her mother had made clear she would have to do.

Walking in the other direction, she planned what she would do to stay in the military. She would have to cut herself off from current friends, but their ranks were already dwindling. She would swear David to silence by threatening to go to the FBI about the ROTC fire and throw herself on Pete's mercy. He would help her again, she knew. And she would keep her focus on being the best nurse she could to save all the Wils she would meet when she got to Vietnam. Pete was right. This would be a real, tangible contribution. She let it work itself through her. She really wouldn't have to do a single thing.

By the time she returned to her room, she had almost forgotten David would be there, waiting for her. The room was dark with smoke of all kinds, and she had to wave it off to see that he was lying on the bottom bunk, shirtless, with the huge ashtray on his stomach, puffing away. It was after twilight now, and the only light was from the closet, where he had left one of the bi-fold doors open. She could see all his stuff thrown at the bottom, under her relatively neat hangers.

She followed the light, cross-hatching across his chest, down the smooth hills around his nipples and wanted to trace its path with her tongue. She longed for them to be able to just lie against each other as simpler forms of life, without thinking brains that knew how to argue.

"I thought maybe you'd gone home with your mother, the way you ran after her," he said, taking a long, dramatic pull on his cigarette.

She took the desk chair her mother had vacated.

"So," he said. "You want to fill me in on the details, or have me tell you what I think I heard?"

What she wanted was for him to take her in his arms and make her feel completely and silently understood.

"All right," she said. "I know it's something I should have told you a long time ago, and I did try a few times, but you must realize now why I couldn't." She took a deep breath and just let it out. Let it be. "Yes, I'm in the army. I'm sure you put that together by now. That's my scholarship."

There was no massive explosion. The world did not come to a cataclysmic end. She wiggled her fingers and saw that she was still intact.

David smoked his cigarette nearly down to its end.

She told him the story, giving him the broad strokes of how the scholarship was her only way to go to college, something he should understand since he knew what it was like not to have money. Then, she backed up to explain about her mother, which was easier now that he had witnessed this afternoon's scene. Finally, she described what had brought her to the Tune Room and why having the same birthday as the Number One had freaked her out so much.

"So you're ROTC?" he asked.

"Essentially."

"This is all starting to make sense," he said. "That's why you weren't in the Lottery Performance, right? And why you kept fighting me on the ROTC campaign?"

She nodded hopefully.

He moved slightly, angling toward her, making the light pattern skitter from skin to sheet and back again.

"Who else knows?"

She shook her head, of all the responses she had anticipated and planned for . . . "That's not what matters, David."

"It matters to me."

The light stopped playing around his form.

"You're the only one who knows, David. The others are dead, Michael and Wil." There was no reason to mention Pete.

"You told Michael?" he asked, sharply. "What did he say?"

"What does that have to do with . . ." She stopped and sank down in the chair. "I never got a chance to talk to him about it. I'm not even sure he heard me."

David sat up, put the ashtray aside, and leaned forward with his elbows on his knees. "Well, I'll tell you what he'd say. He'd say you're supporting the war however you try to justify it. He'd tell you to screw your mother, grow a backbone, and get out."

Judy sighed, expecting as much.

"On the other hand . . ." He paused thoughtfully. "I bet he'd also say, let's use it."

"What?"

He jumped up and started pacing the room. "I mean, holy shit. This could be the biggest thing ever. You're in ROTC, and you give it up publicly as a gesture so we can get it off campus, once and for all. That, on top of Kent State . . . it'll really get the campaign going."

"David, that's *not* going to happen," Judy said. "And you can't tell anyone. Not *anyone*. I could lose my scholarship entirely and have to pay the army back with money I no longer have. I've been AWOL. That's a crime."

He didn't say he understood or fold her in his arms in appreciation of what she had been through for the past semester. He didn't kiss the top of her head or any part of her.

"A crime," she repeated. "Like the one you committed when you set off those fireworks."

DAVID stomped out of the room and slammed the door. Within minutes she heard music blasting at top volume from Vida's room. It wasn't a song she recognized. There was a loud smack against the common wall and the sound of plastic hitting the floor—the Argent album, she was sure. More crashing and thumping sounds followed, startling her at first. Then, she began to guess what they were—books hitting the floor, one at a time, then a whole shelf at once, a chair overturned, hangers pulled from the closet, something fragile shattering against the floor. She tried to visualize Vida's room, hoping he wasn't taking it out on anything she considered sentimental or valuable. She wondered if he was picturing her face as he punched away at Vida's things.

When the sounds stopped, the music got even louder: heavy, heavy metal, with a relentless pounding beat. She hadn't moved from the chair and couldn't think, feeling assaulted by all the noise. None of this was how she imagined this going, when she went over it in her head so many times, as far back as the Moratorium. She thought she'd planned for virtually any scenario, but not her mother revealing her secret, and never David wanting to exploit her like this. Had she been ridiculously naïve about him? Yes, obviously this was the real David. The one she'd loved had been in her head.

When the album was over, there was silence and suspense. When nothing happened, she pulled herself up from the chair heavily and stood in the center of the room, staring at the enormous ashtray sitting in the middle of the bottom bunk.

The door opened, there was movement behind her, and suddenly he was back on the bed, sitting, folding and unfolding his hands, getting ready.

"I don't know who you are anymore?" he said, facing but not exactly looking at her. "How can you call me a criminal? That fire was a necessary statement. You think I could just sit and watch that sick death game and do nothing? Look what happened to Wil? You think I should have done that? What if I'd been Number One? Any of us could have been; that's the whole point." He spoke as if he had rehearsed it in those silent minutes in Vida's room, like he had note cards.

Judy sat back in the chair. She wasn't sure how to begin, or if he even expected her to say anything.

"You know, I thought we were in this together, that you were the woman, I mean a woman who . . ."

Judy's heart started pounding. She wondered if there was something worth saving here, and at the same time wondered why she was even considering it.

"It's not me who's saying you're a criminal, David. I'm just pointing out that you . . . that both of us . . . have done things we could be prosecuted for, and we need to be very careful about what we do now." She spoke very slowly, so he would fully appreciate what she was saying. "So we don't inadvertently get each other in trouble that's much more serious than we intend."

"But do you really think it was a crime?"

"I don't think you meant to blow up the whole block, no. I get the fireworks. I know you thought they'd be harmless. But even then it was a government building, and you had to know they wouldn't just let that go. And then it was just a huge fire. David, people could have been hurt."

"I'm so sick of everyone saying that. It was just property, not people. They deserve to be hit in their pocketbook. It's the only thing they care about. If they cared about people, they wouldn't be sending us to Vietnam."

She sat down next to him and took his hand. "I understand," she said, then checked herself, remembering his tirade about women and understanding before Lottery Night. He didn't seem to notice. Her mind was all over the place. She obviously still cared about him, maybe even loved him, but even so, she needed to get him off the idea about her going public. "Let's take a walk. I keep seeing my mother in that chair. I need to get out of this room."

They went to the lagoon and walked around silently, holding hands, which she felt they both needed in order to remember what they meant to each other, so this political stuff could be pushed away.

David started rustling through the reeds at the shore and came up with a handful of stones he proceeded to skip, one by one, across the water. He gave her a few, and they laughed at each other's skill, or lack of it. Judy relaxed, relieved, and was ready to turn back, remembering how the light had danced across his chest earlier. David finished off with a spectacular skip that went nearly three-quarters across the water toward the other side of the lagoon, then turned to her.

"You know, my situation doesn't even compare to yours," he said, refusing to follow her. He picked up another stone and threw it in the water, not even trying to skip. "You've been lying all this time. You're just like those military freaks, trying to have it both ways."

Here it comes, she knew. He went on, repeating his ROTC rap. She sat on the grass while he paced around her, alternatively waving his arms in frustration and throwing stones with increasing fury. He reminded her of Pete. She kept her head down, knowing he had to say his piece and feeling she deserved the tirade, after her deception.

"How do I know you're *not* a spy for the military?" he said.

"Be serious."

"It could be true. You could be ready to turn me in."

"I would have done it by now, David. Come on."

"There's really only one way I'd believe that," he said. "Do it! Come clean and announce that you're giving it all up, just like I said. Then I'll be able to really trust you."

She got up and started back toward the house. There had really been no progress at all. He followed her, yelling most of the time. He called her a "radical wannabe," and she retaliated by yelling back that he was more interested in being big man on campus than stopping the war, calling him "a kid playing with firecrackers." After defending himself violently, he settled into his usual argumentative tone of voice, relentlessly laying out the options and why this way was the only way . . . and the best thing she could do.

When they got back to her room, she blocked him from coming in.

"Enough," she said. "I will not do this, and you will not say anything about me . . . to anyone. Certainly not in public, like you're suggesting."

"We'll see," he taunted.

She slammed the door.

Later he came back, pushed past the door's pathetic lock and started up again. She didn't want him there but knew it was too risky for him to be out potentially talking to people with his temper up.

They spent the night resetting their relationship, mostly the political side of it. Judy tried to reason, then had to beg, then finally threaten to be sure David wouldn't use her situation for his own ends, which he said were the country's ends, repeatedly, to the point where she made him sleep downstairs in Sheila and RoMo's room. In the morning, he finally agreed to keep her confidence, though she knew it was only because he was unsure about his own potential criminal standing, and that he could change back at any minute.

Chapter 42

THEY WERE WARY OF EACH OTHER AS THEY MADE THEIR way to the SMC meeting the next evening. Attending another meeting was the last thing Judy wanted to do, but she knew she had to keep her eye on David. Aside from that, she was exhausted at the thought of it. She had been to so many of these gatherings and was sure how this one would play out, factions fighting over small victories.

And yet, David was right as he shamed her into coming along; this was no time to hide. She still couldn't believe the National Guard had actually gunned down students, then come to her own campus, ready to do it again. Her friends could have been killed. She could have been killed herself, all for trying to do the right thing by trying to end a war where thousands were getting killed. She felt she was in the middle of one of Sartre's absurdist plays, something that was so bizarre there was no way it could be true. Running from the Guard that night had been the most terrifying moment of her life. If Kent State hadn't started the revolution, nothing would.

She knew she had to be part of what would happen next. The Solidarity March had splintered factions and gotten nowhere. There had been dozens of arrests after the night on the bridge. Achilles was still in jail. And now Vida had heard the administration was going to cancel finals, close the campus for the rest of the semester, and send everyone home, effectively ending the school year, this time for good. If that happened, they would lose months. Worse, it would appear that the students didn't care enough, that Kent State had been acceptable, and that they were fair game.

As they walked to the meeting, Judy listened as David worked out his arguments to the anticipated agenda, trashing his imagined opponents. Phrases and words penetrated her awareness: "need a bigger statement, street action, march, jail, pigs." She tried to concentrate on what David was saying, but she felt distant, like a reporter from another country come to survey the aftermath of a disaster.

The meeting was to be held in Reavis West, the ugliest of the campus high-rises. Inside, dozens of identical, windowless classrooms featured the floor plan that had followed them since grade school—fifty metal chairs lined up in hard rows, each with its own attached writing table. Tonight, one of the rooms had been liberated for the meeting, offering itself up, picked clean and sanitized, with a fresh blackboard and a single, emptied wastebasket.

When they arrived, David raced ahead of her, duster flying, and made his way to the center of the room, shoving chairs out of alignment.

"This is the people's meeting room," David said, heading for the front, pulling chairs out of rows as he went. "We are announcing a new order, as of today, of the people."

Meldrich, Wizard, and others joined in, even some of the SDSers and a few low-level Trots. The crowd filled the seats quickly, then spilled into various sitting, leaning, and standing postures against chair legs, in the middle of the floor, and along the walls. New arrivals picked among extended and crossed legs, ducked under arms, nudged for room. The mostly male sea of jeans and Salvation Army fatigues was mildly unruly but anticipatory, like a class settling down or an imitation army awaiting orders. Within minutes, cigarettes were lit, ashes dropped, wrappers discarded to the floor, books dumped, jackets draped over chairs, and the occupation complete.

But new order aside, there was still a head table, Judy noticed, commandeered by a small band of efficient, blue-jeaned bureaucrats.

"Goddamn Trots," David said to Judy. "Jesus, you take a breath and they take over." He pointed her to a seat next to him right up front, "in their faces," as he put it. He motioned for Vida, RoMo, Meldrich, and Sheila to join them.

Judy watched Lori huddle with Donnell, Sorsa, the usual cast of characters. David was right; the Trots were like locusts, swarming over everything, ready to slam down the opposition and take control for the sake of control.

Tonight, they were angling with David for leadership of the entire movement at CIU. Everyone knew the campus was at a crossroads, and what would happen next was crucial. Were they going to keep on rioting and risk getting shot by the National Guard, or was there something else they could do?

Judy was surprised when Sorsa stood up to chair the meeting. He was still so new, all nervous energy and constantly fluttering fuzzy locks. She assumed he was just a minor Trot. But he *was* black. She figured they must be training him for a bigger role.

"Are we gonna let 'em shut us down, or what?" Sorsa slammed his fist on the table, opening the meeting with a surprise roar that snapped the crowd to attention.

"No way!" A voice said from somewhere in the back of the room, echoed by at least a dozen others.

Sorsa grinned, and it was off. Anyone who wanted to talk did so by yelling louder than whoever had the floor, popping up and down with a better opening line or a savage quip.

"Let me get this straight . . ."

"Oh, anything but that . . ."

But to Judy, it quickly became background noise. She struggled to focus on the usual recommendations, "petitions . . . takeover . . . barricade," but her attention wandered instead across the faces, which were both familiar and not, as if she were bad tripping like Wil and had slipped into that second world where everything was the same but somehow ominous. It was clear there had been little sleep, lots of grass. The room felt thick with the strain of waiting for the next blow, some embracing the tension full out, others just bracing themselves.

Sorsa pranced back and forth like a rock star, playing to the crowd, never straying far from his back-up band at the head table, obviously letting him have his moment. He was so into it, at any minute Judy half expected him to strip off his shirt and spray sweat on the front row.

David took the position as his heckler, and Sorsa pushed him, the two of them peppering cracks among crowd comments.

"What are you gonna do, tell me to vote?"

"Yeah, let's do that. Anyone here twenty-one yet?"

"Right, the good old political process. Didn't we try that? Can anyone spell V . . . E . . . T . . . O?"

The crowd responded as a wave, rising up to cheer as one speaker finished, then receding to rise again and agree with the next.

"Shut it, GagMan." Sorsa finally let it rip. "No one wants you . . ."

"Uncle Sam does," David stood up to acknowledge the raised fists, gleefully regaining the crowd. "He always wants me!"

"I guess he wants me too; I'm seventy-two."

"I'm thirty-seven."

The inevitable one-upping began, and Judy wondered how long it would go on this time before someone was identified as having the lowest lottery number in the room.

Then, surprising them all, Sheila asked, "Did anyone else think they were going to shoot us?"

"Damn straight, they would have," someone said, after a beat of silence, restarting the ping-pong of comments.

"Naw, they wouldn't have dared."

"You think those were play rifles?"

"Oh, were you scared, little girl?" a male voice asked in a sing-song playground taunt. Sheila shrank back.

"We were all scared," Judy said, annoyed at the wobble in her voice.

"Well, then it's a good thing Uncle Sam doesn't want you," Sorsa snapped back at her. Lori was smiling.

The meeting continued. It was raucous, interrupted regularly by cheers of "Yeah!" and "Right On!"

"Is that all we've got?" David said, at one point. "Marches? Meetings?" Judy recognized the opening lines of his argument and knew he was ready for his move. "We have chapters at five universities throughout the state. We should—"

"The state? When we have a whole country at stake?" Sorsa quickly segued to a new option, the plan all along, Judy realized. "They're going to shut us down anyway . . . let them close the campus . . . then align with schools across the country over the summer . . . come back in the fall with a real political response.

"We do this, and we're back in control." Sorsa's volume increased. "We do this, and we *take away their targets!*"

"Yes!" the crowd yelled back.

Sorsa leaned against the head table, smiling. Donnell gave him a soul handshake, gripping him high up by the elbow.

David sat paralyzed, ignored by the crowd.

Then came a voice Judy hadn't heard before, an older guy. "You know how many people will die before fall?"

"Listen, man. Didn't I just say we'd be taking away their targets?" Sorsa said. "We won't even be here to shoot at—"

"I mean how many in Vietnam," the guy said. "Are we here to stop the university administration, or are we here to stop the war?"

"He's got a point," Judy heard someone say.

The crowd sputtered, murmurs started to ramp up in agreement.

"May I finish?" Sorsa said.

"I think we get it," the older guy responded. "You call it taking targets away. I call it cutting and running." He paused. "I say, you leave campus, you've lost. You've got your own casualties now, your own body bags. Kent State gave them to you. Use 'em."

"Like you know."

"I do know a lot about casualties," he said with a half-smile. "I was there."

"Who is that guy?" Judy heard more than one person whisper.

"Connay, Robert Connay," he said.

His name matched the label on his fatigue jacket, and Judy knew they were looking at the real thing. She shifted, tugging at her own army surplus. She had never been this close to an actual Vietnam vet before. No one even pretended not to stare.

Judy and most of the others repositioned themselves to face him. He had survived his six seconds, Judy thought in awe.

He was tall, raw boned, and she wondered how she hadn't seen him earlier. His thick dark hair reached his shoulders, framing cut cheekbones and a gray complexion without a speck of blood. His jacket hung on him, as if he had once been bigger.

Judy reeled off war images like movies in her head: jungles, snipers, tunnels. He did what she was terrified she would never be able to do—stay hyperalert and hear and see everything, just to stay alive. She would have to do that, even as a nurse.

"That's what they want, don't you get that?" the vet said.

"They want you to go home, forget about Kent State and the war, and come back in the fall docile little students again."

"It worked after Lottery Night, didn't it?" Vida reminded them. "No wonder they think it'll work again. He's right."

"Makes sense," she heard someone say quietly.

The head table started buzzing. Chairs scraped.

"So, Connay, Robert," Lori said, coming around to take over. Sorsa, confused, stepped to the side. "Did you kill anybody when you were *there?*" Her angry voice rang out like a warning shot, straight over their heads, startling the room.

Connay looked her in the eye. "It was war," he said. "That's not the point."

"Oh yes, it very definitely *is* the point," Lori fired back. "It's the only goddamn point. Right?" she asked the crowd.

They responded with a weak, "Yeah." Then a stronger, "YEAH!"

"So did you or didn't you?" Lori asked again. "It's a simple question."

Don't answer, Judy wanted to scream.

"Did you or didn't you. . . . Did you or didn't you?" Lori continued, rapid fire.

"Come on, man, it's easy," Sorsa edged his way back in. "You offed 'em or you didn't. Gook got your tongue?"

Stop it! Judy continued to yell in her head. *Someone stop it!* David brushed off Judy's arm grab, his eyes locked on the Trot table.

"Yeah," the vet finally said softly, "I killed some people."

"Well, we don't listen to people who kill people here," Lori said, pushing Sorsa back with a raised arm. "We're here to *stop* people from killing people." She looked from the vet to the crowd. "Right?"

She pumped her fist into the air and started chanting, "Stop the Killing Now! Stop the Killing Now!"

The head table joined in, and soon the whole room was chanting. David started to raise his fist until he saw Judy. She couldn't believe it. She turned to Vida, who was frowning, dumbfounded.

"I bet you think you're a hero?" Lori yelled over the chanting, and it started to quiet down. "You know what I think?" She looked to test the crowd before firing her final salvo, "I think a brave man would have gone to Canada."

The room was dead silent. Judy looked at David and Vida and Wizard. No one would catch her eye.

"Stop the Killing Now," Lori yelled again, her fist back up. The crowd joined her, softly at first, then full-voiced, over and over.

Make it stop! Judy prayed. She couldn't take on Lori again, and this was too public . . . her scholarship. Someone please say something.

"Stop the Killing Now!" David had joined the chanting. Judy could not let this continue and steeled herself to speak. She rose, eyes closed, imagining them all wondering why she would want the floor.

But it was too late.

She opened her eyes.

Robert Connay had stood up. He scanned the room, expressionless, and walked out slowly, right past her, as if she weren't there, a whining, roaring, shattering silence in his wake.

An eternity went by as their wind returned to them.

Judy found her voice. "How dare you?" she glared at them.

She focused on David, who wouldn't look at her, then swept the room.

"How dare us all," she said, then walked out the same door Robert Connay had.

Chapter 43

"WAIT UP." VIDA CALLED.

Judy shrank at the sound of her voice but did slow down, cringing.

What she had done was so lame, and late, and pointless . . . and she felt absolutely contemptible. She wanted to be in pain, as Connay must have been so many times. She yanked on a dried branch of a small tree in front of her and broke it across her knee, hoping it would scratch her hands and she would bleed.

"Judy, wait."

She dropped the branch and sped up, passing the lagoon path, nearly home. She wondered for an instant if Connay was out here, maybe smoking a cigarette, wondering what it had all been for.

"Wait till you hear what happened." Vida caught up with her, panting. "Everyone else left, too."

Judy stopped.

"It's true. The whole place blew up. Lori tried to get the chanting going again, and Meldrich, of all people, told her to just shut the fuck up, and everyone left except her henchman up at the head table."

"What about David?"

"Dunno. He might have hung back with Lori. But you put him in his place." She grabbed Judy's shoulder to look her in the eye. "You put all of us there. We deserved it."

"Lot of good it did Connay," Judy said. "We're doing all this so more of us don't have to do what he had to do." She turned to Vida. "How did we forget that?"

They walked in silence, side by side.

Back at the house, they settled in Judy's room. Vida stretched out on the bottom bunk in David's favorite position with the ashtray on her stomach and lit up. Judy sat in a desk chair to take her boots off. She was moving slowly, like her feet weighed a thousand pounds.

"That was really brave of you, Judy," Vida said. "Frankly, I didn't think you had it in you."

"Apparently, I didn't. Not when it would have counted."

"Don't be so hard on yourself."

"We should never have let it happen, Vida. I should have stood up earlier; we all should have."

"I know why you didn't," Vida said. Judy looked up. "I'm clairvoyant, remember? What I don't get is why you didn't tell me all this time. I'm supposed to be your best friend." She took a drag and blew out a long smoke trail and followed it to Judy's face, dead on. "Why didn't you tell me you were in the army, Judy?"

Judy dropped her boot.

"David, of course," Vida went on. "He probably wasn't supposed to tell anyone, right?"

"He promised he wouldn't," Judy said. "I didn't tell him, Vida. He found out. I would have told you if I could have."

"I admit I was pretty pissed to hear it from him, of all people," Vida said, "but I suppose the signs were there. I knew you were always holding back and hiding, but hell, I thought you were just afraid. Should I be worried?"

"About what?"

"You know . . . everything. What we've planned, what we've done . . ."

"Vida, you can't be serious. I'm still the same person."

She went through her usual, elaborate smoking routine, working slowly with the pack, the match, the light. Then she put the ashtray aside and sat up, knees to knees with Judy.

"Are you? Why did you even walk in the Tune Room that day and let me think you were someone who *knows*? That I was your friend? That Wil was your friend?"

"Because it was true. You were, you are. And you're the one who taught me that I *know*."

Then Judy told her everything, answering all her questions. Unlike David, Vida wanted to know all the details, not only the facts, but what she had been feeling. Judy watched her face change from shock to softness and back again as the story unfolded. She brought her right up to the present, with the dilemma she now had facing her.

"So that's what you're trying to do, get out?" Vida asked.

"I'm still not sure. It's hard to explain."

"I think I get it," Vida said. "See if I have it straight." She inhaled as if she were getting ready to sing a long note. "Get your degree, sell your soul. Get knocked up to keep your soul and end up dropping out and back home with a kid, just like your mom told you was the worst thing you could do with your life. You'd be Maggie with a better conscience."

"I couldn't have put it better."

"And you'd still have all that tuition money to pay back."

"Oh yeah, there's certainly that. I think I could probably get out without having to get pregnant, but I wouldn't earn enough to get back into school for a long time, maybe years. I'd be back where I started from . . . worse."

"Oh, wow, that's heavy," Vida said. "So David's pushing you, I assume."

"He thinks it's all so clear and simple. No life without principles . . . you know."

"As if you'd be in this dilemma without principles. Besides, he can't get pregnant, and despite his bitching, his parents probably pay at least part of his tuition. What's he got to lose?"

Vida stood up and leaned against the windowsill. She ran her finger up and down the length of her nose, thinking, then pointed her cigarette at Judy. "He's planning something."

"I know, but I talked him out of it."

"No, I think it's something with Lori. He's hard enough to trust . . . but her . . ."

"You think it's about me?"

She shrugged. "I'm telling you because that's what friends do. You're still my best friend, get it?"

They hugged. Vida headed towards the door talking about how she would see what more she could find out, then stopped and turned at the threshold.

"This decision you have to make is tough, Judy, but it has to be yours. Be brave. Don't let him use you."

JUDY could no longer think straight and went to bed. She was spent and certainly didn't feel brave. Wil had made a terrible choice, but he hadn't wavered, no matter what they did or said. It was a far greater decision than hers could ever be. Achilles had confronted the National Guard with a question they had all wanted answered, knowing he would be thrown in jail. Even David had taken a risk with the ROTC fireworks, though she still wasn't sure he realized that. And here she was, hiding in the covers.

She drifted in and out of sleep into the late morning, her dreams all over the place. Since tripping with Wil they had become surreal, as if she had plugged into a new palette of disturbing images, vivid colors, and dark, dark scenarios that mixed up all that had been happening. At one point she was dreaming about the drug dealer Sharp, who turned into Robert Connay, who offered her coffee that smelled so good, but she was afraid it was laced with LSD. She didn't want to drink it.

"Judy," a voice said. "Judy."

She opened her eyes.

"I thought you could use this." David was smiling down at her, holding a steaming cup.

She sat up and tried to comb her hair with her fingers and wipe the sleep out of her eyes.

"You look beautiful." He handed her the coffee and plumped the pillows for her to lean against. "How do you feel?"

How did she feel? He had to be kidding. There was a vet somewhere on campus who had to be wondering if what he had to do was worth it, just to try to save our ungrateful asses; Howie and Marsha were destroyed; Achilles had gone off the deep end; her mother and Pete had both written her off; Michael and Wil were dead; and he was about to betray her. On top of it all, she still had to decide whether to continue on a path that no longer seemed to have anything to do with who she believed she really was.

"It was a rough night." She took a sip of coffee and let it work its way through her limbs. He sat next to her.

"It's almost noon," he said. "Are you going to stay in bed all day?"

"Why?" She stretched her arms. "Were any more students shot while I was sleeping?"

"No, but Achilles is gone."

Judy froze, her arms still raised. Gone is what had happened to Michael.

"His parents paid his bail, and he headed back home to Chicago. I think being in the clink for a few days really blew his mind, even if it was just the county jail."

He chuckled. "Don't worry, though. I'm sure Sharp will give him a few Quaaludes before his final court appearance, and he'll be fine."

She wondered why he never had braces for those lower teeth.

"I can't stop thinking about that vet," she said. "I can't believe no one even tried to shut Lori up."

"Probably wouldn't have worked."

She pulled the blanket around her shoulders. "I've always thought of myself as someone who would have been able to stop something like that."

He was watching her carefully, the way Sheila used to watch Michael.

"I guess I'm not the person I thought I was."

"Hey, ease up," he said. "You're the one who talked Wil off the ledge, for chrissake."

"Oh, I'm good at doing what's right in front of me. There's no deciding involved, you just react."

"Maybe nursing is your calling, after all," he said. "I mean, if it wasn't wrapped up in all this army shit."

"That's not the same. There's no . . ." She searched for the words.

"Go on," he said, sounding genuinely interested. He put his hand on her thigh.

"Personal risk," she said. "There was great personal risk for Robert Connay to be there last night. But I didn't stand up for him because I was more concerned about myself. I guess I'd have to say I was a coward."

She wondered why she didn't tear up. She put her hand to her heart.

"Sometimes, you get a moment when you realize what you're made of, like when you talked about that trigger you wondered if you could pull. Well, this was mine. I did worse than cut and run. I stayed silent and expected someone else to do it for me."

"Who?"

"You."

"You're gonna lay this on me?" he asked. "That's not fair." He pulled his hand away and folded his arms.

"I'm not laying it on you, David. That's the point. I shouldn't have expected you or anyone to be braver than I was willing to be. I folded, and someone was wounded because of it. And that's taught me a lot about myself that I have to face."

"And about me too, I suppose."

"I'm talking about *me*, David. But I think . . . I hope we both learned something about ourselves in that room last night."

He stood up and reached for a cigarette. "Yeah, well, if it weren't for this fucking war, none of us would have been in that meeting in the first place." He took a long drag. "But you know it will all be worth it, if it finally makes you do the right thing."

"You're right," she said. "My mother's right. Everyone's right, David. If we try hard enough and talk it to death, we can make anything work. But deep inside, if you look hard enough, you know what you should do."

He stared at her. She didn't look away.

"So, now what?" He didn't seem to realize they were over.

"I lost something last night," she said. "And now I have to see if I can get it back."

SHE missed Wil. He would have told her this moment with David was inevitable. She missed Michael. He would have told her they had gotten themselves embroiled in matters of life and death, making decisions using their teenagers' rules. That's why it was all screwed up, and they had lost the whole point of what they were trying to do.

It was time for her to set things right, as much as she could, for what they had done to Connay and, finally, for herself. She didn't need any more acid trips or walks around the lagoon to figure it out. Pete was right: she had to decide, once and for all, and then, like Wil, she had to just let be what was going to be.

What she knew for certain was what to do next, and that it would all have to be done before the big meeting in the Tune Room that David and Lori had called for tonight. It would be their last stand to keep the university open so they could keep their movement going. They had learned that from Connay. And apparently Judy was to play a significant role. But it wouldn't be the one David and Lori had planned for her.

She knew what it would take, just not how to pull it off. She thought of someone. She had no reason to believe he would help, just a hunch.

Chapter 44

SHE OPENED HER DOOR, AND FOUND HER EXIT BLOCKED by two cops crowding the threshold: one campus, one county.

"You need to come with us," the county cop said.

The shiver of icy dread returned. "Am I under arrest?"

"Now." Their faces were masks.

They bookended her down the stairs, put her in the back of a black-and-white car waiting in the driveway, silently drove her to the police station in town, deposited her into an empty room with a few chairs and a table, and told her to sit. The walls were concrete blocks. It was a step down from the Washington, D.C., interrogation room, but it was clear where she was. Of course, she was being arrested. Pete had been right.

Had he finally had enough and betrayed her? No, she couldn't believe that, no matter what she'd done. He would have tried to talk to her first. It had to be David. This must have been what Vida meant when she told her he was planning something. But that didn't make sense, with his big plans for tonight. He would have waited. With her elbows on the table and head in her hands, she tried to reason it out. There were only three people who knew—Pete, David, and Vida. But it couldn't be Vida, either, unless she told someone before their talk. She had been hurt. It was possible. No, she couldn't believe that, either. She didn't know what was going on, other than the life-changing decision she thought was up to her was now surely off the table.

The door opened, and a female officer walked in and took a seat. She laid a folder on the table.

"I'm Captain Catherine Mark." She didn't need to say she was army. "You can call me Captain Cathy."

The informality shocked Judy as much as Cathy's appearance. She was blindingly beautiful, and astonishingly put together, with perfectly cut chin-length blonde hair, black eyebrows, and bright red lips. Her movie star looks were heightened by the crisp white shirt and black tie of her dark uniform, her precisely angled cap. Judy was mesmerized. In a few years, this could have been her.

Judy moved automatically to stand.

"No, please sit down."

Judy obeyed, suddenly feeling horribly shabby in her jeans and embarrassed by her fatigue jacket. Of all the things to be wearing now.

"So, how will this work?" Judy asked, knowing the boom was about to be lowered.

Captain Cathy eyed her with amusement. "At least, you didn't ask me why you were here."

She opened the folder and read selectively. "Private First Class Judith Talton . . . enlisted August 12, 1968, as a member of the WRAIN program . . . excellent grades . . . top ranked on the list of applicants, impressive." She went on to detail Judy's military family and how both parents had served in World War II. "A picture-perfect recruit."

"And now, apparently, you've become a spy?" Judy was astounded. She had heard this so many times—from Maggie, from Pete, even from David and Vida—but that had meant *for* the army, not against it. What was going on?

Captain Cathy lost her friendly edge and read from another piece of paper in the folder—a list ranging from Judy's attendance at the Moratorium, and her trip to Washington, to her membership in the Student Mobilization Committee. They knew everything she had done from the very beginning. Someone *had* been watching her.

"That was the stupid part," Captain Cathy said. "So smart,

and yet you allowed your name on a list of an organization accused of federal crimes."

My god, Judy thought, this sounded like Pete. Could he really have done this to me?

The inevitable had finally happened . . . from that very first step into the freak side of the Tune Room. Her mother will so enjoy being able to say, "I told you so." Judy just wanted it done and over with.

"So I'm being kicked out of the army and I lose my scholarship, right? And you'll want the tuition money back."

Captain Cathy smiled. "You think it will be that simple?"

She rose, picked up her folder, and walked out.

Judy sat alone for a long time. She had time to imagine all variations of the worst case. They arrived in her mind fully formed, having been considered so many times before. She was sure the captain's comment meant that jail was involved. She hadn't really believed that would happen. What had she done that was so bad? It was what the other military freaks had probably done, no more. She had always assumed that Pete was exaggerating with his warnings to scare her.

She was certainly scared now.

The door opened again. Captain Cathy and the two cops came in together and sat across from her.

"We can make this all go away," she said. Judy was astonished yet again. The captain went through a detailed explanation of how Judy's life could just continue as is, in the WRAIN program, scholarship intact. They would even move her out to Walter Reed immediately and elevate her status from private first class for an acceleration through the program and, of course, more money. It would be like this never happened. They just needed one small piece of information to satisfy the legal authorities.

Judy couldn't believe what she was hearing. "What?"

"A name," said the county cop. "The name or names of the person or persons who set the fire the night of the lottery."

"What makes you think I know that?"

"We'll be back in twenty minutes," Captain Cathy said, rising. "We'll expect you to tell us by then."

Judy knew her conscience, her character, her friends, family, and future were all on the line. It was the most painful twenty minutes of her life, possibly the last she would spend in freedom. She was frantic. How could she give up David? How could she not? Would it be enough to say it was people from Chicago? She didn't know the kazoo guys' names, anyway. And then she had an idea . . . a complicated, absurd, desperate idea.

"I want something in return," she told them when they came back. She said it with authority she didn't feel, showing composure she didn't have.

She made her proposal sound logical and simple, like a piece of cake, even though Judy knew it would rely on convincing others, one she had never actually met. And time was short. It had to happen tonight, at David's meeting.

The details of the deal Captain Cathy and the two policemen were willing to strike made her realize how close to jail she would continue to be, unless she came through. She would have to make it work.

"And another thing," Judy said, once it was all settled, knowing she was pushing it. "I need to know how you found out about me. My plan won't work unless I know who I'm dealing with."

Captain Cathy paged through her folder. "It was an anonymous call," she said.

Judy waited.

"From a woman."

Chapter 45

VIDA HAD BETRAYED HER. FIRST DAVID. AND NOW VIDA. It had to have happened before their talk. She wouldn't believe that hadn't been genuine. She must have felt betrayed herself, or she had told someone else. But who? Judy didn't have it in her to figure out why at this point. She had to put it out of her head and focus on pulling off the deal she had made or she would be finished. But it hurt . . . like hell.

As Judy entered the Tune Room that evening, she noted with relief the coalition David had assembled: the leaders of the SMC, the entire YSA, most of the Student Senate, a few of the Panthers, even the SDS. They were all milling about on center stairs or just below, waiting for the meeting to begin.

Judy sneaked around them and took a seat at one of the tables down by the jukebox, the same table she first sat at, she realized, precisely eight months earlier. Today, she hadn't even considered what side she was sitting on and smiled to herself at how homogenized the protests had made them all after only a semester. The administration had been able to cool them off from time to time, but it had also galvanized them, and they had found their common ground. She took some satisfaction in that.

She fixed on the poster-sized photo of Wil, ensconced over the jukebox, and spent a good long time traveling along the planes of his face, his narrow nose, his tiny eyes. Yes, he had resembled John Lennon, even under the hair and behind the wire rims. She remembered how much it had pleased him.

She saw David as he made his entrance, pausing at center stairs, in his hat and duster, just as she'd seen him that first morning. She let her gaze linger.

He noticed her finally, appeared a bit startled, then hurried over.

"I'm glad you came early." He gave her a wary peck on the cheek. "Come on. We want all the SMC members to sit at this table up front."

She let him walk her to the designated area, their usual table, where Wizard, Meldrich, RoMo, and Sheila had gathered. She studied the new faces that had taken the places of Howie, Marsha, Fish, Achilles, Wil, and Michael, wondering if they deserved their seats or even if they belonged to any of Captain Cathy's undercover agents, waiting to surround her if she didn't name names.

"Anything I can do to help?" she asked, beginning her performance.

David didn't answer, making a show of rearranging a pile of clipboards on the table to clear a place for her.

"Look," she said in a low voice when he bent near. "I know what you're going to do."

"What? *Fuck*." He grabbed her elbow to move her away from the table. "Vida, right? Are you okay with it?"

Judy laughed, thinking he was such an open book.

"It's cool, then? Seriously?" He gave her a hug. "That's so great. It's the right thing, you know, and if we announce it tonight, we can leverage the whole effort. You'll love it. We're gonna make you this big hero. Now, here's the rundown."

She went through the motions of listening to his plans with appropriate enthusiasm. SDS first, the Trot message after that, and finally it would be the SMC with David at the helm to announce the newly recharged ROTC campaign, culminating with her announcement about rejecting the army and walking away from WRAIN/ROTC for the cause.

He didn't ask her what she would say once he introduced her . . . once, as far as he knew, she had given up her future, revealing a secret that could land her in jail . . . once she would be in a position to identify him as the perpetrator of a federal crime. It didn't even occur to him she could betray him back. He was so cocky, he almost deserved it.

She obediently took a seat and watched the Trots assemble—Sorsa, Donnell, and finally, Lori, who kept giving Judy sly glances.

She and David deserved each other, Judy thought.

At the last minute, Vida added a chair to the table and sat next to her. How much harder could this get? She couldn't look at her.

David called the meeting to order. He thanked all of them for not deserting CIU and letting the administration feel that a little time off could calm them down, like a baby with a sucker.

He conducted his usual very effective rally about keeping up the struggle to end the war, especially after Kent State. He introduced the representative from the SDS, who indicated that even they would work together, with the right message, to create nonviolent political action, moving forward.

Lori then joined David at center stairs and, in a move that clearly surprised him, started talking about the assault on the Trot house, the new spies on campus, and how everyone was essentially under surveillance. She alluded to a very close, insidious force that had been working against them since before the lottery.

"Shit," Vida whispered. "She's going to call you out as one of the spies."

Judy felt everything go into slow motion. She saw David's

confusion turn to anger at Lori, who was smiling broadly. She watched Lori lift her arm and point her finger.

Judy stood up and headed toward Lori. The puzzle pieces of what she had worked out rearranged themselves in her mind as she mounted each stair. She needed to get Lori off the stage. She hadn't considered that Lori would go further than David, that she could ruin the plan Judy had agreed to with Captain Cathy.

"About that assault on the Trot House . . ." Judy heard Vida's voice behind her. She paused on the middle stair. Vida was on her feet. "I hear you set that up yourself, Lori."

The room exploded in gasps and stage whispers. "What'd she say?" "They did?" "No way." "Really?"

"What are you talking about?" Lori challenged Vida.

"Well, they never caught anyone, and as I remember it, you Trots weren't too concerned about getting to the bottom of it."

"There's no proof of that," Lori answered. She was watching Donnell in the crowd. He was sitting forward, confused. "Besides, I'm the one who got hurt the worst. You think I hit myself in the face—"

"Well, you did wear your injuries like a badge of honor," Vida said, shrugging. "All we know for sure is the Trots got pretty popular after that. Not a bad strategy, not bad at all."

The room responded with a roar. The remaining Trots rushed toward Donnell, who was shaking his head, genuinely perplexed.

"She didn't clue you in, did she?" Vida shouted to Donnell so everyone could hear.

Lori kept sputtering from the podium. "You can't say that. I didn't . . . we didn't . . ." She seemed more concerned about the darting looks from the Trots than the rest of the crowd. She banged against the podium, trying to regain the floor. "Quiet. Listen to me. I can explain."

Vida sat down and folded her arms, smiling with satisfaction. She winked at Judy, who advanced the rest of the stairs up toward Lori. Judy was totally confused about Vida and had no idea what she was going to say herself.

"This is my spot on the agenda," Lori said. "May I finish?"

"Oh, I think you *are* finished, Lori," Judy said. "I think we'd all like to get back to trying to stop the war instead of trying to stop you."

The words just slid out of her. She nearly gasped, and her hand was on its way to cover her mouth when the room erupted again into applause and laughter. Lori's eyes bugged out, shocked, and she tried to stutter some response, but couldn't. Judy remained with her head cocked toward her until Lori shuffled and stepped down the stairs to the promenade, first haltingly, then in a rush to disappear into the hooting crowd. The Trots scrambled behind David. No one followed her.

All eyes turned to Judy, as if she had planned it.

"I think everyone's waiting for my announcement, so let's just get to it." She noticed Captain Cathy in civilian clothes and no lipstick at a table near the jukebox, the cops lined up outside the door, everyone thinking they were there for the usual security since Riot Night.

She took a deep breath and began. "I know we were all very disappointed by what happened at the Student Senate meeting after Kent State, when our attempt to make the only move we could was vetoed. I know we still feel angry and powerless, and frustrated about what to do next. But the SMC has been working hard behind the scenes." She angled her head toward David, who shook himself out of his confusion to nod back and appear to be in on it.

Captain Cathy had moved into the center of her field of vision.

"I'd like to ask two guests to join me up here on center stairs to explain what's been going on. First, Dr. Swanson." She waited for him to walk up and stand next to her. There was a smattering of applause, as well as a few catcalls about him being the administration's lackey and questions about if he was finally ready to go to Washington.

"And also," Judy continued, "Taylor Adams."

Heads turned and necks stretched. It was the first time Taylor had been seen in public since his veto on Riot Nite. David exchanged looks with the Trots. There were loud boos as Taylor approached. A Styrofoam cup hit him in the back.

"Traitor!" someone yelled, and it was picked up as a chant.

"Traitor! Traitor!"

Judy put her arms out to quell the crowd. "Taylor and Dr. Swanson have something to say. Let's hear them out."

Taylor arranged himself dead center and paused as they quieted down. In jeans and unshaven, as if he had been up all night, he now looked like one of them.

"I know I'm not the most popular guy on campus these days." Taylor was cut off by a deafening rush of agreement and abuse from the crowd.

"All right," he said with his arms out, palms down to silence the racket. "You think I'd be putting myself through this if I didn't have something I thought you'd want to hear?"

The noise receded.

"I still believe in personal choice," Taylor began. "I don't want that to ever go away. It would be the first step in a very bad direction, as I'm sure Dr. Swanson would agree." He gestured to Swanson, who nodded.

There were random snipes from the crowd.

"That said, I do want to acknowledge that we can be too rigid on the other side of the argument, and when the people speak, we need to listen. That's, after all, what's been going on since this war escalated, certainly since December with the lottery and absolutely since Kent State." He paused. "We do have a right to respond, to be heard, to take action.

"Given this, I've done some soul searching since Riot Nite and had some illuminating conversations with some interesting people, including those who have been working quietly but steadily despite personal and professional risk." He opened his palm first in the direction of Swanson and then to Judy, which she wished he hadn't. She flashed a look at Captain Cathy, who was frowning.

"Why should we give a shit?" said someone in the crowd.

Taylor closed his eyes and took a deep breath.

"I've come to realize that there are great, considered opinions on either side. And for this time, at this place, I need to reconsider mine. I've got some legislation here I'd like a vote on."

The crowd rustled, confused.

Taylor's gaze swept the room. "It appears we have a Student Senate quorum here, am I right? Will any attending senators please stand and count yourself off, so we can be sure."

Wizard was the first up. "One," he said loudly.

"Two," Donnell followed.

"Three," another yelled. It went on until the count showed they had the entire Student Senate, short only two.

"Looks like we have enough. I'm officially convening a meeting of the CIU Student Senate as of . . . " he looked at his watch, "8:05 p.m. on Tuesday, May 22, 1970." He pulled a gavel from his trouser pocket and banged it on a nearby table. "This meeting will have one agenda item. I move to hereby lift my veto of the proposal by the Student Senate to remove ROTC from CIU and to reinstate and vote on the original motion. Do I have a second?"

"Second," Wizard yelled.

"All who agree, say 'aye.'"

"Aye," the senators called back.

"Aye," the crowd yelled, drowning out his request for any "nays."

"Motion passed." He banged the gavel again to make it official.

The place went wild. Meldrich said he was sure that if Achilles were here, he would want to throw a chair. The song on the jukebox was changed to "Volunteers."

"Wait," Judy said, "Dr. Swanson has something to say." She waved her hands to get their attention.

The room quieted slightly as Swanson announced they had been able to accommodate the ROTC program off campus for the already enrolled. He tried to explain, but the noise continued and he gave up finally but good-naturedly. Taylor shook his hand, sealing the deal.

Judy put her hand on Swanson's arm to turn him toward her. "Thank you," she said, "for all of this . . . and for what's next."

He covered her hand with his, nodding his head.

The Tune Room became a cacophony of screaming and laughing and even impromptu dancing down the center aisle.

"I wish Michael could have seen this," Sheila said. "The KIA count this week was 41,901."

Taylor took on back claps and other accolades, as the student senators came up to congratulate him, Wizard being first.

Even Donnell paid homage, Lori apparently forgotten. "Better late than never."

"How about we agree I did the wrong thing for the right reason?" Taylor said.

Vida caught Judy's eye, winked, and came up to hug her.

"Oh, wow, I was right about you. You *know*. Always."

Judy didn't know what to think. "Thanks for the heads up and the cover."

Vida grinned. "Hey, that's what friends are for."

Judy turned to David who was approaching her.

"I swear I didn't know what Lori was going to do," he said. "But I admit I got a kick out of how you shot her down." He moved to embrace her, but she stepped back.

"Don't worry," she said. "Let's keep our secrets safe. Go patch it up with Swanson, you need him, and work with Taylor, he's a good guy. You deserve to be in the middle of all this, David. Do it right. Get us back to ending the war. Like Michael said, people are dying and we need to stop it. That's all that counts."

"Roger that." He nodded crisply and headed toward Swanson. As he reached him, he turned and gave Judy a short salute, and a smile.

Judy turned to thank Taylor and ended up facing Captain Cathy.

"You were a little heavy on the antiwar message," she said.

"The 'legal issue' was to ensure we stop the violence," Judy answered. "I believe we accomplished that."

The police came inside the Tune Room, waiting at the door.

"Okay, we did our part, and it wasn't easy," Cathy said. "Now we need the names of those criminals."

"There aren't any criminals, Captain. There were only scared teenagers, trying to make themselves feel better with a little fireworks display. It got out of hand. It was a mistake. It happens to kids.

"They won't be doing it again . . . ," she said, looking at the cops. "That peaceful coalition David talked about, Swanson will keep them in line."

"Are you sure he isn't the one who set the fire?"

Judy shrugged. "As long as he and Swanson stay in SMC leadership, it won't happen again."

Captain Cathy cocked her head and smiled slyly. "It's too bad, you would have done very well."

She started to leave then turned back.

"You think Lori Mueller was involved?"

"Why do you ask?"

"She's the one who gave you up."

Chapter 46

THE RESULTS OF THE CIU ROTC VOTE HIT THE PRESS FAST, attracting the national leadership of the SMC, who had come into town the next week for a huge celebration and kick-off for rolling the campaign throughout the country. There was a genuine possibility that it could succeed, given the Kent State backlash. The government was willing to do virtually anything to stay off campuses. David had finally achieved his goal.

"He's center stage and loving every minute," Vida said, the afternoon of the event, adding that according to the Steering Committee, the positive media attention had caused the feds to hold back on their investigations for now. Judy smiled, glad that Captain Cathy had held up that part of the bargain.

She gave Vida a hug, long and hard.

"What's with all the affection, all of a sudden?" Vida said. "You haven't been able to keep your hands off me since the meeting."

Judy laughed.

"Remember. Six o'clock at the lagoon," Vida said. "You should be there. You've been as much a part of this as anyone. You *will* be there." Judy remembered her shaking the piece of bacon at her with the same words about the Lottery Performance.

Pete had called her that morning to thank her. He had just come from his first off-campus ROTC meeting. They discussed what was coming next.

"I understand," he said. "I hope it works out."

It was the first time he didn't argue against her. It felt so good, she even considered calling her mother. She would in time, she was sure.

She went to the lagoon near six, hearing the noise of the event before she saw it. She climbed up the highest berm and watched it all unfold below her. David was on a center platform with a megaphone surrounded by the stalwarts of Vida, Wizard, even Meldrich and Sheila, but also many new and eager faces. The Trots had been relegated to the crowd, she realized, smiling. Lori was nowhere to be seen.

Judy sat against a tree, the one she had leaned on to read that first awful letter from her mother that seemed so long ago. She thought of the candle lighting up Michael's face as he read from "The Lottery" and Wil's twinkling stars. The country, the war, her family, her life, all played in her head.

She hoped it would be worth it. She remembered David's words. Could anything they did in a cornfield in the middle of nowhere really make enough of an impact to give up her future? But if she really believed the war was wrong, shouldn't she be willing to risk everything like the guys having to start over in Canada?

Wouldn't Wil's life have been worth it? She absolutely knew that if that option, sitting in front of her, was presented, it would never have been a question. But absent that, would leaving the army just be a small, silly gesture, like one of David's grapes rolling off a table?

Swanson's words echoed in her head.

"Your actions today will define who you are . . . and who you will ever hope to become."

Anyway, it was settled. At least, she wasn't going to jail. The police were grateful for the new peaceful coalition and happy to have ROTC removed as a potential future flashpoint. And she wouldn't have to pay the army back for what they had spent on her for the past two years. "Too much paperwork," Captain Cathy had said.

There was some regret in her voice when she told Judy they would have to stick to the deal they had made. It would be an honorable discharge and a clean break.

At first, Judy didn't really feel she had made a decision at all, but then realized it had been in motion since that first day she walked into the Tune Room. That's what she had *known*. That's what Vida and Michael had seen in her.

It was up to her, now, to make her decision count. She did know that. The first step wasn't clear. She knew she could stay around campus and work to get back into school, like she had planned in one of her possible scenarios. That's what her friends wanted. "Look what you've done already," Vida said. But they really didn't need her anymore. And for the first time, her life, however uncertain, didn't seem inevitable. That was frightening but also exciting. She wondered if this is how Michael felt when he deserted, and if the feeling was the same for the guys who left for Canada.

She understood that she could still join the others down below. If she did, it would be one decision, the easiest one, and if she didn't and left, it would be another. She noticed there was a fork in the path leading down the berm that would take her in either direction. She smiled to herself. Both Michael and Wil would have enjoyed that. Perhaps they were, somewhere, watching this.

Noise rose from down on the platform. Another call to action. Judy stood up, brushed the leaves off her faded jeans, and started down the path away from the sound of the megaphone, a ticket for the Greyhound bus in her pocket. The destination was open.

ACKNOWLEDGMENTS

The impetus for this story goes way back to when Tommy Aubry, the "real" guy who screamed, "They're killing us!" the day of Kent State, wrote me a letter several years later saying there was a story in those years, and that I was the one to tell it. This may not have been exactly what he had in mind, but it's how it came out.

I thank those who unwittingly inspired my characters and the long list of those from whom I shamelessly stole a gesture, a tragedy, a way of speaking, or a suggestion, and shaped it to my fictional end, as well as a guy I only remember as Randy who really did claim to have written the words "Let It Be." I honor those who still and forever will remember their destiny-defining lottery numbers and where and what they were doing the blistering nights of each of the Draft Lotteries and the day of Kent State. And I offer an eternal RIP for the real Michael Marek.

I thank my earliest champion, Ken Probst, with whom I exchanged bits of early scenes, as he lobbied for more action, a real war story. And I'm eternally grateful for my first, strongest, and most long-standing supporters (now bosom friends) from the University of Chicago's Graham School, who convinced me I had a story and continually urged me to resist perfectionism and just get on with it: the marvelous instructor Gary Wilson, and fellow students, now novelists, Libby Wheeler and Josh Lohrius.

To my many friends and family members who have supported me through the years as I've toiled on my "phantom novel," I hope the wait was worth it.

I thank the Ragdale Foundation, which allowed me back for

so many residencies, where the majority of this book was written and for the source of an incredible network of friends and resources. It's where I met Barb Shoup, my original editor, with whom I slogged through so many drafts over so many years—never pushing, but always there. And my final editor, Jacquelyn Mitchard, who pulled me over the finish line with her fresh, brilliant eye. Also, my jack of all profile-raising trades, Deborah Siegel, who pointed me to the great team at She Writes Press. And the referral that led to finding my indefatigable copyeditor, Linda Naslund.

I'm also indebted to my intrepid researcher, Allison Porch. And, to JKS Communications founder, Julie Schoerke, such a bright light in her field, and her wonderful team.

Thank you, Tim O'Brien, for the inspiration of "Up a Rainy River," and the soul handshake we shared at a Chicago reading. We should have coffee.

Above all, I'm grateful for the never-say-die spirit of Joe Dragonette. He would have enjoyed seeing our name on the cover. His verdict on the story might have been up or down, but his delivery would certainly have been something off-color and outrageous . . . and then there would have been that look of his. I see it now, and it's worth it all.

CREDITS

"Be Free"
Words and Music by Rod Argent and Chris White
© 1970 by Marquis Songs USA
Used by permission

"Born Under a Bad Sign"
Words and Music by Booker T. Jones and William Bell
Copyright © 1967 IRVING MUSIC, INC.
Copyright Renewed
All Rights Reserved
Used by permission
Reprinted by Permission of Hal Leonard LLC

"I Feel Like I'm Fixing to Die Rag"
Words and Music by Joe McDonald
© 1965 Alkatraz Corner Music
Renewed 1993
Used by permission

"Last Night I Had The Strangest Dream"
Words and Music by Ed McCurdy
TRO – © Copyright 1950 (Renewed), 1951 (Renewed), 1955 (Renewed)
Folkways Music Publishers, Inc., New York, NY
Used by permission

"Let It Be"
Words and Music by John Lennon and Paul McCartney
Copyright © 1970 Sony/ATV Music Publishing LLC
Copyright Renewed
All Rights Administered by Sony/ATV Music Publishing LLC,
424 Church Street, Suite 1200, Nashville, TN 37219
International Copyright Secured
All Rights Reserved
Reprinted by Permission of Hal Leonard LLC

ABOUT THE AUTHOR

RITA DRAGONETTE is a writer who, after nearly thirty years telling the stories of others as an award-winning public relations executive, has returned to her original creative path. Her debut novel, *The Fourteenth of September*, is based upon personal experiences on campus during the Vietnam War, and she is currently at work on her next three books: a World War II-set novel based on her inter-

Photograph by AJ Kane

est in the impact of war on and through women, an homage to *The Sun Also Rises* about expats in San Miguel de Allende, and a memoir in essays. Rita lives and writes in Chicago, where she also hosts literary salons to showcase authors and their new books to avid readers.

ritadragonette.com